"Kathy Herman leaves the city of Baxter and takes readers on a suspenseful journey to the new town of Seaport where gossip threatens to destroy three family's lives. A missing child, fearful heartache, and unfounded rumors make *A Shred of Evidence* a powerful suspense you won't want to miss."

GAIL GAYMER MARIN
Author of *Michigan*

"When I get myself out of bed an hour early in order to keep reading a book, I know I'm hooked! But I also squirmed as Kathy Herman's suspense novel probed that uncomfortable gray zone between what's concern and what's gossip. The book begs for discussion and couldn't be more timely for both church and society."

NETA JACKSON
Author of The Yada Yada Prayer Group novels

"Deception, lies, and slander ensnare the town of Seaport, but there comes as well the power of words to heal and move mountains."

DORIS ELAINE FELL
Author of *Betrayal in Paris* and *The Trumpet at Twisp*

"Kathy Herman's *A Shred of Evidence*, a chilling cautionary tale, exposes the destructive power of suspicion. You'll never again hear a rumor and deem it harmless."

LYN COTE
Author of The Women of Ivy Manor series

"In *A Shred of Evidence*, Kathy Herman gives her readers true-to-life characters, a plot that could be fresh from today's headlines, and plenty of food for thought."

DEANNA JULIE DODSON
Author of In *Honor Bound*, *By Love Redeemed*, and *To Grace Surrendered*

A SHRED
of
EVIDENCE

A Seaport Suspense Novel

KATHY HERMAN

Multnomah® Publishers *Sisters, Oregon*

IF
H55152sh

A SHRED OF EVIDENCE
published by Multnomah Publishers, Inc.
© 2005 by Kathy Herman

International Standard Book Number: 1-59052-348-2

Cover image by Joe Sohm/Alamy
Interior typeset by Katherine Lloyd, The DESK, Bend, Oregon

Scripture quotations are from:
The Holy Bible, New International Version
© 1973, 1984 by International Bible Society,
used by permission of Zondervan Publishing House
Multnomah is a trademark of Multnomah Publishers, Inc.,
and is registered in the U.S. Patent and Trademark Office.
The colophon is a trademark of Multnomah Publishers, Inc.

Printed in the United States of America

For information:
MULTNOMAH PUBLISHERS, INC.
POST OFFICE BOX 1720 • SISTERS, OREGON 97759

Library of Congress Cataloging-in-Publication Data
Herman, Kathy.
  A shred of evidence : a Seaport suspense novel / Kathy Herman.
      p. cm.
ISBN 1-59052-348-2
I. Title.
PS3608.E762S55 2005
813'.6--dc22

                                              2004022960

05 06 07 08 09 10—10 9 8 7 6 5 4 3 2 1 0

To Him who is both the Giver and the Gift

ACKNOWLEDGMENTS

I'm so grateful for those who support me in prayer, those who take time to encourage me—and those who patiently instruct me so that the scenarios I create are realistic.

I owe a special word of thanks to Will Ray, professional investigator, State of Oregon, for taking his valuable time to advise me on the chapters pertinent to DNA evidence, interrogations, and law enforcement procedures. Will, you're always so generous with your time and knowledge; I hope someday we get a chance to meet face to face.

To Melissa Mitchell, director of Loss Prevention at LifeWay Christian Stores in Nashville, Tennessee, for fielding a specific question I had regarding FBI procedures.

I'm grateful also to my friend Carolyn Walker, an ardent advocate for families and children who works with the Texas Foster Family Association, for her input regarding the procedural aspects of child protective services.

I wish to extend a loving thank you to my sister Pat Phillips not only for being a zealous prayer warrior, but also for your perfectly timed words of encouragement. How God is using you, baby girl!

To Susie Killough, Judi Wieghat, and the ladies in my Bible study groups at Bethel Bible Church, and my friends at LifeWay Christian Store in Tyler, Texas, for your heartfelt prayer support.

To my readers who encourage me with e-mails and cards and personal testimonies, thanks for sharing how God has used my words to touch you. He uses you to bless me more often than you know!

To my novelist friends in ChiLibris, thanks for encouraging and challenging me—and for your many prayers on my behalf.

To my editor Rod Morris, thanks for feeding me "all the right stuff" so I can continue to grow as a writer. It amazes me what you see that I don't. How grateful I am for your insights and your gentle way of conveying them.

To the staff at Multnomah, whose commitment to honor God through the power of story is so very evident. Thanks for the privilege of working with such a dedicated group of professionals.

And to my husband, Paul, who knew long before I did that thoughts were stirring in my soul—words that needed to be harnessed and characters who needed to speak. How grateful I am for your nudging. And for all the time you've unselfishly given to accompany me on the journey. It's as though we have but one heartbeat.

And most of all I thank my Heavenly Father, who uses my stories both to challenge and to heal. You have taken my words all over the globe and blessed them beyond measure. What a privilege to be in Your service!

PROLOGUE

The words of a gossip are like choice morsels;
they go down to a man's inmost parts.
PROVERBS 18:8

Julie Hamilton dabbed her eyes, then dropped a limp Kleenex in the waste can and stared at her reflection in the bathroom mirror. At least the puffiness had smoothed out the stress lines around her eyes.

She cupped her hands under the faucet and splashed cool water on her cheeks, breathing slowly through her mouth until the residual sobs finally stopped.

The police had months ago exhausted their questioning of Ross. If only that reporter had been as merciful, perhaps they wouldn't be moving to Seaport. Not that relocating was going to solve their problems. As long as Ross continued to hide behind a wall of silence, her daunting guilt would only scream louder.

Julie exhaled a sigh of desolation. What happened to the life she thought she had signed up for, the girlhood dream-come-true?

She heard Sarah Beth singing in the other room and knew which part of the DVD had come on. Her daughter had been watching the same one over and over for nearly two hours. Julie wondered how long it had been since she had held Sarah Beth's attention for even half that long.

The phone rang. Julie didn't answer it. *This is the Hamiltons'. Leave a message after the beep and we'll call you back.*

"Julie, it's Mother. Would you please pick up? I'm not going to stop calling till you talk to me."

"I don't want to talk to you," Julie mumbled.

"I'm waiting…You might as well pick up the phone because I'm not going to be put off any more…Yoo-hoo, Julie, pick up the phone…I'm not leaving…"

Julie marched into the bedroom and grabbed the receiver off the cradle. "What do you want, Mother?"

"I want you to stop avoiding me."

"Don't be so paranoid. I'm avoiding everyone."

"You can't keep doing this."

"I'm thirty-five years old. If I feel a need to keep avoiding people, that's my business."

"It's not healthy."

"It's a way to cope. Why can't you understand that? Ross and I need space to deal with what's happened. The media's driving us crazy."

"You don't think your father and I are hurting?"

"Of course, you are. But you can't possibly understand what this has done to us."

"How can we when your *husband* won't let us come visit?"

"Will you stop calling him that? Having you stay here is just too difficult right now."

"I never would've believed my own daughter would think I'm a burden."

"I never said you were a burden." Julie exhaled loudly enough to make her point. "We need time to get over this. Ross can't do it with a house full of people."

"We're *family*, not people. Let us take Sarah Beth for a couple of weeks. The break would do you good."

"Are you kidding? The empty house would send Ross over the edge."

"You think it's fair to punish her just because your husband can't cope with what he did?"

"Mother, stop it! I can't deal with this right now. I love you, but I'm hanging up." *Click.*

Julie sat hugging herself, her body trembling, and willed away the emotion, then got up and went into the bathroom.

She squeezed a small amount of foundation onto her index finger, applied it lightly to her face, and watched the red blotches disappear the way they always did. What good would it do for Ross to know that after an entire year, she still had bouts of uncontrollable weeping? He'd already suffered enough. They both had.

I

Julie Hamilton ambled down the front steps and picked up Monday and Tuesday's newspapers, wondering if she dropped dead on the sidewalk if anyone would even notice. Except for a half-hearted wave from a shriveled man living next door, none of the neighbors had even acknowledged that her family had moved in. It wasn't as though they could have missed the U-haul parked in the driveway.

A checker at the grocery store had told her that Seaport functions like several smaller towns within a town. He said that once she found her niche, she'd like it there.

And just how was she supposed to find her niche when she'd hardly spoken to an adult in days? Ross stayed conveniently busy at his Uncle Hank's body shop and found more and more excuses to work late. Much of the time he didn't make it home until just before Sarah Beth went down for the night. He always made time for his daughter, but would be snoring on the couch before Julie got the dinner dishes done.

She went out to the curb and opened the mailbox and found it empty. *Like everything else in my life,* she thought.

"Mama!"

Julie looked up and saw two tiny bare feet and a smile the size of Texas. Sarah Beth toddled toward her giggling, arms outstretched, red curls setting off her clear blue eyes.

"You didn't take a very long nap," Julie said, scooping her daughter into her arms.

Sarah Beth laid her head on Julie's shoulder. "I wuv Mama."

"I love you, too. But you need to sleep longer so you can stay up and see Daddy when he gets home."

"Not sweepy. Watch songs." Sarah Beth raised her head, her tiny hands cupped around Julie's face. "Pwease?"

"Oh, all right." How could she say no to those pleading eyes?

Julie carried her daughter inside and sat her in front of the TV, then slipped the *Toddler-Sing-Along* disc into the DVD player. The phone rang, and she hurried out to the kitchen. "Hello."

"It's me," Ross Hamilton said. "I've gotta stay late and finish painting Adam Spalding's Corvette."

"What am I supposed to do about dinner?"

"Go ahead without me. I'll microwave the leftovers when I get home."

"How late will you be this time?"

"I don't know. Eight. Maybe later. Uncle Hank bumped another job and made this one the priority. Spalding throws his weight around here—and his old man's money. Hank wants to keep him happy."

"Well, by all means, let's keep everyone else happy." Julie cringed at the sarcasm in her voice but decided to make no apology for it.

"Sorry. I'm the only one my uncle trusts to get this done right. Plus, we need the extra money. I'll be home in time to say goodnight to Sarah Beth."

"And then you'll crash in front of the TV and I'll be left twiddling my thumbs. Moving here was supposed to help us reconnect, not push us further apart."

Ross lowered his voice. "I can't talk about this on the phone. I'll see you when I see you. Bye."

Love you, too, she thought.

Julie hung up the phone, then peeked around the corner and saw Sarah Beth in front of the TV, singing off key and happily swaying to the sing-along tunes.

Julie wiped a tear from her cheek. She'd always heard that

time heals all wounds. Then why did hers still feel so fresh—and so incurable?

Ellen Jones popped a chocolate caramel into her mouth and typed as fast as the words came to her, then scrolled up the page and reread chapter eleven of her novel. She turned off her laptop, smiling with satisfaction, and threw a pile of empty candy wrappers in the trash.

She got up from her desk and looked outside, her eyes drinking in the calm, glimmering water of Seaport Beach. She heard the front door open, and then her husband's voice calling her name. What was he doing home from Tallahassee on a Tuesday afternoon?

"Guy, I'm up here."

Ellen heard footsteps on the circular staircase that led to the third-story widow's watch she had made into her workplace. She turned around just as he walked in the door.

"Surprise!" Guy Jones put his arms around her and lifted her off the floor.

"You're home a day early, Counselor. Judging from your frivolous mood, I'm assuming all is well at McAllister, Norton, Riley, and *Jones*?"

Guy's smile scrunched the crow's feet around his eyes. "Indeed. Brent McAllister wants me to take on a toxic chemical case. He thought I might be more efficient working at home this week, so here I am. I know you're busy, and I probably should've called so you could shift gears. But I wanted to surprise you."

"Actually your timing is perfect." Ellen straightened his tie and brushed a piece of lint off his sleek Italian suit. "So tell me about this big case."

"Brinkmont Labs is being sued by residents of Marble River who claim the plant has polluted the river and is responsible for all kinds of health problems. Some aspiring young litigator is just out to make a name for himself. Documentation of samples taken from the river over the past seven years is in line with EPA standards. Should be a slam dunk."

Ellen brushed her hand through his hair and noticed a glint in his eyes she hadn't seen since his law school days. "Good. It's about time Brent let you show him what you can do." She turned around in his arms, his chin resting on her shoulder, and looked out over water. "Oh, look, the skimmers are back—there, flying along the beach. See them?"

"Uh-huh. What did you call them?"

"Skimmers. They glide above the water and dip their bills in the water to feed. I read about them in my bird book."

"So did you make any progress on your novel?"

Ellen turned around, feeling almost giddy. "I just finished chapter eleven. That's probably about the halfway point."

"So when do I get to read it? Is it any good? Ellen, are you blushing? I was just kidding."

"No, I'm not blushing."

"Yes, you are," he said, pinching her cheek with his thumb and forefinger.

Ellen laughed in spite of herself. "*I* think it's good, though getting a publisher to agree with me might prove to be an interesting challenge."

"Thought of a title yet?"

"I haven't gotten that far. I'm just relishing the joy of writing."

"And I'm relishing being home," Guy said. "Why don't you change and let me take you to dinner—some place with candles and soft music?"

"That's awfully generous of you, Counselor, considering you've been eating out all week."

"Yes, but Brent McAllister's not exactly my idea of a dinner date."

Ellen chuckled. "I thought you'd be ready to eat at home."

"Honey, anytime I'm with you, I *am* home. Besides, you've

been working, too. You shouldn't have to cook just because I'm here."

"I've been eating entirely too much sugar," Ellen said. "I'm craving seafood. Why don't we eat at The Sandpiper and watch the sunset?"

"Okay. Most of the snowbirds have left and I doubt it's busy on a Tuesday night. I'll try to reserve a table by the window. Why don't you put on that sassy sundress—the one with the floral print? You can watch the sunset, and I'll watch you."

Ellen prodded him toward the door. "This partnership really agrees with you. I don't know when I've seen you more light-hearted."

"Get used to it, Madam Novelist. Things are just going to get better and better."

Ellen listened to her husband's descending footsteps and thought how happy she and Guy had been since the move to Seaport. It hadn't been easy for her to walk away from a satisfying ten-year career as editor of the *Baxter Daily News*—or from the close-knit community she had grown up in. But watching Guy thriving as a partner in Brent McAllister's law firm had been worth any sacrifice she had made. And now that she was writing a novel, she didn't even mind Guy working out of his office in Tallahassee a few days a week.

She sauntered over to the doorway and turned around, her arms folded, and admired her workplace. Quaint. Uncluttered. The wood floor bore the scars of decades of foot traffic, and Ellen wondered who else had spent time up here.

A bank of windows formed a semi-circular alcove and provided abundant light. Sometimes she would lose herself in the beauty outside, always amazed when her thoughts came together and her fingers moved on the keyboard.

"Ellen? We have reservations in thirty minutes. Better hurry if you want to watch the sunset."

"I'm coming."

She let her eyes flit around the room one more time, wondering how long it would take to finish her novel. She had spent fourteen months doing little else. But for now, it seemed enough.

2

Wednesday's sun was high and hot when Gordon Jameson stood outside Gordy's Crab Shack and admired the rustic new sign that had been hung just in time to impress the lunch crowd. Light gray. Crisp blue lettering. Red crab claws up in the left corner. He decided it stood out well against the weathered shingles.

"Hey, the sign finally came!" called a voice behind him.

Gordy turned around and saw Adam Spalding walking down the pier toward him. "Yeah. The guy just hung it. Whaddya think?"

"Looks great. You pleased?"

"Yeah. Adds a little class without detractin' from the character of the place. So'd you get your Corvette back?"

"Not yet, but Hank's got his top man working on it. I'm starved. What's the special?"

"All-you-can-eat crab cakes." Gordy tried to pinch Adam around the middle and got only a wad of his Polo shirt. "Wouldn't hurt you to put on a few pounds."

Adam laughed. "Why? So I can have love handles like yours?"

"Hey, don't be badmouthin' me. Your day's comin'. One of these days you'll wake up and *you'll* be fifty—and all that muscle will've turned to flab and shifted to your belly. Hope I'm still around to rub it in."

"No way." Adam shook his head, his perfect smile worthy of a toothpaste ad. "Just takes a little self-discipline."

"Yeah, I remember thinkin' that, too. And you see where it got me."

Adam smirked. "Well, *thinkin'* sure didn't cause that roll around your middle."

"You're a real wiseacre, you know it?" Gordy gave Adam a playful jab on the arm. "Come on inside. I'll pour you a fresh-squeezed limeade."

Weezie Taylor poked her head out the front door of Gordy's. "Boss, I just reserved the meeting room for 6:00. The mayor's bringin' some brass and some guests from the Sister Cities Program—eighteen of 'em."

"Wow, that's the kind of press I like," Gordy said.

"Yeah, unless they all order crab. We're gettin' low."

"All right, call and get whatever we need." Gordy looked at Adam, his eyebrows raised. "The mayor, eh? We oughta at least get a mention in the newspaper over this."

"Might want to think about getting your hair trimmed." Adam's palms assumed a defensive posture. "Just a suggestion."

"What's wrong with my hair?" Gordy said.

Adam pulled the back of Gordy's hair out of his collar and held it with his thumb and forefinger "Don't you want to make a good impression? You know someone from the newspaper's going to be snapping pictures. Probably couldn't hurt to change your shirt either."

"Hmm… I suppose I could wear somethin' nicer than a T-shirt."

"How about that yellow shirt you got in Brazil—the one you don't have to tuck in?"

Gordy rolled his eyes. "Okay. I get the hint. Cover the flab. Get my hair trimmed. Anything else you want me to do?"

"Remember to smile," Adam said. "That's your best trait."

"Looks like Eddie and Captain are here," Gordy said, waving to the two men walking down the pier. "You guys save me a place out back. I'll join you when the crowd thins out."

Gordy glanced at his watch and could hardly believe an hour had passed. He went into the kitchen and fixed himself a plate of crab cakes.

"Weezie, I'll be out on the deck with the guys. Can you handle it without me?"

"With one hand tied behind me."

Gordy blew her a kiss and went out the back door onto the deck and flopped in an empty chair next to Adam and across from Eddie Drummond and Captain Jack. "Since when do you get this long for lunch?" he said to Eddie.

"I took the afternoon off." Eddie rolled his eyes. "Had about all I can take of Mr. Perfect."

"That new guy?"

"Yeah, Hank's got him working on Adam's Corvette—won't let anybody else touch it."

"Thank you!" Adam said, his hands folded, his eyes looking up to the sky.

Eddie fished an ice cube out of his water and tossed it at Adam. "I've been doing body work for twenty years. I don't need some newbie hotshot trying to show me up. Suddenly I'm chopped liver."

"So, he's kissin' up to Hank?" Captain said.

"You got that right. Hardly says a word to the rest of us. Drives me crazy."

"Is he any good?" Gordy said.

"Of course, he's good. We're *all* good. That's why Hank hired us. I just don't like playing second fiddle to a guy who's only been there a month."

Adam lifted his eyebrows. "Well, it's not as though he hasn't done this kind of work before. I'm sure he had references."

Eddie sneered. "Whose side are you on anyway?"

"I'll let you know after I get my Vet back."

Eddie dismissed him with a wave of his hand. "I don't care how good it turns out, I could do as good a job. Really ticks me off Hank's singling out this hick from Biloxi like he's better than the rest of us."

"Mee-ow," Captain said. "You gonna scratch his eyes out?"

"Go ahead and laugh. What does a retired fishing captain know about getting squeezed out? Jobs aren't secure anymore, in case you haven't heard."

Captain slapped him on the back. "Lighten up. Since when are you tease bait?"

"Okay. I admit it sounds like sour grapes, but I've put in twenty years with Hank. At my age, I'd hate to be out on the street looking for a job."

Weezie came out on the deck and walked up to Gordy. "That order of crab'll be here before five."

"Which reminds me," Gordy said. "Since the mayor is comin' to my fine establishment, I need to go get my hair trimmed."

"At the barber shop or the beauty parlor?" Captain said.

Gordy smiled and rose to his feet. "I liked you better when you were pickin' on Eddie. Now, if you all will excuse me, I need to go get gussied up. Rich boy here says I need to make a good impression."

"While you're at it, why don't you splash on a little cologne?" Adam winked. "Never can tell when a lady might take notice."

"Yeah, right."

3

On Wednesday afternoon, Ellen Jones came out of Publix pushing a cart full of groceries and was met with the warm, sweet breath of orange blossoms. She walked to her car and let the cart rest against her bumper, then began placing the bags of groceries in the trunk.

She was distracted by a child's giggling and squealing and peeked around the side of her car and saw a redheaded toddler running between two parked cars, headed in her direction. A young woman was in pursuit, shouting for the child to stop.

Ellen's heart sank as the tiny girl darted across the traffic aisle, narrowly escaping the front bumper of a blue SUV. Ellen stepped between her own car and the one parked next to her, blocking the toddler's path, then grabbed hold of her arm.

In the next instant, the woman caught up with them, and applied two firm whacks to the child's behind, then picked her up.

"Mama told you not to get out of your car seat!" the woman scolded. "How can I protect you if you won't listen?"

The bewildered child rubbed her eyes, then laid her head on her mother's shoulder and clung to her.

"Thank the Lord she's not hurt," Ellen said.

The mother was silent for a few seconds as if consoling herself, then looked at Ellen. "Thank you. I pushed the grocery cart over to the return area, and she was out the door before I realized what was happening. I guess I'm the one who deserves the spanking."

"Don't be too hard on yourself," Ellen said. "An energetic

toddler is a handful. I remember chasing after my boys a few times when they were little."

The woman balanced the little girl on her left hip, and then held out her right hand to Ellen. "I'm Julie Hamilton. This is my daughter Sarah Beth."

"Ellen Jones. It's good to meet you both."

"Would you believe you're the first person I've met in Seaport," Julie said, "besides store clerks, the mailman, and the guy at the gas station? And we've been here a month."

"I've lived here over a year; and truthfully, I haven't met all that many people either. What brought *you* here?"

"My husband went to work at Hank's Body Shop, down by the pier."

"Yes, I know where that is."

"What about you?"

"My husband accepted a partnership in a law firm in Tallahassee."

"So he commutes?"

"Not exactly. He tries to spend half the week in Tallahassee, and the other half working out of our house."

"Do you work?"

Ellen smiled without meaning to. "I'm attempting to write a novel. At the moment, it seems more like playing."

"Sounds exciting."

"It is. But the downside is that I haven't taken the time to make friends."

Julie lifted her eyebrows. "I haven't found people all that friendly. I thought it would be easier here than in Biloxi— Seaport being so much smaller and all."

"It's not close-knit the way you might expect," Ellen said. "Half of the population has been here less than five years."

"Maybe that's what the checker at the grocery store was hinting at. He said once I found my niche I'd like it here. I hope he's right."

Ellen touched the tip of Sarah Beth's nose and got her to smile. "Why don't the two of you come to my house and have a glass of lemonade? I live just a few blocks from here."

"That's really nice of you, but I've got milk and eggs in the car."

"You can put them in my refrigerator."

Julie looked at Sarah Beth. "If only it were that easy to contain Little Miss Sprinter here."

Ellen smiled. "I have a long covered porch out back, where Sarah Beth can run and play to her heart's content while we visit. Please say yes. At least then both of us can say we've made a friend."

Ellen sat in a wicker rocker on the covered veranda of her home, her fingers wrapped around a second glass of lemonade, her eyes studying Julie Hamilton. Ellen guessed her to be thirty something. Thick auburn hair. Pretty face, in spite of the dark circles under her eyes. Nice figure. Ellen noticed her fingernails had been bitten down to the quick. She wondered why Julie had seemed eager to accept her invitation, yet contributed surprisingly little to the conversation.

Ellen turned her attention to Sarah Beth, who squatted on the floor next to the magazine rack, enthralled with the pictures in *National Geographic*.

"Your daughter seems so self-contained," Ellen said. "Her attention span is really quite amazing."

Julie took a sip of lemonade, but offered no response.

"I guess that's often the case with only children," Ellen said.

Julie raised her eyes and looked at Sarah Beth. "Yes, I suppose it is."

Ellen heard sorrow in Julie's voice and couldn't imagine that she had said anything to cause it. "She's a beautiful little girl. Someday, I hope to have a granddaughter."

"Didn't you say you had two grown sons?"

Ellen nodded. "Yes, Brandon's single. Owen got married over the holidays. It might be a while before we have grandchildren. But I'm looking forward to it."

"I remember how excited my folks were when I was pregnant."

"Do your parents see Sarah Beth often?"

Julie stared at her glass, her nose suddenly red, her chin slightly quivering. "Not since…let's just say there's some friction between them and my husband."

Ellen toyed with the urge to play psychologist, but couldn't bring herself to ask questions.

Julie looked at her watch, then set her glass on the coaster. "We really need to be going. Sarah Beth needs a nap, and I have a mound of laundry to tackle."

"Did I say something to upset you?" Ellen said.

"No. It's been a hard year. I guess I'm not ready to talk about it." She got up and went over to Sarah Beth and held out her arms. "Come on. Mama's ready to go. Give the magazine back to Miss Ellen."

"No! Mine!"

"The magazine isn't Sarah Beth's. It belongs to Miss Ellen."

The little girl looked at Ellen, her lower lip pushed out, then clutched the magazine tightly to her chest. "*My* book!"

Ellen covered her smile with her hand and looked at Julie. "She can have the magazine. I'm finished reading it."

"She's been so headstrong lately, I hate to give in to her."

"But she's been an angel since you got here. The magazine is no big deal."

"Are you sure?"

"Yes." Ellen winked. "I have a feeling the ride home will be much more pleasant if you take it with you."

Julie picked up Sarah Beth and held her on one hip. "Miss Ellen says you may have the magazine. What do you say?"

"Thank you."

"You're welcome, cutie." Ellen stroked the child's curls,

amazed at how soft they were. "You were such a good girl. I'm glad you came."

"Thanks for being so nice," Julie said. "I was beginning to think moving here was a mistake."

"Relocating is stressful," Ellen said. "Give it time. Here's my phone number if you need to talk." Ellen jotted the number on the magazine cover.

"Thanks."

"Oh, wait, don't forget your sack in the refrigerator."

Ellen sat on the veranda, enjoying the cool south breeze blowing off the gulf. She heard footsteps inside the house, and then the French doors open.

"I've been on the phone for hours," Guy Jones said. "I thought I heard voices. Was someone here?"

"A young woman and her daughter I met at the grocery store." Ellen told him about how she had apprehended Sarah Beth in the parking lot, and how that had led to a conversation with Julie, and Ellen inviting them over.

Guy walked to the other wicker rocker and sat. "Is she nice?"

"Yes, very nice," Ellen said. "But deeply troubled about something."

Guy arched his eyebrows. "And you know this because...?"

"Because she got emotional when she mentioned a problem between her husband and her parents. And she's clinically depressed. I'd stake my life on it."

"You can't fix her, Ellen."

"I know. But I can't ignore her either."

"Well, you were a good Samaritan, inviting her to your home, then listening to her talk. What more can you do?"

"Probably nothing. I gave her my phone number."

Guy shook his head. "I hope you don't live to regret it. She sounds like one of those people who will drain you."

"I won't let it go that far. But maybe she doesn't even know she's depressed. She seemed detached much of the time, even from Sarah Beth."

"Ellen, you're not a shrink."

She smiled. "I would've made a good one, though."

"Come on, honey, use your energy for writing. You can't save every stray you find."

"Oh, for heaven's sake. I'm nice to one lonely young mother and now I'm trying to save every stray I find? That's a weak and unfounded accusation, wouldn't you say, *Counselor*?"

He held her gaze, the corners of his mouth turning up. "Yes, I'd say. And if you get tired of writing or playing psychologist, you can always try law school."

Julie slid the meatloaf into the oven, dreading the thought of another dinner alone and trying to talk herself into a proper perspective about her husband's long hours. It was hard to say how long it would take to sell their house in Biloxi—especially after all the media hype. But without Ross's overtime, she would have to go back to work.

Julie took in a breath and forced it out. Sometimes she wished she were teaching school again and able to get her mind on something positive. Ross wouldn't hear of her leaving Sarah Beth in daycare, but what kind of stay-at-home mom was she in her current state of mind? She shuddered to think what could have happened to Sarah Beth in the grocery store parking lot. How could she have forgotten to fasten her daughter's seatbelt?

Julie's eyes clouded over and she laid the potholders on the countertop. Ross was too preoccupied with his own inward battle to realize how fragile she was. How was she supposed to cope?

"Mama?"

Julie batted her eyes until they cleared and she saw Sarah Beth standing in the doorway. "What is it, sweetie?"

The little girl stood quietly for a moment, then came over and wrapped her arms around Julie's legs and held tightly. "Be happy, Mama."

Julie squatted in front of her daughter and brushed the unruly curls out of her eyes. "Do you know Mama loves you very much?"

An elfin grin spread across Sarah Beth's face, her tiny arms stretched out as far as they would go, her eyes wide and expressive. "I wuv Mama berry, berry, berry, berry, *berry* much!"

"I know you do. And that's why Mama's happy."

Sarah Beth put her hands on either side of Julie's mouth and pulled up. "Put on happy face."

Julie smiled in spite of herself and then took hold of her daughter's hands and kissed them, thinking if only she could be as direct with Ross as Sarah Beth was with her, maybe things would start to get better.

4

Ellen Jones closed her Bible and walked through the open French doors onto the veranda. She took a whiff of damp, salty air and saw patches of hot pink sky through the sprawling branches of the live oak tree.

"What a gorgeous morning." Guy came out and stood next to her, holding a tray. "Your coffee and newspaper, Madam."

Ellen smiled and sat in the wicker rocker. "Thanks. It's hard to break the ritual after all those years at the *Daily News.*"

Guy set the tray on the side table. "Enjoy the quiet. I'm going to start reading through the Brinkmont files."

"You're not going to your Thursday Bible study?"

"No, I've got too much work to do."

"That's what you said last week."

"I need to stay focused. That was the whole point of coming home early from Tallahassee."

Ellen held his gaze. "It would be a shame not to finish your study of John after all the weeks you've invested."

"There will always be another Bible study, honey. This case is demanding all my energy right now."

Ellen didn't say what she was thinking. She waited until he left, then poured a cup of coffee and opened the *North Coast Messenger* and began reading the lead story:

BOY KILLED BY HIT-AND-RUN DRIVER

Seaport police are looking for clues in the hit-and-run death of an eight-year-old boy, Jeremy Maxwell Hudson. The boy's mother, Kimberly Hudson (37), told police that late Wednesday afternoon she heard a motor vehicle speeding through her south side neighborhood and was on her way outside to investigate, when one of her son's playmates pounded on her front door, screaming that Jeremy had been hit by a truck.

The ten-year-old playmate, whose name is being withheld, told police that a man with dark hair and a mustache sped down the street, his blue truck weaving back and forth, and struck Jeremy who was riding his bicycle along the right side of the street.

Jeremy was thrown into a neighbor's yard by the impact and suffered broken bones as well as multiple head and internal injuries. He was pronounced dead on arrival at Seaport Community Hospital.

Authorities have no suspects and are asking anyone who has information that might help to uncover the identity of the hit-and-run driver to contact the Seaport Police.

Ellen sighed and shook her head. What kind of monster runs down a child and keeps on going?

She sat perusing the paper, and saw a picture of Gordy's Crab Shack and began to read the article under it. She was vaguely aware of Guy coming out on the veranda.

"Honey, have you seen my good fountain pen?" he said.

"I thought I saw it on your desk."

"No, it's not there. I've looked everywhere I can think of."

Ellen looked over the top of the newspaper. "Maybe we should try Gordy's Crab Shack. The mayor took a group from the city council and the Sister's City Program there for dinner last night. The food critic even did an article on it. Sounds impressive."

"Isn't Gordy's a casual place?"

"Very. And it's practically a landmark. Food sounds really good. Not too pricey either."

"Well, I suppose if it's good enough for the mayor, it'd be fun to try."

"Did you check your pocket?" Ellen said.

Guy patted his pocket, then reached in and pulled out his fountain pen. "I must be getting old."

Ellen smiled. "You've got too much on your plate, Counselor."

"Not really. I just need to concentrate. I'm going to hibernate all day. What've you got on your agenda?"

"Think I'll go upstairs and start on chapter twelve."

"I'm glad you're enjoying the writing."

"More than I thought I would. The headlines this morning about the hit-and-run reminded me what I *don't* miss about being close to the story."

Gordy Jameson sat on a bench outside Gordy's Crab Shack, his arms folded and his eyes closed, and let the April sun warm the side of his face. He heard a familiar whistle and his eyes flung open.

"Sleeping on the job?" Adam Spalding said.

"Is it already lunchtime?" Gordy looked at his watch. "I must've snoozed for a minute."

"After schmoozing last night? You got some great press in this morning's paper."

"Yeah, the *Messenger* really talked up the place. That food critic fella, what's-his-name, really did me proud. Wish my folks were alive to hear it."

31

"I didn't realize this place had been here more than fifty years," Adam said.

"Yeah, I remember playin' in the back room before I was old enough to go to school."

Eddie Drummond came across the pier, a finger to his lips, and snuck behind Adam and put him in a headlock. "Hey, rich boy, where's that beautiful blond you keep telling us you're dating?"

"As far away from you as I can keep her."

Eddie laughed. "Afraid she might prefer my type?"

"No, she's not a dog person."

Gordy watched with amusement, aware of Captain Jack standing beside him.

"Who's got who?" Captain said.

"Eddie's razzin' Adam about his mystery girl. Guess I better make sure my cook's got those clams ready."

"You're gonna lose money on me today," Captain said. "I'm so hungry I could eat the whole lot of 'em raw."

"Well, come on then. Weezie's got us set up out back."

Gordy followed his friends through the restaurant and out to the back deck and took a seat. A brisk breeze was spinning the umbrellas on the tables, and a row of scruffy-looking pelicans lined the wood railing in hopes of a handout.

"Gordo, you sure got high praise in the paper this morning," Eddie said.

Captain nodded. "Yeah, congratulations."

"Thanks. I was pretty pleased about it."

"Didn't hurt that you got a hair cut either," Adam said, and quickly added, "You looked professional in the picture."

Gordy felt his face get hot. "Looks can be deceivin', eh?"

Weezie Taylor came outside and walked up to the table. "Everybody want the special?"

All heads bobbed.

"I knew that," she said. "I'll be right back."

Gordy noticed Eddie tapping his fingers on the table, a far-away look in his eyes. "Somethin' buggin' you, Drummond?"

"Oh, I'm still miffed that Ross Hamilton's sucking up to Hank."

"I hope you don't hold it against *me*," Adam said. "All I wanted was my Vet fixed."

"Nah. I just can't figure why Hank's so hot on this new guy doing the detail work."

"What's the guy like?" Captain said.

Eddie rolled his eyes. "How should I know? Hardly ever opens his mouth."

"Ever try talkin' to him?" Gordy said.

"He keeps to himself. Even eats lunch in his truck. A real strange duck."

Gordy took a sip of water and wiped his mouth with the back of his hand. "So maybe he's shy."

"More like antisocial. There's something *off* about this guy."

Captain poked Eddie in the ribs with his elbow. "Sounds like sour grapes to me. Whine. Whine. Whine." He bellowed a hearty laugh that made the people at the next table turn their heads.

"Think what you want, man. But I'm telling you, something's not right.

"Then why do you suppose Hank hired him?" Adam said.

Eddie lifted his eyebrows. "Good question."

Julie Hamilton folded the last piece of laundry and was ready to get off her feet, when she remembered that a lady from J.C. Penney had called and left a message that her new bedroom curtains were in.

She walked into the living room where Sarah Beth was swaying happily to the music of a DVD. "Sweetie, I need you to come to the store with Mama."

Sarah Beth jumped up and down and clapped her hands. "Yipeeeeee!"

Julie turned off the DVD player, then wet her thumb and wiped a smudge off her daughter's cheek. "If you're a good girl while Mama's in the store, we'll stop by the dairy and get ice cream."

Sarah Beth giggled, seemingly beside herself, and dashed into her bedroom and came back clutching a white teddy bear. "Pwincess wants ice cweam."

"Okay, she can go with us." Julie picked up her purse and headed for the front door, aware that Sarah Beth had walked over to the bookshelves. "Mama's ready to leave now. What are you doing?"

The little girl rummaged through a drawer and took out a string of bright blue beads and pulled them over her head. She picked up a pink yarn purse and hung the strap on her shoulder, then stuffed Princess under her arm and toddled back to Julie. "Weady now," she announced, holding up her hand.

Julie smiled and took Sarah Beth's tiny hand into hers, thinking this child deserved so much more attention than she had the energy to give.

Ellen walked out of the alteration's shop carrying Guy's new suit on a hanger and spotted a woman and a little redheaded girl.

"Julie!" Ellen waved and walked over to them. "Small world. What are you two up to?"

"I just picked up my new curtains at Penney's, and Sarah Beth and I were on our way to the Old Seaport Dairy."

"We go to ice cweam!" Sarah Beth held up a white teddy bear as if to show it off.

"And who is this?" Ellen said.

"Pwincess."

"Are you going to share your ice cream with Princess?"

Sarah Beth gave a firm nod. "I nice to her."

"Why don't you go with us?" Julie said. "I promise you they have the best milkshakes in the known world."

Ellen looked at her watch, already trying to decide which flavor she would choose. "Sure, why not? Guy's at home working and I doubt he'll come up for air for another couple hours."

Ceiling fans whirred like helicopter blades above the white tile floor and red brick walls of the Old Seaport Dairy. Customers packed the booths and tables and the noise level made it impossible to be heard when speaking in a normal tone of voice.

Ellen sipped the last of her strawberry-banana shake, her eyes fixed on an old-fashioned metal sign in the middle of the back wall: a redheaded girl in pigtails sharing an ice cream cone with a puppy. She couldn't quite make out the slogan.

"Isn't that a cute sign ?" Julie said. "The owner said it's been hanging in the dairy for seventy years."

"The little girl on the sign looks like Sarah Beth."

"I guess she does. A little."

"I'm really glad I ran into you. This has been fun, and the shake really is wonderful. Thanks."

"I'm glad you like it," Julie said. "I can't tell you how nice it was to finally run into someone I recognize."

Sarah Beth took her thumb and forefinger and pushed a glob of chocolate ice cream onto her spoon, then offered it to Ellen.

"Sweetie, Miss Ellen has her own ice cream," Julie said.

"Oh, but I want a taste of Sarah Beth's." Ellen leaned over and pretended to take a bite. "Mmm...it's delicious. Thank you for sharing."

Sarah Beth giggled and repeated the offer several more times, then began to hum contentedly, stirring what was left of her ice cream until it was soupy.

"What an absolutely beautiful child," Ellen said. "You are so blessed."

Julie's eyes turned watery and she looked away.

Ellen pretended not to notice but was no less surprised than she had been the day before when Julie got emotional.

Half a minute later, Julie looked up. "Sorry, I get teary-eyed over nothing lately. It's probably PMS."

Or depression, Ellen thought.

Julie reached in a zippered bag and plucked a couple of wet wipes and began wiping the chocolate off Sarah Beth's face and hands. "I need to get her down for a nap so she can stay awake till Ross gets home. His day will be ruined if he doesn't get his time with her."

"He works late?"

Julie nodded. "His Uncle Hank gives him the more detailed bodywork. That's not a complaint. Until our house in Biloxi sells, we can really use the overtime. Sometimes I wish I were teaching again. It would make things a whole lot easier."

"I don't remember you mentioning you were a teacher."

"Yes, I taught second grade for eight years. I quit when I got pregnant."

"You haven't been out of it long. Shouldn't be hard to get back into it when you're ready."

"Well, actually, it's been—uh, you're right. It shouldn't." Julie lifted Sarah Beth out of the booster chair and stood her on the floor. "Mama's ready to go. Can you tell Miss Ellen goodbye?"

Sarah Beth laid Princess on the chair, then wrapped her arms around Ellen's legs, squeezed with all her might, and said, "Bye-bye, sweetie."

Ellen laughed and then laughed harder. She squatted next to Sarah Beth and brushed the curls from her face. "Maybe your mama will let you stay at my house for a couple of hours when she needs a little quiet time. I have a tea set tucked away and no little girl to play with."

"What a nice offer," Julie said. "Are you serious?"

"Yes, very. Call me. I'd enjoy spending a couple of hours with her."

Ellen pushed open the kitchen door, dropped her purse on the countertop, and carried Guy's suit to the bedroom closet and hung it up.

"There you are," Guy Jones stood in the doorway, his arms crossed. "I was about to send out a posse."

"Sorry, I didn't call because I didn't want to disturb you. I ran into Julie and Sarah Beth Hamilton when I was coming out of the alterations shop. We went to the Old Seaport Dairy and had the best time. That little Sarah Beth is a character. I'd forgotten how cute two-year-olds can be."

"What about Julie? Was she different this time?"

"She still seemed depressed to me, but she was more sociable. Going to the dairy was her idea. But it was the strangest thing: I expressed my feeling that Sarah Beth was an absolutely beautiful child, and that Julie was so blessed—and she got choked up. She passed it off as PMS, but I'm not buying it."

Guy shook his head and came over to her and put his hands on her shoulders. "Honey, don't take this wrong, but I'm really not interested in Julie Hamilton's problems. Can't we just have a nice quiet evening together?"

Ellen slipped into his arms and rested her head on his chest. "I did offer to keep Sarah Beth sometime—for a couple of hours."

"Why don't you focus on getting your book finished?"

"I am. But truthfully, I'd enjoy the diversion. She really is a sweet little girl. She'd have *you* wrapped around her little finger in no time."

"Wrong. I'm not getting involved. I've got more than I can say grace over now. What little leisure time I have, I want to spend with you."

"That's fine. There will be plenty of time when you're in Tallahassee for me to be a Good Samaritan."

"I don't know why you do this to yourself."

Ellen leaned her head back and looked up at him. "Do what?"

"Try to fix people."

"I didn't say anything about fixing anyone. But it's hard for me to ignore a need when I see it."

"Good." He kissed her forehead. "You can start right here at home because I *need* a relaxing evening."

5

Ellen Jones sat on the veranda, mulling over Friday's devotion in *The Upper Room,* and distracted by a huge plant that, for weeks, seemed as though it were begging to be moved out to the patio. She decided it was time to heed its call.

She got up and crouched next to it, gripped the sides of the pot with both hands, then slowly rose to her feet. She quickly realized it was too heavy. She slid her right hand to the bottom of the pot and lugged it over to the table and dropped it.

"Ouch!" Ellen felt as if someone had hit her hand with a hammer. She tilted the pot slightly by pushing with her shoulder and pulled out the throbbing fingers of her right hand.

Guy came out on the veranda, carrying a tray with her coffee and newspaper. "What's wrong?"

Ellen held out her hand and barely found her voice. "I dropped the plant on it."

Guy set the tray down and examined her hand. "You really mashed those fingers, honey. That thing must weigh forty pounds. What were you thinking?"

"Obviously I wasn't." Ellen winced when she finally saw her fingers. "I didn't want to bother you with something so trivial. I should've just waited till you could help me."

Guy took her by the arm and led her over to the rocker. "Sit down. I'll get you some ice."

Ellen sat staring at her fingers, bemoaning her impulsiveness and wishing she could turn back the clock five minutes.

"Here, put this on it," Guy said, handing her a small ice

pack. "Maybe you should have the doctor take a look at it."

"I don't know what good it would do. Nothing's broken. It's more of a colossal inconvenience than anything else."

Guy stood behind the chair and rubbed her shoulders. "You want me to set the plant out on the patio?"

"Please."

Guy picked up the plant and carried it down the back steps. A minute later he was back. "Is the ice helping?"

"A little. At least it's numbing the pain."

Guy sat in the other rocker, his hands clasped between his knees. "I'm not sure what else I can do for you."

"I'll be fine. Get back to work." She felt her face soften. "Brent's going to be pleased when he sees all the data you're compiling on the Brinkmont case."

"I hope so. I'm glad he trusted me to take the lead on this one."

"I'm so proud of you. God's been good to us, hasn't He?"

Guy gave her a blank look. "I'm sure He has, but I'm not following you."

"This move to Seaport has been a blessing. The Lord opened the door to everything you ever wanted *and* blessed us financially."

"I'd like to think I had something to do with it, Ellen. I've worked hard for this. It's not as though He just poured out the blessing and all I did was show up."

"I just meant that His hand was certainly evident."

"Well, He may have had a hand in it. Just don't forget I'm the one who jumped in with both feet." Guy got up and pressed his lips to hers. "I love you. I'll be in my study if you need me."

Ellen heard his footsteps in the hallway, then the study door open and close. She never quite knew how to discuss spiritual things with Guy. One minute he seemed on the same page, and the next it was as though he didn't understand the most basic biblical concepts. At least he had made a profession of faith. Why couldn't she just be content with that?

Ellen tried to wiggle her swollen fingers and decided it hurt too much. She leaned her head against the back of the rocker. So much for working on her novel.

Julie Hamilton put a scoop of scrambled eggs and three strips of bacon on Ross's plate and set it in front of him. "Why are you so quiet?"

"It's early."

"When I asked you the same question last night, you said you had nothing to say because it was too late."

"Julie, don't start. I'm busting my tail to keep us afloat till the house sells. I'm sorry I'm not conversational enough for you."

Julie turned to Sarah Beth and forced a smile, then set some orange slices on her plate. "Think we could use a civil tone of voice when you-know-who is at the table?"

Ross reached over and stroked Sarah Beth's cheek. "How's my baby doll?"

She reached over and put her sticky fingers on one side of his mouth and pulled up. "Be happy, Daddy."

Julie smiled in spite of herself and locked gazes with Ross.

"There." A phony smile stretched his cheeks. "Is that better?"

Sarah Beth gave an emphatic nod and began to hum as she rubbed an orange slice around her plate.

"Are you going to work late this week?" Julie said.

"Probably."

"Ross, we have to go on with our lives. We can't just stay stuck in all this pain."

"Look whose talking." He hung his head over his plate and took a bite. "This is the wrong time to get into this."

"Then when is the right time? Nighttime doesn't work. Morning doesn't work. You're unavailable every second in between. You've been completely shut down for over a year."

"What do you want me to say? I'm not over it, okay? I'm doing the best I can."

"You're not dealing with it, you're being consumed by it. Do you have any idea how alone that makes *me* feel?" Julie could almost hear the door of his heart slamming shut.

Ross pushed himself away from the table. "Yeah, you tell me a hundred times a day." He got up and grabbed his lunch pail off the counter, then kissed Sarah Beth on the top of the head. "Bye, darlin'. Daddy loves you."

"You need to eat breakfast," Julie said.

"I'm not hungry anymore. I'll see you when I see you."

Julie sat with elbows on the table, her chin resting on her palms, and listened to Ross slam the front door, start his truck, and back out of the driveway. Her eyes brimmed with tears and she blinked rapidly to clear them.

Sarah Beth tugged at the sleeve of Julie's bathrobe. "No cwy, Mama. Be *happy*."

Julie brushed the hair out of Sarah Beth's searching eyes and managed a weak smile, then hurried out of the kitchen. She groped her way to the bathroom, locked the door, and wept.

Ellen managed to dress herself in spite of her sore fingers. If she couldn't work on the book, there was no reason why she should just sit home feeling sorry for herself.

She thought about calling Julie Hamilton, then decided against it, not wanting to seem too available. Once she was working on her novel again, she wouldn't have the time or emotional energy to nurture a friendship with someone as needy as Julie. Keeping Sarah Beth for a few hours was one thing, but Ellen thought it best not to open herself up to Julie until she was sure they had established some boundaries.

She remembered reading about a sale at Beall's and decided

to use this stroke of misfortune as an opportunity to freshen her wardrobe. And maybe try out Gordy's Crab Shack.

Gordy Jameson walked out the back door of his crab shack and onto the deck, delighted to see every table occupied. He let his eyes wander over the lunch crowd and walked up to an attractive lady about his age who was sitting alone.

"I'm Gordy Jameson, the owner. I trust you're enjoyin' your meal?"

"Indeed, I am," the woman said. "This is my first time here, and I just love the seafood salad." She started to extend her right hand, and instead put down her fork and offered him her left. "My name's Ellen Jones. Sorry for the awkward handshake." She smiled sheepishly and held up the bruised and swollen fingers of her right hand. "I tried to lift a plant that was much too heavy for me and dropped the thing on my fingers. Not one of my brighter decisions"

Gordy shook his head. "That looks painful. I'm really sorry." He reached in his pocket and gave her a coupon. "Why don't you try a piece of key lime pie on the house? Guaranteed to cure whatever ails you—or at least distract you from it for a while."

"Thanks, I will. How kind of you. I'm enjoying the food, but also the view from out here. I'm glad I read the article in the newspaper. I'm going to bring my husband with me next time."

"Great. That's what I like to hear. Hope your fingers feel better soon."

Gordy greeted a few more customers he didn't recognize, then walked over to the table where his friends were sitting and dropped into the chair next to Eddie Drummond. "Whew, this place is hoppin'!"

"Must be all that good press," Captain Jack said.

"Yeah, I suppose. I had Weezie call in an extra waitress. If this keeps up, I may be waitin' tables. So, what'd I miss?"

"I got my Corvette back," Adam Spalding said. "Can't tell it's ever been sideswiped."

Eddie rolled his eyes. "Glad *you're* happy."

"Come on, Drummond," Gordy said. "Don't make Adam feel bad just because Hank gave the job to that new guy."

Eddie didn't say anything, but kept stabbing the ice in his glass with the straw.

Weezie Taylor came to the table carrying a big round tray. "Key lime pie all around." She set a piece of pie in front of everyone at the table except Gordy. "You want one, boss?"

"Nah, I can't sit while it's this busy. I'll come back inside in a minute."

Two police officers came out on the deck and sat at the far table.

"Wonder if they've made any progress on that hit-and-run case?" Eddie said. "We never had problems like that till all these outsiders started movin' here."

"Why don't you go ask 'em?" Captain leaned forward, his elbows on the table. "I'm sure they'd be honored to discuss police business with a fine upstanding citizen such as yourself."

Eddie swatted the air. "Joke about it all you want, but crime's on the rise."

"We're talking *one* hit-and-run," Adam said. "It's not like we're becoming another Miami."

"Yeah, well, that's why I don't live there."

Gordy pushed back his chair. "I'll let you guys handle the heavy stuff. I'd better go pitch in if I wanna keep Weezie on the payroll."

Ellen heard bellowing laughter and looked over at the group at the next table, smiling at the owner as he walked past her table.

She let the warm breeze wash over her and took a bite of

key lime pie and let it melt in her mouth. The gulf waters shimmered in the noonday sun; and in the distance, a flock of frenzied gulls were hovering over a fishing boat and diving into the water. Near her feet, several pesky grackles meandered, stealing whatever scraps they found.

She let her mind wander and soon had an idea where her novel would take her when she was able to type again. Why hadn't she brought something to jot notes on? Then again, how fast could she write with her left hand? She pictured in her mind the setting of the next chapter and tried to memorize the details. She visualized the new characters and rehearsed the dialog over and over until she was sure she wouldn't forget it.

Ellen came back to the present and realized all the customers had left the deck except those seated at the table next to her.

"Okay, you wanna know what's eatin' me?" she heard a man say. "I overheard some real scary stuff about Ross Hamilton."

"Like what?"

The man lowered his voice and Ellen strained to hear. "I heard Hank talking on the phone. Sounded to me like Hamilton's a *child molester.*"

"Hank actually said that?"

"More or less."

"Has the guy done time?"

"I don't know, but he must have."

"What were Hank's exact words, Eddie?"

"I can't remember *exactly.* But he was talking with someone on the phone about Ross Hamilton being accused of doing something to a little boy named Nathaniel in Biloxi. Then the other person must've said something because Hank sounded mad and said that nosy reporter couldn't prove Ross was involved in the deaths of those *other* boys or the disappearance of those young women."

"That doesn't sound good."

"No kidding. What if the guy's a pedophile and a murderer?

Heaven knows how many other victims there might be. You can't cure these guys."

"Man, that's scary."

"Then Hank said, and I quote, 'Like it or not, Ross is family. And he's got nowhere else to go.' Wanna bet that's the only reason Hank hired him?"

"No wonder Hamilton's keeping to himself. You think he's a registered sex offender?"

"I dunno, but I'm sure as heck gonna find out. I don't want him near *my* kids."

Ellen opened a menu, her heart racing, and pretended to be engrossed. She stole a glance at the table and saw that the man talking had a crew cut and wore blue coveralls, the name Eddie embroidered above the pocket. One of the other men told him to lower his voice; and after that, she couldn't hear any more of the conversation.

She thought back on Julie's sad eyes and her seeming depression. Had the Hamiltons moved here to escape the wrath of people in Biloxi who didn't want them living next door? And what about Sarah Beth? Was Julie in denial—or naïve enough to think a pedophile husband wouldn't hurt his own child? Is that what had caused the friction between Ross and her parents? Or caused her to cry when Ellen told her how blessed she was?

Out of the corner of her eye, Ellen saw the three men at the table get up. She kept her eyes on the menu as they filed past her and went inside.

6

Ellen Jones walked in the kitchen, set her purse on the island, and hurried down the hallway. She stood in front of the closed door to Guy's study and started to knock, then thought better of it. Would he think what she had just overheard was important enough to interrupt his work? She decided it could wait.

She walked softly down the hall, through the living room, and out onto the veranda. The muggy air turned her around and sent her right back inside. She sank into the couch.

If only she hadn't chosen today to go to Gordy's! The last thing she needed was time on her hands and a story that begged to be reported—especially when it involved someone she knew. When she left Baxter, hadn't she vowed to leave her newspaper career behind and take up something tamer and less obsessive?

She jumped up from the couch, went out to the kitchen, and poured a glass of lemonade. She sat on a stool at the breakfast bar, her mind reeling with the implications of Julie's husband being a child molester.

Ellen started to pour another glass of lemonade and realized she hadn't touched the one in front of her. If Ross was abusing Sarah Beth, it was unconscionable that Julie would simply ignore it. Then again, Cynthia's mother had.

Ellen had never forgotten her friend Cynthia's emotional retelling of how her father had abused her when she was a child. Cynthia had never told anyone until she and Ellen were roommates in college. But once Ellen showed herself to be a compassionate listener, it was as though Cynthia couldn't stop talking until she had rid herself of the dark, oppressive secret. Some of the images filed in Ellen's mind still bothered her. How could she ignore what might be happening to Sarah Beth?

Ellen considered calling Julie and telling her what Eddie had said. But it seemed wiser to call Cynthia and ask her advice.

Ellen reached in the drawer and took out her address book. She found Cynthia's number and dialed, and then hung up. What if Cynthia resented her bringing this up after all these years? And did Ellen really want to get involved in the Hamiltons' situation?

She thought of Sarah Beth and dialed again.

"Hello."

"Cynthia?"

"Yes."

"It's Ellen Madison—Jones."

"Oh, for heaven's sake. How in the world are you? I got your Christmas letter and couldn't be happier about Guy's law partnership. And you're writing a novel! How exciting. Though I've got to tell you, it was a bit sobering to find out Owen got married. Last time I saw him he was just a smidgen taller than the kitchen table."

"Tell me about it. Seems like only yesterday we were in college. And now our *kids* have graduated from college."

There was an awkward stretch of silence. Ellen suddenly lost her nerve and wished she hadn't made the call.

"You haven't phoned me in years," Cynthia said. "Is everything all right?"

"With us, yes. But I do have a situation I'm not sure how to handle. I hesitated to call you, but I don't know who else could offer the input I need. I recently met a young woman with a two-year-old daughter. I think her husband is a pedophile."

"Go on," Cynthia said.

Ellen spent the next couple of minutes telling Cynthia

everything she knew about Julie, Ross, and Sarah Beth Hamilton, and about the conversation she had overheard at Gordy's. "Should I confront Julie with what I overheard?"

"If you don't have a close relationship with her, I can't imagine she would open up on something that sensitive," Cynthia said. "But someone needs to protect that little girl. Her mother obviously isn't."

"How do I start?"

"I guess you'll have to report the situation to the police. Or social services."

"That seems drastic since I don't have proof."

"Come on, Ellen. Where there's smoke, there's fire. You could always confront Ross's employer since he seems to know what's going on."

Ellen put her elbow on the breakfast bar and rested her chin on her palm. "I hate to go behind Julie's back. What if Ross gets fired?"

"I'd be more concerned about getting an innocent two-year-old out of his clutches. I wish someone had rescued me."

"I definitely have to do *something*. But there's a lot at stake here. I don't want to get ahead of myself."

"Why don't you sleep on it? You're too compassionate and too principled to let this go. Once your head is clear, you'll do the right thing."

"Thanks, Cynthia. I'll talk it over with Guy, too. He's a good sounding board."

Gordy Jameson rode his bicycle to Hank's Body Shop and spotted Billy Lewis wiping down the garage door. "Hey Billy, how's it goin'?"

"I am fine, Mister G. How are *you* do-ing?"

Gordy patted his young friend's shoulder. "I'm good, Billy.

Have you seen Eddie?"

"Yes, I have. Ed-die is leav-ing now." Billy pointed to a white truck parked along the curb.

"Thanks." Gordy ran over to the truck. "Hey, Eddie. Wait up! Captain told me what you said at lunch. Did you ask Hank about this Hamilton character?"

"Not yet. I was going to, but he left early. He and the missus drove over to Panama City to pick up her new car. I told you something was wrong. The guy's spooky. Makes me mad Hank hired him, knowing what he is." Eddie traced the letters on his steering wheel. "I guess we're supposed to just sit around and wait till some kid goes missing."

"You *sure* you heard Hank right?"

"Positive."

Gordy shook his head. "Doesn't seem like Hank just to blow off somethin' like this."

"Yeah, well Hamilton's *family*. People do weird things to cover up family secrets."

Gordy pushed away from the truck and stood up straight. "I wanna hear what Hank has to say. Why don't you give me a call after you talk to him? I'll be up late."

"I will." Eddie rolled up his window and pulled away from the curb.

Gordy went over to Billy who was wiping down the door to the garage. "You're workin' mighty hard over here."

"Yes, I am. Mister Ord-man pays me."

"I talked to your dad this morning and he said you're lookin' for more work. I'd sure like to hire you to keep things clean on my back deck. You interested?"

"Yes, I am. I would do a very good job—an *ex-cel-lent* job."

"How about you come talk to me in the morning at eight-thirty—show me what you can do? We'll work out your salary and schedule."

"Oh, yes," Billy said, his eyes wide and animated. "I will

come."

"Great." Gordy shook Billy's hand and slapped him on the back. He hesitated and then decided it couldn't hurt to ask. "Whaddya think of Ross Hamilton? Does he seem like a nice guy?"

"He does not talk to me."

"How come?"

Billy shrugged. "Maybe because I am slow."

"Slow? Why you're the whiz kid when it comes to clean." Gordy delighted in seeing Billy's face light up the way it did when he was little. "See you in the morning."

Ellen sat in the chair in her bedroom, her mind reeling and her emotions in turmoil.

"There you are." Guy came in and sat on the side of the bed, his hands clasped between his knees. "Sorry it took me so long to surface, but I can't believe how much I got done. How're your fingers?"

"About the same. But that's the least of my worries."

"What's up?"

"You won't believe what's going on."

Ellen told Guy about the conversation she had overheard at Gordy's, and about her subsequent conversation with Cynthia.

"I have the sickest feeling that Julie knows and that's why she's depressed."

"Good grief, Ellen. You really know how to pick them."

"You think I wanted *this*?"

"Take it easy, I'm just kidding. What are you going to do?"

Ellen rested her head against the back of the chair. "I'm driving myself crazy trying to decide. I don't have the courage to talk to Julie. I don't think I could handle her reaction. She's either going to be devastated or hopping mad. But I can't simply turn my back on Sarah Beth. Someone has to fight to get that child removed from what's going on."

"What's *allegedly* going on."

"You don't have to correct me, Counselor. I'm well aware I'm walking on eggshells here. What do I do?"

"I agree with Cynthia. Seems reasonable to talk to Eddie's boss."

Ellen's stomach felt as if an army of ants were marching inside it. "I dread sneaking around behind Julie's back. How did I end up in the middle of this mess?"

"Far be it from me to say, 'I told you so.' But you won't be able to leave it alone until you've satisfied your conscience."

Gordy Jameson sat back in his chair, his feet on the ottoman, and took a bite of peach ice cream. He picked up the remote and turned on the TV just as the phone rang.

"Hello."

"Gordo, it's Eddie. Hank's dancing around the Hamilton issue. Says I overheard him wrong. Well, I *didn't*. He says Hamilton's his nephew, and that's why he hired him. Told me to back off and mind my own business. I get the feeling he could make my job miserable if I bring it up again. What's he hiding?"

Gordy stuck his spoon in the ice cream left in the carton. "Maybe he's not hidin' anything. Is it possible you misunderstood what he meant in the telephone conversation?"

"No way."

"Then maybe you should talk to Will about it."

"What's the point? Your friend the police chief thinks I'm a troublemaker since I got into that fight down at The Cove."

"You never could hold your liquor, Eddie. Sounds like you've had one too many tonight."

"I tipped a few. So what? Doesn't mean I'm not right about Hamilton. I'm not done with this. Far as I'm concerned, Hamilton can move his perverted little mind somewhere else."

7

Gordy Jameson stood at the window, skimming Saturday's newspaper while he observed Billy Lewis scrubbing the last of the umbrellas on the back deck. He waited until ten-thirty, then opened the back door and went outside. "About ready to call it a morning?"

Billy's head bobbed, perspiration running down his temples. "I have no more tables to clean now. I did an ex-cel-lent job."

"You sure did. Look how bright these umbrellas are without all that mildew." Gordy ran his hand across the plastic table. "Spotless. Good job, Billy."

"I am a hard worker, right Mister G?"

Gordy put his arm around Billy's sweaty shoulder. "The hardest. I'd like to hire you to come in a couple hours in the mornings. Whaddya think?"

Billy smiled. "I think yes."

"How about Monday through Saturday from eight-thirty till ten-thirty? That shouldn't interfere with your schedule at Hank's."

"Oh, yes. I can come."

Gordy shook his hand. "It's a deal then. Oh, by the way, did Ross Hamilton show up at the body shop this morning?"

Billy nodded. "He was there. Ed-die does not like Ross Ham-il-ton."

"What makes you say that?"

"Ed-die called Ross Ham-il-ton a name I do not understand. I heard Mr. Ord-man yelling at Ed-die. I could not hear all the words, but Mr. Ord-man was not happy. I do not like yelling."

"Well, try to stay out of their way," Gordy said. "I'm sure the guys will work it out. I'm glad you're gonna be on my crew, Billy. I'll see you Monday morning."

Ellen pulled her Thunderbird behind a blue pickup and turned off the motor. She looked into the garage at Hank's Body Shop and saw Eddie with his head under the hood of a black sports car. He glanced up but didn't act as though he recognized her.

Ellen rehearsed what she planned to say, then got out of the car and went into the office and up to the customer service window.

A bleach blond in jeans and a tank top put out her cigarette and rose to her feet. "Can I help you?"

"Yes, I called earlier and was told Hank would be here until noon. I'd like to speak with him, please."

"Wait here. I'll get him."

Ellen looked around the waiting room and read the service policy posted on the wall, signed by *Hank Ordman, owner*. She perused the framed photographs of the service crew. Eddie Drummond looked to be forty-five, give or take. Ross Hamilton appeared to be much younger. And rather harmless-looking. Clean cut. Dark hair. Mustache. The kind of face a child might trust.

A door opened and a gray-haired man dressed in blue coveralls came into the waiting area. "Yes, ma'am. I'm Hank. What can I do for ya?"

"Is there a place we could talk privately?" Ellen said.

Hank stared at her a moment. "You sellin' somethin'?"

"No, this is a personal matter. I won't keep you long."

"All right. Follow me."

Ellen followed Hank through the business office and into a smaller office.

"This private enough?" he said.

"Actually, would you mind closing the door?"

The ridges on Hank's forehead deepened. He got up and shut the door, then sat at the desk facing Ellen. "Okay, who *are* ya and what's this about?"

"My name is Ellen Jones. I realize this is awkward, Mr. Ordman, but I stumbled upon some troubling information about one of your employees, Ross Hamilton, and feel a moral obligation to see if there's any truth to it."

The old man dropped his head and shook it from side to side. "You reporters just never give up, do ya?"

"I'm not with the media," Ellen said. "I'm just a resident who overheard a private conversation. Someone said he heard you on the telephone and the implication was that Mr. Hamilton is a child molester. If it's true, I feel an obligation to be sure he's registered as a sex offender."

"Yeah, and who would this person be who *overheard* me talkin'?"

"That's really not important, it's either true or it isn't."

"Ya see, that's the trouble. All that he-said-she-said malarkey ain't worth anything."

"Are you saying it's not true?"

"Lady, first off, it's none of your business. Second, I ain't givin' you ammunition to put this boy through anything else."

Ellen was glad a gush of cold air came out of the ceiling vent. "Honestly, I'm not trying to hurt the man. I don't even know him. I just—"

"You just what—wanna protect the public? I've heard it all before. So who's gonna protect Ross and his family, wanna tell me *that*?"

Ellen felt the color scald her cheeks. "Actually, that's exactly my concern—that someone should be looking out for his little girl."

Hank sighed and shook his head again, then rose to his feet. "We're done. Git out."

"Sir, are you protecting a pedophile?" Ellen said. "You know I can't just drop this."

"Well, you ain't gittin' me to help you." He held open the door. "You can leave the same way you come in."

Ellen went in the house and looked down the hall to see if the door to Guy's study was closed. It was. She got a bottle of water out of the refrigerator and sat at the breakfast bar.

If Ross Hamilton wasn't guilty, why hadn't Hank Ordman answered her question instead of rudely talking around the issue? There had to be a way to find out. Ellen left the kitchen and went up the winding stairs to the widow's watch. She turned on her laptop and got online.

She pulled up Google, and then with the forefinger of her left hand pecked out, "r-e-g-i-s-t-e-r-e-d s-e-x o-f-f-e-n-d-e-r-s F-l-o-r-i-d-a," and hit Enter, surprised at the long list of pertinent information options that appeared on the screen. She scrolled down till she found the Florida Sex Offenders home page, then clicked on to the site and typed in Ross Hamilton's name and the county. A long list of sex offenders and predators appeared. *No Ross Hamilton.*

She went back to Google and followed the same procedure for sex offenders in Mississippi, Georgia, and Alabama and got the same results. She turned off the computer and sat back in her chair.

Should she tell the police what she'd overheard Eddie say? Should she talk to Julie first? Or should she mind her own business and just try plotting the next chapter of her novel?

Julie Hamilton pulled up in front of Hank's Body Shop and spotted Ross with his head buried under the hood of a blue sports car. She tooted the horn.

Ross looked up, then wiped his hands with a rag and walked over to the car, the lines across his forehead revealing his mood. "What're you doing here?"

"I brought your lunch." She took his lunch pail off the passenger seat and handed it to him through the open window. "You walked off without it."

"I wish you'd have called first. I'm coming home at noon." He looked in the backseat, the lines disappearing from his forehead. "Hear that, baby doll? Daddy's got the rest of the weekend off."

"Good," Julie said. "That'll give us some time to talk."

Ross dropped his head and shook it from side to side. "Here we go again."

"It's not as though I'm asking for the moon," she said. "I just want things to be the way they used to be. Do you know how awful it makes me feel when you avoid me?"

Ross lifted his eyes and shot her a disgusted look. "No, tell me again. I've only heard it now about a thousand times."

"Don't you find it alarming we can't seem to carry on a normal conversation since Nathaniel—"

"I told you I'm not over it. Anyway, I need to finish this car. The customer's waiting." He turned on his heel and started walking toward the service garage.

"Ross, please don't turn your back and walk away mad. It upsets me for the whole day."

"Yeah, well, my day hasn't been a picnic either."

Julie blinked the stinging from her eyes, wondering if anything would bring back the man she married.

Ellen sat in the Seaport police station, her hands folded on a big oak table. She glanced up at the clock and wondered what was taking Police Chief Will Seevers so long. She was eager to turn this matter over to him and get herself uninvolved as quickly as possible.

The door opened and the police chief came in the room and sat across from Ellen. "Okay, Mrs. Jones. You did your civic duty. We'll take it from here."

"Are you going to tell me whether Ross Hamilton's a sex offender?"

"He doesn't have a criminal record, ma'am."

"Aren't you at least going to question him—or Eddie or Hank Ordman?"

"We'll look into it. But unless someone presses charges or produces evidence, this kind of information isn't terribly useful."

Ellen leaned forward on her elbows. "Chief, I was a newspaper editor for ten years, and a reporter for many years before that. I've been in the thick of some serious situations. I wouldn't have brought this to your attention if I didn't think it warranted investigation. My instincts are pretty good. Something's wrong in that family. I can feel it."

"Yes, ma'am. Like I said, we'll look into it."

He had the audacity to patronize her? "I sincerely hope you do. If what Eddie overheard is true, Ross Hamilton poses a threat to the children of this community, not to mention his own daughter."

The chief's intense gray eyes locked on to hers. "*Nobody* wants to keep kids safe any more than I do. Why don't you let *me* do my job?"

"Very well." Ellen pushed back her chair and stood.

She left Chief Seevers's office with an uneasy feeling that he didn't take this seriously enough. She remembered Eddie saying that Ross Hamilton had been accused of doing something to a little boy named Nathaniel in Biloxi. She decided to go online and check the Biloxi newspaper and see if she could find anything archived.

Ellen opened her eyes wide and blinked several times to get rid of the grainy sensation, then took another sip of coffee. She had been online all afternoon and had already accessed the news articles that appeared in the Biloxi-Gulfport *Sun-Herald* over the past three years and found no mention of Ross Hamilton or a boy named Nathaniel.

She took in a breath and forced it out. She backed out of the *Sun-Herald* website and noticed a website listed for a *Biloxi Telegraph*. She went to the home page and clicked on to Archived Articles and began to scroll backwards.

Ellen looked through all the articles in April and March and started reading February's when she started to nod off. She was just about to quit her search and take a break when her eyes fell on a February 15 article:

TIME TO WAKE UP
By staff reporter Valerie Mink Hodges

Four-year-old Nathaniel Hamilton died one year ago today, and I'm still bothered by it. Biloxi police have closed the case, concluding it was a tragic accident that the boy's father, Ross Hamilton, backed over Nathaniel with the family car.

But why are the police reluctant to comment on a series of accidental deaths and mysterious disappearances for which Ross Hamilton was the only witness—not to mention an unresolved hit-and-run?

The first incident happened on April 14, 1980, when Hamilton was ten. He accidentally discharged a rifle and shot and killed his eight-year-old brother William.

Then on October 30, 1982, Hamilton witnessed his best friend Daniel Slocum fall to his death when the boys were climbing at the Pritchard rock quarry. Slocum's death was ruled an accident.

On June 23, 1986, Hamilton was parked in a secluded area of Griswold State Park with his girlfriend Alicia Derringer (16), when the young woman mysteriously disappeared while Hamilton was thirty yards away in the park restroom. Her body was never found.

On November 18, 1991, Stacey Lincoln (21) failed to show up at her parent's home for Thanksgiving break after being dropped off at the bus station by Ross Hamilton. Records show Miss Lincoln never boarded the bus. She has not been heard from since.

According to articles in the Biloxi-Gulfport *Sun-Herald* following each of these incidents, police questioned Hamilton at length and conducted a thorough investigation, but found no incriminating evidence.

Then on August 11, 1998, a hit-and-run driver killed six-year-old Jana Gilbert on the 700 block of North Hemlock Street. Though the description of the car and driver didn't yield any viable suspects and the crime remains unsolved, it is interesting in hindsight that the vehicle, described as a white late model Ford Taurus, was also the type of car Ross Hamilton owned at that time.

Does anyone else wonder why the police are snoozing on this one?

Ellen sat back in her chair and tried to assimilate the magnitude. Nathaniel was Ross's *son*? How horrible that must have been for Julie! Ellen reread the article. Not once was it even implied that Ross Hamilton was a child molester. Why hadn't Hank just said that?

But this new information gave Ellen a sinking feeling. Was Ross Hamilton an unusual type of serial killer? She thought of the hit-and-run in Seaport. Blue pickup. Mustached man. She remembered parking behind a blue pickup when she went to talk to Hank Ordman.

Ellen turned off her laptop and skipped down the winding staircase to the kitchen, where Guy sat at the breakfast bar, drinking a glass of lemonade.

"So what did you decide to do about Ross Hamilton?" he said.

Ellen told Guy everything that had happened from her confrontation with Hank Ordman to her encounter with Chief Seevers to her finding the article in the *Biloxi Telegraph*.

"You're a news magnet, you know that?" Guy said.

"I didn't go looking for this. But I can't just ignore it."

"I agree. So, what's the next step?"

"I'll have to go back to Chief Seevers on Monday and give him the article. Even if Ross Hamilton doesn't have a record, the chief should be made aware of his suspicious history."

8

On Monday morning, Ellen Jones awoke to the inviting aroma of freshly brewed coffee. When had she finally dropped off to sleep? Her body would have been content to lie right there, but her mind was already in high gear. She threw off the covers and heard Guy singing in the shower. She put on her bathrobe and headed for the kitchen, aware of the dull throbbing in her fingers.

She took two Advil, then poured a cup of coffee and went out on the veranda. She sat in her wicker rocker and tried to get quiet inside. She closed her eyes and absorbed the sounds—the chirping of birds, the stirring of palm fronds in the warm breeze, and the deep, resonating blast of a freighter's horn in the distance.

She prayed for Julie and Sarah Beth—and for courage and wisdom to appropriately handle the encounter she would have with the police chief later this morning.

Ellen sat quietly for a few minutes, then opened her eyes and took a sip of lukewarm coffee. The chirping of a tiny Carolina wren filled the backyard, and she wondered if what she had to tell Chief Seevers would create as much stir at the police station.

Guy came out on the veranda. "Okay, honey, I'm off to Tallahassee. I'll call you tonight." He pressed his lips to hers. "Thanks for giving me space to work. I know it's been difficult trying to decide what to do about Ross Hamilton. Maybe by the time I get home Wednesday afternoon, we can put this behind us and spend next weekend doing something fun."

Julie Hamilton stirred fresh blueberries into the bubbly oatmeal, then put the lid on the pan and turned off the burner. The front door slammed so hard the kitchen window rattled.

"It's okay, sweetie," she said to Sarah Beth. "Mama will be right back."

Julie went into the living just as Ross flung the newspaper at the far wall and let out a string of curse words.

"What's wrong?" she shouted in a whisper. "Sarah Beth can hear you."

Ross pushed open the front door. "Take a look. I'm sure half of Seaport has by now!"

Julie went out on the porch and noticed cars slowing and drivers looking up at the house. She went down the steps and halfway down the front walk, then turned around. On the garage door, the words "Child Molester" had been written in black spray paint. She stood staring until her eyes clouded over, and then stormed up the steps and back into the house.

"Ross, what's this about?"

"I'm gonna kill Eddie Drummond, that's what this is about! He overheard Uncle Hank talking to Aunt Alice about what that reporter in Biloxi wrote and came up with some stupid notion that I'm a child molester."

"*What?*" Julie threw up her hands. "Hello? I'm your wife! I can't believe you didn't bother to tell me!"

"I was too upset. That's what was wrong with me when you brought my lunch Saturday."

"You've known since *Saturday*?"

"Yeah, Eddie came in early, loaded for bear. Said I was a sicko pervert. Hank set him straight, but you should've seen his face. I can't prove it, but I know Eddie's behind this."

"I'm calling the police," Julie said.

Ross grabbed her arm. "The *last* thing we need is for the police to get involved. I'll handle it."

"How? By having a fistfight with Eddie? This is more than name-calling. Think of the implications!"

"Why should I? I'm not a child molester!"

"*Something* Uncle Hank said gave Eddie the impression you were. Didn't you even ask Hank what it was?" Julie sat on the couch, her fingers massaging her temples.

"I told you he was talking to Aunt Alice about everything that reporter wrote. Eddie must've gotten bits and pieces and put his pea brain to work overtime."

"I must be missing something. Are you sure you've told me everything?"

"So now I have to defend myself with you, too?"

"I'm just trying to understand how something could get so radically misconstrued."

Ross put his hands flat against the wall and hung his head. "If you wanna know what Uncle Hank said, ask him yourself. It doesn't really matter. Eddie's way off base."

"Then report this to the police and stand your ground."

"Why should I have to? It's absurd."

"Ross, listen to me. We have to refute this. They could take Sarah Beth away from us!"

"Mama?"

Julie's heart sank. She turned and saw Sarah Beth standing in the doorway, her eyes wide and questioning. "Come here, sweetie."

Sarah Beth ran to Julie's open arms. "It's okay." Julie picked up her daughter and rocked from side to side. "Mama and Daddy are angry with someone, but not Sarah Beth."

Julie looked over at Ross and held his gaze. "You have to make this go away."

Ross headed for the door. "That's exactly what I'm going to do—starting with that bigmouthed weasel Eddie Drummond."

Gordy Jameson rode up to Hank's Body Shop and leaned his ten-speed against the side of the building. He didn't see Eddie, though his truck was parked out front.

"Hello Mister G," Billy Lewis said. "I am fine. How are you doing?"

Gordy slapped him on the back. "Just great, Billy. I'm anxious to put you on my payroll this morning. We still on for eight-thirty?"

"Yes, eight-thir-ty."

"Any idea where Eddie is?"

Billy nodded toward the office. "Everyone's face is mad."

"Okay, thanks." Gordy walked in the customer service door and heard deep, muffled voices in another room. He stood at the service window, straining to hear.

"I don't care *what* you think you know," a man shouted, "I'm not a child molester! I've never even been arrested! How dare you vandalize my home and trash my reputation with that filth!"

"Settle down," Eddie said, "it wasn't me."

"Well, don't look at me," another man said. "I was home with the missus all night."

"Well, I sure as shootin' didn't do it!" a young man exclaimed. "I don't even know what the heck you're talkin' about!"

"Maybe you should ask that lady who talked to Hank," Eddie said. "She's the one who's got it in for you."

"I just want it stopped! You got that, Eddie? It's nothing but a bunch of—"

Gordy was suddenly aware of someone standing behind him.

"Is Ross Ham-il-ton a bad man?" Billy said.

"I'm not sure. Why do you ask?"

The young man hung his head, his hands in the pockets of his cutoffs. "People think I do not hear things. But I do."

"Things about Ross?"

Billy nodded. "Ed-die says he does bad things—touches chil-dren in wrong ways, and *kills* them. I am afraid of Ross Ham-il-ton."

Gordy heard a door open, and then through the customer service window saw a young man with a mustache rush out of Hank's office and yank open the door to the waiting area. He paused in the doorway, seemingly stunned to see Gordy and Billy, and then brushed past them and went outside.

Eddie Drummond came out of the back, a smirk on his face. "I doubt he'll be around much longer. Somebody spray-painted 'Child Molester' across the front of his garage."

Ellen walked into the Seaport Police Station and asked to see Chief Seevers. After waiting twenty minutes, she was escorted to his office.

"Back again so soon?" the chief asked.

"I promise I won't keep you long. I thought you should be made aware of this." Ellen handed him the Valerie Mink Hodges article she had printed out.

"Sit down and let me take a look." Chief Seevers put on his glasses, his eyes moving from left to right down the page. "Where'd you get this?"

"In the *Biloxi Telegraph* archives, February 15 of this year."

"I don't see sex offender mentioned anywhere."

"No, but I find the deaths and disappearances equally alarming. I thought you should be apprised."

"Hamilton's never been charged with anything."

"Yes, I know," Ellen said. "But there's still that unsolved hit-and-run in August of '98. Doesn't it strike you as odd that Seaport had a hit-and-run—one month after Ross Hamilton moved here? I assume you know he drives a blue truck and has a mustache, which fits the description of the driver?"

"And a hundred other guys."

"But under the circumstances, surely you can understand my concern."

"Sure I can." Seevers looked over the top of half-glasses. "Now, I have a question for you: Where were you last night?"

"Excuse me?"

"My phone's been ringing off the hook since early this morning. Seems someone spray painted the words 'Child Molester' across the front of Ross Hamilton's garage."

"Surely you don't think I had anything to do with it?"

"Why not?"

Ellen felt the heat scald her cheeks. "I'm insulted that you would even imply such a thing! I'm the one who came to you!"

The chief folded his hands on his desk. "Relax, Mrs. Jones, I don't suspect you. But can you see how easy it is to jump to conclusions? You had motive. Opportunity. Why *not* you?"

"Because I would never do something like that."

"My point exactly. Look, I had a heart-to-heart with Hank Ordman. Ross is his nephew. He told me all about the things written in this article and the suspicions surrounding Ross. There simply hasn't been evidence to support his wrongdoing in any of the deaths or the disappearances. And there's no point in trying to reopen the 1998 hit-and-run case because the man who bought Ross's white Taurus totaled it shortly afterwards." The chief leaned back in his chair, his hands behind his head. "And unless someone comes forward with a legitimate accusation of child molestation, there's nothing to investigate."

Ellen picked up a pencil and twirled it over and over like a baton. "I think it's important that Ross Hamilton know that *you* know he's living in Seaport. If he's innocent, he shouldn't mind you keeping a watchful eye. If he's hiding something, then he deserves to squirm."

Chief Seevers got up and stood by the window, his hands in his pockets. "I've known Hank Ordman all my life. If he had the slightest suspicion that Ross was guilty of any of these charges, he never would've hired him. He says Ross isn't capable of hurting anyone on purpose."

Ellen sighed. "With all due respect, Mr. Ordman can hardly be objective. I'm not looking to persecute Ross Hamilton. But it seems you owe it to this community to keep an eye on him. You have to admit trouble seems to follow him wherever he goes."

Will Seevers pulled his squad car in front of Ross Hamilton's house and saw the words "Child Molester" bleeding through a fresh coat of white paint.

He got out of the car and pushed his way past a handful of reporters and a blue pickup in the driveway. Just as he put his finger on the doorbell, a pretty young woman with frightened eyes opened the door.

"Mrs. Hamilton? I'm Police Chief Seevers. I called earlier."

"Please come in."

Mrs. Hamilton led him into the living room where a thirty-something man with a mustache sat on the couch, his arms folded, his jaw set.

"Please sit down," Mrs. Hamilton said. "My name's Julie, and this is my husband, Ross."

Will started to offer his hand and then changed his mind. "Mr. Hamilton, I appreciate your agreeing to meet with me here instead of at the station. I didn't see any reason to cause you more embarrassment. I know my officers have already questioned you, but Hank asked me to talk to you myself."

"I'm *not* a child molester," Ross said.

"Can you think of any reason why someone would accuse you?"

"No."

"Why didn't you report the vandalism to the police?"

Ross glanced over at his wife and then at the chief. "With all the freaky things that have happened to me, I assumed you'd believe it. I didn't want to be interrogated all over again. Guess I can forget that."

"Hank seems sure you're not a child molester. And he thinks that lady reporter in Biloxi is way outta line, too."

"Yeah, well, try telling that to her readers."

"I spoke with your coworkers. Eddie Drummond admitted talking to some friends down at Gordy's about you. That's where the lady who spoke to me overheard the conversation."

"Here we go again," Ross said, throwing up his hands. "Telegraph. Telephone. Tell a *woman*."

"Might wanna cut her some slack," Will said. "This woman is the *only* one who's going through proper channels. Said she was alarmed and didn't feel comfortable not checking it out. I honestly think she has your daughter's best interest at heart."

Ross rolled his eyes. "Yeah, I'll bet."

Will paused for a moment, studying Ross's face. "Can you account for your whereabouts last Wednesday afternoon at 4:00?"

Ross put his hand on the back of his neck and rolled his head from side to side. "I'm not your hit-and-run driver either. You can go over my truck with a fine-tooth comb. You won't find anything because I didn't do it."

"Do you remember where you were at the time?"

"Hank sent me to Auto Supply to pick up a part. I'm sure you can find my signature on the paperwork. I wasn't anywhere near that hit-and-run."

"Mr. Hamilton, I can only imagine how frustrated you must be. But I assure you that if you're innocent of any wrongdoing, you have nothing to fear from the Seaport police."

"*If?*" Ross leaned his head on the back of the couch. "I'd like to rip those two letters out of the alphabet."

Julie stood at the front door until the chief's squad car pulled away from the curb. She cracked the door to Sarah Beth's room and peeked inside, then went back into the living room.

Ross sat on the couch, his arms folded. "She still asleep?"

Julie nodded. "I think the police chief believes you."

"Yeah, well, let's see how long that lasts once the media puts their own spin on it. It's gonna be the same wherever we go."

Julie sat next to Ross and wished he would hold her hand. "Sarah Beth and I love you. We're in this together."

"I miss Nathaniel so much. I don't think I can handle anything else…"

She blinked the stinging from her eyes. "I know."

There was a long stretch of silence.

"Julie, you believe me, don't you?"

"Of course, I believe you. You'd never be inappropriate with Sarah Beth."

"Well, after the way you reacted this morning, I got the uneasy feeling you were doubting me."

"It's just beyond me how Eddie came up with such a gross accusation based on anything Hank would've said. Why would he just make up something like that out of the clear blue?"

"Because he's a moron."

"Obviously."

Julie sat in silence, her hands folded in her lap, all-too-aware of the oppressive, impenetrable wall between Ross and her. She felt a twinge of doubt and quickly dismissed it. He wasn't capable of such a thing. He just wasn't.

9

Late Monday afternoon, Will Seevers sat in his office, the ceiling fan rustling the papers on his desk, and perused a FAX that had just come in from the Biloxi police department.

Nothing on file indicated Ross Hamilton had ever been accused of child molestation. But the department had kept an eye on him after Valerie Mink Hodges from the *Biloxi Telegraph* wrote an article summarizing Hamilton's questionable history and insinuating that the police were sleeping on the job.

The chief read through several pages, which essentially outlined what he already knew. His eyes dropped to the final paragraph:

Over a twenty-six year span, Ross Hamilton has been the sole witness of three accidental deaths. And was the last person to see two young women alive before each mysteriously disappeared in two separate incidents. But there has been no evidence whatsoever linking him to a crime.

Will removed his glasses and rubbed his eyes. The phone rang and he picked it up. "Seevers."

"Will, it's Gordy. I'm not askin' for a special favor, but can you tell me *anything* about Ross Hamilton?"

"Yeah, the Biloxi police have nothing on him. But listen to this." Will picked up Valerie Mink Hodges's article and read it aloud. "How uncanny is that? Hamilton's either one slick operator or the unluckiest chump on the planet. The media ought to have a heyday with this."

"It's hard to blame Eddie for bein' rattled after overhearin' Hank say the guy's a child molester."

"Yeah, but Hank says your buddy Eddie interpreted the phone conversation all wrong. He insists that Ross is a victim of cruel circumstances."

"Come on, Will. Hank's his uncle, whaddya expect him to say? I'll tell you one thing: Billy Lewis is sure uncomfortable around Hamilton."

Will leaned back in his chair, his hands clasped behind his head. "Yeah, that's what he told my officers. Think he knows something he's not saying?"

"Nah, Billy wears his feelings on his sleeve," Gordy said. "But it's worth notin' that he doesn't want anything to do with Ross Hamilton."

"Hear anything down at your place?"

"I'm startin' to. But wait'll that garage door is shown on the news. That oughta set off a chain reaction."

The chief picked up a pencil and started doodling. "I'm gonna keep an eye on Hamilton. But Hank thinks he's innocent, and I put a lot of stock in Hank's judgment."

"Why—because he picked *you* to pitch the final inning in that championship game?"

Will laughed. "We won, didn't we? Listen, I gotta get back to work. By the way, did you ever ask out that lady who runs the clothing shop?"

"Nah, I haven't had time."

"You big chicken."

Gordy sighed. "I don't think I'm ready, Will. It's a big step."

"Listen, friend, life's too short to put off the good stuff. Why don't you just jump in with both feet and ask her out?"

"Every time I see her I get so flustered one foot ends up in my mouth."

"You just need to build up your confidence."

"You really think any woman's gonna get cranked up over

a guy with a spare tire that would put Goodyear to shame?"

"Yeah, I do. You're a big teddy bear. Women like that. But would it be so bad to get a haircut a little more often and learn to skip second helpings? You've got a lot to offer. Don't sell yourself short."

Ellen looked at her watch, then picked up the remote and turned on the TV.

"Good evening, this is Shannon Pate…"

"And Stephen Rounds. Welcome to Regional News at Six. Seaport police are trying to uncover the motivation behind a blatant and troubling act of vandalism in north Seaport.

"Shortly after sunrise this morning, Seaport police began getting calls from concerned citizens who had driven past the home of Ross and Julie Hamilton in the 900 block of Whitmore and saw the words 'Child Molester' spray painted on the garage door. Jared Downing is at the scene. Jared, tell us what you know."

"Stephen, I'm standing outside the Hamilton residence, and you can see the words 'Child Molester' are still visible, even after being painted over. Police have investigated the situation and have made no arrests in the case. But sources inside the police department told WRGL News that the incident may have occurred in response to a February 15th article that appeared in the *Biloxi Telegraph*, and which outlined a series of accidental deaths involving Ross Hamilton, including the death of his four-year-old son Nathaniel—and the unexplained disappearances of two young women.

"It's unclear at this hour what precipitated the vandal to write 'Child Molester' on the garage. But given Ross Hamilton's history, local residents want answers, fearing that someone may be pointing a finger at a sexual predator. Hamilton and his wife, who have a two-year-old daughter, have refused to comment.

"Police Chief Will Seevers would not comment on the case,

but did say that Biloxi police had no evidence to indicate Hamilton was guilty of a crime, nor has he ever been charged with a crime. This is Jared Downing, reporting live. Stephen…"

"Thanks, Jared. We'll continue to bring you breaking news as it happens. In other news tonight…"

Ellen turned off the TV and sat for a moment, trying to absorb the impact of what had happened. She shuddered to think of Sarah Beth being in that house.

The phone rang and Ellen went out to the kitchen and picked it up.

"Hello."

"It's me," Guy said. "Brent and I are getting ready to go out for dinner, but I wanted to check in first and see how your day went. How's your hand?"

"About the same. But you're not going to believe the latest in the Hamilton situation."

Ellen told him about the vandalism at the Hamiltons' and the stir it had created in the community. She also told him about her meeting with Chief Seevers.

"Did the police chief comment on the article?" Guy said.

"Very little, since it didn't allude to child molestation and that's the crime in question. The fact that Hank Ordman thinks Ross is innocent seems to carry a lot of weight with him."

"Yes, but no police chief worth his salt is going to decide a man's guilt or innocence based on the opinion of one man— especially a blood relative."

"Let's hope you're right, Counselor. I just wish the Department of Children and Families would remove Sarah Beth from the home until this is resolved."

There was a long pause.

"I'm surprised you're even thinking that DCF should take action at this stage," Guy said. "You would favor tearing that little girl away from her parents based on what—something you overheard about something Eddie overheard? And words spray-painted on a garage door? Since when is that your style?"

"I'm not acting as a newspaperwoman, just a concerned citizen."

"So that makes it okay to get sloppy? Assumptions like this can destroy a person's reputation without a shred of evidence. You've always been above that."

"Come on, Guy, I read you the article. There was just cause to wonder about Ross Hamilton before this happened."

"Wonder all you want. But he was never charged with anything."

Ellen sighed and leaned her head on the back of the couch. "Okay, you're right. I'm way ahead of myself. But something's wrong in that family. I can feel it."

"Since when does *feeling* supercede fact? Ellen, either find the evidence—or let it go."

10

Julie Hamilton stared at the picture of her house on the front page of Tuesday's *North Coast Messenger*, then folded the newspaper in half and threw it in the trash. She peeked out the kitchen curtains and saw a WRGL-TV truck parked across the street.

Ross came into the kitchen and kissed Sarah Beth on the top of her head, then sat at the kitchen table next to her. "Are the vultures still out there?"

Julie nodded. "I doubt this will just blow over. I'm wondering how long before some social worker comes knocking on our door."

"We have rights. Just because somebody spray-painted an accusation of abuse on our garage door doesn't entitle the state to march in here and tell us what to do. The whole thing's bunk."

Julie walked over to the stove and stirred the oatmeal, then took it off the burner. "I don't know how much power they have, but I think we need to brace ourselves." Julie put her fist to her mouth and choked back the intense fear that felt like chalk in her throat. "What if they try to take you-know-who away from us?"

"Over my dead body!"

Sarah Beth reached over and pushed up the side of Ross's mouth. "Be happy, Daddy."

"Okay. Daddy's happy. See?" He faked an exaggerated smile.

"We don't have anything to hide," Julie said. "Maybe we

should just make the first move and invite them to come talk to us."

"Absolutely not! I won't play this game. I haven't done anything."

"But—"

"But nothing! Why should I make it easy for them when I'm the victim here? If they want anything from me, they can get a court order."

Julie glared at him. "And what if they do? What then? I don't know that we have a whole lot of say-so."

"Oh, yes, we do. We're not caving in to this. I'm going to work, and you do what you always do. Let's just go about our normal lives."

Normal lives? Julie spooned oatmeal into three bowls, wondering if Ross realized the absurdity of what he had just said.

Julie lay with her arm draped over Sarah Beth until the child fell asleep, then went out to the kitchen table and sat, vaguely aware of the faucet dripping.

She closed her eyes and called up a memory that still seemed as clear to her as if she were there, one she could go back to again and again and remember what it felt like when life *was* normal…

Nathaniel had been riding on Ross's shoulders, his auburn curls tossed about in the sea breeze, his tiny hands clinging tightly to the sides of his daddy's head.

"It's gonna *get* you!" Ross said, making shrieking noises as he ran away from the approaching surf, the sound of Nathaniel's belly laugh drawing smiles from onlookers.

Julie watched with delight as Ross repeated the game over and over, running from the surf and squealing playfully when the waves flattened out and whooshed onto the sand, covering his feet. Nathaniel's giggling was so intense that it continued without sound until he finally caught his breath. Julie memorized the moment, wondering if the child in her womb could bring them as much happiness as Nathaniel had.

But she never imagined the happiness would turn to sorrow.

"Okay, hon, I'm going to the store," Ross had said. "Do you need anything besides milk and diapers?"

"That's all for now."

"You want me to take Nathaniel with me?"

"No, I think he's finally fallen asleep. I don't know why he fights his nap so hard, but he's started this new routine where he hides from me and won't come when I call him. It's about to drive me crazy."

"Probably just a phase." Ross pressed his lips to her cheek. "I'll be back in a few minutes. If you think of something else, call my cell phone."

Julie went to the nursery door and peeked in on Sarah Beth and saw the rise and fall of the pink thermal blanket in her crib.

She closed the door and then peeked in on Nathaniel and saw his bed was empty. She looked in the toy chest and checked the closet. "Nathaniel, stop hiding. It's time for your nap. Mama's losing patience—"

"Julie, help! Somebody help. *Heeeelp!*"

She raced outside and saw Ross kneeling on the driveway, Nathaniel limp in his arms, blood trickling from her son's nose and mouth. Ross looked up at her, terror in his eyes. "Call 911! I backed over Nathaniel!" Ross held the boy to his chest and rocked. "Stay with me, son. Hang in there, buddy. Daddy's here. Daddy loves you…"

Julie dashed into the house and dialed 911. After that, everything was a blur. Sirens. Paramedics. Police. Voices. The baby crying. The phone ringing. Someone holding her hand. Someone holding the baby. The dazed look on Ross's face—and the sheet being pulled over Nathaniel's…

Julie got up from the kitchen table and tore a paper towel off the roll and wiped her eyes. She'd been over this a hundred times. Nathaniel must have been hiding under the car. Had he fallen asleep there? Why hadn't she seen him sneak out of the house? If only she had checked on him a minute earlier.

She sat again, her elbows on the kitchen table, her warm hands pressed against the sides of her neck, remembering all-too-vividly that rainy Tuesday morning at Resurrection Cemetery...

Julie hadn't been able to take her eyes off the tiny casket covered with a spray of baby roses and a pale blue ribbon with the word "Son."

Pastor Helms dabbed his eyes, then held tightly to her hand and Ross's, struggling to maintain his composure through the final prayer, something about Nathaniel being in the arms of his Heavenly Father, and everyone seeing him again in that place where pain and weeping will be no more.

But the pastor's closing words were sobering—and unforgettable.

"Father in heaven, we bless Your Name in spite of the sorrow and the questions—and even the doubts. We trust in Your higher purpose and await that glorious day when we, too, will be called into Your presence."

Julie dutifully squeezed the pastor's hand, but stood silently and defiantly against his words. How could she trust a God who would allow a cruel tragedy like this to destroy their family—and especially after what Ross had already been through?

She got in the black limousine, wanting no more to do with Him or His church...

Julie got up and tore another paper towel off the roll. She wiped the tears off her cheeks and blew her nose. Things had only gotten worse since Nathaniel's death. That reporter at the *Telegraph* had twisted and manipulated the events of Ross's past and set him up to look like some sort of serial killer.

But child molestation? That accusation had caught her

completely off guard. Everything else Ross was accused of had at least originated from an incident that actually happened. Why this? Why would anyone just make this up?

Julie dabbed her eyes. The more Ross pulled away from her, the less certain she felt about anything.

Ellen Jones realized she'd been watching a TV program for a half hour and had no idea what was going on. She picked up the remote and turned off the TV, then went out to the kitchen, poured a glass of milk, and grabbed a bag of Oreos out of the pantry. She sat at the breakfast bar and took a cookie out of the bag, pulled it apart, and scraped the icing off one side with her teeth.

She knew Guy had been right to point out her premature conclusion of Ross Hamilton's guilt. But what else could she think when all the pieces seemed to fit? She'd spent the entire day trying to talk herself out of her feelings about Ross. Certainly what she saw on the news hadn't worked to swing her opinion a different direction.

Ellen wondered if she should call and introduce herself to Valerie Mink Hodges at the *Biloxi Telegraph* and see if the woman would open up to her, journalist to journalist. It was worth a try. It might be helpful to know how she had researched Ross Hamilton's background.

Ellen trusted her intuition in spite of the facts she didn't have. But years of experience had taught her that only a conclusion based on fact would be just.

Experience had also taught her that until she had satisfied her own mind, she wasn't going to find peace.

Gordy Jameson scraped the last of the peach ice cream out of the carton and set it in the kitchen sink. He suspected Eddie of spray-painting the Hamilton's garage but had seen no reason to pass his suspicion on to Will Seevers when it wouldn't change what had happened—or why.

He went into the living room and flopped in his chair to wait for the eleven o'clock news when the phone rang.

"Hello."

"It's Eddie. What'd your buddy the police chief have to say?"

"Nothin' that's not a matter of public record."

"Come on, Gordo, you two go way back."

"Those are the rules, Eddie. And that's how you and me hafta deal with this, too. Don't tell me anything I don't need to know."

"You think *I* know something?"

Gordy didn't answer.

"I didn't set foot in the Hamilton's driveway! I don't even own a can of spray paint."

"Hey, like I said, don't tell me anything. But if you know who was behind this—"

"I don't. And I already told the cops that."

"Okay. But Will's gonna nail you if you're lyin' about this."

"I'm not. Did he tell you he suspects me?"

"We didn't discuss it. But I'd be disappointed if he didn't."

"I don't believe this!"

"Look, Eddie, you're the one who let the cat outta the bag about Hank's phone call, and far as I know, the only one who suspected Hamilton of bein' a child molester. What would *you* think?"

Dead air.

"Okay, look," Eddie said. "You know how I get after a few beers. I might've shot off my mouth around some of the guys. But I swear I was nowhere near the Hamiltons' house."

"Take it easy. It's not like I'm hung up about it. I don't like the idea of a child molester livin' in this town either."

Julie woke up at 3:00 AM with a stomachache. She went to the kitchen and took some more Pepto-Bismol, then poked her head in Sarah Beth's room and saw a tiny mound in the center of the bed completely covered with the Hello Kitty blanket they had bought her for Christmas.

Julie tiptoed over to the bed and folded down the blanket a few inches and saw only the face of a white teddy bear. She threw back the covers. "Sarah Beth?"

She turned on the light and looked around the room, then went to the hall bathroom and flipped the light switch. "Sarah Beth, where are you? Mama needs to see you." She pushed back the shower curtain and saw an empty tub.

"What's wrong?" Ross said sleepily.

"Sarah Beth's not in her bed or in the bathroom."

"She's here somewhere," Ross said. "I'll help you look."

Julie went down the hall and turned on the lights in the living room, dining room, and kitchen and searched thoroughly, even behind furniture and in the coat closet, all the while calling her daughter's name. A sense of panic gripped her. Had Sarah Beth gone outside?

Julie checked the front door and then the kitchen door and found them locked. She was suddenly aware of Ross's hands on her shoulders.

"She's not in the other end of the house," he said.

Julie turned around, her pulse racing. "She's got to be here. The doors are locked." She hurried back to Sarah Beth's room, Ross on her heels, and rummaged again through the closet and the toy chest, and looked under the bed, willing away a vivid flashback of the afternoon she went looking for Nathaniel.

"I found something!" Ross said.

Julie rose to her feet and saw Ross trying to push the window up and then down.

"The window's stuck open about an inch," he said. "Was it like that before?"

"No, I don't think it's been opened since we moved in. But there's no way she could've—"

"Someone's been in here." Ross turned on his heel, his eyes pooled with dread.

Julie stood trapped in silence, then clutched Ross's pajama top. "No, she's here! She's hiding! We'll find her! Let's look some more! She's here! She has to be here—"

Ross took hold of her wrists and held her gaze. "Julie, listen to me: She's gone. We need to call the police."

"No!" Julie flailed until Ross let go of her wrists, then she raced down the hall. She fumbled with the lock on the front door, then ran down the steps and over to the window of her daughter's room. She saw something lying on the bushes and realized it was Sarah Beth's tattered and faded blanket.

II

Police Chief Will Seevers stood looking through the two-way mirror, a cup of coffee in his hand, and observed Ross Hamilton being questioned by Investigator Al Backus.

"Tell me again," Backus said, "what time you discovered your daughter missing."

"Just after three this morning," Ross said. "Julie got up to take something for an upset stomach and checked in on her and saw the covers were over her head. She went to pull them off her face and discovered the teddy bear."

"What did she do then?"

"Checked the hall bathroom. That's where I heard her calling for Sarah Beth. I helped her look, but we couldn't find her anywhere in the house."

"Tell me again when you discovered the window open."

Ross raked his hands through his hair and rested his elbows on the table. "We ran out of places to look so we went back to Sarah Beth's room and looked some more. That's when we noticed the window was stuck open."

"And *you* were the one to discover it?"

Ross nodded. "Yeah."

"Why do you think your wife didn't notice the window?"

"Why would she check it? She didn't know Sarah Beth wasn't in the house."

Backus gazed intently at Ross. "And you didn't discover the window open till you and your wife went back in there?"

"That's right."

"But you said you had already checked that end of the house. How could you have missed it?"

"I don't know. I was pretty rattled."

Backus leaned forward on his elbows. "Or maybe *you* opened the window so it would look like someone else had been in there?"

"*What?*" Ross turned ashen. "I don't believe this. You're wasting time trying to make me look like the guilty one when you should be out looking for my daughter!"

"Don't worry," Backus said. "We've got a whole team on it. But right now, I'm interested in what *you* have to tell me."

"But I've already told you everything I know."

Backus sat back in his chair, his arms folded. "Maybe you have. And maybe you haven't."

Will felt his cell phone vibrate. He took it out of pocket and hit the talk button. "Yeah?"

"Sir, it's Rutgers. Eddie Drummond was home sound asleep. His old lady swears he's been home all evening. Says he doesn't know anything about the missing girl."

"You believe him?"

"He was pretty convincing. You want us to bring him in for questioning?"

"No, let's see what we can get out of the Hamiltons. Thanks, Jack."

Will disconnected the call and watched as Backus continued to pound Ross with questions.

"You've been under a great deal of stress," Backus said, "with your son's death, and then that lady reporter in Biloxi writing a, shall we say, *questioning* article. Then someone spray-painting 'Child Molester' on your garage door."

"Yeah, it's been a nightmare," Ross said.

"With all that on your shoulders, it wouldn't take much for a kid in the terrible twos to push you to the brink. Maybe you spanked her harder than you meant to and then realized she wasn't breathing. Maybe you panicked and got rid of the body. It'd be understandable."

"*Understandable?* Are you nuts?" Ross threw up his hands. "I'd never hurt Sarah Beth!"

"Then again," Backus said, "If you were guilty of molesting your daughter, you'd have to get rid of the evidence."

"I didn't have anything to do with Sarah Beth's disappearance! Please, just…issue an Amber Alert." Ross buried his face in his hands.

"Relax," Backus said. "We already have. But all we have to go on is your daughter's description. At least a redhead will be easier to spot than most."

Ross looked up at Backus. "Do you have children?"

"Three."

"Then surely you can understand my desperation. I'll cooperate any way I can, just please find my little girl."

Backus got up and sat in the chair next to Ross, his demeanor more casual, his voice softer. "Believe me, I understand how you feel about Sarah Beth. I have two girls of my own. I'm trying to be your friend, but I need you to shoot straight with me. If you think of anything else that might help us find Sarah Beth, I want you to call *me*—nobody else. We have to trust each other. I have to know I can count on you."

Ross nodded.

Chief Seevers walked back in his office and poured another cup of coffee, then sat at his desk and stifled a yawn. He glanced at the clock. 4:55.

If they didn't find some solid evidence either pointing a finger at Hamilton or absolving him, Will was going to have his hands full with community outrage.

Investigator Backus appeared in the doorway. "Whaddya think?"

"I think I'm glad I don't have to do the dirty work anymore. You believe him?"

"I don't know. The emotion seems real. Then again, he's had a lot of practice. Could be a darned good actor. So how'd the questioning go with the missus?"

"Her statement backs up his story. I don't think she knows anything. Broke down several times during questioning."

Backus smirked. "Yeah, well, don't forget Susan Smith and her big crocodile tears staring into the cameras pleading for her sons' lives. By the way, how'd you get the Amber Alert activated with so little information?"

"I had to rattle a few chains," Will said. "But we can't afford not to handle this like it's legit. I know the likelihood of the perp being someone close to the family. But I can't imagine Ross is dumb enough to do away with his daughter when the whole town's breathing down his neck."

Backus shrugged. "Maybe the pressure got to him. Or he just thrives on danger."

"Did he ask to speak to an attorney?"

"Says he doesn't need one. I'd just as soon keep it that way as long as possible."

"Just make sure you're not violating his rights. I don't want this thing blowing up in our faces."

Gordy Jameson made sure the lunch traffic was under control, then went out on the back deck of Gordy's Crab Shack and flopped in the chair next to Adam Spalding. "Where'd we leave off?"

"The cops were banging on my door before the sun was up," Eddie Drummond said. "Talk about humiliating. My wife nearly freaked out."

"Well, after all, you were bumpin' your gums about this guy," Captain Jack said. "Cops gotta check every avenue."

Eddie rolled his eyes. "Well, they're wasting time and money talking to me. I don't have a clue what happened to that little girl. Ross Hamilton's the one they oughta be asking."

"You think *he* knows something?" Gordy said.

Eddie shrugged. "Hey, there's a reason someone wrote 'Child Molester' on his garage door!"

"Will you keep your voice down?" Adam said. "We don't need the whole world in on this."

Eddie leaned forward and lowered his voice. "Why do you think that reporter was trying to get the Biloxi police to wake up? Look at the guy's history. He's capable of anything."

"I don't see how he could've snowed the police," Adam said. "Cops today have pretty sophisticated ways of proving a guy's guilt."

Eddie smirked. "Maybe his luck just ran out."

"Guess that'd solve a big problem for you," Captain said. "If Hamilton got arrested, you'd go back to bein' number one down at Hank's."

"Yeah, I suppose I would," Eddie said. "But we'd all be better off without vermin like him on the street."

Ellen Jones picked up the phone and dialed the number she had gotten from Directory Service and scribbled on a notepad.

"Good afternoon, *Biloxi Telegraph*. How may I direct your call?"

"I'm trying to reach Valerie Mink Hodges."

"Who should I say is calling?"

"Ellen Jones."

"I'll see if she's in. If not, would you like to leave a message on her voice mail?"

"Yes, thank you." Ellen didn't know if the butterflies she felt were more a result of her feeling like a cub reporter or her intense concern about Sarah Beth Hamilton's disappearance. Ellen heard the phone ring and then a click.

Hello, you've reached the voice mail of Valerie Mink Hodges. Please leave a message and I'll get back to you. Beep...

"Valerie, this is Ellen Jones. I'm a former newspaper editor who read your February 15 article expressing your concerns about Ross Hamilton. I'm concerned, too. Ross and Julie Hamilton are living here in Seaport, Florida, and their two-year-old daughter is missing. Would you please call me at—"

"Ms. Jones, I'm here. This is Valerie."

"I'm so glad I caught you. Please, call me Ellen."

"Okay, Ellen. How long has the Hamiltons' daughter been missing?"

"According to our local TV station, Mrs. Hamilton discovered Sarah Beth missing at three this morning. They've issued an Amber Alert. The details are sketchy, but I understand the police are questioning the parents. Let me back up a minute and fill you in on what's been happening here and how I came to know about it."

Ellen told Valerie everything that had happened from the time she ran into Julie and Sarah Beth in the grocery store parking lot until someone spray-painted the Hamilton's garage door. "Even though Sarah Beth seems like a bright, affectionate, adorable little girl, I've felt all along that something is wrong in that family."

"I'm with you," Valerie said. "But frankly, I never would've figured the guy for a child molester. I just thought he was one of those people who keeps having accidents that aren't really accidents, but nobody can prove otherwise. But hey, this'll make a great follow up article."

"I trust you'll at least wait and see what happens before you add your own spin."

"Why? Juicy information sells newspapers. That's the name of the game."

"But without facts, it's no better than tabloid gossip."

"Come on, Ellen, people will eat this up. There's enough fact here to counter a few raised eyebrows. Let the readers sort it out."

"That's what they expect *you* to do."

"I can't help what their expectations might be. My job is to report what I know."

"But what do you really *know*: That the Hamiltons' daughter is missing forty-eight hours after someone wrote 'Child Molester' on their garage door? That sounds a little suspect, even with his history."

There was a long moment of dead air.

"Okay, I'm confused," Valerie said. "Then why did you call me?"

"Because the unanswered questions bother me and I wanted to talk to someone else who feels the same way. I was hoping you'd remember something in your investigation of Ross's background that might point to his being a pedophile. Obviously, you didn't."

"But you gave me enough now to create overwhelming suspicion that he is."

Ellen sat back in her chair and put down her pencil. "It was never my intention to *create* overwhelming suspicion. I just wanted to determine if there were any grounds for it. I really wish you'd hold off until—"

"Until what…they find a body? Sorry, timing is everything."

"I was going to say until the police make some sort of statement. It's possible that Sarah Beth *was* abducted. We can't discount that possibility." Ellen paused and then decided to ask. "How did you obtain the information you put in your article about Ross Hamilton?"

"After Nathaniel Hamilton died, I received an anonymous phone call from a man who lived in the neighborhood where Ross grew up. He gave me dates and told me to check old newspaper articles in the *Sun-Herald*. Everything I reported is a matter of public record."

"Did you talk to the Biloxi police?" Ellen said.

"I tried, but they couldn't tell me anything since he was never charged."

"Did you ever ask Ross Hamilton for his side of the story?"

"He never returned my call. Look," Valerie said, "it's not easy competing with the *Sun-Herald*. The *Telegraph* can't afford to pass up a chance to draw readers. This story had sizzle to start with. But now that the Hamilton girl is missing, it's juicy enough to buy me a little job security."

Ellen exhaled loudly. "I'd appreciate it if you'd consider everything I told you as off the record."

Ellen logged off the Internet and turned off her laptop. She had been browsing the website of the National Center for Missing and Exploited Children for over an hour. She sat for a few minutes, staring at nothing, suddenly aware of her head throbbing.

She went downstairs, took two Advil, and lay on the couch, hugging a pillow. She couldn't stop thinking about Sarah Beth. She blinked away the image that popped into her mind and replaced it with a pair of bright blue eyes and a cherub face framed with carrot-colored curls. How could anyone harm such a sweet little girl? *Lord, if she's still alive, please protect her. Show the police how to find her.*

As disgusted as she was with Valerie Mink Hodges's questionable ethics, Ellen was no closer to resolving her own feeling that Ross Hamilton was somehow involved in his daughter's disappearance.

She heard the cuckoo clock strike four. Guy would be home from Tallahassee in time for dinner. She wondered if the news about Sarah Beth's disappearance had raised his level of suspicion about Ross Hamilton's guilt.

Will Seevers took off his glasses and rubbed his eyes. The Hamilton girl had been missing for sixteen hours. If she had fallen into the hands of a sexual predator, the odds of her still being alive were slim. There had been only two responses to the Amber Alert, and both proved to be false alarms.

Everything about this case bothered him. Ross's history made it easy enough to believe he might have repeated the pattern and could be responsible for another mysterious disappearance. But right after being accused of child molestation? Would he be that brazen—or that stupid?

Plus, the Hamiltons had been cooperative, even pleaded with the police to search their home for clues. Crime scene investigators had found a few white cotton fibers stuck in the window frame and determined they were from a Fruit-of-the-Loom T-shirt that could've been purchased at almost any department store in the country. The fact investigators didn't find that brand in the Hamiltons' home didn't prove anything.

No evidence was found inside the house. And nothing on the ground outside the child's window proved to be helpful, especially since Mrs. Hamilton had trampled over whatever impressions or footprints might've been out there.

The bottom portion of the window frame yielded numerous fingerprints, including Ross Hamilton's—and probably those of previous tenants.

But investigators also found two sets of prints that could have been left only by someone entering from outside. Yet those prints weren't found on the satin edging of the little girl's blanket and weren't on file at NCIC.

Will heard a knock on the door and looked up at the face of Investigator Backus.

"You looking for me?" Backus said.

"Yeah, come in. Take a load off."

Backus flopped into a chair. "Man, I'm fried!"

"Yeah, me, too. I keep going over this thing in my mind, but it just doesn't jibe. I've asked the feds to help."

"Come on, you don't really think the girl was abducted?"

Will sighed. "I don't know, but we're not getting anywhere with the Hamiltons."

"They could've hidden her, afraid DCF would take her from the home."

"Yeah, I thought of that. But they're so broken up over it…I don't think they could *both* fake their emotions that well."

"It wouldn't be the first time guilty parents put on a good performance," Al said.

"Yeah, I know that, too. But somebody entered that little girl's room from outside, and I'm going to do everything I can to find out who."

"So when are you bringing in the feds?"

Will leaned back in his chair, his hands behind his head. "They're on the way. We owe it to that little girl to find her— dead or alive—and punish whoever's responsible."

12

J ulie Hamilton lay on the couch as Wednesday turned into Thursday. The grandfather clock struck twelve times, each gong piercing her heart. The FBI had explained how critical it was to find Sarah Beth within the first few hours. After that, the chances of finding her alive dwindled with each tick of the clock.

She focused her eyes on the family portrait taken shortly before Nathaniel's accident.

Ross stood with his hand firmly planted on Nathaniel's shoulder, his face beaming with happiness, his eyes full of light that had since gone out.

Nathaniel was a handsome bundle of energy and the spitting image of his Grandfather Gardner.

Sarah Beth's bright blue eyes and red hair were outshined only by her adoring smile as she reached up to touch her brother's face just as the photographer snapped the picture.

Julie looked relaxed and youthful minus all the stress lines the past year had etched on her face. She relished for a moment how happy she had felt—and how alive.

She let the tears roll down her cheeks. If only she had paid more attention to Sarah Beth. If only she had appreciated what a gift her daughter was instead of spending so much emotional energy on the son she couldn't bring back.

Ellen Jones sat at the breakfast bar in the kitchen, sipping a cup of warm milk, vaguely aware that Guy had stumbled through the doorway.

He put his hand over his mouth and stifled a yawn. "What are you doing up? I hoped you'd sleep better now that I'm home."

"I'm stressed about Sarah Beth. I've been praying for over an hour. Since I'm wide awake, I decided I might as well get up."

"Must be a horrible ordeal for her parents," Guy said.

"I just hope it's because they want her back and not because they *don't* want her found."

"The police routinely hold family members suspect in cases like this."

Ellen mused. "In spite of his strange history, it's hard to believe Ross Hamilton would molest and murder his daughter while he's in the spotlight."

"No one's saying he did."

"I know. But I'm bothered by my phone call to Valerie Hodges."

"Good. At least you still recognize sloppy journalism when you see it."

"In all fairness to Valerie, she started out with a perfectly valid lead," Ellen said. "And she uncovered some disturbing facts. Too bad she never made a serious attempt to contact Ross and get his side of the story. I got the impression she didn't really care if he was guilty or innocent or how much her article might have hurt him. All she wanted was credit for a good story. I have no respect for that."

"So are you waffling in your assessment of Ross?"

Ellen put her head back and downed the last of the warm milk. "No. I just don't have the facts yet to back up my suspicion."

"That's more like it."

"I'm glad you're happy. I'm not going to sleep unless I unwind. I think I'll put on my sweats and go running on the beach."

"It's too late to be down there alone. I'll go with you."

Ellen ran with Guy along the surf until she reached her favorite spot at the far end of Seaport Beach, then turned around and ran back to where she had started. She dropped into the warm sand and tried to catch her breath. "I can't believe...how good...it feels to run."

Guy stretched out in the sand next to her. "I don't know...why we haven't done...more running since we moved here. The beach is a great place for it."

Ellen lay staring at the starry sky, the damp breeze tickling her face, and became immersed in the sheer magnificence of the heavens. "The last time we saw stars like this was on that dinner cruise in the Cayman Islands."

Guy took her hand in his. "Makes you realize how small we are and how big God is, doesn't it?"

"You haven't talked much about the Lord lately. I was beginning to wonder if you'd changed your mind about Him."

"Of course not. I've just been preoccupied trying to impress Brent McAllister. I'll get back to Bible study and church soon."

Ellen didn't tell him how relieved she was. "How's the case coming?"

"Great. Brent's decided to let me do the opening."

Ellen squeezed his hand. "That's exciting."

"Yeah, that's what I wanted."

"You nervous?"

"Not really. I'm confident that what I have to say will set the tone."

"You sound sure of yourself."

"Absolutely. Brinkmont's done everything by the books."

Ellen wrinkled her nose. "Considering all the sick people in Marble River, that's hardly comforting."

"True. But Brinkmont's done nothing illegal."

"I don't know how you stay objective," Ellen said.

"I look at the facts and try not to let my feelings color the issue—just like you're trying to do with Ross Hamilton."

"Then it's just as well I'm not writing an article *or* defending him," Ellen said. "Because everything in me feels as though the man must've had some part in each of those deaths and disappearances even if the police have never found anything to charge him with."

"But that's the name of the game: Innocent until proven guilty."

"I'm aware of that, Counselor. But I trust my feelings more than you trust yours."

"I can't afford that luxury," Guy said. "Feelings can mislead you. Facts don't."

Ellen kept her eyes fixed on the night sky in an effort to keep thoughts of Sarah Beth's demise from turning into images. If Ross had killed her, surely the police would find enough evidence to charge him. The thought that he might get away with it was almost more than she could bear.

"You're awfully quiet over there," Guy said.

"I'm so afraid they're not going to find Sarah Beth alive. It's been twenty-two hours—" Ellen's voice cracked.

"Come on, honey, don't cry. Let's pray about it." Guy tightened his grip on her hand and paused for a moment. "Lord, we know that You have each of us in your sight at all times. If Sarah Beth is alive, we pray You would protect her and bring her to safety. If she's with You, we pray that the authorities will find her body and bring the perpetrator to justice. Help everyone involved in this case to do a fair and thorough job. We ask it in Jesus' name."

Ellen wiped a tear off her cheek.

"Did I upset you?" Guy said.

"No, I always feel close to you when we pray together. I'm just preparing myself for bad news."

"You ready to head back to the house?"

"You mind if we stay a little longer? It's so peaceful out here."

Guy turned on his side and draped his arm over her. "We can stay as long as you like. Pretend we're on vacation. That ought to relax you."

Ellen nestled in the sand and listened to the surf whooshing up on the beach. Her eyelids grew heavy, and she lost herself in the smells and the sounds of the sea.

Ellen was aware of a blinding light and a deep voice. She held up her hand in front of her eyes and tried to remember where she was.

"Do you folks know it's against the law to spend the night on the beach?" a man said. "You'll have to move on."

Ellen sat up and could see the man's silhouette in the moonlight and recognized his voice. *Chief Seevers!*

Guy sat up and combed his fingers through his hair. "What time is it?"

"4:30 AM."

"No kidding? My wife and I were out jogging last night and stopped here to rest. Must've gone out like a light."

Chief Seevers shone the light on Guy and then on Ellen. "Oh…it's *you*, Mrs. Jones. Want me to drive you home?"

"Well, actually I—"

"We just live up the street," Guy said. "No need to rattle the neighbors by chauffeuring us home in a squad car."

"Sorry to run you off, but there's a city ordinance against congregating, partying, or camping on the beach after dark. It's an effective means of keeping out the wild kids and the homeless."

"Well," Guy said, "we're not wild or homeless—just a couple of aging baby boomers who fell asleep after a good run." Guy put his hands on his lower back and stretched. "Come on, honey, let's head up the hill and find a better mattress."

Ellen took his hand and trudged through the sand, glad it was too dark for the chief to see her face burning with embarrassment. She stopped and looked over her shoulder. "Have you found Sarah Beth Hamilton?"

"No. Someone reported seeing her with a man at a McDonald's in Pensacola, but it turned out to be a false alarm. Sure you don't want a ride home?"

"No, we're fine," she said.

The chief tipped the brim of his hat and then walked over to his squad car and got in.

Ellen and Guy crossed Beach Shore Drive and began walking up the hill. When the chief pulled his car away from the curb and drove past them, Guy began to laugh and then laugh harder.

"I'm glad *you* think it's funny," Ellen said.

"I wish you could've seen your face. You looked like a teenager caught in the dark with her boyfriend."

"You do realize that was Chief Seevers? I'm sure he thinks I'm a real loon. My credibility just dropped to zero."

Guy laughed and slipped his arm around Ellen and pulled her close. "Oh, come on. This'll make a cute story to tell our grandkids someday."

Chief Seevers plugged in the coffee pot just as his watch beeped. Five o'clock was too early to be in the office two days in a row. Not that he'd ever fallen asleep.

He heard a knock and saw FBI Special Agent Bryce Moore standing in the doorway. "Just the man I'm looking for. Come in."

Bryce dropped down in the chair next to Will's desk. "We've

questioned all registered sex offenders within a hundred miles. As far as we can tell, each has followed the conditions of his parole. Plus, that set of prints on the window doesn't belong to any of them. Or Hamilton's coworkers. Or the previous tenant."

"Where does that leave us?" Will said.

"Other than hanging by our thumbs?" Bryce heaved a sigh. "I'd like to be positive, but it's time we started looking for a body. I've got my agents and some of your officers searching the warehouses and docks in Old Seaport. It doesn't look like anyone's been down there in years, except a bunch of pelicans and some kids who painted graffiti all over the place."

"Seems like a good spot to dump a body," Will said.

"That's what I thought. I had my divers take a look before the tide went out. Nothing."

Will sat back in his chair. "On my way over here, I spotted something lying on the beach and got out to investigate. Turned out to be a couple joggers who fell asleep. And that was the closest thing to a lead I've had. Pathetic, eh?"

"More and more I'm thinking Hamilton was involved in this," Bryce said. "I'll need a lot more than a hunch to prove it. But he has the strangest history I've ever seen for a man without a criminal record."

"Yeah, I know." Will got up and went over to the coffee pot. "Can I pour you a cup?"

"No, thanks. I'm due for a little shut-eye." Bryce yawned and rose to his feet. "My agents will be working around the clock. You've got my cell number if anything breaks."

"Yeah, okay. Get some rest."

Will put his feet up on his desk and took a sip of coffee, aware of Bryce's footsteps moving down the hall. If Ross Hamilton was involved in his daughter's disappearance, then whose unidentified fingerprints were found on the windowsill?

13

Gordy Jameson picked up Thursday morning's newspaper and tucked it under his arm. He turned the key in the front door of Gordy's Crab Shack and stepped inside, the scent of old wood bringing a smile to his face. He paused for a moment and looked around at cherished reminders of happier times: The prized peacock bass his father had caught in Brazil; the grouping of autographed photos Jenny had taken of celebrities who'd eaten there; the collection of shells, starfish, and seahorses his mother had attached to the fish netting draped from the ceiling; and the rod and reel his uncle had given him after Gordy caught his first sailfish. How old had he been— nine? Maybe ten? Not much taller than the side rail on the old Boston Whaler.

He walked over to a framed eight-by-ten photo of him standing with Jenny and his parents as his father handed Gordy the keys to the crab shack. How present they seemed in this place that felt as comfortable as an old shoe and held more memories for him than any place else.

Gordy heard the door open and saw a glint of sunlight flash on the wall. He turned around. "Mornin', Billy."

"Good mor-ning, Mister G," Billy Lewis said, heading straight for the supply closet. "I will work now."

"Whoa, where's the fire? Hold on a minute. Let me unlock that back door for you."

Gordy went over and unlocked the deadbolt, then pushed it open. "There you go. Have at it."

Billy brushed past Gordy without looking up, his bucket of supplies in hand, and went out on the back deck. Within seconds, he began spraying Clorox water on the nearest table.

Gordy chuckled and shook his head. When Billy was focused on a task, there was no stopping him.

The front door opened again and Eddie Drummond walked in.

"Mornin', Eddie. What're you doin' here this early?"

"I snuck out for a coffee break. I need to talk to you privately."

"Sure, okay. I'm the only one here except for Billy, and he's out cleaning the deck. What's on your mind?"

Eddie slid into a booth next to a window, and Gordy sat across from him.

"You want coffee?" Gordy said.

"No, I can't stay long."

"You looked stressed. What's wrong?"

Eddie cracked his knuckles. "I know who spray-painted the Hamiltons' garage door, but I don't want to get him in trouble with the cops—and especially not the FBI."

"I doubt the FBI has much interest in the spray-painter unless he was involved in takin' Hamilton's daughter."

"No, no. Nothing like that," Eddie said. "He's just a good ol' boy who got fired up about scarin' off a child molester."

Come on, Eddie, fess up. You'll feel better. "Guess he'd better be talkin' to Will about this."

Eddie sighed. "That's why I'm here. Would you do it?"

"Me?"

"I can't snitch on a buddy. I could never show my face at The Cove again."

"I thought you were talkin' about *you*," Gordy said. "So this is one of your drinkin' buddies?"

"Yeah. Took me aside last night. Told me everything."

"Did anyone else hear him?"

"I don't think so." Eddie wrung his hands. "Look, if the cops realize how harmless this guy is, it's bound to broaden their thinking and help in the search for the little girl. He had nothing to do with it."

"And it might make Hamilton look even more suspicious? Nice try."

"Come on, Gordo. It would be wrong for me keep this to myself, and you know it."

"As long as *I'm* the one to tell the cops?"

Eddie's eyebrows formed an arch. "Please?"

"Who's the guy?"

"Charlie Pan."

"The gorilla with the red beard?"

"Yeah. Look, the guy's really a pussycat. He heard me raggin' on Ross Hamilton at a poker game Sunday night. After downing a couple of six-packs, Charlie got a little bold. He'd like to admit what he's done and get it out of the way. Says he's nervous about getting involved with the FBI. But I'm sure he'd talk to Chief Seevers."

"And how do you propose I tell Will I found out this information? A little birdie told me?"

Eddie threw up his hands. "Please, Gordo. I really don't wanna get in the middle of this; I'm in enough trouble as it is. I know the guy had nothing to do with the Hamilton girl's disappearance. He wouldn't hurt a flea."

Gordy mulled over everything Eddie had said. "You've always shot straight with me."

"And I am now, I swear."

"All right. I'll pass this on to Will. But I'm not takin' the heat if it blows up. Deal?"

Eddie nodded. "Man, I hope they find the little girl alive. The whole thing makes me sick. It's all I can do not to lock my daughter in the house till this is over."

"You're absolutely sure this Charlie Pan couldn't have done it?"

"I'd stake my life on it, Gordo. Really."

Ellen Jones felt warm lips pressed to her cheek and opened her eyes.

"Good morning, sleepyhead," Guy said. "It's going on nine. You going to sleep all day?"

Ellen stretched and rolled on her side facing him. "Why'd you let me sleep so late?"

"Is there someplace you need to be?"

She smiled. "No, I'm retired, remember?"

"Ah, but I'm not. And I need to go in my study and close the door and concentrate on the Brinkmont case. Your coffee and newspaper are on the veranda, Madam."

"You're so good to me. I don't deserve you."

"No, you don't." Guy laughed and hurried to the door, as if he were waiting for her to fire a pillow at him. "I'm just a prince of a guy. See you at lunch."

Ellen chuckled and lay quietly listening to his footsteps grow faint, then got up and put on her bathrobe.

She flipped on the TV and surfed channels for several minutes, hoping for some breaking news about Sarah Beth, but all she found was regular programming.

She went out to the veranda and poured herself a cup of coffee, then sat in the wicker rocker, opened the *North Coast Messenger*, and read the headlines:

HAMILTON GIRL VANISHES WITHOUT A TRACE

Seaport police are working feverishly with the FBI to uncover any clue that might lead to the whereabouts of Sarah Beth Hamilton, the two-year-old daughter of Julie Hamilton (35) and Ross Hamilton (36), the Seaport couple whose garage door was spray-painted with the words, "Child Molester," earlier this week.

Last evening, Police Chief Will Seevers spoke to reporters.

"We've pulled out all the stops," Seevers said. "The department is working around the clock with the FBI, and every effort is being made to uncover information. We're committed to finding this little girl."

Sarah Beth Hamilton was reported missing from her bedroom by her parents just after 3:00 AM Wednesday morning, forty-eight hours after the spray-painting incident.

An Amber Alert was quickly issued. Sources inside the police department told reporters that four different individuals have reported seeing Sarah Beth, but in each case, the sightings turned out to be a false alarm.

Chief Seevers and FBI Special Agent Bryce Moore would not comment on the specifics of the case, or whether the girl's parents are suspects in the child's disappearance. However, sources inside the police department say the parents have been interrogated at length and have not been eliminated as suspects.

A neighbor of the Hamiltons who asked not to be named told reporters that the couple has been "stand-offish" since they moved in just over a month ago and that Sarah Beth has rarely been seen outside the house.

If you have seen this child or have any information as to her whereabouts or who may have abducted her, please contact the Seaport police or the FBI at the numbers listed below.

Ellen studied the color photograph of the cute little redhead until her eyes clouded over. She'd almost given up hope Sarah Beth would be found alive.

Ellen was at the same time angry and sorrowful. This did not have to happen. If only DCF would have moved more quickly to remove Sarah Beth from the home!

Gordy went in his office and dialed Police Chief Seevers's cell phone.

"Seevers."

"Will, it's Gordy. I heard somethin' you need to know. There's a good chance a guy named Charlie Pan spray-painted the Hamiltons' house. He's a real moose—stands about six five. Red beard. Hangs out at the—"

"Yeah, I'm familiar with the guy. Where'd you hear this?"

"I'm not at liberty to say."

"There's no such thing as snitch-snitchee privilege. Give me a name."

"Sorry, Will. Would you just talk to Charlie and see if he confesses? He got a little drunk and thought he was doin' the town a favor. I'm pretty sure he had nothin' to do with the Hamilton girl's disappearance. He's nervous about talkin' to the FBI, but he'd talk to you."

"Anything else I ought to know?"

"That's all I've got."

"Okay, Gordy, thanks. I'll get it checked out. Keep your ears open for anything else. Oh, I almost forgot: Margaret wants you to come to dinner Sunday. Think you could leave that restaurant of yours for a few hours and let her serve you a home-cooked meal?"

"Sure, sounds great. Wait a minute…is this a set up?"

Will chuckled. "Would it be so bad if she tried to fix you up with someone?"

"Depends on the someone. No lady's gonna come close to bein' like Jenny. You know that."

"Come on, Gordy. It's been three years. It's time you moved on with your life."

"I like my life. Where do you think I oughta move it?"

"Be honest. Don't you get lonely?"

"Not at work. Jenny's so much a part of this place it helps me cope."

"Aren't you ready to do better than just *cope*?"

"I don't know how. That woman was the best thing that ever happened to me."

"I know. So why not let yourself feel that way about someone else? Moving on doesn't erase the past."

Gordy fiddled with the loose knob on a desk drawer. "So who's the lady?"

"Margaret'll kill me if I tell you."

"I'm not showin' up without some kinda hint."

"Okay, the woman's sweet, attractive, talkative, easy to be with. I think she even likes to fish."

"So why isn't she taken?"

"After her husband was killed in a boating accident four years ago, she had her hands full getting two kids through college. I really think you'll like her."

"What am I gonna wear? I don't have dress up clothes anymore."

"Relax. It's just a casual dinner, that's all. If you don't find her attractive, you can walk away and never see her again."

"What if the Hamilton case isn't solved by Sunday and you can't break free for dinner? What am I gonna talk about if there's no other guy around?"

"I'll be there, Gordy. Chill out. This is going to be enjoyable."

"Easy for you to say."

"Margaret's serving barbequed brisket, au gratin potatoes, and her special green beans. And guess what's she's having for dessert? Your favorite."

"Strawberry shortcake! You're makin' this awful temptin'. I'm a little burned out on seafood and don't think I could eat another piece of key lime pie if my life depended on it."

"Great. This'll be a nice change of pace. So you'll be there...? Gordy...?"

"Let me think about it. I haven't done anything like this in over thirty years."

"Fair enough. Thanks for the lead on Charlie Pan. And don't wait too long to give Margaret your answer or I won't be able to live with her."

"All right," Gordy said. "I gotta get to work."

"Catch you later."

Gordy hung up the phone, his eyes fixed on the photograph of Jenny on his desk—the one of her fighting a huge black marlin off the coast of Panama. Her face was a vision of pure joy and pure agony—eyes closed, head tilted back, mouth stretched into a broad, toothy smile as she defiantly gripped the rod, which was bent like a horseshoe by more than a quarter of a ton of sheer strength. No other woman he knew had brought a six hundred pounder to the boat—man either, for that matter. Jenny had insisted the black beauty be released immediately. She didn't want its survival threatened just so she could get brag pictures. Gordy respected her for it and wondered if he would have been as unselfish had it been *his* trophy.

For a split second the sound of Jenny's laughter echoed in his head, and emotion caught in his throat and clouded his eyes. He pressed his lips to his index finger and gently touched the glass over Jenny's face, wondering if he would ever be ready to move on.

The wonderful smell of rolls baking wafted into Gordy's office and made him hungry. He thought about going out to the kitchen, but instead grabbed the thick roll around his middle and changed his mind.

He glanced at his watch and remembered the stack of orders he had to go through before the guys arrived for lunch.

14

On Thursday afternoon, Police Chief Will Seevers sat at his desk, reviewing the file on the Hamilton case and listening to the tapes of Julie and Ross's separate interrogations. He heard someone cough and looked up at Special Agent Bryce Moore standing in the doorway. "How long've you been there?"

"Long enough to know something's eating you," Bryce said.

Will sat back in his chair and exhaled. "The desperation in the parents' voices…it sounds so real."

"You think sick people can't *sound* convincing?"

"Yeah, but if we didn't know Ross Hamilton's background, we wouldn't suspect him of this. And no one who really knows him thinks he's capable—not even his in-laws who don't seem all that fond of him."

"You waffling, Chief?"

"Yeah, I suppose I am."

Bryce raised his eyebrows. "There is another possibility I've been batting around."

"Sit down and let's hear it. You want coffee?"

"Sure, black."

Will poured two cups of coffee and handed one to Bryce, then leaned against the front of his desk. "I'm listening."

"I'm nowhere near convinced Ross Hamilton's innocent," Bryce said. "But for the sake of argument, let's eliminate him as a suspect. Who else would be motivated to take Sarah Beth?"

"You mean other than a sexual predator? I suppose someone

who was worried Ross might be abusing her. But you already eliminated the grandparents and everyone close to the family."

Bryce nodded. "Ever heard of a group called RISK—Rapid Intervention to Safeguard Kids?"

"Doesn't ring a bell."

"Well, the bureau's been on to this group for a long time. It's an underground movement that snatches kids from homes they think are abusive."

"Is it a cult?" Will said.

"I wouldn't go that far. But these people are fanatics who don't trust the system. They're well-connected and waste no time giving the children new identities and placing them in new families."

"How'd you find out about them?"

Bryce took a sip of coffee. "Two summers ago in Miami, some dope dealer fingered the group in exchange for a lesser charge. They were headquartered at his sister's house at the time. We busted them, but they claimed to have safe houses all over the state of Florida and beyond. We were able to locate and break up two of them and found five missing kids—all unharmed and well cared for. But by the time we located the other safe houses, they'd already moved."

"What makes you think RISK is responsible for Sarah Beth's disappearance?" Will said.

"I'm not sure they are. But the spray-painting incident made the news and would've been enough to send these people into high gear, especially with Ross Hamilton's history. We can't discount the possibility. We got a tip on a possible RISK safe house in Tallahassee, and agents are en route as we speak."

"Man, I've gotta get out of Seaport more often," Will said. "I've never heard of these guys."

"Don't feel bad. The bureau's tried to keep it quiet, hoping we could get a few of our people inside the group."

"Does this mean you don't think Hamilton's guilty of foul play?"

Bryce chugged the last of his coffee and stood. "I didn't say that. I'm just not ready to bet the farm on it."

"You say this RISK has cells all over the state?"

"We think so."

Will stroked his chin. "Then it's possible some of the members could be living in this area."

"That would certainly account for the ability to pull off a rescue within forty-eight hours."

Ellen Jones sat on the veranda, wishing Guy had the day off and lamenting that her fingers were still too sore to type. She was losing momentum on her novel. The doorbell rang, and she went inside and looked through the peephole.

Oh, no, Chief Seevers! She was tempted to pretend she wasn't home but was afraid he'd ring the bell again and disturb Guy. She unlocked the door and opened it, determined not to let her embarrassment over last night show.

The chief tipped the brim of his hat. "Good afternoon, Mrs. Jones. I'm sorry to stop by unannounced but was wondering if I could ask you a few questions pertinent to the Hamilton case?"

"Have you found Sarah Beth?"

"No ma'am. Not yet."

Ellen ushered the police chief into the living room and offered him a seat on the couch, then sat on the loveseat opposite him.

"I'll be glad to help anyway I can," Ellen said. "I'm heartbroken over Sarah Beth's disappearance."

"And I suppose you suspect Ross Hamilton?"

"I'd sure have him under a microscope if I were working this case."

"Well, that's exactly where we've got him. So far, we haven't found any evidence. We're looking at other possibilities."

Ellen rolled her eyes. "I don't know what it is about this

man. How many times does he have to strike before he's stopped?"

"The law says he's innocent until we can prove he isn't."

"Try telling that to his poor daughter!" Ellen paused and took a slow, deep breath. "I'm sorry, but it's impossible for me to stay objective about this after having been around Sarah Beth. Just the thought that he might have been abusing that sweet little girl..."

"I understand how you feel. I struggle with it, too. Trust me, we're doing everything we can. You might be interested to know that the man who spray-painted the Hamiltons' garage door turned out to be a buddy of Eddie Drummond."

"Really?" Ellen said. "I don't remember hearing that on the news."

"You will. He confessed, and I just finished talking to the media. And after questioning him, we have no reason to suspect him of abducting the girl. He had one beer too many while listening to Drummond mouth off about Hamilton and decided to send a message. He'll get slapped with a big fine and community service."

Ellen raised her eyes and looked into the chief's. "And Ross Hamilton will go Scott free—just like all the other times."

"This investigation is far from over, ma'am."

"It's beyond me why you can't find *something* to charge him with! He's obviously trying to keep the Department of Children and Families and everyone else from proving he was abusing her. Look at the man's history. Is it so hard to believe that he would kill her to hide the evidence?"

"You seem awfully passionate about this."

"What I am, Chief Seevers, is *appalled* that DCF didn't remove her from that house before something like this happened! Though I don't know why I should be surprised. How many children have to be abused and even killed before we fix the system?"

"To tell you the truth, I'm more inclined to think someone else took Sarah Beth to protect her from her father."

Ellen paused and tried to process the implication. "I'd honestly never considered that possibility."

"You sure about that?" The chief's eyes locked on to hers.

"Are you implying I had something to do with it?" Ellen felt her face turn hot. "It never occurred to me to take matters into my own hands. But if someone else did, you ought to thank him! Someone needed to protect that child!"

"Maybe they did. Ever heard of a group called RISK—Rapid Intervention to Safeguard Kids?"

Ellen looked into the chief's probing eyes, trying to recall if she had ever heard of them. "No. Are you saying they took—"

"What's going on in here?" Guy Jones said. "I can hear you down the hall."

Ellen dabbed the moisture from her upper lip and lowered her voice. "Chief Seevers came by to ask me a few questions about the Hamilton case."

"Your wife seems quite passionate about Sarah Beth's situation."

"Ellen's passionate about a lot of issues," Guy said. "Is there a reason you're grilling her?"

The chief smiled politely. "Sorry if you perceive my questions as grilling. I'm just exploring the possibility that someone may have taken Sarah Beth to protect her."

"What does that have to do with my wife?"

"Apparently nothing," the chief said. "But I felt compelled to pose the question. After all, she's the one who first came to me about Ross Hamilton. And I know how protective she feels toward his daughter. We can't leave any stone unturned."

"Ask her whatever you want; she has nothing to hide." Guy put his hands on her shoulders. "But as Ellen's attorney, I don't want her answering any more questions unless I'm present."

Ellen heard the front door close and Guy's footsteps moving in her direction. He walked into the living room and sat next to her on the loveseat.

"What in the world possessed you to raise your voice to the police chief?"

"I don't know. The more he talked about the case, the madder I got. It's beyond me how the system can fail a helpless child. Then when he implied maybe I had something to do with Sarah Beth's disappearance, I lost it."

"Back up and tell me everything."

Ellen relayed the conversation to Guy exactly as she remembered it. "Chief Seevers came over here with the sole intention of tripping me up."

"Honey, he's just doing his job. When you reacted, his antenna went up. Now he's probably racking his brain to figure out why you're so ouchy."

"Ouchy? Is that what you call it? When was the last time someone implicated you in a crime, Counselor?"

"Ellen, he asked you a simple question, and you turned it into a counteroffensive. You've got nothing to hide. Don't act like you do."

"Well, thanks for your support."

"Whatever happened to your resolve not to decide Ross Hamilton's guilt or innocence until there's sufficient evidence? You were all over that reporter for jumping the gun. Now you're doing the same thing."

"Well, it's not as though I'm putting it in *print*."

Guy's face softened and the corners of his mouth turned up slightly. "I *was* impressed that you held your own with Chief Seevers. You haven't been on your soapbox like that since you worked for the newspaper."

"I'm glad you're amused." She felt Guy staring at her and

smiled without meaning to. "Why can't I just blow things off like other people?"

"I don't want you to be like other people. Just don't antagonize the good guys, okay? I've got to get back to work. You all right?"

"I'm fine. I think I'll go take a brisk walk and let off some of this steam. I'm even more upset about Sarah Beth than I realized."

Ellen carried her sandals and strolled along the wet sand, letting the waves wash up over her feet and the breeze tussle with her hair.

"Lord, why am I so intense about everything?" she mumbled. "Life would be so much easier if I didn't care."

Ellen strolled another hundred yards and approached an elderly man kneeling in the sand, his skin dark from the sun, his thin white hair blown in all directions.

"Hello," she said. "Sorry to intrude on your quiet."

"I'm glad for the company," the man said. "You're probably wondering why a grown man's out here all alone, building a sandcastle. It's good therapy. Keeps me out of trouble."

Ellen smiled. "Sounds like what I need."

The man looked up at her, his blue eyes nearly as faded as the denim cutoffs he wore. "Why don't you sit for a spell? The name's Ned Norton, but please just call me Ned. Makes me feel old when a pretty young lady addresses me as mister."

"Nice to meet you, Ned." She flopped down in the dry sand, putting a comfortable distance between her and the stranger. "I'm Ellen Jones."

"Name suits you. You live around here?"

"Yes, my husband and I have a house just up the hill."

Ned's eyebrows went up. "Some stately old homes up there."

"We chose this area because of the flowering trees and live oaks. Neither of us wanted to buy a new place and wait for all the foliage to grow up." Ellen smiled. "*And* because it has the neatest widow's watch I've ever seen. I've turned it into an office."

Ned took a scoop of wet sand and began to form what appeared to be a tower on the top of his sculpture. "What do you do?"

"I was a newspaper editor before we moved to Seaport last year. Now I'm trying to write a novel—at least I was until I mashed my fingers." Ellen held out her right hand. "If they don't heal soon I may be forced into early retirement. I feel the momentum of the story waning."

Ned smiled at a brown pelican that landed on the beach, just a few yards from him. "I always thought I'd like to be a writer. Ended up being a high school teacher instead."

"Have you always lived here?"

"Born and raised. I remember when the docks down in Old Seaport were the busiest place in town—freighters coming and going all the time. Now the docks are deader than a doornail, and retail construction is generating all the excitement."

"I understand the population has doubled in the past five years. That must be a culture shock for a native."

Ned took his index finger and carved a door into the front of the sculpture. "I've come to accept it. Don't like the traffic, though. Most of the time I walk or ride my bike."

"Do you have family here?"

"Not any more. My wife passed away a few years ago. I have a son in Atlanta who just retired. He suffers with arthritis and isn't able to get down here often. I've got two grandsons, one in Alaska and the other in Saudi Arabia. Hardly ever get to see them. What about you?"

"My husband Guy is the only relative I've got in Seaport. He's a partner in a law firm in Tallahassee. My two sons live in Raleigh. Brandon is single, and Owen recently married, so I also have a sweet daughter-in-law, Hailey. We see the boys a few times a year. That'll probably increase when they start having kids."

Ned glanced over at the pelican, then opened a pouch and took out a small fish and held it between his thumb and index finger. "Come and get it, Porky. Mind your manners. We have a lady visitor."

The pelican waddled over and snatched the fish from his fingers, gulped it down with one swallow, and stood staring at Ned.

"Okay, I've got two left, then you're on your own. It's a lot cheaper for you to go fishing than for me to buy you baitfish."

Ellen laughed. "So is Porky one of your beach buddies?"

"Yeah, he's a rascal. Knows right where to find me."

"You must really love it out here. This end of the beach is almost secluded."

Ned picked up another handful of wet sand and added it to the base of what was starting to look like a work of art. "I spend a good part of my days building sandcastles that won't last long—a good reminder not to get hung up on the here-and-now."

"Are you a religious man?"

"Religious sounds sanctimonious. I'm a sinner saved by grace who loves the Lord."

"So am I! I've been a Christian almost three years now."

"It's been more than fifty for me. After my wife died, I wondered why the Lord kept me alive down here when everything I'd been living for was up there. I felt old and useless, like I had nothing to contribute anymore. But He gave me a new way of looking at things. When I build my sandcastles, my mind is free and I can do a lot of intercessory praying. You know, Ellen, it's amazing how connected you get to people when you pray for them—people you don't even know."

"Can you explain what you mean?"

Ned sat cross-legged in the sand and looked at her. "I pay attention to people I see around town or read about in the newspaper or see on the news—victims, criminals, political figures, terrorists, nice folks, nasty folks. Doesn't matter. Some stand out more than others and those are the ones I pray for. Before long, I start to really care what happens to them. I can't explain why, but praying for people makes me feel connected to heaven *and* earth—and it's something I look forward to when I wake up and realize I'm still here."

"This is a whole new concept for me." Ellen sat quietly for a moment. "Ned, do you pray for Ross Hamilton?"

"Sure."

"Doesn't it matter to you whether or not he's guilty?"

"Kind of hard to sit in judgment when I'm asking the Lord to touch his heart." Ned drew a cross in the wet sand. "What matters to me most is that he might be unsaved."

"Do you pray for his wife—and for Sarah Beth?"

"Everyday. Sometimes three or four times."

"You put me to shame," Ellen mumbled.

"Sorry?"

"Oh, I was just thinking how much more spiritually mature you are than I am. I'm ashamed to say that I haven't once prayed for Ross Hamilton—just his wife and daughter. I guess I figured he's so despicable he doesn't deserve the time of day. How Christian is that?"

Ned looked up and held her gaze. "Maybe you just need a little time building sandcastles. Never know what it might do for your perspective."

Chief Will Seevers walked into his office and saw Special Agent Bryce Moore sitting at his table.

"Oh, sorry," Bryce said. "I was taking you up on your offer to borrow your office. I'll get out of your way."

"Stay put. Let me fill you in," Will said. "I went to see Ellen Jones."

"And?"

"She's livid about Ross Hamilton, but I don't think she had anything to do with his daughter's disappearance. You should've seen the blank stare she gave me when I mentioned RISK."

"She could've been faking."

"I don't think so. She lost her cool right off the bat. If she was hiding something, she wouldn't have let me have it with both barrels."

Bryce smiled wryly. "She told you off?"

"It wasn't personal. She's in a real lather over Hamilton's history. Afraid he's going to get off again. Her concern for Sarah Beth is genuine, but other than her emotions, I don't think she's mixed up in this."

Bryce folded his arms and let out a sigh of exasperation. "Well, this won't make your day either. The tip on the RISK safe house in Tallahassee turned out to be a dead end."

Will's phone rang and he reached over and picked it up. "Seevers."

"Chief, it's Rutgers."

"Yeah, Jack, what's up?"

"You might wanna come out to the Hamilton's house and take a look. I think we've got a *situation*."

15

Police Chief Will Seevers waited for police officers to clear the street of angry protestors, then pulled his squad car into the Hamiltons' driveway and turned off the motor.

He got out of the car and saw a row of flowers, candles, notes, and stuffed animals along the bottom of the fence, and a yellow ribbon tied around one of the posts. He turned and faced the crowd, aware that someone was standing next to him.

"It's gotten worse since I called," Officer Jack Rutgers said. "We don't have enough manpower if this thing gets out of hand. More than half our force is working with the FBI."

Will took a handkerchief and wiped the perspiration off his forehead. "Who organized this?"

"We haven't determined that," Rutgers said. "All I know is they gathered in front of city hall and marched over here. The media's already jumped on it—and some pushy reporter from Biloxi. There…the blond in the blue dress."

"Yeah, I see her. I'll try talking to them. Maybe I can persuade them to back off and save us all a lot of grief."

Will walked to the edge of the driveway and stood quietly until all eyes were on him and the shouting died down to a whisper.

"Most of you know me. I'm Police Chief Will Seevers. Do you have a spokesperson?"

Will heard scores of people hollering at the same time and raised his hand to silence them.

The lady in the blue dress stepped forward. "I'm Valerie

Mink Hodges of the *Biloxi Telegraph,* and I demand to know why you haven't arrested Ross Hamilton."

"Ma'am, how about you holding off on your questions and let me talk to the citizens of Seaport since this is *our* community business?"

"Well, I've written articles about Ross Ham—"

"Again...I'd like to hear from the people of *this* town first."

Officer Rutgers came and stood next to the chief, his feet planted firmly on the edge of the driveway, his arms folded across his chest.

Ms. Hodges took a step backwards, her lips pursed, her eyes defiant.

"Okay, folks," the chief said, "can somebody explain to me what it is you're protesting?"

"We want that pervert out of here!" a man shouted.

The crowd started hollering again, and Will couldn't understand what anyone was saying. He looked out at a waving sea of picket signs and scanned the sentiments written on the placards:

YOUR CHILD COULD BE NEXT!
PERVERTS HAVE NO RIGHTS!
LOCK HIM UP—THROW AWAY THE KEYS!
KID KILLER!
THIS IS NOT THE FIRST TIME—IT HAD BETTER BE
THE LAST!
PROTECT OUR KIDS!
PEDOPHILES CANNOT BE CURED!

Will stood motionless until the noise died down to a hum and then jumped in. "I hear your voices! And see your picket signs! Let me assure you that my department is working with the FBI to do everything possible to find Sarah Beth Hamilton. You should also be made aware that the man who spray-painted the Hamiltons' house has come forward—and admitted that the only reason he thought Ross Hamilton was a child molester was because a drinking buddy said so."

The crowd began to mumble among themselves and Will held up his palm again. "Please, let me finish…no one wants justice any more than I do. This investigation is far from over, but let's be clear: All the talk about Ross Hamilton being a child molester is hearsay. There's no evidence to support that he is— or ever was—a child molester. This has gotten blown way out of proportion."

"Open your eyes, Chief," a man shouted. "This guy's an experienced liar! You gonna wait till another kid dies before you do something?"

Valerie Mink Hodges stepped forward and began to chant. "We-want-the-truth. We-want-the-truth." She turned around and faced the others, her hands waving as if she were directing an orchestra. "We-want-the-truth. We-want-the-truth."

The noise went up another decibel as the crowd began to chant with one voice, their placards lifted higher in a show of unity.

Will put his lips to Rutger's ear. "So much for persuasion."

Julie Hamilton pulled back the kitchen curtain and watched the protesters marching along the sidewalk.

"There are more of them now than there were an hour ago," she said to Ross. "Chief Seevers said something to them, but nobody's leaving."

"They can call me anything they want," Ross said. "The only thing I care about is getting Sarah Beth home safe and sound."

It's been too long, Julie thought. She let the curtain fall back and glanced over at Sarah Beth's empty booster chair, desperation tearing at her heart. And how could Ross really think if they found her alive they would return her to them now? Didn't he get it? Either way, they were going to lose her.

Ellen turned on the six o'clock news, then took an onion and a bell pepper from the refrigerator and placed them on the counter. She was only half listening until she heard Chief Seevers's name mentioned and looked up at the TV and saw a crowd of people carrying picket signs.

"....And the tension continues to mount this evening outside the Hamilton residence where protesters have been gathering since early afternoon. More than a hundred local residents have joined together to send a message to Chief Seevers and the FBI that they feel Ross Hamilton is a danger to their children, and should not be allowed to reside in Seaport.

"WRGL News got this statement from Chief Seevers after he spoke to the crowd just after two this afternoon. 'I don't know how much clearer I can state my position regarding the Hamilton case. Every effort is being made by my department, the county sheriff's department, and the FBI to find Sarah Beth Hamilton. But we've uncovered no evidence that the girl's father is guilty of sexual abuse or that he had anything at all to do with the child's disappearance. Any speculation to that effect is based on hearsay and gossip and only serves to confuse and distort the facts.'

"Also present in the crowd was reporter Valerie Mink Hodges of the *Biloxi Telegraph*, who has written several articles about Ross Hamilton's questionable history of accidental deaths and disappearances. Hodges had this to say: 'How many children does this insidious predator have to kill before the people rise up and demand justice?'

"Chief Seevers would not comment on the specifics of the case. But sources inside the police department confirm that Ross Hamilton is not the chief suspect at this time. We will continue to keep you apprised of all new developments.

"In other news tonight, the president and vice president have..."

Ellen turned off the TV and sat at the breakfast bar, annoyed that Valerie had had the audacity to come here, and wondering what Ned Norton's reaction would be to the flood of public opinion. She was aware of Guy standing in the doorway.

"Honey, why are you trying to chop vegetables with that sore hand. Let me take you out."

"Oh...I wasn't thinking."

Guy came in the kitchen and sat on the stool beside her. "You still mad about your little run-in with the police chief?"

"No, but you should see how things have escalated." She relayed to Guy the scene she had just witnessed on the news.

"Well, you shouldn't be surprised. People feel safer when they have someone to blame. But the crowd mentality worries me. I just wish they'd sit tight and let the police do their job."

"*They* meaning *me*?" Ellen arched her eyebrows.

"At least you've confined your opinions to me and the police chief. By the way, how was your walk?"

"Very nice. I met the most interesting man on the beach." Ellen told Guy everything she could remember about Ned Norton and her conversation with him.

"Sounds like a wise fellow. And a better person than I am."

"Yeah, me too." Ellen rested her elbows on the breakfast bar, her chin on her palms. "I never even considered praying for Ross Hamilton. Doesn't say much for my spiritual life, does it?"

"Oh, don't be so hard on yourself."

"How sincere could my prayers be? I believe Ross Hamilton should be punished for what he's done."

Guy shook his head. "Ellen, for the umpteenth time, you don't know what he's done or not done. And I've yet to see God's forgiveness keep a convicted criminal out of jail. Natural consequences and eternal consequences are entirely different. Why don't you pray that Ross Hamilton comes to the understanding that God is far more forgiving than people are?"

Ellen held her husband's gaze. *Now you decide to get spiritual on me!*

Gordy Jameson shook hands with the new customers at table ten and looked up just as Will Seevers walked in the front door of the crab shack.

"Enjoy your meal," Gordy said, "and the key lime pie's on the house." Gordy noticed the deep lines on Will's forehead and walked over to him. "You here for dinner? Where's Margaret?"

"She plays Mahjong on Thursday night. I was hoping I might be able to get a fried shrimp dinner and eat it in your office—and maybe unload a little, if you're free."

Gordy slapped Will on the back. "Good timin'. I've made the rounds. Go on back, and I'll tell Weezie what I'm doin'. You want a baked potato and blue cheese on the salad?"

Will nodded. "Yeah, same as always."

Gordy waited by the kitchen door until Weezie approached with a handful of orders.

"Busy night," she said. "The grilled grouper's goin' fast."

"Will Seevers is here and wants his usual. Think you can handle things while I sit with him in my office?"

Weezie smiled. "With one arm in a sling. You want me to deliver?"

"Would you mind—and make that two?"

"You got it."

"What did I do before you started workin' here?"

She laughed. "A whole lot more than you're doin' now."

Gordy went down the hall and into his office where Will Seevers sat, his feet on the desk. "You look lousy. I heard about what's goin' on. So what's the story?"

Will moved his head to one side and then the other until his neck cracked. "In a nutshell: A growing group of locals are organizing. If we don't arrest Ross Hamilton, they're threatening to run him out of town."

"Can they do that?"

Will stifled a yawn. "Not legally. But public sentiment is building against the guy, and I'm worried it could get violent. I can't imagine he'd want to live here when this over."

"You say that like he's not gonna get charged."

"Come on, Gordy, don't start with me. I've had about all—"

"Hey, I'm not carryin' a picket sign. Did I hear right? Hamilton's not a suspect anymore?"

"I *never* said that. I said the investigation is far from over, but there's no evidence to support that he is, or ever was, a child molester. Not that anybody bothered to listen." Will opened his eyes wide and blinked several times. "Man, I'm beat up. All I need is an angry mob when half the department's out working with the FBI. And to add insult to injury, we have no solid leads on the Hamilton girl."

"Have you seen the parents lately?"

"Yeah, they look like they could lay down and die. Breaks my heart. I keep hoping something will split this case wide open."

"You don't think he did it, do you?"

"Doesn't matter what I think, Gordy. My job is to weigh the facts. And right now, we've got zilch."

16

Ellen Jones stopped jogging and looked eastward at the glowing golden rim separating earth and sky and the streaks of orangey pink and purple that looked to her as surreal as every artist's expression of it on canvas.

She inhaled the damp, salty air and listened to the surf hiss as it washed up on the sand, and the sound of laughing gulls echoing across the expanse. She was aware of a boat whistle and a dog barking and the Friday morning traffic in the distance.

Ellen walked away from the surf and sat cross-legged in the dry sand, relieved that Guy had been too busy this morning to run with her. She'd tossed and turned all night, her conscience nagging her to pray for Ross Hamilton. She couldn't seem to find the words and didn't see how praying would change how she felt.

It will. Ellen didn't argue with that still small voice. She closed her eyes and let her heart get quiet and waited for the words she didn't feel. Finally, she began to speak in a whisper.

"Father, I'm sorry for the way I've judged Ross Hamilton and for the things I've said about him. I don't have to know anything more than he's a sinner who needs salvation. You forgave me when I didn't deserve it, and I ask the same mercy for Ross. I'm making the assumption that he hasn't asked Jesus to take control of his life. So, Father, please put someone in his path that will point him toward Your Son. Soften his heart and make him receptive to Your saving grace.

"And be with Julie throughout this nightmare. Comfort her. Draw her to Your Son. Put someone in her path that will make a difference. I pray these things in Jesus' Name."

Ellen sat in silence for a minute, then opened her eyes. She didn't feel differently, but got up and started jogging again, satisfied that she had at least made a breakthrough.

Gordy Jameson heard the front door of the crab shack open and glanced at his watch. "That you, Billy?"

"I am here, Mister G," Billy Lewis said. "I will work now."

Gordy got up from his desk and walked out into the dining area and caught Billy before he went out on the deck. "You're forty minutes late, son. Is everything all right?"

"I—I was need-ed at home." Billy shifted his weight from one foot to the other, his eyes darting from side to side, his cheeks flushed. "I will do an ex-cel-lent job. An *ex-cel-lent* job!"

Gordy felt bad he had embarrassed Billy and wondered if the groom had been romancing his bride. "I know you will. But I expect you to be here on time, just like the rest of my crew. You're scheduled to work from 8:30 to 10:30 so you'll be finished in time for us to get the deck ready for the lunch crowd."

Billy's head bobbed. "Yes, I will work faster to-day."

"I'll let it slide this time. Don't go disappointin' me now. By the way, how's that sweet wife of yours? I don't think I've seen her since the wedding."

"Lisa is happy."

"Remind me how long you've been married?"

"Jan-u-ary thir-teenth. I will work now."

Gordy opened the back door and held it while Billy went outside. "I don't think those umbrellas have ever been this clean."

Billy looked over his shoulder, a broad smile revealing a row of crooked teeth. "You ain't seen no-thin' yet."

Gordy chuckled and shut the door. It was easy to forget that Billy's thick tongue and childlike manner didn't negate his sense of humor—or his emotional needs.

He still remembered the glow on Billy's face as he watched Lisa come down the aisle. And at the reception, how Billy held tightly to her hand and led her around from guest to guest, looking as if he'd just won the lottery.

There were those who had questioned whether these two mentally challenged adults should be allowed to take on the responsibilities of married life. But Gordy was glad Billy had found someone to love.

The sound of a woman's voice broke Gordy's concentration, and he realized Weezie Taylor was standing there, her hand on her hip.

"You comin' back to the real world, or am I gonna have to send out a posse?" Weezie's hearty laugh resonated throughout the room. "What in the world has its hooks in your mind?"

"Oh, nothin' much," Gordy said. "I thought you weren't comin' in till ten."

"Somebody's gotta be sure you're plugged in." She poked his chest with her index finger. "Actually, I wanna get my work done so I'll have time for a bowl of that clam chowder before customers start comin'."

Gordy smiled. "I'll stay outta your way. I've got plenty to keep me busy."

Julie Hamilton sat on the couch, her eyes closed, aware of the mantle clock ticking and Ross out in the kitchen turning the pages of the newspaper. It had seemed cruel asking her parents not to come stay right now, but she couldn't handle the added tension of their ongoing anger at Ross.

After Nathaniel's death, her parents had begun driving down from Meridian and spending the weekends. Ross had tried to be tactful with them, explaining that he needed to be alone with his thoughts. They honored his wishes, but had registered their hurt by not talking to him since.

Julie's eyes brimmed with tears. All the hard feelings seemed petty in light of the present crisis. How would *any* of them be able to deal Sarah Beth's death when they hadn't even come to peace with Nathaniel's?

Julie got up and looked through the blinds on the living room window, touched by the flowers, cards, and stuffed animals along the fence where someone had tied a yellow ribbon. She glanced at the crowd but avoided rereading the picket signs, choosing to believe that those who had misjudged her husband were at least sincere in their concern for Sarah Beth. It was hard to hate them for that. But how she hated the media! How merciless it had been in those horrific months following Nathaniel's accident!

And just when things had started to die down, that Hodges woman from the *Biloxi Telegraph* called and left a message, but Ross had been too depressed to talk to her. It never occurred to Julie that the woman would print all those things about Ross without talking to him. Julie still seethed, thinking about their telephone confrontation...

"Ms. Hodges, this is Ross Hamilton's wife," Julie had said. "Where do you get off trashing my husband? You have no idea what he's been through!"

"He didn't return my call," Valerie said. "The public deserved to know the facts."

"You twisted the facts! You made Ross out to be some kind of serial killer! He's a kind and decent man—a wonderful father! How could you do this to him?"

"Like I said, I gave him a chance to comment."

"You left your name and phone number on our answering machine with no explanation. How were we supposed to know you had dredged up the past and put your own spin on it?"

"It's all a matter of public record, Mrs. Hamilton."

"Well, thanks to you, so is the *suspicion* you created. Our lives are a living hell. We can't sleep. The phone never stops ringing. We're getting hate mail. We can't go anywhere without people staring and whispering!"

"Look, I was just doing my job."

"Well, your *job* ruined my husband's reputation! There's no way we'll ever find peace in this town…"

Julie was aware of her pulse racing. She let go of the blinds and went and sat on the couch, overwhelmed again with all the old feelings. She had been shocked to hear on last night's news that Valerie Mink Hodges was in Seaport—and in the thick of the protests against Ross. It seemed so unfair that the woman's first amendment rights were being protected when no one seemed to care about Ross's.

Perverts have no rights. Julie cringed at the words she remembered seeing on one of the picket signs. It was just as well her parents weren't here to see this.

Gordy put a paper clip on the stack of food orders he'd completed, then attached a Post-it note with Weezie's name on it and dropped the stack in her to-do box. He left his office and went out into the kitchen, where Weezie stood leaning against the stainless steel sink, spooning the last of the clam chowder out of her mug.

"So what's the verdict?" Gordy said.

Weezie smiled and licked her spoon. "I do believe this is the best I've ever tasted. You'd better be good to that new cook of yours."

"Hear that, Micah? Weezie's braggin' on you."

A dark face with a broad grin peered around the center post. "Preach it, sister."

"Wooooeeee!" Weezie hollered. "Get me out of here before I put on another five pounds."

"Aw, come on," Gordy said, "have a piece of key lime pie."

"Get thee behind me, Satan! I have the victory!" Weezie let out a robust, contagious laugh. "Time to go to work and burn off my lunch." She put on her name tag and disappeared into the dining room.

Gordy winked at Micah and then went into the dining room just as Adam Spalding, Eddie Drummond, and Captain Jack walked in the door together.

"Good timin', guys," Gordy said.

Captain slapped him on the back. "You gonna eat with us today?"

"Yeah, I've got three waitresses scheduled in. Weezie'll watch things." Gordy followed the group out to the deck and sat between Adam and Captain and across from Eddie.

"So how's your Vet runnin'?" Gordy said to Adam.

"Fine, but I feel like I should boil it in hot water or something after Hamilton's had his hands all over it."

Eddie smirked. "That was unkind. True, but unkind."

"How about those picketers outside the Hamiltons' house?" Captain leaned forward, his elbows on the table. "I think they've got guts. *Somebody* needed to get it out in the open."

"How can you say that when the facts don't line up?" Gordy jabbed Captain in the ribs with his elbow. "This is the same kinda crowd mentality that causes people to riot and loot and do lots of other stupid things."

"I didn't see any rioting or looting goin' on," Captain said. "Just a lot of opinions bein' expressed."

Gordy raised his eyebrows. "Just wait till they try runnin' Hamilton outta town on a rail. This could turn ugly real quick."

"I take it you don't approve of the protesting?" Adam said.

Gordy poked at the ice in his glass with a straw. "What I don't approve of is people makin' up their minds without even listenin' to what the authorities are sayin'."

"Oh, I get it," Eddie said. "Because your friend the police

chief says they can't find anything on Hamilton, that's supposed to make us feel better?"

Gordy locked on to Eddie's gaze. "Will made it clear the investigation is far from over. But right now, they've got nothin' to prove Hamilton's a child molester. I think it makes sense to listen to the authorities who have facts instead of jumpin' to conclusions. That's how people get hurt."

"Is that so?" Eddie said. "Why don't you tell that to Sarah Beth Hamilton—and her brother—and all those other victims?"

Gordy exhaled a sigh of exasperation and shook his head from side to side. "Let's not forget how this mess got started, Eddie. You're the one who overheard Hank talkin' on the phone about Ross Hamilton. Hank says you heard wrong, and the cops and the FBI can't find anything to show otherwise. Why can't you leave it alone and let them do their job?"

"Well, excuuuuse me!" Eddie threw up his hands and sat back in his chair. "Then suppose *you* tell us what happened to Sarah Beth?"

Gordy was aware of his face burning, and the customers at the next table staring. He leaned forward on his elbows and lowered his voice. "We go back a long way, Eddie. Let's not let this thing come between friends. We both want the same thing: justice served and that little girl found."

Eddie cracked his knuckles and didn't say anything for what seemed like an eternity. Finally the lines on his forehead relaxed. "Yeah, you're right. Sorry. Guess I'm too wrapped up in this thing."

Police Chief Will Seevers read and reread the case notes in the Hamilton file, looking for something—anything—that would make him feel less helpless. The odds that Sarah Beth was still alive were so remote that he no longer considered the possibility. The ending of this story wasn't going to be filled with celebration, and he wondered what shocking revelation it might bring.

He heard footsteps running down the hall and looked up just as FBI Special Agent Bryce Moore came rushing through the doorway and put his palms on the top of Will's desk.

"We just got a hot tip that there's a RISK safe house in Port Smyth."

"Man, that's practically on our door step!" Will said.

"Come on, let's head over there. I'll fill you in on the way. I've got a good feeling about this one."

17

Julie Hamilton sat with Ross on the living room couch and listened intently to FBI Special Agent Danny Connor tell them that a possible RISK safe house had been located in Port Smyth. Did she dare cling to the hope that Sarah Beth might be alive—might actually be unharmed?

"Often these tips don't pan out," Connor said. "But Special Agent Moore wants you to know what's going on. The bureau's got agents and a SWAT team headed that way. We'll let you know as soon as we know anything."

"Why do you need a SWAT team if this group won't harm the children?" Julie said.

"Because they have every incentive to run, ma'am. The last thing they want is to get caught and risk exposing the entire operation. Our SWAT team is precise. They won't take chances with the children's safety."

Julie was surprised when Ross took her hand in his and couldn't remember the last time he had shown her affection. She realized he was shaking—or was it she?

"You folks have any other questions?"

"I do," Ross said. "If you find Sarah Beth, will you bring her home to us?"

Connor sat forward, his hands clasped between his knees. "If the allegation of sexual abuse is determined to be false, yes, sir."

"And if someone else—" Ross choked on the words and paused until he gathered his composure. "If someone else has abused my daughter, how will I ever be able to prove my innocence?"

Connor didn't look up. "For right now, let's just concentrate on finding Sarah Beth."

Police Chief Will Seevers peeked around the side of Special Agent Bryce Moore's car, which was parked in front of a dilapidated beach house near the old pier at Port Smyth. There was no sign that anyone might be inside the house, other than a white delivery van parked out back.

FBI agents had the house surrounded in less than a minute.

Bryce held the walkie-talkie to his ear. "Okay, hold your positions and don't fire unless I tell you to. Out."

He picked up the bullhorn. "This is Special Agent Bryce Moore of the FBI. We know this is a RISK safe house. We have you surrounded. Put down your weapons and come outside with your hands in the air."

A deafening staccato of automatic gunfire sent everyone diving for cover. Will dropped down behind the squad car, bullets kicking up puffs of dirt just a few feet from him.

Bryce crouched next to Will, his walkie-talkie already in his hand. "Do not return fire! Repeat: *Do not* return fire! Out." Bryce turned to Will. "You okay?"

"Yeah. Some safe house."

"Idiots!" Bryce spoke again through the bullhorn. "This is Special Agent Moore of the FBI. You are surrounded. You cannot escape. We're as concerned for the safety of the children as you are. Put down your weapons and come out with your hands in the air, and you will not be harmed."

Bryce switched to the walkie-talkie. "Spiderman, this is Moore, do you read me, over?...I don't care how you do it, find a way in—"

"Look!" Will said. "The front door's opening."

"Cancel, Spiderman, hold your position. Out."

Will watched intently as what appeared to be a broomstick

with a white towel draped over the bristles was pushed out through the crack in the door.

"White flag!" Bryce said. "Hold your fire! Repeat: Hold your fire!"

In the next second the door opened wide, and a hand reached out and laid the broomstick on the porch. A young man emerged, both hands high in the air, his face filled with terror. "No shoot! No shoot!"

The man walked slowly down the steps and was apprehended by FBI agents and yanked out of the line of fire. In the next instant, three other men filed down the steps, hands in the air, and were pulled off to the side.

Bryce put the walkie-talkie to his lips. "Go!"

Instantly, the SWAT team stormed the house.

Will stood up, his heart racing faster than his mind.

The seconds seemed to drag by, and Will kept looking at his watch. What was the SWAT team doing? They'd been in there three minutes.

He turned his head just as Bryce put the walkie-talkie to his ear. "I read you, Spiderman, over...You've gotta be kidding... How many are in there...? Where...? Did they tell you that...? Figures. Okay, bring them out."

Bryce stood motionless for a moment, then kicked the gravel so hard he nearly lost his footing. He walked away from the car, his hands turned to fists, and grumbled under his breath. A minute later he came back and put his palms flat against the car, hung his head, and let out a loud sigh.

"I take it we didn't find Sarah Beth?" Will said.

"No, what we found was a band of illegals who've got enough marijuana in there to sink the Queen Mary. There are women and kids in the house. They hardly speak English."

Will's heart sank. "I was actually starting to believe we might find Sarah Beth alive."

"Me, too. Come on, we don't need to hang around for this part."

Julie's eyes flew open when the phone rang, and she realized she had dozed off with her head on Ross's shoulder. She sat up straight on the edge of the couch and rubbed her eyes.

Special Agent Connor got up and turned his back to her and lowered his voice, and she couldn't make out what he was saying. She put her hand on her husband's arm and shook him. "Ross, wake up. Something's going on."

"I'm not asleep," he said.

"Okay, sir. I'll tell them." Connor put his cell phone in his shirt pocket and sat in the chair facing the couch, his fingers forming a tent. "False alarm…it wasn't a RISK safe house. We didn't find Sarah Beth."

"I can't take any more of this!" Julie shouted.

"I'm sorry, Mrs. Hamilton," Connor said. "I told you these things don't always pan out. We went to the location given by the informant, but it turned out to be a house full of illegals involved in drug trafficking."

"How can someone be that far off in their assessment?" Ross said.

"There were several families living in the house—half a dozen kids. Guess it looked suspicious."

Julie got up and started pacing. "We might as well accept it. Sarah Beth's never coming home!"

Ross rubbed his hands through his hair. "Aren't there other RISK safe houses you can check out?"

"If there were, we'd have done it. We're doing everything we possibly can to locate them."

"Then go to the media," Ross said. "Get the word out about this group. Maybe if people know what to look for, they'll remember seeing something."

"Sir, the bureau's trying to pinpoint whoever's orchestrating the RISK movement. We don't want them to know we're on to them. That's the whole point."

"I thought the *point* was getting our daughter back!" Ross looked up at Julie. "We have a right to talk to the media, don't we?"

Julie went over and sat on the couch next to Ross. "Look, Agent Connor, we've stayed silent as the FBI suggested. The past sixty hours have been a living hell, and it hasn't gotten us anywhere."

Connor glanced at Ross and then at Julie. "With all due respect, your going to the public will have little to no impact. That's part of the reason we've steered you away from it."

Ellen Jones sat at the breakfast bar, sipping a glass of lemonade and half listening to CNN Headline News. She heard Seaport's name mentioned and turned up the volume.

"Authorities in this seaside community are still without clues in the mysterious disappearance of Sarah Beth Hamilton, two-year-old daughter of Ross Hamilton who is currently under investigation for child molestation and has been a key suspect in the child's disappearance.

"FBI Special Agent Bryce Moore and Seaport's Police Chief Will Seevers have consistently refused to comment on the open investigation.

"However, Chief Seevers did address a crowd of protestors outside the Hamilton home yesterday, and told them, quote: 'No one wants justice any more than I do,' and 'All the talk about Ross Hamilton being a child molester is hearsay. There's no evidence to support that he is—or ever was—a child molester.' End quote.

"Chief Seevers's comments seemed to fall on deaf ears as more than a hundred protestors continue to rally outside Ross Hamilton's home.

"In Washington today, the Senate is preparing to vote on..."

Ellen sat for a moment, thinking back on her experiences as editor of the *Baxter Daily News,* and remembering how explosive public outrage over a missing child can be.

"Ellen?"

She looked up into Guy's searching brown eyes and wondered how long he'd been standing there.

"What are you thinking about so intently?"

"Oh, I just saw a sound bite on CNN about the Hamilton case. It made me remember the anger and pain we all experienced when Sherry Kennsington was kidnapped and murdered."

"Did they find Sarah Beth's body?"

"Not yet. But there are scores of protesters outside the Hamiltons' home who would like to see Ross's head on a platter."

"That should make you happy."

Ellen winced. "I suppose I deserved that. But there's still no proof, and people shouldn't take things into their own hands."

Guy sat on the stool next to her, his hands folded on the breakfast bar. "What's going on with you? You've been pensive all day."

"I'm not sure. I've been praying for Ross off and on since this morning. Suddenly, he seems like a real person, not just some monster."

"You've changed your mind about him?"

"No, that's the puzzling part. I still don't trust him."

"Then I'm not following you."

Ellen locked her fingers together and stared at the curio shelf on the far wall. "I don't know, Guy. Everybody is somebody's baby. Ross was a little boy once—probably no different from Owen and Brandon. What happened in his life that caused him to end up like this?"

"Assuming he's even guilty, I doubt that will matter."

"But *he* matters." Ellen sighed. "I guess that's what's bothering me. Suddenly, I'm asking myself how the Lord looks at people like Ross Hamilton."

Will Seevers sat at his desk staring out the window, aware of a knock and a male voice and then Bryce Moore standing in front of his desk.

"What are you thinking so hard about?" Bryce said.

"Oh…my eleven-year-old, Meagan." Will held a pencil and bounced the eraser on his desk. "What happened to the world *we* grew up in—where kids could roam and play outside, walk to school or a friend's house or baseball practice without fear that some pervert would snatch us?"

"I don't know. I've seen so much on this job, I sometimes wish I'd chosen a different occupation."

"Like what?"

Bryce sat in the chair next to Will's desk, a boyish grin on his face. "When I was a kid I wanted to be an ice cream man. I always thought it'd be great fun driving one of those trucks around, ringing the bell, being every kid's best friend."

"Funny," Will said, "I always thought being a policeman would be like that—riding around in a squad car with a cool siren and being every kid's hero…but I never imagined how bad it would feel when I failed."

"You didn't fail Sarah Beth," Bryce said. "Everybody did. And nobody did. Some things just aren't in our power to control."

Will studied Bryce's face and thought the stress lines were more pronounced than they were when they'd first met. "I thought you were taking off early?"

"No, that's why I'm here. The Hamiltons want to talk to the media and plead for their daughter's life."

"You comfortable with that?"

Bryce lifted his eyebrows. "This could give us a perfect opportunity to talk openly about RISK. An informed public is more likely to spot something suspicious."

"I thought the bureau was keeping that information under wraps?"

"We were. But this case has forced us to rethink our position. Talking about the group's existence won't hurt our surveillance and might actually cause them to move some of the safe houses and possibly help us home in on the ringleaders. *If RISK is responsible for the Hamilton girl's disappearance, they may never tell us where she is. But the watchful eyes of John and Jane Q Public might.*"

"Then you're okay with it?"

"I better be. The field office just gave the green light."

18

As the Friday afternoon traffic came to a crawl along Main Street, Police Chief Will Seevers stood on the steps outside city hall, his arms folded, his eyes focused on police officers, sheriff's deputies, and FBI agents who were sectioning off the area and directing media people.

Investigator Al Backus came out the front door and stood next to him. "Okay, Chief. Agent Connors and I briefed the Hamiltons. They won't say anything they shouldn't."

"Thanks. I know Ross trusts you."

"Wish I could say I trusted *him*." Al looked down where the microphones were being set up. "I hate this kind of dog-and-pony show. We've seen it all before."

"The Hamiltons deserve to have their say in front of the cameras."

"Think anyone's going to believe them?"

"Doesn't matter, Al. This has as much to do with the FBI's plan to talk about RISK as it does the Hamiltons."

"Come on, you don't really believe some obscure group was organized enough to snatch the Hamilton girl forty-eight hours after the molestation thing hit the fan?"

"Regardless, Bryce thinks that by exposing RISK's activities while public sentiment is high, we stand a good chance of someone fingering the ringleader."

Backus put his hands in his pockets. "Radicals like that would gladly go to jail before selling out the group or handing over a child they think needs protecting."

"It's Bryce's call, not mine."

"We're gonna look pretty stupid if it turns out Ross's been guilty all along."

"Yep. But I'd rather be criticized for looking stupid than acting stupid. We aren't even close to being able to nail him for this."

Will saw the door swing open and Bryce Moore walking toward them. "Al, give me a couple minutes with Bryce and then bring the Hamiltons out."

"All right. Think I'll go take some Maalox first so I won't lose my lunch when the tears start to roll."

Bryce nodded at Al as they passed each other, and then went and stood next to Will. "Amazing how fast the troops rally, isn't it?"

"There's a lot of media, all right. Decided what you're going to say?"

"Pretty much," Bryce said. "I'm convinced it's a timely move. Exposing the RISK movement is bound to yield information."

"That's one perspective. What if it backfires? People could empathize with this group if they actually believe it's protecting kids from abuse. I mean, there're plenty of angry protestors at the Hamiltons' house who would probably applaud the actions of RISK."

"Then it's my job to make them see a bigger picture."

Julie Hamilton held tightly to Ross's arm and kept her eyes down as she descended the steps behind Special Agent Bryce Moore and approached the microphones. She glanced out into the crowd, her heart beating wildly, and hoped her legs would hold her up long enough to plead for her daughter's return. She was grateful when Moore stepped up to the microphone and blocked her view.

"I'm FBI Special Agent Bryce Moore, the agent in charge of this case. Mr. and Mrs. Hamilton will each address the media, but have been instructed not to answer questions since the investigation is ongoing." He stepped aside and motioned for Julie and Ross to come forward.

Julie stood trembling, her eyes moving across a sea of faces and flashing cameras on the other side of a barricade. "I—I'm Sarah Beth Hamilton's mother. And I love my daughter very much. Somebody out there knows where she is, or what has—" Julie paused to gather her composure. She could do this. She had to do this. "Or what has happened to her. Please, tell the FBI what you know or even what you *think* you know. Help them bring my little girl home and stop this nightmare." Julie wiped a tear from her cheek. "Most of you are parents. You know what it is to love a child. *Please*…please help us get our daughter back." Julie turned and buried herself in Ross's embrace.

He held her for a moment, then turned and looked out at the media. "I can't tell you how much I love my daughter." Ross's chin quivered and so did his voice. "I'd trade my life for hers if I could. Please, if you know something—*anything*—tell the police or the FBI. Help us end this torment, *and* Sarah Beth's." Ross stood for several seconds without saying anything, and then continued. "Whoever has my little girl, please don't hurt her…let her go…it's never too late to do the right thing." Ross stepped away from the microphone, his shaking hand holding tightly to Julie's.

Bryce Moore stepped up to the microphone again.

"As you know, the FBI is working closely with the Seaport police department and the county sheriff's department in the search for Sarah Beth Hamilton. We have concurrently agreed to reveal new information that would heighten public awareness and might possibly lead to a break in this case.

"In the past few months, the FBI has become increasingly aware of a covert vigilante group that uses the acronym RISK, which stands for Rapid Intervention to Safeguard Kids. These extremists kidnap children from homes where abuse has been alleged—and they do so without waiting for proof, without regard for the law, and without giving the agencies already in place a chance to intervene on behalf of these children.

"By all indications, RISK is well-connected and is able to give the children they abduct new identities and place them with new families very quickly.

"We believe RISK safe houses exist throughout the state of Florida and into neighboring states. Make no mistake: this underground operation is illegal. It is nothing more than vigilantism. And it operates in direct opposition to a system already in place that seeks to counsel, reconcile, and restore families whenever it's in the best interest of the child.

"Persons assuming illegal custody of these children will be prosecuted to the fullest extent of the law. And anyone found to be withholding information that would lead to the location of safe houses or the people involved in this group will be prosecuted accordingly.

"If you have information about this group, the location of safe houses, or someone who may have illegally adopted one of these children, we urge you to contact the FBI or your local law enforcement agency. That's all I'm prepared to say at this time."

Moore stepped away from the microphone and ushered Julie and Ross up the steps and in the side door of city hall.

Julie walked into the room where she and Ross had been schooled on what would be prudent to say or not say and collapsed in a chair.

"You all right?" Ross said.

"No, but I will be."

Ross sat in the chair next to hers. "I'm not giving up hope that Sarah Beth will be returned to us."

"I wish I had your confidence. At least now the public has heard from *us*. There's no way people can believe we had anything to do with her disappearance."

"She's coming back to us, Julie. I feel it in my gut."

Julie blinked an awful image from her mind and clutched Ross's hand as if to grasp the hope she so desperately wanted to feel.

Investigator Al Backus walked over to them. "How're you holding up?"

"We should've spoken out sooner," Ross said. "We should've listened to our instincts instead of letting you think for us."

"It didn't seem wise to put you in front of a microphone when public sentiment was so negative toward you."

"It's still negative. I don't care anymore. I know I'm not guilty of doing anything wrong, and I'm fighting back!"

Backus put his hand on Ross's shoulder, and Ross pushed it off. "Stop trying to be my friend and just find my daughter!"

Backus's eyes moved to Julie. "It's been a trying day for both of you. Go home and get some rest."

"Rest?" Julie said. "I don't even know what that means anymore."

"Look, I know how you feel—"

"You *know*?" Julie felt the heat radiating from her face. "When's the last time *your* daughter was ripped away from you—when all you could do was wait helplessly, trying not to think about the horrific and despicable things that could be happening to her? When's the last time someone accused you of molesting and killing the person you love most in the whole world? With all due respect, Investigator Backus, you don't know *anything* about how we feel!"

Police Chief Seevers walked over and whispered something to Backus.

"If you'll excuse me," Backus said, "I need to go take care of something."

Julie waited until Backus was gone and looked up at Chief Seevers. "I'm sorry. I just feel so angry at the way he seems to patronize us."

"Investigator Backus is a good man. He was trying to help."

"The only thing that's going to help is getting Sarah Beth back alive."

Ellen Jones listened to the news anchor give a lengthy spin on what the Hamiltons had said to the media, then put the TV on mute, disturbed at how broken Julie and Ross had looked.

Ellen hadn't thought any more about RISK since Chief Seevers mentioned it during his impromptu questioning of her. But after hearing the FBI's explanation, how could she not consider the group a viable suspect in Sarah Beth's disappearance?

Lord, show the authorities how to proceed. Put Your arms of love around Ross and Julie. Comfort them and give them peace.

Guy came in the living room and stood staring at her. "I thought you were going to change? Gordy's is going to fill up fast on a Friday night. You know how I hate waiting."

"Sorry, I lost track of time. Ross and Julie Hamilton just spoke to the media."

"Why didn't you come get me?"

"I didn't want to miss any of it. They're going to show it again on the news tonight."

"Good. So what did you think?"

Ellen sighed. "I'm beginning to wonder if anything I *think* is even worth repeating."

19

Gordy Jameson was working on next week's staffing schedule, suddenly aware of voices and dishes clanking. He glanced at his watch: 5:30! Where had the time gone? He put on his name tag and hurried toward his office door and almost ran headlong into Will Seevers.

"Got a minute?" Will said.

"Yeah, sure. I was just about to hit the floor runnin'." Gordy backed out of the doorway and let Will come in, instantly aware of the aroma of the take out order Will held in a sack. "What's up?"

"Did you happen to hear the Hamiltons' statement to the media?"

"No. When was it?"

"About forty-five minutes ago. It'll be on the eleven o'clock news. I'm anxious to get your reaction."

"Yeah, okay. You wanna give me a hint what it is you're after?"

"No. I just want you to watch and then give me a call."

Gordy folded his arms, an eyebrow raised. "Guess that means I'll have to give Margaret an answer about comin' to dinner on Sunday."

Will smiled. "That, too. I need to scoot. She'll flip if this food gets cold before I get home."

Gordy followed Will out of his office and through the dining room to the front entrance, pleased to see Ellen Jones waiting to be seated.

"Will, don't say anything to Margaret," Gordy said.

"Okay, call me after the news."

Gordy slapped Will on the back, and then walked over and extended his hand to Ellen, who introduced him to her husband.

"My wife hasn't stopped talking about this place since she had lunch here," Guy said.

Gordy smiled. "That's what I like to hear. I'd like to offer each of you a cup of clam chowder with your meal—just my way of sayin' I appreciate your business."

Weezie came over with a bright smile and menus in hand. "Right this way, folks."

Ellen followed Weezie to a corner table, and Guy held the back of her chair until she was seated comfortably, then walked around and sat across from her.

"I'm glad Chief Seevers didn't see us," Ellen said. "I'm still embarrassed about being run off the beach, not to mention my little soapbox incident."

"I'm sure he's got more important things to think about." Guy picked up his menu and opened it. "What are you staring at?"

"Gordy reminds me of someone, but I can't think who it is."

"A king-sized hippie with an AARP card?"

"Be serious."

"He doesn't remind me of anyone, honey. He seems very nice—friendly and accommodating. And considering his age, a little on the edge for letting the back of his hair grow down over his collar."

"I like it. I think it suits him."

Guy looked over the top of his menu at Ellen. "Did you notice he called Chief Seevers by his first name?"

"No, I was too busy being glad the chief didn't stop to talk to us." Ellen read quickly down the menu and closed it.

"You folks ready to order?"

Ellen and Guy placed their order and then engaged in small talk while they sampled a variety of delicious breads and sipped fresh-squeezed limeades.

Guy spread butter on the last piece of Jalapeno cheese bread and took a bite. "Mmm…so much for watching my cholesterol. By the way, we never finished our earlier conversation. Why are you beginning to wonder if anything you think is worth repeating?"

"Because after watching Ross Hamilton plead for Sarah Beth's life, everything I've thought about him went out the window."

"He was that convincing?"

"I think transparent is a better word." Ellen told Guy about the plea the Hamiltons had made and how Ross had come across to her as a man genuinely broken and desperate for his daughter's safe return.

"Guy, I was so sure I would see right through him. But after listening to the anguish in his voice and seeing the torment in his eyes, I have the most horrible feeling I've been wrong about him."

Guy started to say something and then didn't.

"Don't misunderstand, I don't feel sorry for *suspecting* Ross. There were signs that something wasn't right, and a little girl's safety was at stake. It seemed like a precarious situation, and I believe I acted appropriately in going to the police. I make no apology for that. But I decided Ross's guilt the minute Hank Ordman threw me out of his office. You tried to tell me what I was doing, but I decided to trust my feelings instead of waiting for the facts."

"So now you think he's innocent?"

Ellen sighed. "I don't know. I'm afraid to trust my feelings. But the man I saw in front of the cameras struck me as anything but an abusive father. He came across as a *daddy* who'd lost his little girl and whose heart was crushed. I'm no better than those protesters. I've said the very same things about him. I can only imagine how much he's suffered—how much Julie has suffered."

Guy covered her hand with his. "Honey, I had no idea you were feeling this way or I wouldn't have brought it up here."

"I didn't realize it either. I haven't had time to process everything that's happened today."

"Just keep in mind that regardless of how he came across, we still don't know whether or not Ross Hamilton's guilty."

Ellen nodded. "I think that's the point."

Julie Hamilton sat watching herself on the eleven o'clock news, hating that her nervousness had caused her to tremble and stutter. Now that she could see Ross's face from the camera's angle, she decided he had come across even better than she thought.

She listened again to Special Agent Moore as he described the RISK movement, surprised that she didn't remember hearing most of what he had said at the time.

A commercial came on and she muted the TV. "Did you remember Agent Moore saying all that?"

Ross shook his head. "I hardly remember anything."

"I thought my knees were going to buckle."

"I know the feeling."

"Do you think the FBI really believes RISK took Sarah Beth?"

Ross pursed his lips. "With the public up in arms, you can bet they're feeling pressured to find someone to blame. Must be driving them nuts they can't find anything to hang me with."

Yet. Julie fiddled with the fringe on the couch pillow. She didn't really mean that. How could she doubt him, even for a second?

Ross jumped up and went to the window, then pulled up the blinds and looked defiantly at the protesters. "I'll never rest till I know what happened to her."

Julie was thinking she might never rest if she knew what did.

Gordy turned off the TV and stared for a minute at the picture of Jenny on the end table, then picked up the phone and dialed.

"Hello."

"Hey, Will. It's Gordy."

"So what'd you think?"

"About which part?"

"Did Ross Hamilton seem sincere?"

"Yeah, but I kept tellin' myself this could be a big act. Why are you askin' me?"

"Because you read people pretty well. And I want your knee jerk reaction to what you saw. Don't clean it up."

"Okay. I think the emotion was real, but I can't tell where it was comin' from. I mean, if the guy's guilty, he could be sorry for what he did and that's why he got all teary-eyed."

"What about his wife?"

"The missus came across like a grievin' mother. I don't think she was puttin' on. Is that what you want?"

"Yeah, Gordy. Thanks."

"If I wasn't such a loyal friend, I might be tempted to violate our agreement by askin' what the heck's goin' on."

"And if I wasn't such a good cop, I might be tempted to tell you. Margaret's tapping me on the shoulder. She wants to talk to you."

"Yeah, okay. Put her on."

"Gordy! How are you?"

"I'm fine, Margaret. I suppose you want my R.S.V.P. for Sunday dinner? I'll be there. What time?"

"Why don't you come around five-thirty?"

"You realize I haven't done this in thirty years?"

"Just be yourself," Margaret said. "Don't feel pressured about meeting Pam. She doesn't have any expectation other than meeting a very good friend of the family's."

"Pam, eh?"

"I'm sure you'll like her. Whether or not you like her enough to date her is your choice. I promise not to meddle. I just think the world of both of you and thought it couldn't hurt for your paths to cross."

"Hmm…Will said the dress is casual."

"Very. Wear what you wear to work."

"Khaki shorts and a T-shirt?"

"Sure. Whatever you're comfortable in."

"I'm not all that good of a conversationalist. What am I supposed to talk about?"

"I've known you for twenty years, and you've never been at a loss for words."

"Well, I might be this time."

"Honestly, Gordy. Do you think I'd set you up with just *anybody?* Pam loves fishing. Loves being on the water. She's crazy about seafood. Loves to play dominoes. And her favorite dessert? Strawberry shortcake. You've got a lot in common."

Gordy smiled. "Will said you're makin' pound cake to go under all those strawberries."

"From scratch. Just the way you like it. It's going to be an enjoyable evening all the way around. Promise me you won't worry?"

"I'll do my best. See you Sunday at five-thirty."

Gordy hung up the phone, thinking he needed his head examined. What if he didn't like this Pam? What if he did? He wasn't sure which scared him more.

Julie lay wide-awake, feeling alone and empty. She thought back on the first time her two children met…

"Nathaniel, sit here in the big brother chair," Ross had said. "When I put your baby sister in your arms, you need to hold her head like daddy showed you, okay?"

Nathaniel nodded and held out his arms.

Ross took Sarah Beth from Julie and ever so gently placed her in Nathaniel's arms.

Nathaniel giggled, his blue eyes wide with wonder, a toothy grin stretching his dimpled cheeks. He leaned over and pressed his lips to Sarah Beth's cheek. "She smells good."

Ross chuckled. "We'll see how long *that* lasts."

"Why is her face pink?"

"Her skin's pink because it's brand new," Julie said. "And she smells good because Mama put baby lotion on her skin. When we get home, you can help me. Big brothers are good helpers."

Nathaniel's head bobbed. "I'm a big helper."

Julie sat quietly in her hospital bed, enjoying the sight of Ross and Nathaniel making over Sarah Beth as if she were a long-awaited princess. If there was a greater blessing than having these three to love, she couldn't imagine what it was…

Julie let the tears run down the sides of her face and onto her pillow. *God, why have You taken everything I love away from me?*

She was surprised when Ross turned over and pulled her into his arms. She buried her face in his chest; and for the first time since Nathaniel's death, the two of them wept as one.

20

At 10:30 Saturday morning, Gordy Jameson looked out on the back deck of Gordy's Crab Shack and saw Billy Lewis hurriedly packing up his cleaning supplies.

Gordy stepped outside and stood with his hand on Billy's sweaty shoulder, admiring the clean umbrellas and tables. "I appreciate your hard work, Billy, but I'm serious about you stickin' to your work schedule. Fifteen minutes late may not seem like much, but it's a bad habit I've never tolerated with people who wanna work here. You've gotta do better, hear?"

Billy nodded, trickles of perspiration dripping off his chin. "I am a good worker. I will go now." Billy grabbed the bucket and headed for the door.

Gordy grabbed his arm. "What's your hurry? Why don't you sit under one of those umbrellas and cool off, and I'll get us something cold to drink?"

"I like Sprite," Billy said.

"Okay, I'll be right back."

Gordy went inside and got two cans of Sprite, then went out on the deck and sat next to Billy. "There you go. Ice cold."

Billy took the can with one hand and covered a yawn with the other.

"Looks like you could use a nap," Gordy said. "You're not workin' *too* hard, are you?"

Billy took a long gulp of Sprite and stared at Gordy over the top of the can, then wiped his mouth on the sleeve of his T-shirt. "I am paint-ing outside. The house is yel-low now."

Gordy tried to picture Billy and Lisa settled in the little frame house Billy inherited from his grandmother. "I'm sure Mattie would be very proud of how you're keepin' the place up."

"I do an *ex-cel-lent* job!"

Gordy smiled. "So whaddya hear down at the body shop?"

"Ed-die does not like Ross Ham-il-ton." Billy's eyebrows met in the middle. "He says Ross Ham-il-ton did bad things to his daugh-ter."

"Hank Ordman doesn't agree with him, Billy. And the police can't prove it."

"I think Ross Ham-il-ton does not tell the truth."

"Because of all those protestors on TV?"

Billy shook his head. "I do not watch TV. Ed-die told me. I am afraid of Ross Ham-il-ton."

"Aw, don't be. Even if he turns out to be a child molester, he's not gonna bother a grown man like you."

"Ed-die said the police cannot protect chil-dren from Ross Ham-il-ton."

Gordy crushed his empty Sprite can. "Eddie's chock-full of opinions he oughta keep to himself."

Weezie poked her head out the door. "Boss, we need to get those tables set up. The lunch crowd's gonna start traipsin' in here any minute."

"Okay, we're outta here."

Billy tipped his can and gulped down the last of his Sprite. "I will go now."

"Okay, Billy. See you Monday morning—at 8:30 sharp."

Gordy got up and stretched his back, then went inside. "Sorry to hold you up," he said to Weezie. "Kinda nice havin' a few minutes to talk with Billy man-to-man. I doubt he gets much of that."

The front door opened and Eddie Drummond walked in.

"*You're* early," Gordy said.

Eddie grinned. "Can't stay. Hank's giving me the good jobs

again. I'm working on a BMW that needs to be ready by five."

"Does that mean you want takeout?"

"Yeah, give me the special. Maybe a couple of extra rolls."

Weezie turned and walked toward the kitchen. "Comin' right up."

Gordy gave Eddie a slight shove. "So what've you been sayin' to Billy Lewis to make him scared of Ross Hamilton?"

"Like he needed *me* for that."

"Billy's so innocent. What's the point of fillin' him with fear?"

"I just want to make sure Billy stays away from him."

"Gimme a break, Eddie. Hamilton's never comin' back to Hank's, and you know it. If he doesn't end up in jail, he'll have to move. People here won't let this go."

"Suits me just fine. I'm glad to be rid of him."

"Did you watch him on the news last night?" Gordy asked.

"Yeah, so what?"

"You think it was all an act?"

Eddie's eyes narrowed. "Oh, he's good. But the cops'll wise up eventually. They're gonna find proof he did it."

"Maybe they will. But till they do, how about not fillin' Billy's head full of stuff he doesn't need to know?"

"Sure. Whatever. You happy with his job performance?"

"Yeah, he works hard. Never complains. Wish I had a few more like him."

Eddie smirked. "Well, if that wife of his gets pregnant, you may get your wish. Let's hope their parents were smart enough to get them fixed."

Gordy held Eddie's gaze and resisted the urge to grab him by the collar. "You've got no call to be talkin' about 'em like they're animals. Billy and Lisa may be slow, but they have feelings just like you and me! Why are you so cynical anyway? You never used to be like this."

Eddie cheeks matched the red name embroidered above the pocket of his coveralls. He glanced over at the waitresses and then stared at the floor. "Sorry, I didn't really mean that."

"Yeah, you did. You're not feelin' good about yourself, Eddie. That's your problem and you better deal with it. But don't you ever say anything like that to me about Billy again."

Gordy heard the snapping of Weezie's sandals moving in his direction.

"Okay, Eddie, here you go," Weezie said. "One fried oyster dinner with extra rolls. I put it on your tab."

"Thanks. I need to get back to the body shop. See you, Gordo."

Ellen Jones sat in bed reading the newspaper, a pillow behind her back and a breakfast tray in her lap. She popped the last bite of cinnamon roll into her mouth then chased it with a swallow of coffee. She set down her cup and picked up the red rose Guy had put on the tray and brought it to her nose. "I love our Saturday morning tradition."

"I do make a mean cinnamon roll," Guy said.

"And I look so forward to them—and to you bringing me breakfast in bed."

Guy turned and kissed her cheek. "It's worth it just to see that girlish look on your face when the aroma of warm cinnamon rolls wafts under your nose. You want another one?"

"No, thanks. I don't know where I'd put it. I sure hope I can get back to my writing soon." Ellen opened and closed her right hand. "My fingers are getting better."

"You ever miss working for the newspaper?"

"I don't dwell on it." Ellen closed her eyes and let her thoughts drift back to the past. "Sometimes I miss the smell of the ink. The sound of the presses. The feel of barely dry paper. I miss the satisfaction of being able to report breaking news before the electronic media does. I miss working with Margie. I miss the relationship I built with the community. And I suppose

I miss knowing that what I do makes a difference."

"That's a whole lot more *missing* than I realized," Guy said. "I hope the novel writing will be enough to satisfy you."

"I think it will. Every now and then, I feel a pang of longing for the old profession. But just a pang. I really need to make friends, though. That's a big void."

Guy climbed out of bed and took the tray off Ellen's lap. "What're you going to do today?"

"Everything I can to avoid the horde of weekend shoppers. Maybe I'll take my binoculars and bird book and go walking on the beach."

"I'll get this mess cleaned up, then I need to go hide in my office."

Ellen followed Guy out to the kitchen. She came up behind him, put her arms around his waist, and rested her cheek on his back. "Did I mention I love you?"

"No, I assume you want me only for my cinnamon rolls."

Ellen smiled and tightened her embrace around his middle. "That's not true. I love *all* your rolls."

"It's a good thing. All this fine eating is starting to hang over my belt buckle."

Ellen chuckled and nuzzled a moment longer. "I really do enjoy our Saturday mornings. Thanks for making the time."

Guy set the breakfast trays on the countertop and turned around, his hands resting on Ellen's shoulders. "It bothers me that you miss your old profession."

"I hardly ever think about it," Ellen said.

"Yes, but the minute you did it all came flooding back. I hope my asking you to get out of the newspaper business hasn't put you in a box."

Ellen shook her head. "It's challenging enough writing a novel." She stood on her toes and pressed her lips to his cheek. "You need to get to work. I'm going bird watching."

Ellen reached the far end of Seaport Beach, pleased to have recorded seventeen species of birds on today's list. She fixed her eyes on a couple dozen shore birds meandering in the sudsy surf. Several bore distinctive black-and-white markings and a pinkish tan head and neck. She looked them up in her bird book and decided they were American Avocets—not common in the Panhandle. She marveled at the detail of God's handiwork and wrote the name on her list, then lay in the warm sand, listening to the sounds of the wind and the surf and the gulls.

Ross Hamilton's face popped into her head, and she felt compelled to pray. *Lord, comfort Ross today. Draw him to Your Son. Help the authorities find Sarah Beth, and Ross and Julie to find closure. Lord, he needs Your forgiveness. He needs to come to a saving knowledge of You. I pray You would use these circumstances to cause him to turn to You. Somehow let him know that You haven't abandoned Him. That nothing he's done is beyond the forgiving power of the cross.*

Ellen felt something brush across her arm and her eyes flew open. A scruffy, plump pelican stood staring at her. She sat up and backed away, hoping the creature wouldn't bite her.

The bird inched forward and looked almost comical as he moved his eyes and tilted his head.

"Oh, you little rascal," a man said.

Ellen turned around and saw Ned Norton hobbling toward her.

"Porky, you little beggar, leave the lady alone. Oh…Ellen, I didn't realize it was you."

Ellen smiled and held up her hand to block the sun. "Nice to see you both again."

"Mind if I plop down in the sand next to you?" Ned said.

"Not at all. I hope you brought something to feed your friend here."

Ned sat in the sand and opened the same pouch Ellen remembered from last time. He opened a Ziploc bag and took out a small fish and held it out. "Come on."

Porky snatched the fish with his bill and swallowed it with one big gulp, then stood staring at Ned.

"I've only got two left, and you can jolly well wait a while." Ned chuckled and closed the pouch. "So how have you been?"

"I've done a lot of thinking since we talked the other day."

"That so?"

Ellen hugged her knees. "I took your advice and started praying for Ross Hamilton. You were right. It's hard to judge someone when you're asking the Lord to touch his heart."

Ned smiled knowingly.

"Did you see the Hamiltons speak to the media?" Ellen said.

"Yes, I did. I've invested a lot of prayer in those folks. I wanted to hear what they had to say. I've been praying for you, too."

"Me?"

"I told you I pray for lots of folks."

"Well, I appreciate it," Ellen said. "I've struggled so much with my attitude about Ross, and that's starting to change. I'm really glad I listened to you, or I might still be judging him and harboring all kinds of bad feelings, which wouldn't have served either of us."

"Sounds like you've been building sandcastles."

Ellen smiled and held out her sore fingers. "Not on the beach, but certainly in my heart. I'm more interested in how God is going to touch Ross than in what the authorities find out about him."

Ned picked up her left hand and gave it a squeeze. "That's good. That's real good."

Ellen noticed a woman walking a white poodle along the surf. She kept glancing up at them. "Do you know that lady, Ned?"

"Can't say as I do. But she keeps looking at us like she knows us."

21

Julie Hamilton awakened to the sound of church bells and for a fleeting moment forgot she was mad at God. But the grief that immobilized her was a grim reminder why she had severed all ties with Him.

She glanced at the clock and could hardly believe it was ten. She wasn't sure what time she had finally fallen sleep, but it had been long after midnight. She looked over at Ross and could tell by his breathing that he was in a deep sleep. She took his hand and held it to her cheek, trying not to cry and wondering how she would find the courage to face another day—and the bad news it might hold.

She blinked away the vile images that tormented her and thought back on the first time she saw Sarah Beth, even before she was born. It seemed like only yesterday that Dr. Hogan had done the ultrasound...

"Okay, here we go," Dr. Hogan had said.

Julie looked at Ross. "You *sure* you want to know the gender?"

"Are you kidding? I'm dying to know."

Julie felt Ross holding her hand and something cold on her abdomen, but she focused on the monitor and the image of the child in her womb.

Ross laughed. "Look, the baby's sucking its thumb!"

Julie was amazed. "I'll never understand how anyone can argue that's not a baby."

"Has a strong, healthy heartbeat," Dr. Hogan said. "And look up here—a head full of hair."

Julie watched in wonderment as Dr. Hogan helped them identify arms and legs and two tiny, perfect feet.

Dr. Hogan got quiet and stood intensely studying the monitor. "Well, that didn't take long. Okay, last chance. Do you really want to know, or do you want to be surprised?"

Julie clung to Ross's hand. "I want to know."

Ross nodded.

Dr. Hogan looked at them, a twinkle in his eyes, the corners of his mouth turning up. "I hope you like pink."

Julie put her hands to her mouth and breathed in without exhaling.

Dr. Hogan pointed to something on the monitor, but Julie was only half listening. She had always dreamed of having a son *and* a daughter—and now it was becoming a reality.

Six months later, she stood before the congregation at Harmony Community Church, her beautiful baby daughter in her arms, and Ross and Nathaniel standing proudly at her side. With Pastor Helms leading the prayers, they dedicated Sarah Beth to God and promised to raise her to love and follow Jesus…

Julie let go of Ross's hand and wiped a tear from her cheek. She turned over and hugged her pillow, wondering why she had ever trusted God with the lives of her children. Where was He when Nathaniel lay crushed and dying, and when some monster had stolen her daughter's innocence and perhaps her life?

Julie felt the sting of betrayal all over again and felt justified for wanting nothing to do with God or the church.

Ellen Jones stood in the third row of Crossroads Bible Church, singing the last stanza of the final hymn and trying not to feel annoyed that Guy had opted out for a third consecutive Sunday.

When the singing stopped, Pastor Peter Crawford said a

closing prayer, then dismissed the congregation with a blessing.

Ellen greeted a few people she and Guy had gotten to know in Sunday school and was glad when they didn't press her about why he wasn't with her.

She filed out the front door and shook the pastor's hand. "Wonderful sermon. I don't know how you do it week after week."

"Thankfully, I'm just the vessel." Pastor Crawford leaned closer to her and lowered his voice. "Ellen, do you have a few minutes? I need to speak with you before you leave."

And I know what about. "I'm not in a hurry," she said. "I'll just wait over there."

"Actually, would you mind waiting in my office? I won't be long."

Ellen went down the front steps and across the courtyard to the door marked *Pastor's Office*. She went inside and decided to wait in the reception area. She strolled around the room, admiring the framed Ron DiCianni prints on the walls, thinking about what she could say to defend Guy without justifying his choice of priorities.

"Here we are." Pastor Crawford breezed through the door with his wife Dorothy. "Please, let's go in my office."

Ellen followed them into what Guy had jokingly called the *inner sanctum*. She sat in a chair facing the couch where the pastor and his wife sat side-by-side, their expressions like stone.

Pastor Crawford coughed and then locked his fingers together. "Ellen, something was brought to our attention last night. I'm not one to pry into other people's business unless it involves an issue of faith and morals, but I can't in all conscience ignore this."

Ellen stared at him blankly. "Ignore what?"

"I've noticed that Guy has been absent from church and Bible study for a while now. And I know he spends several days a week in Tallahassee."

Ellen nodded. "His law firm has him working on a big case. He's got his priorities a little out of whack, but he—"

"This isn't about Guy," Pastor Crawford said. "It's about what you're doing while he's gone."

"What do you mean?"

"We were hoping you would tell us," Dorothy said. "We certainly understand how difficult it must be having all that time alone."

Ellen held Dorothy's gaze and tried to make sense of what she had said. "I *need* time alone. I'm writing a novel. Would you please tell me what this is about?"

Pastor Crawford glanced at Dorothy and then at Ellen. "A lady who said she's your neighbor came to us and told us you're having an affair."

"An affair? How ridiculous. What in the world would make her think that?"

"She claims she saw the police run you and a gentleman off the beach in the middle of the night. She also claims she saw you in a secluded area of the beach with that same man two other times—including yesterday when she saw you holding hands. Knowing your husband has been gone, this information is very disconcerting—"

"Pastor, stop right there," Ellen said. "I would *never* cheat on Guy! There's a simple explanation for all this."

Ellen told the pastor and his wife about Chief Seevers having found her and Guy asleep on the beach and how embarrassing it had been. She also explained her two brief encounters with Ned Norton and how they had impacted her spiritual life.

"Good heavens," Ellen said. "Ned must be in his mid-eighties! Maybe if this busybody would put on her glasses, she would at least get *one* of her facts straight!"

The pastor's face suddenly looked sunburned and he shifted his position. "Ellen, forgive us for putting you through this.

Surely you can understand why we have to pursue this type of accusation?"

"I don't blame you, Pastor, but I sure would like the name of the lady who's gossiping about things she knows nothing about. How dare she attack my integrity!"

"She wouldn't give her name," Dorothy said. "That made me skeptical from the beginning. But we couldn't just let this go without addressing it. I assure you, we haven't said anything to anyone else. I do hope this won't cause you to leave the church."

Ellen sighed. "No, of course not. I'm just appalled that someone would actually accuse me of something this serious without confronting me first."

Gordy Jameson lay between the sticky sheets, wishing away the obnoxious buzzing noise that had invaded his slumber. He groped for the alarm clock and brought his hand down on the off button.

He sat up, his feet flat on the floor, and listened to the soothing sound of the surf washing up on the sand. He slipped into his cutoffs, then stumbled barefoot out to the kitchen and turned on the coffeemaker.

He sat at the table and watched the condensation drip from the Bahamas shudders outside the window, wondering if he could go through with his promise to have dinner at Will and Margaret's.

In five short hours, he would be sitting across the table from some stranger named Pam—a dear friend of Margaret's and probably a big waste of his time. Could he ever have feelings for another woman? Did he even want to?

Will's words wouldn't leave him alone. *Why not let yourself feel that way about someone else? Moving on doesn't erase the past.*

So why was he already starting with the nervous stomach and the sweaty palms? It was almost enough to make him start smoking again. He smiled without meaning to, remembering that Jenny had threatened to come back and haunt him if he did.

"Well, sweetheart, I wish you were here. I wish I didn't have to try to get on with my life. I'll never love anyone else the way I love you."

Gordy blinked several times to clear his eyes and wondered if she knew what he was about to do.

Ellen came in the kitchen door and slammed it. She tossed her purse on the countertop and stormed into the living room, almost running headlong into Guy.

"Whoa, where are you going in such a hurry?" he said.

Ellen turned away from him and flopped on the couch. "I am sooooo mad!"

"What happened?"

"Pastor Crawford and Dorothy had a little meeting with me in the inner sanctum. Seems they've been told by some busybody neighbor of ours that I'm having an affair."

"You've got to be kidding." Guy sat in the loveseat facing her. "Who's the busybody?"

"The woman wouldn't give her name. Talk about lily-livered. How dare she make such a disgusting accusation and not even identify herself."

"Wonder where she got an idea like that?" Guy said.

Ellen told him every detail of her conversation with the Crawfords, and then got up and started pacing. "You still think the beach incident with Chief Seevers will be something cute to tell our grandkids someday?"

"Honey, settle down. We both know this is absurd. Unless, of course, you've got a thing for ol' Ned you're not telling me about."

Ellen glared at him.

"Just kidding."

"I don't find anything humorous about this," Ellen said. "I don't want someone casting aspersions on my character. What if your partners hear about it? Once the suspicion is raised, people will always wonder. You can't erase that."

"Come on, no one in Tallahassee is going to hear about this."

"Well, I don't want to be the subject of gossip—period!"

"Ellen, we're talking about one cheap-shot busybody. I doubt if anyone even listens to someone like that."

Ellen lifted her eyebrows. "Pastor Crawford and Dorothy sure did."

Gordy looked through his closet and selected a Navy-blue golf shirt to go with his khakis. He decided to wear long pants instead of shorts, and navy socks with his topsiders. He laid everything on the bed and then had second thoughts. What if being nervous made him sweat? What if he was too hot in long pants and socks? Would Pam think he was awful if he just wore shorts and topsiders and skipped the socks? He looked down at his hairy legs and decided long pants were best.

He stared at the clothes he had laid out on the bed and raked his hands through his hair. This was exhausting. He was just going to have to be himself—and Pam could take him or leave him. He hung up the long pants and put the socks back in the drawer.

He looked at his watch, then sat on the side of the bed, picked up the phone, and dialed.

"Gordy's Crab Shack, this is Weezie."

"Hi, beautiful. Thought I'd check in before I head over to Will's."

"You sound nervous as a kid goin' to his first prom."

"I feel like it, too. I've been goin' round and round tryin' to decide what I should wear. Finally decided just to wear what I always wear. This Pam needs to see the real me. No point in pretendin' to be someone I'm not."

"Listen, boss, you're a real prize. Don't you go sellin' yourself short. Why, if I wasn't workin' for you, I'd be chasin' after you myself."

"Yeah, right. That'd turn a few heads."

"Hey, it's not your fault you're not black."

Gordy smiled and shook his head. "So how's it goin'?"

"Busy. Just the way I like it. I've got Micah crankin' out orders at top speed and four waitresses runnin' relays. Honey, I'm in my element."

"Thanks for handlin' things. I never worry when you're in charge." Gordy looked at his watch. "I need to get dressed and splash on some cologne. If I have a heart attack and don't make it back, promise me you'll keep the place runnin'."

"Oh, you're gonna do just fine. I'll be sayin' a prayer that the Lord either opens this door or slams it shut. Give it a chance, boss. Could be the Lord has handpicked this one just for you."

Gordy hung up the phone and looked at the picture of Jenny on the dresser. *That* was the woman God had handpicked for him. And he sure didn't expect that kind of happiness twice in a lifetime.

22

Late Sunday afternoon, Police Chief Will Seevers walked out of the police station and across the street to the employee parking lot and saw FBI Special Agent Bryce Moore getting out of his car.

"Any leads?" Will said.

Bryce raised his eyebrows. "Nothing worth a hoot. I can't believe we haven't gotten one decent lead after going public."

"Maybe RISK *wasn't* involved."

"Their fingerprints are all over it. But regardless, they've got to be stopped."

"I've been meaning to ask, did you personally interrogate the members you busted in Miami two years ago?"

"Yeah, why?"

"I'm curious what kind of people they were."

"Fanatics—just like the pinheads who try to stop women from going into abortion clinics. They're on a mission and don't care what the law has to say about it."

"Did their concern for the kids seem real?"

Bryce shut the door to his car. "Doesn't matter. They should've let the system handle it."

"Kind of hard to do when they don't trust it. Guess they figured a caring stranger, even a fanatic, was better than an abusive parent."

Bryce caught his gaze and held it. "Look, Will, nobody disagrees with that. But we can't have vigilante groups deciding the fate of these kids."

"Yeah, I know. It's just easier to think that RISK might be sheltering Sarah Beth than the other chilling possibilities. But if she's never found, it's going to be tough for her parents to find closure."

"At least one of them. I still don't know if I believe Ross. Look, I need to get to work. You done for the day?"

"Yeah, Margaret's playing matchmaker with two friends of the family under the guise of *Sunday dinner*." Will rolled his eyes. "I promised I'd be there to support the male half of this little cupid caper."

Gordy Jameson rode his bicycle into Will Seevers's driveway, then walked it to the side of house and set the kickstand. He caught a whiff of cologne and started to cough.

He stood for a moment, fighting the temptation to get back on his bicycle and forget the whole thing. He heard a car approaching and looked up, relieved to see Will's squad car pull into the driveway.

"Man, I was afraid you were gonna stand me up," Gordy said.

Will laughed. "I told you I'd be here. Will you calm down?"

Gordy walked over and poked his head in the open window. "Do I smell too strong? I think I mighta dumped too much cologne on me."

"Yeah, you're pretty stout, but we can fix that." Will got out of the car and went to the side yard, picked up the garden hose, and turned it on. "Give me your hands." Gordy held out his hands and Will got them wet. "Rub the water on your face and neck."

Gordy splashed the water on his face and neck and rubbed until the breeze dried it. "Is that better?"

Will moved closer and took a whiff. "Yeah, smells good."

"It's Polo. Weezie gave it to me for my birthday. This is the first time I've used it."

"Look, Gordy, I know you're nervous, but Pam's really easy to be around. Just be yourself. If you don't hit it off, it's no big deal."

"That's good because you keep assumin' she's gonna like me. I'm not exactly Tom Cruise, you know."

"Will you give yourself a break? You're a sensitive guy and women love that. I wouldn't introduce you to Pam unless I thought she was good enough for *you*."

"Yeah, but you're prejudiced."

"Maybe. But I'm right. Come on, let's get the hard part over with."

Gordy smoothed his hair with his hands, his stomach feeling as if a company of tiny soldiers were marching all over it. He followed Will into the house and was comforted by Margaret's smiling face and the fact that she had on shorts.

Margaret put her arms around him and squeezed. "I'm so glad you came." She took his hand and led him into the living room and over to the couch, where a woman sat talking to Meagan Seevers.

The woman's face seemed to light up when she saw him, her round blue eyes looking into his and not at the spare tire around his middle.

"Gordy," Margaret said, "this is Pam Townsend. Pam, Gordy Jameson."

He wondered if Pam was disappointed. If she was, her pretty smile graciously concealed it. He held out his hand and shook hers. "Nice to meet you, Pam."

"Nice to meet *you*," she said, sounding both relaxed and sincere.

Gordy decided she was fiftyish. Pixie haircut. Nice tan.

"Everyone make yourselves comfortable," Margaret said, "and I'll get us something to drink. I've got lemonade, Coke and Diet Coke, Seven-Up, iced spice tea, or water."

Gordy sat in the chair opposite the couch and stole a few

glances at Pam. She wore denim pedal pusher-type pants and a floral print top and Birkenstocks. Her toenails were painted pink. She seemed energetic and earthy—and pleasantly feminine.

"Gordy?" Margaret said.

"Oh, uh, lemonade sounds great."

Ellen Jones sat at her desk in the widow's watch, chagrined that her fingers were still too sore to type. What difference did it make? Her creative juices had dried up.

With her left index finger, she finished composing a letter to the busybody who was gossiping about her, thinking it felt good to get it out of her system.

She heard footsteps ascending the winding staircase and then, out of the corner of her eye, saw Guy walk through the doorway.

"Were you able to get anything done on your novel?" he said.

"No, I'm much too angry to be creative. Not that my fingers would cooperate anyhow. I've written a scathing letter to that gossip, whoever she is. I wonder if the woman has any idea how hurtful this is?"

"I doubt it," Guy said. "Probably thinks she's doing *me* a favor."

"Some favor. I wonder who else she's told?"

"Ellen, don't look for trouble. Maybe the woman felt compelled to go to your pastor, and that's it."

"Easy for you to say. You're not the one being gossiped about."

He raised his eyebrows. "You think this doesn't affect me?"

"No, of course it does. That's part of the reason I'm so mad. How will we ever know which neighbors she's told—and what they think of us?"

"I don't suppose we will. But worrying about it won't change anything. Maybe you need to pray for her, just like you're praying for Ross. At least then you won't feel like lynching her from the nearest tree."

Ellen sighed. "The last thing I feel like doing is praying for someone who's poisoning people's minds about me."

"I don't blame you. But have you got a better idea?"

Ellen looked at the letter on her laptop screen. It was so perfectly worded. So satisfying. She glanced up at Guy and fought with herself for several seconds and pressed the delete button.

"Okay, it's gone. But I don't feel any better."

"Come on, I'll take you out to dinner."

"I won't be very good company."

"I don't know, you're kind of cute when you're pouting."

"Don't patronize me, Counselor. I'm not pouting. I'm seething with indignation!"

"Okay, withdrawn. How about a short recess?" Guy put his arm around her. "Honey, I know this is hurtful. But what really matters is that *we* know the truth. I don't believe for a moment that you'd ever cheat on me. And you know I wouldn't. You're the one who always says God has a plan and uses all things for good. Maybe if we turn this situation over to Him, something good will come of it. Letting it eat you up isn't helpful."

There he went again, getting spiritual on her. "Okay, let's go out for dinner," Ellen said. "Though I doubt a full stomach will do anything to squelch my desire to tell this woman off."

Gordy sat at the Seeverses' dining room table, Will and Margaret sitting at opposite ends, and Pam and Meagan across from him. The dinner conversation had been more comfortable than he had anticipated, and eleven-year-old Meagan had kept them entertained.

Gordy took the last bite of strawberry shortcake, suddenly aware he was the only one still eating. He put down his fork, wiped his mouth with a napkin, and sat back in his chair. "Excellent. Really a great meal, Margaret."

"Would you like more dessert?"

"Sure I would. But I don't know where I'd put it."

"Anyone want more coffee?" Margaret said.

All heads nodded.

"I'll get it." Meagan jumped up and headed for the kitchen. She stopped in the doorway and looked back at Gordy, a big grin on her face, and mouthed the words, "She likes you."

Gordy chuckled to himself. Like mother, like daughter.

Will leaned forward, his elbows on the table. "After we have coffee, anyone game for dominoes?"

"I am!" Meagan shouted from the kitchen. "Mexican Train!"

Will rolled his eyes. "Such a bashful child."

"Gordy, how long have you owned your restaurant?" Pam asked.

"My folks founded the place fifty years ago. Gave me the keys about fifteen years ago. I practically grew up there. Spent more time playin' in the backroom than I ever did at home. In some ways, it *is* home."

"Did you work for your parents before they passed the business on to you?"

"Oh, yeah. I was bussin' tables by the time I was nine or ten. Eventually they paid me to clean the place. Little by little, I learned to strip and wax floors, fix the plumbing, paint, do repairs—just about anything you can think of except cookin' or keepin' the financials. Then after I dropped out of college, my dad had a little heart-to-heart with me. Told me it was time to fish or cut bait—either get serious about the business or find somethin' else to do with my life. That's when I decided I was in for the long haul. Dad took me under his wing and taught me everything he knew. I've never regretted it."

Pam smiled. "I remember your parents. I used to eat there fairly often, though I haven't since Todd died."

Gordy was relieved to leave the conversation there and was glad when Meagan came out of the kitchen.

"Okay, fresh coffee." Meagan held a full pot of coffee in one hand and a potholder underneath it with the other. "I sure wish this stuff tasted as good as it smells."

Gordy studied Pam for a moment while all eyes were on Meagan. He definitely found her attractive. He wondered if she was the least bit interested in him—and if she was finding it as difficult to let go of Todd as he was Jenny.

The phone rang and Will excused himself and went out to the kitchen. A minute later he came back and stood holding the back of Margaret's chair. "I hate to be a party pooper, but I have to go down to the station. Sounds like we found the south side hit-and-run driver."

23

Ellen Jones sat in her rocker on the veranda, the sounds of night alive around her, and the conversation she'd had with Pastor and Dorothy Crawford replaying in her mind. How anyone could have made a case for adultery out of such innocent circumstances was beyond her.

"Ellen, come in here. You need to see this."

She got up and went into the living room, where Guy sat watching TV.

"The news is about to come on," he said. "They've made an arrest in the hit-and-run case."

"Good evening, this is Shannon Pate…"

"And Stephen Rounds. Welcome to Regional News at Eleven. Seaport Police may have found the hit-and-run driver responsible for the death of Jeremy Maxwell Hudson, the eight-year-old who was run down ten days ago while riding his bicycle in a south side neighborhood.

"Terrance Michael Adams, a thirty-four-year old-commercial fisherman, is being held tonight without bond in the Beacon County jail. Jared Downing is reporting live from Old Seaport, where Adams was arrested earlier this evening. Jared…"

"Stephen, 911 dispatchers received a call just after six o'clock this evening from Rick Ramirez, a west side resident, who, with his next-door neighbor Juan Martinez, was in pursuit of a blue pickup that had been driving erratically up and down Magnolia Lane where Ramirez's children and other neighbor children were playing.

"According to police, Ramirez and Martinez were outside talking when the incident happened, and remembered the description of the driver involved in the south side hit-and-run. The two men got in Ramirez's SUV and followed the blue pickup, then called 911 in an effort to get police help.

"Minutes later, two Seaport police cruisers had picked up the chase and motioned Ramirez to back off. The officers, lights flashing and sirens blaring, pursued the blue pickup through Old Seaport where the driver made an abrupt turn onto a gravel road and continued at high speed until the road came to a dead end. The truck then spun around, its right rear slamming into this loading dock warehouse behind me.

"Officers ordered Adams from the car, after which he failed an onsite sobriety test, and registered a blood alcohol level of .20. According to the arresting officers, Adams was, quote, 'Disoriented, belligerent, and clueless.' End quote.

"Crime Scene Investigators were called in to gather evidence from previous damage to Adams's right front bumper, grill, and headlight. Though investigators refused to comment, a source inside the department confirmed they might have found DNA evidence. If the DNA matches that of Jeremy Hudson, Adams will be charged in the boy's death. Police Chief Will Seevers is expected to make that announcement tomorrow morning.

"In the meantime, WRGL News has learned that Adams had been charged in two previous DUIs and was driving with a revoked driver's license. Adams was also recently fired from J and R Commercial Fisheries for being intoxicated while on the job. This is Jared Downing, reporting live from Old Seaport. Stephen…"

"WRGL News will bring you the latest on this developing story as it is made available to us. In other news tonight, frustration abounds in the disappearance of two-year-old Sarah Beth Hamilton. Police and the FBI continue to sort through leads, which have not yielded anything useful in determining the little girl's whereabouts, even after the child's parents, Julie and Ross Hamilton, addressed the media in a plea for their daughter's life.

"At least three dozen protesters still hold a vigil outside the Hamiltons' home tonight, an indication that some here still believe Ross Hamilton may have been involved in the early Wednesday morning disappearance of his daughter..."

Ellen tuned out the anchorman's words, which were starting to feel oppressive.

A commercial came on and Guy muted the TV. "What's wrong?"

"Everything," Ellen said. "Who am I to talk about being falsely accused? I'm the one who told Chief Seevers that Ross Hamilton might be the south side hit-and-run driver."

"It was a valid hunch, honey. You just overstepped."

"That's an understatement." Ellen laid her head against the back of the couch. "I know how betrayed I feel. I can only imagine what Ross must be going through."

"If he's innocent of any wrongdoing with his daughter. We still don't know that."

Ellen jabbed him with her elbow. "You're playing both sides of the fence, Counselor."

"Not really. The only facts I have are what the media's reported."

"But more and more it's looking as if Ross may have been falsely accused."

"No, more and more it's feeling as if he may have been falsely accused. Stick with the facts, Ellen. The hit-and-run has nothing to do with the other allegations."

Gordy Jameson scraped the bottom of the carton for the last bite of peach ice cream and then threw it in the trash. He turned out the lights and went to the bedroom. He undressed and flopped on the bed, his mind racing with the events of the day.

He had studied everything about Pam Townsend while he played dominoes with her, Margaret, and Meagan. He felt the chemistry, but promptly shut it down. Pam was nice enough—friendly, sensitive, talkative. He liked her laugh. And the way she seemed interested in the things that were important to him. In fact, he couldn't remember the last time any woman had shown a real interest in his business.

But it bothered him that he saw pain in her eyes when she mentioned Todd. He wondered if she had seen that same look in his eyes when Jenny's name came up. He also wondered why he said he'd call sometime and maybe they could have dinner. He wasn't sure he even knew how to carry on a meaningful conversation with a woman anymore. And how could he find time for a relationship when he had to work every night? He owned a business. He had responsibilities.

Gordy watched the ceiling fan go round and round in the dark. Who was he kidding? Weezie would jump at the chance to be assistant manager. She already knew how to run the place. He hadn't promoted her because having to run the restaurant was a convenient excuse not to move on with his life.

Gordy's heart raced. He felt jittery all over and wanted to run. Jenny had told him these anxiety attacks only happened when he felt trapped—like the day he found out her chemotherapy hadn't worked. Why was he feeling trapped now? He had the choice to pursue a relationship with Pam or to walk away. Will and Margaret had promised not to press him about it.

Gordy lay on his back with his arms outstretched and let the ceiling fan dry his perspiration. Something Jenny had said before she died came rushing back to him, something he'd forgotten—or didn't want to remember.

I know you can't imagine going on without me, but don't keep your love bottled up for long. Find someone to give it to. Otherwise, you'll self-destruct.

Gordy reached for Jenny's pillow and clutched it to his

chest, painfully aware that it had long ago lost the scent of her perfume. He buried his face in the downy softness, his chest convulsing with the anguish of her absence, and muffled the sound of his weeping.

Julie Hamilton carried a mug of Sleepy Time herb tea into the living room and handed it to Ross. "Maybe this will help you sleep."

She sat next to him on the couch, thinking the only thing that would put either of them to sleep was total exhaustion.

Ross blew on the tea and then took a sip. "You've been quiet today."

"I'm trying to cope. I wasn't doing too well even before this happened." *Not that you ever noticed.*

"At least be glad they've stopped suspecting me for the hit-and-run. Our lives can get back to normal once Sarah Beth is home."

Julie felt her neck and shoulders tighten. "Ross, we have to start dealing with the possibility that she's not coming home."

"Don't say that. She's—"

"She's what...? It's been five days! The odds of us finding her—"

"I don't wanna get into this."

"Well, we have to! What if they find her body and we have to bury her?" Julie put her hand over her mouth and choked back the emotion. "While we can still think, we need to decide if we want her buried in Biloxi with Nathaniel. There's no way I'm leaving my daughter in this godforsaken town. And there's no way we can stay here after this."

Ross sat with his arms folded and stared at the wall. She just wanted to shake him.

"Don't talk to me about burying another child," he said. "We're getting Sarah Beth back."

"How can you say that so matter-of-factly?" Julie pulled at

the fringe on the couch pillow. Doubt began to gnaw at her again. Was she brave enough to ask him? "Ross, if you knew where Sarah Beth was…you'd tell me, wouldn't you? Because I keep picturing her in the clutches of some monster, and it's all I can do to make it through the day." Julie's voice failed.

"What are you asking?" Ross stood and threw up his hands. "I can't believe this. My own wife…"

"I know you wouldn't hurt Sarah Beth. Just tell me if you've got her hidden somewhere."

"I wish I did! At least she'd be safe." Ross raked his hands through his hair. "How could you think I'd do something like that without telling you? I'd never put you through this torment. What kind of man do you think I am?"

Julie stood and grasped his arm. "I don't know what to think anymore! We never communicate!"

Ross stared at her, his eyes brimming with tears, his chin quivering.

Julie cupped his face in her hands. "I'm sorry. Don't make me feel worse than I already do. I *had* to ask."

Ross closed his eyes, a tear trickling down one side of his face.

Will Seevers closed the April issue of *Salt Water Sportsman* and realized he didn't remember anything he'd read. He turned off the lamp in the living room and walked down the hall to the bedroom. He ever so quietly opened and closed the door, then walked softly toward the closet.

"I'm wide awake," Margaret said.

Will went over and sat on the side of the bed. "How come?"

"I heard you come in two hours ago. I figured you needed to unwind. So *is* this guy the south side hit-and-run driver?"

"Yeah. And he's a stinking drunk. Didn't even remember hitting the kid. Saw the damage on his truck after he sobered up and thought he'd hit a deer. Ran his truck through a car wash.

CSIs found traces of hair, blood, and skin embedded in the chrome around the right headlight. The DNA matches the boy's."

Margaret put her hand on his. "How horrible. Those poor parents."

"This guy should've been locked up a long time ago. He's got a string of DUIs in three states and was driving with a revoked license. One more slosh head falls through the system." Will sighed. "And to make matters worse, I'm sure MADD will show up with picket signs before I even have time to swallow my breakfast. Then I get to deal with two groups of protesters, two dead kids, and two sets of devastated parents."

"Where are you with the Hamilton case?"

"Hanging by our thumbs. At least Jeremy Hudson's parents can find some closure now, though closure sounds trite when you're struggling to deal with the death of a child."

"You're not going to sleep tonight, are you?" Margaret said.

"Probably not. But I need to at least rest my eyes. How'd the evening go with Pam and Gordy?"

"Good. After you left, Meagan and I got out the dominoes. Everyone seemed to be having fun."

"What time did Gordy leave?"

"Around eight-thirty. Pam said she thought he was nice and enjoyed the evening. I heard Gordy say maybe they could have dinner sometime."

Will smiled. "That's a big step."

"I think they hit it off. But both of them are so closed-mouthed, we may never know unless it develops into something. I'm not holding my breath.

24

Ellen Jones sat on the veranda hiding behind Monday's newspaper. She was vaguely aware of the glowing pink sky visible between the live oak branches, a Carolina wren chirping, and Guy stirring inside the house. But all she could focus on at the moment was finding out which neighbor had had the audacity to go to Pastor Crawford and tell him she was having an affair.

"Honey, I'm ready to head out." Guy came out onto the veranda and pressed his lips to hers. "I'll see you Wednesday night."

"I hope your meeting with the Brinkmont people goes well. I'll be praying for you."

"Thanks. I feel prepared. Sorry I had to work all weekend."

"That's all right. You've certainly done your share of week-ending it alone."

"Ah, the good ol' days," Guy said. "I didn't always like playing second fiddle to the newspaper."

Ellen smiled. "I'm not looking to be a weekend widow. Things will get back to normal once you get a handle on this case."

"What're your plans?"

"My hand feels a lot better today and I'd like to get back to writing. Only now I'm distracted by my disgust at the gossip-monger who lurks about."

"Like I said, maybe the woman went to the pastor, thinking that was the proper way to handle it. She'll probably never bring it up again."

"In the meantime, my reputation is in the toilet."

"Not with me it isn't."

Ellen sighed. "Unfortunately, I care a whole lot more about what other people think than you do."

"I care, honey. Just not enough to lose sleep over it. Do yourself a favor and sink your energy into writing and get your mind off this—and off the Hamilton case."

"I wish I were feeling creative."

"Maybe a few hours up in the widow's watch will get you back into the story." He looked at his watch, and kissed her hand. "I've got to run before the traffic gets horrendous. I love you."

"I love you, too."

Ellen was aware of the kitchen door opening and closing and Guy's Mercedes backing out of the garage. She held out her right hand and wiggled her fingers. He was right. She just needed to get back to work.

Gordy Jameson put the last of the stock orders in Weezie's to-do box and heard the front door open. "That you, Billy?"

Gordy got up and hurried out to the dining room and saw Billy Lewis pulling on the knob of the locked door to the deck. He put his hand on Billy's shoulder and turned him around. "Almost on time doesn't cut it. Ten minutes late is still late."

Billy looked down, and Gordy was sure he was blushing. "I did not mean to be late. I am a good worker."

"Yes, you are. But there's more to bein' a good employee than just bein' a good worker. I see a trend startin', and I want it stopped before it becomes a problem. I'm a fair boss, and you have to follow the schedule if you want to work for me—just like all my other employees."

Billy nodded, his weight shifting back and forth from one foot to the other. "I will come at eight-thirty. I will work now."

Gordy unlocked the door and held it open. "Okay, but I'm serious about this."

Billy walked outside and looked over his shoulder. "I will do an ex-cel-lent job—an ex-cel-lent job!"

Gordy closed the door and shook his head. Billy Lewis was at the same time predictable and unpredictable.

Weezie walked in the front door, a grin on her face that was anything but subtle. "I came in early to get the scoop. How was the blind date?"

"It wasn't a date. I was invited to dinner at Will and Margaret's."

"What'd you think of Pam?"

"She's a nice lady."

Weezie put her hand on her hip and held his gaze.

"Okay, I had a nice time. You happy?"

Weezie's smile looked like a half moon against her mahogany skin. "I'm so proud of you for takin' that first step. I've watched you dyin' inside since Jenny passed away. It doesn't matter to me whether this thing goes anywhere. What matters is you gettin' your life unstuck, gettin' out of the mire and movin' on."

"Hmm. Think you know me pretty well, don't you?"

Weezie took her index finger and poked his chest. "And don't you forget it. I've been prayin' the Lord would heal that heart of yours. He can help you feel good about what *is* without diminishin' what *was*." She put her arms around him.

Gordy blinked several times to clear his eyes. "I could do without all this mush, you know."

Weezie gave him one last squeeze then let go. "Wait'll you see the figures from last night. This place was packed out from five till closin' time."

"Did you have enough staff?"

"Honey, I was the grease on a finely tuned machine. Not only were we enough, we done you proud."

Gordy heard the passion in her voice and saw the excitement

on her face. It seemed foolish to put off the inevitable. "Let's go in my office. I've got somethin' I wanna run by you."

Gordy followed her into his office and sat in the chair next to her. "How many years have you worked for me, Weezie?"

"Nine, if you count that summer I started part time."

"You're the best employee I've ever had, bar none. In many ways, you seem like family. Jenny always thought so, too."

"I feel that way. Guess when you work with people, you get to know them real well."

"But I think we have a workin' relationship that's pretty unusual. You've always done anything I've asked you to do and never complained that I didn't pay you more."

"You've always been fair with me. I love my job here. Never saw any cause to make waves when you asked me to do more. I was always flattered you trusted me to get it done."

Gordy put his fingers to his chin. "I think it's high time I made you assistant manager. Does that have any appeal?"

Weezie's eyes were round and wide. "You serious?"

"Very. Of course, I'd adjust your salary. It would be a big increase. I'd need to rely on you to do the scheduling and to close several nights a week. That would free me up some. I might actually find time to do somethin' besides work. Interested?"

"Absolutely!" She laughed. "Assistant manager? Imagine that. When do I start?"

He picked up a ruler and held it on her shoulder. "I dub thee assistant manager. That oughta work. Why don't you go order a new nametag?"

"I can't believe it. I'm the assistant manager of Gordy's Crab Shack. Whoooeee, does that ever sound nice!"

Gordy tilted her chin up and looked into her eyes. "Don't you let the new title go to your head, now. I'm countin' on you *not* to change. You're the best asset I've got. That's why I'm promotin' you."

"Don't you worry, boss, I won't. My Joshua, rest his soul, must be dancin' across those streets of gold."

Gordy smiled. "And would you please stop calling me boss and call me by my first name."

"That might take some gettin' used to."

"Okay, scram. Let me work on the details, and we'll discuss the new salary before you go home. Don't say anything to the others. I'll announce it tomorrow."

Weezie went to the door and then turned around. "Thank you. I never dreamed I'd be assistant manager."

"Aw, I should've done it a long time ago, Weezie. I just wasn't ready to have time on my hands."

Gordy got up and sat at his desk, his eyes fixed on the picture of Jenny catching the big marlin. He wondered if Pam had ever been deep-sea fishing. And if she'd thought about him at all since last night.

Will Seevers walked into the officer's lounge and got a can of Coke out of the vending machine.

"Bravo," Special Agent Bryce Moore said, clapping his hands. "You weren't even at the plate and you got a hit-and-run."

Will popped the top off the Coke and took a sip. "I got lucky. A couple of citizens were on the ball."

"And that's exactly what I'm hoping will happen with the RISK organization."

"Anything new?"

"There might be. It's premature to get into details, but one of our undercover agents thinks she's getting some subtle hints about RISK. But we're going to take this one slower than the last. We can't take a chance on blowing it."

Will nodded. "Now that we know Hamilton wasn't our hit-and-run driver, it's looking less and less like we're going to get him for anything."

"Don't count on it," Bryce said. "I still don't trust the guy. Can't really put my finger on it, other than his bizarre history. But I'm not through putting him under a microscope."

"Where do we go from here? Without a body and without incriminating evidence, Hamilton's out of my reach."

Bryce started to say something, and then didn't.

"What?"

"Oh, just something that's been running through my mind. Probably way off base."

"Give it a shot."

"Okay," Bryce said. "Between you and me and that wall over there, I wonder if Hamilton could've handed Sarah Beth over to the RISK group to cover his tail."

"I'm not following you."

"Supposing he knew where to find them—or they knew where to find him. How hard could it be to strike a deal? These people would've jumped at anything to protect Sarah Beth from an abusive father and keep her out of the system—even agreeing to overlook his guilt."

"Are you saying Ross might've *let* them take his daughter so the Department of Children and Families wouldn't find out he was abusing her?"

Will lifted his eyebrows. "Let's just say nothing would surprise me."

Julie Hamilton sat looking at her hands and heard the mantel clock chime twelve times. She couldn't remember what day it was.

Ross walked into the living room. "I just ate the last of the bread and peanut butter. And the refrigerator's almost empty."

"I'll go to the grocery store," Julie said.

"You can't use the car with the media camped outside. They'll follow you."

"I've already figured it out. I'll go out the back gate and cut through the yard behind us. I can walk to the grocery store and bring a few things back. I'll wear my hair up and put on sunglasses. Nobody will recognize me."

"You don't have to do that," Ross said. "Make a list. I'll go."

"You'd be easier to recognize. Besides, if I don't get out of here, I'm going to scream."

He walked over to the couch and sat next to her. He was quiet for a moment, then began cracking his knuckles. "I know I haven't been communicating worth a hoot. I don't mean to add to your pain."

"Or I yours." Julie blinked to clear the stinging from her eyes. She started to ask his forgiveness again and then decided not to grovel. At least having confronted him with her doubt had opened him up—a little.

"Why don't you call that lady you made friends with?" Ross said. "She'd probably help you get groceries."

"I'm just sure Ellen Jones would like to be seen with *me* right now. Her husband's a prominent attorney. You should see the house they live in."

"You won't know if you don't ask. She was awfully sweet to you and Sarah Beth."

"I don't know that I have the courage to ask her, under the circumstances."

Ross jumped up off the couch, went to the window, and looked through the blinds. "Fine, then I'll go to the store myself. I'm not gonna be intimidated anymore. And I sure as heck am not going hungry rather than face up to a bunch of thugs who call themselves concerned citizens! I don't care if they stare at me! I don't care what they think! Or say! Or do! Or threaten!"

Julie got up and put her arms around him. "Okay, okay. Calm down. I'll call her."

Ellen turned off her laptop and sat back in her chair. It was no use. Until she worked through her anger, she wasn't going to get anything written on the book. The phone rang and she picked it up.

"Hello…? Hello…? Is anybody—"

"Ellen, it's Julie Hamilton."

Ellen's heart raced and she could hardly catch her breath. "I—I didn't expect to hear from you. I'm so sorry about Sarah Beth. I've been praying for you."

"You have?" Julie sounded surprised.

"Yes. I'm sorry I haven't called. It's hard to know what to say."

There was a long pause and Ellen thought she heard Julie sniffling.

"This is so hard," Julie said. "But I don't know who else to ask. Could you possibly take me to the grocery store? We're really down to the bottom of the barrel. The media's planted outside my house, and I don't dare drive the car. I can cut through the yard behind me and meet you on the corner of Orange Blossom and Flamboyant. I'll wear my hair up and put on dark glasses. No one will know who I am."

Ellen's mind was reeling. It didn't seem wise to get that close to the Hamiltons, and yet…*Lord, what should I do?* In her mind's eye, Ellen saw an image of the man beaten by robbers and left on the side of the road, and the Good Samaritan stopping to help.

"What will you be wearing?" Ellen said.

"Yellow crop pants and a white blouse."

"Okay, I'll pick you up at the corner of Orange Blossom and Flamboyant in ten minutes."

"I can't thank you enough…" Julie's voice trailed off. *Click.*

Ellen hung up the phone, her hands shaking, and was flooded with doubt—and fear that she had acted impulsively and Guy would be furious with her. *Lord, if I heard You wrong, please cover me.*

25

Will Seevers stood at his office window, his arms folded, his eyes fixed on the gathering outside. He counted twenty-two members of Mothers Against Drunk Driving picketing along the sidewalk, demanding that Terrance Adams be prosecuted to the fullest extent of the law.

Special Agent Bryce Moore came and stood next to Will. "Hey, Chief, you did a good job with your statement to the media. The community ought to rest better tonight knowing your hit-and-run is behind bars."

"I doubt if Jeremy Hudson's parents will." Will's eyes followed the marchers up and down the sidewalk. "I wonder if they really care or are just looking for a cause."

"How can you say that?" Bryce said. "MADD's been proactive for a lot of years in getting tougher drunk driving laws passed and enforced. It's not like you to be so negative."

Will glanced at Bryce out of the corner of his eye. "My old man was a drunk. He routinely beat the tar out of me, and I figured one day he'd kill me. Would've been nice if someone had rallied for tougher laws to protect me from his fist."

"Yeah, domestic violence can get really nasty. I take it your mother couldn't protect you?"

"Nope. I can't remember a time when she wasn't black and blue. He pretty much terrorized the whole family. They say alcoholism's a disease, but that always seemed to me like a cop out."

"I guess unless you're addicted, it's hard to understand or sympathize."

Will put his hands in his pockets. "How sympathetic should I be toward a guy like Terrance Adams who got behind the wheel after drinking himself into such a stupor that he ran down a kid and didn't even know it? I mean the creep took his truck to the carwash and rinsed off the fragments of somebody's child like bugs off his windshield."

"He thought he hit a deer."

"He hit a dear, all right—just not the kind he thought. I'll never understand why a guy like Adams was put back on the street."

"The guy's driver's license had been revoked. He wasn't supposed to be behind the wheel."

"Come on, Bryce. We turn these guys loose, knowing full well they're addicts and will likely do the same thing again. It's the same with sex offenders. I'm sick and tired of it."

Bryce's eyes locked on to his. "Is that why you've been asking me so many questions about RISK—you're sympathetic to the cause?"

Will felt the heat color his face. "I uphold every law whether I agree with it or not. I don't make exceptions."

"But you would if you could?"

"Look, I totally agree that vigilante groups like RISK cannot be allowed to take the law into their own hands. But I also understand why they *do*. The system needs fixing, Bryce. You know it, and I know it."

Ellen Jones drove slowly down Flamboyant Street and let the traffic go around her so she had a clear view of the next intersection. She spotted Julie standing on the sidewalk waving her arms and pulled over to the curb. Julie got in on the passenger side and fumbled with her seatbelt.

"Is Publix okay?" Ellen said.

"Yes, that's fine. I really appreciate your doing this."

Ellen pulled away from the curb, her mind racing with platitudes that she couldn't make herself say. Finally, she could stand the silence no longer and turned the car down a side street and shut off the motor.

"Julie, I cannot tell you how sorry I am about Sarah Beth. I can only imagine the suffering you've endured…" Ellen's voice cracked. "Don't feel as though you have to talk about it. But I'm here if you need to."

Julie reached up under her dark glasses and dabbed her eyes. "Thank you. That's the nicest thing anyone's said to me in a long time."

"Would you like me to drive around a while before we go to the store, maybe give your emotions time to settle down?"

Julie nodded. "If you don't mind. I'm a little nervous. I haven't gone anywhere public since this nightmare started."

"I'm here to do whatever you need." Ellen meant what she said, but wondered if she were merely trying to salve her guilty conscience. "You know what always helps me get my mind focused? A walk on the beach."

"I loved going to the beach when we lived in Biloxi," Julie said. "But I haven't been since we moved here."

"I'll be glad to show you my favorite place."

"Thanks. I'd like that."

Ellen started the car and made a U-turn, and headed toward Beach Shore Drive.

Gordy Jameson sat out on the deck, enjoying the shade of the umbrella, the last of a limeade, and the laughter of his lunch buddies. He couldn't remember the last time he had felt this lighthearted.

"Hey, Gordo," Eddie Drummond said. "You ever gonna get that boat of yours back in the water?"

"Thinkin' about it. What I'd really like to do is trailer it down to Miami Beach and take it offshore for sailfish."

Captain Jack lifted his eyebrows. "Better not wait too long. Season'll be over before you know it."

"I didn't know you had a boat," Adam Spalding said. "How long has it been since you've had it out?"

Gordy shrugged. "I don't know. Three, maybe four years."

"He's been threatening to get that thing out of mothballs for-ever and a day," Eddie said.

"Well, it's finally gonna happen." Gordy lowered his voice. "I'll have some time off now that I've hired an assistant manager."

"An assistant manager?" Eddie said. "Where've *I* been?"

"Shhh!" Gordy put his finger to his lips. "Keep your voice down. I'm about to let you in on a little secret."

Everyone leaned forward, elbows on the table.

"Now, I'm not announcin' this officially till tomorrow, you understand, but just between the four of us and those grackles over there, Weezie's agreed to accept the position."

"Hear, hear," Adam said, holding up his limeade.

Eddie gave Gordy a high five. "Wow, that's great news."

"Couldn't be happier for her," Captain said. "*And* you."

"Yeah, I'm pretty fired up about it." Gordy glanced up and saw Weezie come out the back door and walk toward the table. "Shhh. Here she comes."

"Sorry to interrupt," Weezie said, turning her attention to Gordy. "I've got Pete talked into cuttin' us a deal. If we double our order of fresh grouper, he'll knock off another thirty percent. Can't beat that with a stick. I say we do it. Micah's been workin' on a dynamite recipe that'll make a wonderful weekend special."

Gordy winked. "You go, girl."

Weezie put her hand on her hip, her eyes moving slowly around the table. "Somebody wanna tell me why you're all lookin' at me like the cat that ate the canary?"

Eddie put his hand over his smile. "Meow."

"Oh, what the heck." Gordy stood up and put his arm

around Weezie's shoulder. "I just told them our good news."

"You stinker. You're the one who wanted to wait till tomorrow."

"I know. But I wanted my friends to hear it first."

Ellen pulled her Thunderbird into a parking space and turned off the motor. "I love this end of the beach because it's not crowded."

She got out of the car and took off her sandals and put them on the floor in the backseat. Julie did the same.

"Come on," Ellen said. "Let's go get our feet wet."

Ellen walked with Julie about a hundred yards along the wet sand, her hands in her pockets and her thoughts unspoken, growing increasingly uncomfortable with the silence. "You mind if we sit a while?"

"No, that's fine," Julie said.

The two women sat side-by-side, facing the water.

Ellen closed her eyes and tilted her face toward the sun. Minutes passed without a word between them. She wondered if it had been a mistake coming here.

"Sarah Beth would've loved it out here." Julie drew a happy face in the sand with her finger. "But I never brought her."

"You had your hands full with unpacking and getting settled."

"I was still trying to deal with Nathaniel's death."

Ellen started to comment and then felt impressed not to.

"I'm sure you read everything in the newspaper. Nathaniel's accident was devastating. Ross and I used to be close, but losing Nathaniel nearly destroyed that—and left us too drained to be there for Sarah Beth. We tried. But we were so empty…" Julie's voice cracked. She took off her sunglasses and wiped her eyes. "The day you caught Sarah Beth in the parking lot, I was so preoccupied that I forgot to fasten her in her car seat. What kind of mother forgets to protect her child? Now that she's gone, she's all I can think about. I just want the chance to make it up to her." Julie let the tears fall and didn't wipe them away.

Ellen swallowed the emotion that seemed caught in her throat.

"In case you were wondering, that reporter at the *Biloxi Telegraph* twisted everything about Ross's life. She never even talked to us. After that article appeared in the newspaper, we were devastated. The phone never stopped ringing and we got all kinds of hate mail. All we wanted was privacy so we could work through Nathaniel's death. That's why we moved. But the lies and the gossip just followed us."

"Did the Seaport police explain to you how the allegations got started here?"

"Yes, some lady overheard one of Ross's coworkers tell some friends that he heard his boss say Ross was a child molester." Julie wiped her eyes. "That's so ridiculous. Ross's boss is his Uncle Hank. He'd never say that because it's not true."

"But the lady couldn't know that," Ellen said.

"Obviously, she believed it because she went to the body shop and asked Uncle Hank if Ross was registered as a sex offender. He threw her out and told her all the gossip she heard wasn't worth anything." Julie sighed. "Try telling that to the guy who spray painted our garage, or the protesters carrying their hateful signs, or the police, or the FBI, or just about anyone else in town. Why don't people find out the truth before they go ruining someone's life?"

"Maybe the woman was worried about Sarah Beth—since she didn't know whether or not what Eddie told his friends was true."

Julie finally made eye contact and held Ellen's gaze. "I never told you it was Eddie."

Will Seevers sat on a wrought-iron bench near the center of Bougainvillea Park, glad to be away from the office and alone with his thoughts. Nestled here amongst the longleaf pines, lush green flora, and deep purple and magenta bougainvilleas, he felt as though he had his hand on Mother Nature's pulse—a welcome contrast to the heartless concrete jungle he would return to in less than an hour.

He took his sub sandwich out of the sack and took a bite, savoring the distinctive taste of each of his chosen ingredients.

Until this morning's conversation with Bryce, Will hadn't realized how sympathetic he was to the RISK movement—if not its methodology, certainly its ideology. Was that a character flaw? He didn't think so. He'd never stand by and let them break the law, but he was nonetheless comforted that somebody cared enough about kids who were being abused to make sure they would never have to endure it again.

He felt his cell phone vibrate and was tempted not to answer it. He took the phone out of his pocket and hit the talk button.

"Chief Seevers."

"It's Gordy. You eatin' lunch?"

"Yeah, what's up? Sorry I had to leave last night."

"Glad you got your hit-and-run," Gordy said. "That oughta make you feel good."

"It might if it weren't for the dead kid. You didn't call me to talk about that, though."

"No, I just got through talkin' to Margaret. I just wanted to say thanks for nudgin' me to meet Pam. She's real nice."

"And…?"

"Hey, you said you weren't gonna push."

Will chuckled. "So I did. Is that the only reason you called?"

"No, I thought you might like to know I promoted Weezie to assistant manager. She's gonna be great at it. And it'll give me some free time."

"That's something you haven't had in a long time."

"Yeah, and who knows? Maybe I'll get up the nerve to call Pam and see if she wants to head out to the blue water with me."

"Do you even remember where it is?"

"You're a real wiseacre, you know that? I thought maybe this weekend I'd get the boat out of storage, clean it up, and do some fishin'."

"And maybe some *catching?*"

"Man, you're worse than Margaret."

Will laughed. "I doubt that. Seriously, whether or not this thing with Pam goes anywhere, I'm just happy you're moving forward."

"Yeah, thanks, Will. That means a lot. Talk to you later."

Will put his phone back in his pocket and took another bite of his sandwich. The phone vibrated again.

"Chief Seevers."

"Hi, it's me," Margaret said. "Where are you?"

"Hiding in the park, having a sub sandwich. What about you?"

"I just picked up the dry cleaning. I thought I'd grab something to eat and then head for the grocery store. I wanted to tell you what a good job you did in front of the cameras. I know how much you hate it."

"It came off okay, huh?"

"You looked and sounded like the professional you are. Let's hope Terrance Adams is behind bars for a long, long time."

Will sighed. "I keep asking myself why an innocent child had to die before we could get this guy locked up."

"You did what you could. At least he won't hurt anyone else."

"Let's hope he doesn't have a brother with the same bad gene."

"Did Gordy call you?" Margaret said.

"Yeah, right before you did. Something's going on. He promoted Weezie to assistant manager to free up his time and is thinking about taking Pam out in the boat. Didn't have a lot to say about her. But actions speak louder than words."

"My thoughts exactly. Pam didn't say much more than he did. Okay, Chief, I've gotta run. Have a good afternoon. I love you."

"Love you, too."

Will put the phone in his pocket and took another bite of his sandwich. He looked beyond the live oaks and caught a glimmer of the gulf in the distance. His phone vibrated again, and he pulled it out of his pocket.

"Chief Seevers. This better be important."

"I'm on my way to the Hamiltons'," Bryce said. "A protester called 911 and reported hearing a gun go off inside the house."

26

Ellen Jones sat on the beach, the midday sun hidden behind a glowing thunderhead, and explained to Julie Hamilton how she had overheard Eddie Drummond talking about Ross and then had gone to Hank Ordman and Police Chief Seevers—and eventually to Valerie Mink Hodges.

"Julie, I can understand your anger, but you have to realize I really don't know you and Ross. I had a moral obligation to pursue what I heard Eddie say for Sarah Beth's sake—and the other children in the community."

Julie hugged her knees and seemed to be staring out at the water.

"At least I went through proper channels," Ellen said.

Julie looked over at Ellen, her eyes brimming with tears. "You never asked *me* about it."

"No, I guess I didn't want to get that close to it."

Ellen was aware of sirens in the distance and a band of black skimmers about fifty yards off the coastline. She watched the birds glide above the water until they blended into the glare, then stole a glance at Julie.

Finally, the silence again seemed oppressive. "Julie, look at me. I'm sorry I didn't come to you with this. Perhaps if I had, things would've turned out differently. I have to live with that. But please believe me when I tell you that I was deeply concerned for Sarah Beth. Protecting her was my only motivation."

Julie looked away and dabbed her eyes. "I'm so tired of always having to defend my husband."

"I'm sure it must be exhausting."

"You have no idea," Julie said. "That reporter ruined him. I suppose you think she had the right to report the news. But she twisted everything. It's so unfair and no one cares."

"I do." Ellen reached over and touched Julie's arm. "I admit her article alarmed me. I asked myself how one man could have been innocent all those times, and—"

"But he was! The problem is no one ever bothered to talk to Ross and find out his heart. They just decided he was some strange breed of serial killer. And why not? It sells a whole lot more newspapers than the truth would."

Thanks, Valerie, for making all of us journalists look like self-serving jerks! "Julie, for what it's worth, I'm not proud of jumping to conclusions about Ross. I finally decided to start praying for him instead of judging him. It's really softened my heart."

"Great," Julie said sarcastically. "Now if you can just pray our daughter back to life, maybe we'll have a reason to get out of bed in the morning."

Police Chief Will Seevers slowed when he reached the Hamiltons' house, and a wave of picketers parted and let his squad car through. He pulled into the driveway, flung open the car door, and jogged to the front door.

An FBI agent he didn't recognize held the door open. "In the kitchen, sir."

Will hurried out to the kitchen, prepared to see the gruesome remains of a suicide–murder. He stopped in the doorway, surprised to see Ross Hamilton sitting at the kitchen table, a blank stare on his face, and Bryce Moore sitting next to him.

"What happened?" Will said. "Where's his wife?"

"At the grocery store." Bryce arched his eyebrows. "Ross was going to shoot himself and then changed his mind at the last second. The gun went off, but he's fine."

"I just want the pain to stop," Ross said, his shaking fingers laced together and folded on the table.

Will heard a man's voice behind him. "Excuse me, Chief. I'm Special Agent Newt Clifford. I'm here to see Ross Hamilton."

Will stepped aside and listened as Agent Clifford introduced himself to Ross and motioned for everyone else to leave the room.

Will went into the living room with Bryce. "Man, I was expecting blood up to my elbows."

"Yeah, me, too."

Will realized his knees were a little weak, and he leaned against the wall. "I suppose we shouldn't be surprised."

"Oh, I'm not surprised at all," Bryce said. "I think he staged the whole thing."

"Faked it?"

"Yep. It's one more way to seem like the grieving father."

"Come on, Bryce. The guy looks wasted."

"Sure he does, he's had years of practice. By the way, Clifford's one of our profilers. He's been baffled by this case from the beginning. Maybe now he can get a psych eval on Hamilton."

"Yeah, well, when he's done with Ross, maybe he can give me one. This thing's about to drive me crazy."

Ellen followed Julie through the back gate of the Hamiltons' home, each woman carrying two plastic bags of groceries in each hand.

Julie set the bags on the back stoop and opened the door, then picked up the bags and went inside. Ellen waited in the doorway, feeling as if crossing the threshold would somehow thrust her more deeply into Julie's life.

"You can put the groceries on the countertop," Julie said.

Ellen hesitated and then went into the kitchen and set down

the bags. "Do you want me to help you put them away?"

"No, I'll get them. Thanks for your help. I—"

"Mrs. Hamilton?" A man walked into the kitchen from another room.

"Yes, who are you?"

"I'm Special Agent Newt Clifford."

"Why are you in my house?"

Agent Clifford looked at Ellen and then at Julie. "May I speak to you privately, ma'am?"

"You can speak in front of Ellen. What's going on?"

"Your husband attempted to take his life."

Julie put her hands to her mouth, a deep groan coming from within, and began to weep.

"He's fine, ma'am. He's okay. He's sitting in the living room."

"Julie, I should probably go," Ellen said.

"No! Please stay. I can't face this alone."

Ellen didn't want to stay. But how could she not? "Go be with Ross. I'll put things away."

Julie left the kitchen with Agent Clifford, and Ellen put the perishables in the nearly-empty refrigerator. She opened the pantry and was flooded with guilt that she had never even thought to send them a meal. She began putting away the canned goods when she heard footsteps and turned around—and looked up into the eyes of Police Chief Will Seevers.

"Well, Mrs. Jones…you're just full of surprises."

Julie waited until Chief Seevers and the FBI agents had left, then flopped in a chair, her arms tightly folded, and glared at Ross. "How could you?"

Ross looked down at his hands. "All I'm doing is causing you grief."

"And you didn't think killing yourself would *add* to it?"

"I just wanted the pain to stop."

"And what about mine? Do you really think I could cope with *another* death? I love you, Ross, and I've stood beside you through every accusation, every heartache."

"Not *every* one."

Julie sat forward, her elbows on her knees. "You wanted to kill yourself because I dared to ask if you'd hidden Sarah Beth? What should I have done—ignored my doubt and hoped it would go away? I had a right to know."

"I told you I didn't do it."

"And I believed you! I apologized all over myself. What more can I do? Was killing yourself supposed to punish me? I can't believe you'd be selfish enough to even think of leaving me to suffer through this nightmare alone."

"Come on, Julie. You don't need me. You've cut me off ever since Nathaniel died."

"That's not true."

"No? Why do you think we never have a real conversation?"

"Because you're never home!" Julie shouted. "You don't want to know how I feel!"

"Give me a break. I listen to you ad nauseum about how lonely you are because I never talk to you. Well, you don't talk to me either—except to blame me over and over for making you unhappy. If you're so big on sharing, why don't you just admit what's really bothering you? Then maybe we'd have something to talk about."

"I don't know what you mean."

"You think I don't know you cry all the time? How do you think that makes *me* feel? I'm the one who ran over Nathaniel. *I killed our son!* Do you have any idea the guilt I'm carrying around?"

"You? What about me?"

The expression faded from Ross's face. "What are you talking about?"

"I'm the one who didn't check to make sure Nathaniel was in his bed. If I'd paid more attention, he wouldn't have gone outside. It's *my* fault he's dead." Julie's voice quivered and tears soaked her face. "I've been aching to hear you say you forgive me. But every day the chasm between us just gets bigger. I'm sorry. I'm so sorry."

Ross got up and pulled her to her feet, his arms engulfing her, his hand stroking her hair. "Shhh…I never blamed you. Never."

"Why didn't you just tell me that? All this time I thought you did."

Ellen sat at the table in the Hamiltons' kitchen, thinking she had no business hearing the conversation in the next room.

She went through the drawers, looking for something to write with. Finally, she found a yellow pad and a pen and sat at the table and began writing:

Dear Julie,

I've been waiting in the kitchen for forty minutes and think it's best if I leave and give you privacy to deal with what's happened.

I'm glad I had a chance to at least explain how I got involved in your personal business and want you to know that I will be praying fervently for you and Ross.

I didn't say much about Sarah Beth because I could tell you were fragile. I can only imagine the grief you must be feeling and don't want to add to it. But if you ever need to talk, please call me. I really do care terribly about your loss.

Sincerely, Ellen

Ellen put a kitchen timer on top of the note and left it on the table, then went out the back door and quietly pulled it shut. She paused for a moment. *Father, I pray a blessing upon this house and upon Julie and Ross. Only You know the layers of pain that compound this situation. I offer myself to be used in any way You see fit and pray for wisdom and clear direction to do whatever You desire. I ask these things in Jesus' name.*

Ellen blinked to clear her eyes, surprised at the attachment she was starting to feel to this couple. She went out the back gate, wondering if she were brave enough to do what she had just prayed.

Chief Will Seevers sat in his office with Special Agents Bryce Moore and Newt Clifford, and Investigator Al Backus.

"I'm glad Hamilton pulled this stunt," Bryce said. "It's given us a green light to get inside this guy's head. Newt has the psyche testing scheduled for tomorrow."

"A few hours with him should be very telling," Newt said. "I'm anxious to talk to him when his wife isn't present. I need to get him in touch with his feelings and see where it goes."

"Has he ever been in counseling before?" Will said.

Newt shook his head. "According to him, just crisis counseling after the shooting accident with his brother. Ross was ten."

"What will your testing prove?" Will said.

"Nothing is foolproof, Chief. But I can tell whether or not this guy is operating on all cylinders. I should be able to determine if the suicide attempt was real or faked."

Will got up and leaned against the file cabinet, his hands in his pockets. "Even if he staged the attempt, it won't prove anything."

"Proof is a relative term when you're dealing with the complexities of the human mind," Newt said. "My job is to determine how he's thinking and what he's trying to escape from."

Backus snickered. "How about life behind bars?"

Will shot Backus a reproving look. "Hamilton's managed to

avoid being charged all these years. What makes you think you can get him to admit anything?"

"He's on the edge," Newt said. "He probably wants to confess what's on his heart. It's a matter of knowing how far to push him."

Backus shifted in his chair. "I've done everything short of pushing him over a cliff, and he hasn't given up anything."

Newt nodded. "Interrogation tactics are one thing. I'm more interested in understanding how his mind works. That'll tell me a lot about what he's capable of."

"Which means we need to get back to work and find something to charge him with," Bryce said, rising to his feet. "Let's meet back here tomorrow after Newt's finished with Hamilton's evaluation."

Ellen walked in the door and heard the phone ringing. She set her purse on the kitchen counter and picked up the phone.

"Hello."

"Hi, it's me," Guy said.

"How'd the meeting go?"

"I think I hit a home run. We're about ready to go back in and finish up, but it sounds like we're ready to proceed. Thanks for your prayers. What's going on there? Have you written any more on your book?"

"No, not yet. I tried, but just don't feel creative today."

"So what are you doing? Not brooding about the gossip, I hope."

"I've been really busy. I'll talk to you about it tonight when you're not on the run."

"Okay. Look, I see Brent walking down the hall. I need to go. Love you."

Ellen hung up the phone and sat at the breakfast bar, her

body trembling. She thought back on her conversation with Guy the day she had met Julie Hamilton.

"Well, you were a Good Samaritan, inviting her to your home, then listening to her talk. What more can you do?"

"Probably nothing. I gave her my phone number."

"Ellen, you're not a shrink."

"I would've made a good one, though."

Ellen breathed in slowly and let it out. Me and my big mouth!

27

Two hours after Ross's averted suicide attempt, Julie sat with her head resting against the back of the couch, her eyes closed, her hand holding tightly to his. She shuddered to think how close she had come to losing him, but was grateful that the incident had caused them to finally get honest with each other.

"You can stop worrying," Ross said. "I'm not gonna try it again. It was stupid."

It was worse than stupid, Julie thought. She couldn't imagine where she would have found the strength to cope with the loss of her entire family.

She retreated to silence and sat staring at the coffee table, at the *National Geographic* Sarah Beth had brought home from Ellen's. She was aware of the grandfather clock ticking and the kitchen faucet dripping and a jet flying overhead.

"Julie, can I ask you something?" Ross said.

"Uh-huh."

"You've admitted having doubt, so be honest with me. Do you ever wonder if all those accidents were really accidents?"

"Of course not. Why would I?"

"Because even I wonder. I mean, if I were nuts, would I even know it?"

"Stop talking like that. *I* would know."

"Maybe not. A lot of criminals have fooled their families."

"Ross, quit. You're scaring me."

He looked at her, his eyes hollow, his face expressionless. "If

I flunk the mental evaluation, they'll finally have an excuse to lock me up."

"There's nothing wrong with your mind."

He sank into the couch and heaved a desolate sigh. "How can you be so sure? I don't know what to believe about myself any more."

Ellen Jones strolled along her favorite stretch of beach, replaying the events of the past couple hours. She had been touched by Julie and Ross's private conversation and knew it was too late for her to be emotionally detached from the situation.

She saw a mound of sand about fifty yards in front of her, and as she got closer, she saw it was an impressive-looking sand-castle. She looked around but didn't see Ned Norton.

She squatted next to the sand sculpture and admired the detail, thinking if she could pick anyone to talk to about what had happened today, it would be a prayer warrior like Ned.

Ellen looked out at the gulf, its waters glistening like millions of diamonds in the afternoon sun. For a split second, it was as though she got a glimpse of the Eternal City that would one day be her home. And her heart yearned for the peace.

"Well, look who's here!" said a male voice.

Ellen turned and saw her white-haired friend walking toward her carrying a yellow pail. "I knew this work of art had to be yours. Where were you?"

"Looking for shells," Ned said, pointing back at an outcropping of jagged rocks that formed a small cove. "Got me a whole bucketful."

Ellen smiled. "What will you do with them?"

"I'm not just an eccentric old man gathering shells that'll end up in somebody's garage sale, if that's what you're thinking. These are designated treasures."

"Designated for what?"

Ned looked at her, a twinkle in his eye. "For starters, a lady named Blanche Davis. Thought I'd string her a pretty shell necklace."

"Is Blanche someone you're fond of?" Ellen said.

Ned glanced up at her, the corners of his mouth turning up. "Not yet. You see, I say a blessing for each shell I string on the necklace. I do this for people I have a particularly hard time with."

"Is she a real pill?"

"I'll say. All she does is gossip and gripe. Most people at church run the other way when they see her coming. I have to admit, I've done the same."

"What gave you this idea?"

"Oh, I imagine it was the Lord since I've been praying about it. He doesn't take lightly her petty gossip *or* my ignoring her because of it. We're supposed to love everybody. Blessing her will help me do that."

Ellen stared at this dear old man who fascinated her more by the minute. "How many of these necklaces have you made?"

"Oh, I don't know, maybe a dozen. I'll tell you what: it hasn't failed to work yet. Blessing people who bug me changes my perspective—and sometimes it even changes them."

"Why do you suppose that is?"

Ned shrugged. "Maybe because I treat them differently, and they respond kindly to it. I suspect Blanche needs a touch from God. And we're His body, right?" Ned held out his hands. "Isn't that what these are for? It's a whole lot easier not getting them dirty, eh?"

"Ned, how did you get to be so wise?"

He tilted back his head and laughed. "The hard way, dear girl, the hard way. So what have you been up to?"

"How much time do you have?"

Ned caught her gaze. "As much time as you need."

Ellen began by telling Ned about being called into Pastor Crawford's office because of the woman who was gossiping about her, and then told him the details of her time with Julie Hamilton, about Ross's attempted suicide, and the conversation she'd overheard.

"Goodness, you have been through it," Ned said. "Sounds like your plate is mighty full."

"I'm disgusted about the gossip," Ellen said. "I'm sure I'll eventually resolve it in my own mind and maybe even figure out who to confront. But right now, my attention is on the Hamiltons' situation, which seems to be coming to a head. I was hoping to run into you so I could fill you in and ask you to pray."

"Oh, I'll do that, all right."

"I'm a little afraid," Ellen confessed. "I don't know anything about Ross except what the media's reported and the little bit Julie told me. I hope I haven't walked into something I can't handle."

"What's the Lord telling you?"

Ellen picked up a handful of sand and sifted it through her fingers. "I'm not sure yet. But I've told Him I'm willing to be used in this situation. I guess if that's what He wants, He'll keep opening doors."

Gordy Jameson sat in his office, finishing up a conversation with Weezie Taylor about her promotion to assistant manager.

Weezie stared at the piece of paper in her hand. "You're really gonna give me this much increase right off the bat?"

"You've been doin' lots of this stuff already," Gordy said. "I'm just makin' it official."

Weezie planted a kiss on the paper. "Whooee! I never did think I'd be assistant manager. It's like a dream come true."

Gordy chuckled. "Let's work it out so that your dream doesn't turn into a nightmare. Notice I changed your hours: lots of evenings and weekends. That's the tradeoff."

"Fine by me. Only one thing buggin' me about it."

"What's that?"

"I won't be workin' with you as much."

Gordy picked up her hand and gave it a gentle squeeze. "Aw, we'll see each other plenty. I'll be in and out even when you're in charge. Plus, we'll need to schedule weekly meetings. You got any questions?"

"No, I think you've about covered it."

"Okay, then. Get on outta here and enjoy your evening off."

Weezie sprang to her feet. "Praise the Lord for this! I can't wait to tell my mama. I'm allowed to tell my mama, right?"

Gordy nodded. "It's official. Tell whoever you want."

The phone rang and he picked it up. "Gordy's Crab Shack."

"Hi, it's Will. Got a minute?"

"Yeah, but that's about all. The dinner traffic's gonna start up pretty quick. What's up?"

"I just need to dump. Can you keep your mouth shut about something?"

"Sure."

"Ross Hamilton tried to commit suicide. Put a pistol to his head and then changed his mind at the last second. Some protester outside heard the shot and called 911."

"Is he hurt?"

"No, not a scratch. His wife had gone to the grocery store when it happened."

"I guess that's a good thing," Gordy said. "Think it was a cry for help?"

"There are those who think Ross staged the whole thing to make himself look like the grieving father—another way to mask his guilt."

"Are you in that camp?" Gordy said.

"No."

"Just *no*? The least you can do is throw me a bone."

"I can't really discuss the details of the investigation,

Gordy. The attempted suicide rattled me, that's all. I wanted to unload before I leave the office. I don't like taking my work home to Margaret."

"So do you feel sorry for the guy?"

"I didn't say that."

"Sounded to me like you did."

"It's taking a toll on his wife," Will said. "I'd like to get this case solved."

"You think findin' a body's gonna give her closure?"

"In a sad sort of way, yes."

Ellen turned off the eleven o'clock news just as the phone rang. "Hello, Guy. You're right on time."

"How'd your day go?" he said.

"I think I'd rather hear about yours."

"We finished our meeting on a positive note. I think we're all on the same page now. I feel ready. We're going to try to settle this out of court first, but I'm not confident the other side will accept the offer. They want millions in compensatory and punitive damages. They'll never get it, but we may have to play it out."

"Are you going to have to work these long hours much longer?"

"For a while. But I hope to take at least Sundays off. So tell me about your day."

"You're not going to believe what's happened. I spent the morning in the widow's watch, trying to get creative when the phone rang…" Ellen told Guy every detail she could remember, beginning with her phone call from Julie until her parting prayer with Ned. "It's not as though I went looking for this. Should I have refused to help Julie get her groceries?"

"Not if you felt the Lord nudging you," Guy said. "I imagine Julie will call again since you gave her a green light."

"She may not. She was really angry with me for going to

Hank Ordman instead of to her with my questions about Ross."

"Oh, she'll call. You're the only one she has to talk to. Just don't forget the Lord's leading you to talk to her, *not him*. I'd just as soon you keep your distance from Ross."

"Should I invite her here?"

There was a long pause.

"I'd really rather you didn't," Guy said. "The media might find out, and the last thing I need with the trial so close is negative publicity."

28

On Tuesday morning, Gordy Jameson finished stringing balloons around the customer waiting area of Gordy's Crab Shack, then stood back and admired his sign:

CONGRATULATIONS, WEEZIE TAYLOR,
ON YOUR PROMOTION TO ASSISTANT MANAGER!

The front door opened behind him, and he glanced at his watch.

"Good morn-ing, Mister G." Billy Lewis scurried toward the supply closet, his head down.

"Hold it right there," Gordy said.

Billy turned around, his face flushed, eyes darting from side to side. "I will do an ex-cel-lent job! An ex-cel-lent job!"

Gordy went over and placed his hands on Billy's shoulders. "It's five till nine, son. I know you can tell time. You wanna tell me what's goin' on?"

Billy looked down and shifted his weight from one foot to the other. "I—I was needed at home."

"That's not a good excuse, Billy. Your job here begins at 8:30. Maybe you need to get up earlier and get your tail in here on time."

"I am sorry, Mister G. I did not want to be late."

Gordy looked at Billy's pleading eyes and wondered if he was expecting too much. "I'll give you another chance. But if you want to keep this job, you need to be ready to work at 8:30.

Go on now and get to work. I'm not lettin' anything spoil this special day."

Billy looked beyond Gordy at the balloons. "Whose birthday is to-day?"

"We're celebrating something different: Miss Weezie has been promoted to assistant manager. That means she's the boss when I'm not here."

"I like Miss Wee-zie. She laughs funny. I will work now."

Billy got the bucket of supplies out of the closet and went out the back door, just as Eddie Drummond came in the front.

"What're you doing here so early?" Gordy said.

Eddie grinned sheepishly. "I was hoping I could bum a cup of coffee. Nice sign. Weezie ought to get a kick out of it."

"Yeah, I hope so." Gordy walked into the kitchen, Eddie on his heels. He poured coffee into a Styrofoam cup and handed it to Eddie. "Has Hank got you runnin' your wheels off?"

"Yeah, I started this morning at 6:30. By the way, do you know anything about the shot fired at the Hamiltons'?"

"What shot?" Gordy said.

"I heard on the news some protester called 911 and reported hearing a shot inside the house, but nobody was hurt."

"Then it must not've amounted to anything."

Eddie took a sip of coffee, his eyes peering over the cup. "So when are you going to ask Pam out?"

Gordy felt the heat rush to his face. "What're you talkin' about?"

"A lady my wife knows has a friend who's a friend of Pam Townsend's ex-mother-in-law. She said the police chief was trying to get you and Pam hooked up."

"You can tell that friend of your wife's and all her little whisperers to kindly mind their own business."

"Well, is it true? Are the Seevers trying to get you and Pam hooked up?"

"Back off, Eddie."

"It's not like the cat's not out of the bag. My wife's bridge club was talking about it last night."

"*What?*"

"Will you lighten up? Why are you being so squirrelly about it?"

Gordy grabbed Eddie firmly by the arm. "What I decide to do or not do in my personal life is my business, you got that?"

"I hear you, man. If I'd have known you were gonna go postal on me, I wouldn't have brought it up."

"Why don't you start thinkin' about how the other person might feel before you go shootin' off your mouth?"

"I still don't understand what the big deal is. So what if you're seeing someone?"

"Did you hear *me* say I'm seein' someone? I've struggled every day since Jenny died! I haven't dated anyone because I haven't wanted to!"

"Do you now?"

"Tell you what, Eddie, when I decide I'm ready to talk about it, I'll keep you in the loop. Till then, my personal life is off limits."

Police Chief Will Seevers heard voices and recognized one of them as Ross Hamilton's. He got up and went out into the hallway and saw Special Agent Newt Clifford walking into the staff meeting room behind Ross.

"I didn't realize you were going to get started so early," Will said.

Newt nodded. "Ross wanted to get this out of the way first thing."

Will's eyes locked on to Ross's and he studied him for a moment. "Okay, I'll make sure you're not disturbed. Buzz me if I can do anything."

"Thanks." Newt went inside and closed the door.

Will went back in his office and saw Special Agent Bryce Moore sitting in his chair, his feet on Will's desk, his hands clasped behind his head.

Will smiled. "You're getting way too comfortable in here."

"Trust me," Bryce said. "I'd love nothing more than to solve this thing so I could go home."

"Tallahassee, right?"

Bryce nodded. "Last time I checked."

"So what's on your agenda for today?"

"That's what I'm here to talk to you about. We're a heartbeat away from arresting the brains behind the RISK movement."

Ellen Jones heard the phone ring and debated whether to let the answering machine get it. She picked it up on the fourth ring. "Hello."

"Ellen, it's Julie. I'm sorry I left you sitting out in the kitchen. I was pretty shaken about Ross. I spaced out everything else."

"I understand. Is he all right?"

"Yes, but the FBI is doing a complete psychological evaluation on him this morning."

"When?"

"Now. I'm about to climb the walls here by myself. It's going to take hours."

"You want me to come get you?" Ellen heard herself say.

"If you wouldn't mind. It's difficult being alone right now."

"Okay, why don't I pick you up on the same corner in ten minutes?"

"Thanks. I'll be there."

Ellen hung up the phone and closed her eyes.

Lord, You're obviously putting us together for a reason. I'm really nervous about this, but I want to be obedient to whatever You want. Please give me wisdom and let my words be Your words.

Ellen picked up her purse and went out to the garage. She backed her Thunderbird out of the driveway and headed for the corner of Orange Blossom and Flamboyant.

Will Seevers passed by the closed door to the meeting room and heard muffled voices. He was eager to find out what Ross Hamilton's psychological evaluation would reveal.

Will got a Dr. Pepper out of the vending machine and popped the top just as the paging system clicked on.

"Chief Seevers, would you report to your office please? Chief Seevers, report to your office."

Will hurried down the hall where he found Bryce Moore pacing in his office.

"We've made an arrest," Bryce said. "My agents are bringing her in now. Name's Moira McDaniel. She's a thirty-seven-year-old social worker from Port Smyth."

"A *social* worker?"

"Yeah, a RISK implant, no doubt. Can you hang around for the interrogation?" Bryce said.

"Absolutely. How'd you find this lady?"

Bryce lifted his eyebrows. "We got a tip a few months back that someone in the Port Smyth Department of Children and Families was a RISK operative. We sent in an undercover agent posing as a caseworker and made sure she was vocal about the flaws in the system. Nothing happened for months. Then one day a few weeks ago, this Moira McDaniel made an overt attempt to befriend our undercover. And after a few coffee breaks and lunches together, and a few dinners out, our undercover confided to Daniels how mad she was about being forced to send a six-year-old back to her parents, that she knew the kid was being abused but couldn't prove it. Bingo! McDaniel starts talking about *options* and finally tells her there's a guardian group of concerned citizens called RISK. Says they have ways to make children disappear from abusive homes. Our undercover pushes the envelope a little too hard, and McDaniel senses she's been had and shuts down. So our gal pulls out her badge and reads McDaniel her rights. Guess we'll have to do the rest of it the hard way. Better make sure the coffeepot's on."

Ellen drove around Bougainvillea Park until she came to the central parking area. "Is this okay?" she said to Julie.

"Yes, it's beautiful here. Thanks for getting me out of the house."

Ellen spotted an empty park bench under some towering shade trees about thirty yards away. "Why don't we take our bagels and coffee over there?"

The two women got out of the car and walked across the wet grass, then sat on the park bench.

Ellen took half a bagel out of the sack, spread it with cream cheese, and handed it to Julie. "There's jelly in here if you'd like some."

"No, this is fine."

Ellen spread cream cheese on the other half and savored the first bite, then took a sip of coffee, her eyes taking in her surroundings. "Look, there's a rufous-sided towhee. Right there, next to that purple Bougainvillea bush."

"What's a rufous-sided…what did you call it?"

"Towhee." Ellen smiled. "I forgot to mention I'm into birds. It's a relatively new hobby."

"It's nice to have a hobby," Julie said. "I used to do a lot of needlework till we had kids…"

Ellen pretended not to see Julie's chin quivering. "How long is Ross's evaluation supposed to take?"

"I don't know. The FBI agent said he'd bring Ross home when he was finished, but it wouldn't be until after lunch. The testing's a waste of time. There's nothing wrong with Ross's mind.

His heart's on overload. Time is the only cure for that—*if* there's a cure at all."

"Where did you two meet?" Ellen said.

"On a blind date eleven years ago. His mother taught at the same school I did and set it up." Julie smiled. "We went to a bluegrass concert in the park. Seemed safe enough in case we didn't hit it off. We stayed all afternoon and eventually ended up at an all-night coffee shop. I don't remember what time I got home, but I remember my roommate was shocked. I knew from the start I was going to marry him."

"How long before you did?"

"Six months." Julie took a sip of coffee and seemed to be staring at nothing. "I know what you're thinking: how well did I really know him—considering his history and all? Ross told me early on about the painful things that had happened in his life. I don't think he's ever gotten over shooting his little brother. They had gotten out their father's hunting rifle and were fighting over it when it went off. His mother told me Ross cried off and on for a year after that. Used to draw pictures and take them to Billy's grave."

"And his best friend's fall?"

"Devastating. Danny and Ross were practically inseparable. They grew up together and seemed even closer after Billy died. When Danny slipped at the rock quarry and was hanging by his hands, Ross tried desperately to pull him up but felt him slowly slipping away. When Danny fell to his death, something in Ross died, too. He flunked school that year and had to repeat the seventh grade. He had stomach problems for years after that."

Ellen studied Julie's face. "I'm sure the disappearances of those two young women must have been equally horrible."

"Alicia's sure was. She was his first love. Ross had just given her his class ring the night she disappeared at the park. He'd left to go to the restroom and when he came back, he thought she was playing a trick on him. He looked for her for a half hour before he panicked and called the police. No one has ever seen her again. Ross said the police interrogation and the unanswered questions in the minds of everyone made his life a nightmare. He never had space and time to grieve."

"What about the other girl?"

"Stacey? Ross didn't even know her last name. She dated one of his buddies, and Ross agreed to give her a lift to the train station because his buddy had to catch a flight home for Thanksgiving. He let her off outside the station. No one knows what happened after that. And all the talk about the hit-and-run in Biloxi is baloney. So what if Ross drove a white Taurus? There must be a million of them. That reporter just wanted to make a name for herself."

"Julie, haven't you *ever* had doubts? You have to admit this is quite peculiar."

"The man I love wouldn't hurt a flea."

Ellen started to ask about Nathaniel and then decided not to.

Police Chief Will Seevers sat next to Special Agent Moore in the interrogation room. Across the table sat Moira McDaniel, her eyes full of fire and defiance, and her arms tightly folded in front of her.

"We know you're a link in the RISK movement," Bryce said. "You could make this a whole lot easier on yourself if you'd just tell us where Sarah Beth Hamilton is."

Moira sneered and said nothing.

"I could certainly understand your desire to save her from an abusive father," Will said. "You were desperate. No one seemed to be protecting this little girl. You had to do something."

"I didn't *have* to do anything," Moira said.

Bryce held her gaze. "But did you?"

Moira looked as though she were trying to stare him down. Bryce blinked first.

"You seem to think so," Moira said. "I never heard of RISK."

"Really?" Bryce took his finger and pushed the play button on a tape recorder.

"You don't have to sacrifice this little girl. There is another way. Have you ever heard of RISK?

"No, what is it?"

"An amazing group of people—like the guardian angels of abused children. They know how to snatch innocent victims and relocate them in safe houses till they can place them in new families. If you don't want this child to suffer any more, let me get them in touch with you—

Bryce turned off the recorder. "Won't do you any good to deny it, Moira. We'll just get a voice match."

She glared at Bryce. "I want to call my attorney."

"Be my guest. But we can cut you a deal and save you an awful lot of heartache. Tell us where Sarah Beth Hamilton is, and we can get the judge to go really easy on you."

Moira snickered. "You don't get it, do you? We aren't paying homage to a broken system any more. I'll rot in jail before I'll tell you anything about any of the kids we've helped."

29

Ellen Jones strolled with Julie Hamilton along the walking trail that wound around Bougainvillea Park, admiring the lush beauty of the flowering plants and leafy trees and pines—and trying not to react to Julie's seeming naïveté regarding her husband's emotional state. What would she do if the psychological evaluation indicated he needed to be confined? Was she capable of handling any more stress?

Ellen was glad that Julie had given her a different perspective on the events of Ross's tragic past. She would have loved to confront Valerie Mink Hodges with this information.

"How come you never ask about my children?" Julie said.

"I'm afraid it might add to your grief."

"It's worse when we talk around them as if they never existed."

Ellen put her hand on Julie's arm. "I'm sorry. I've wanted to ask about them, but didn't know if it would be too much for you."

"I wish you could've met Nathaniel. He was a handsome little boy—auburn curls, the biggest blue eyes you ever saw. His laughter was adorable, downright contagious. It was impossible to be with him and not get caught up in his excitement about *everything*. He had a presence that drew you in. If it's possible for a little boy to have charisma, he did. Part of it was because he was so darned cute. But it was more than that. If he had lived long enough to develop his personality, I'll bet he would've been some public figure—or maybe a motivational speaker or even an evangelist."

"I'm sorry for your loss," Ellen said. "I have two sons and can hardly imagine what it would feel like to lose either."

"I guess the best way to describe how it feels is *empty*. But even in the emptiness there's something dark and heavy and oppressive that keeps reminding you every second that he's never coming back."

"Has your faith helped get you through?"

Julie's face turned to stone. "I don't have any faith."

"I'm sorry, when you said Nathaniel could've been an evangelist, I just assumed—"

"I gave up on God and the Church the day we buried Nathaniel."

"Why?"

"What was the point? After all Ross had been through, God didn't protect Nathaniel or spare us the grief and guilt. I couldn't very well walk away from God and stay in church. So we stopped going."

"How do you deal with all the pain in your life?" Ellen said.

"I've gotten used to it."

"And you don't think God could help bear that burden?"

Julie looked at Ellen, her eyes piercing. "Why would I want His help when He's the One who caused it?"

Ellen, just listen. "Julie, what actually happened to Nathaniel? I only know what I read in the newspaper."

Julie told Ellen what had transpired that afternoon, and how Nathaniel must have been hiding from Julie and fallen asleep under the car. "I can't get the image out of my mind of my precious little boy dying in his daddy's arms." Julie wiped her cheeks. "It haunts me to this day."

Ellen stopped and put her arms around Julie. "I'm so sorry. What a horrific experience."

"I don't know that I'll ever get over it. It consumed my life for the past year—until Sarah Beth disappeared. Now my pain

vacillates between the two. And then when Ross tried to—"
Julie's voice failed.

Ellen squeezed Julie a little tighter and then let go and
started walking again. *Lord, there's nothing I can say.*

Will Seevers walked back into the police station, the lunch he'd
barely had time to chew feeling like a brick in his stomach. He
popped two Maalox into his mouth and nodded at the recep-
tionist.

He walked toward his office when he saw Special Agent
Newt Clifford come out of the meeting room and walk across
the hall to the men's room.

"Hey, Newt, did you finish with Ross Hamilton?"

"Not yet. We're close."

"Are you satisfied that you're getting what you need?"

"Definitely."

"Not going to give me a teaser?"

"I'll need the rest of the day to process everything. Might be
tomorrow before I reveal my findings."

"Okay," Will said. "Let me know where and when you want
to meet."

Will walked into his office and flipped the light switch. He
heard footsteps behind him and turned just as Bryce Moore
landed in the doorway.

"When you said quick bite, you weren't kidding," Bryce said.

"Anything happen while I was gone?"

"McDaniel's shrewd defense attorney arrived. He's not going
to let her answer many questions, but maybe he'll talk her into
dealing."

"When do you want us to talk to her again?" Will said.

"The sooner the better."

"Okay, let's go."

Will walked with Bryce into the interrogation room and extended his hand to the man seated next to Moira McDaniel. "I'm Police Chief Seevers."

"Godfrey Hawkins, Ms. McDaniel's attorney."

Will sat at the table and glanced at Moira. She seemed even smugger than she had earlier.

Bryce sat next to Will, his elbows on the table, and his fingers linked together. "Let me get to the point, Mr. Hawkins. In addition to the tape you've already heard, my agents have searched Moira's apartment and found a desk containing files that allude to various RISK safe houses. Being the clever organizer that she is, she chose to list the files with code names so the locations of the safe houses aren't revealed. Make no mistake: our number one goal is to find Sarah Beth Hamilton. But we also want the locations of those safe houses. We can make things a lot easier for your client if she gives us what we want. Frankly, I have little interest in seeing her prosecuted. I'm more interested in gleaning useful information."

Attorney Hawkins put his lips to Moira's ear and she shook her head. He whispered something else and she pushed away from him, her arms folded in front of her.

"May I have a moment alone with my client?" Hawkins said.

Will and Bryce left the room and waited in the hallway.

"There's no way that woman's gonna deal," Will said.

Bryce put his hands in his pockets and leaned against the wall. "She will if she's smart. It's either that or prison."

"People like her don't fear prison as much as selling out a cause."

There was a knock on the door. Will opened it and followed Mr. Hawkins back to the table, each resuming his place.

Mr. Hawkins took off his glasses and folded them. "Ms. McDaniel isn't interested in dealing. She has nothing else to say."

"You're making a big mistake," Bryce said to Moira. "Why be a martyr for a cause that's doomed. We *will* find the safe houses.

And you *will* go to prison. The only way to redeem yourself is to cooperate."

"Redeem myself?" she said. "You think betraying innocent children by returning them to abusive parents or passing them from one foster home after another as if they had no more value than a football is *redeeming* myself?"

"Moira, don't say anything!" Hawkins cautioned.

"Let me tell you something, Special Agent Moore. These are little human beings we're talking about. They aren't resilient. They don't adjust. The scars don't just go away! The system failed them! What they have now are loving, stable homes! And I'm not about to take that away from them! If I have to stay in jail to keep them safe, then so be it!"

Hawkins sank into his chair and let out a loud sigh.

"Okay, Moira," Bryce said. "Have it your way. Will you at least tell us whether or not Sarah Beth Hamilton is safe?"

"Why would I give DCF that satisfaction after they did nothing to help her? You figure it out."

Ellen glanced at her watch. "You want to get a sandwich before I take you home? Ross will be home soon."

"Truthfully, I'm not really hungry."

"Me either," Ellen said. "Why don't we sit in the shade for a while?"

Ellen walked over to a park bench some distance from a duck pond that was partially hidden behind a live oak tree. "This place is lovely. I don't know why I haven't come here more often."

"It is beautiful," Julie said. "But Seaport has such horrible memories, all I can think about is getting away from here."

Ellen sat quietly for a long time. "Julie, if you don't mind my asking, how long had you been a Christian before Nathaniel died?"

"I got saved at youth camp when I was sixteen."

"Did you have a close relationship with the Lord after that?"

"I thought so."

"Did Ross?"

"Yes, why?"

"I'm just puzzled why you blame God for what appear to be human failings."

"Call them whatever you want, but He had the power to stop them. Why didn't He?"

Ellen paused for a moment, her eyes focused on a couple of Mallards in the pond. "We'll never understand why. But He promises He will never leave us or forsake us, and that nothing can separate us from His love because of Jesus."

"Well, *I chose* to separate us."

"You can't stop His love, Julie. No matter how hard you try. His love for you is even stronger than yours for Nathaniel and Sarah Beth."

"He sure has a weird way of showing it."

Ellen hesitated, but felt impressed to share something. "A few years ago in the little community where we lived before moving here, a sixteen-year-old named Sherry Kennsington was kidnapped and murdered. It was a terrible ordeal for the entire community. I was newspaper editor then, and was in the thick of things. I wasn't a Christian yet; I was an agnostic.

"At Sherry's funeral, her best friend Taylor, who had also been kidnapped but survived, got up and gave a very moving account of how Sherry's determination not to hate her kidnapper even in the face of death had dramatically changed Taylor's perspective and caused her to accept Jesus."

Ellen looked at Julie. "There's a lot more to the story, but suffice it to say I was so stirred by the faith of those two young girls in the midst of such horrible circumstances that I began my own search for truth—and eventually chose to trust Jesus as my Lord and Savior. Then my husband did. And our two boys. And my daughter-in-law."

"What's your point?"

"Just that we rarely understand why terrible things happen—but can rest assured that God does. And that He's faithful to His promise to cause all things to work together for the good of those who love Him and are called according to His purpose. That's you, Julie. He loves you, and nothing will ever change that. So why not fall into His arms of grace and let Him comfort you?"

Will Seevers led Attorney Hawkins and Moira McDaniel out of the interrogation room and down the hall toward the side entrance just as Special Agent Newt Clifford and Ross Hamilton came out of the meeting room.

Moira did a double take, then stopped and turned on her heel. "You lying piece of garbage! I hope you get what you deserve!"

Ross stared at her dumbfounded. "Who the heck are you?"

"Come on, Ross. This way." Newt took him by the arm and led him in the other direction.

Will and Bryce escorted Moira to the side entrance and handed her off to FBI agents, and then went to Will's office and shut the door.

"Did you see how she looked at Ross?" Bryce said.

"Probably recognized him from TV."

"Or in person when they made a deal."

"I'm not convinced there was ever a deal," Will said. "But if Moira knows for sure that Sarah Beth is safe, why doesn't she just say so? You'd think she'd jump at the chance to throw it in DCF's face."

Bryce raised his eyebrows. "Maybe she's playing both sides. If RISK cut a deal with Ross to turn his head while they abducted Sarah Beth, then RISK also erased any chance that he'll be punished for abusing her. Maybe Moira thinks it's sweet revenge to let him sweat it out as a suspect as long as possible."

Will sighed. "You've got experience with this kind of stuff. I don't. I'm anxious to hear what Newt has to say in his report."

Ellen took hold of Julie's hand and was relieved when she didn't resist. "Would it be all right with you if I prayed?"

Julie nodded and tightened her grip on Ellen's hand.

Ellen closed her eyes and sat quietly for a moment. "God of all comfort, please draw Julie and Ross close to Your heart. Be their strength, their comfort, and their healing. I pray that You would restore their hope, faith, and trust in You and each other. Help them believe that no matter what happens, You will use it for good in their lives. Father, give them grace to face the future one day at a time and to trust You with the outcome. In Jesus' name I pray. Amen."

Ellen took her thumb and forefinger and dabbed her eyes. "You don't have to face this alone."

Julie nodded but seemed too overcome to say anything. She sat with her hands folded, her eyes closed, and seemed to be praying.

Ellen sat quietly and looked out at the pond. A couple with a small child was feeding the ducks. The little girl wore a pink sundress and matching bonnet. She threw something into the water that the ducks seemed happy to get, then jumped up and down and clapped. Ellen smiled. The child reminded her of Sarah Beth. She started to say something to Julie and then thought it might be too painful.

Ellen glanced at her watch and waited a few more minutes. "I should probably get you home. It's almost one o'clock. Ross may already be there."

Julie opened her eyes and looked over at Ellen. "Thanks for caring enough to listen and draw me out. I would never have realized how desperate I am for the Lord without your willingness to risk stepping on my toes. For the first time in over a year, I feel His touch. I can't tell you how grateful I am."

"Me, too. The Lord obviously orchestrated this whole thing."

Ellen got on her feet, Julie next to her, and headed toward the parking lot, amazed at how her perspective on the Hamiltons' situation had changed.

30

Julie Hamilton walked into the kitchen and heard the TV playing in the other room. She sorted out the hate mail and dumped it in the trash, then went into the living room where Ross was sitting on the couch, eating a bologna sandwich.

"I'm sorry I wasn't here when you got back," she said. "Ellen was nice enough to get me out of the house but I was hoping I'd be home before you."

Ross held out the remote and put the TV on mute. "I haven't been home long. The FBI's arrested some RISK operative. There's nothing on the news yet, but they brought her in when I was there. She almost bumped into me in the hallway when I was leaving. Looked right at me and called me a lying piece of garbage and said she hoped I get what I deserve."

"How'd she know who you were?"

Ross shrugged. "Must've seen me on TV. Special Agent Moore says they'll keep us informed if she tells them anything. But he didn't sound very positive."

"As if he ever does. So how'd your testing go?"

"It was all right. Special Agent Clifford had me answer a ton of written questions, then dug into my past and tried to get me to talk about it. He sure knew where all the hot buttons were."

"I hope he was gentle."

"Yeah, he was great," Ross said. "To the point where I almost believe he cares about me. But I'm sure the big guns are waiting in the shadows to find out what's inside the head of the infamous Ross Hamilton."

"There's nothing wrong with your mind. I'm sure that's the only conclusion they can come to."

"Frankly, I'm more interested in what they're able to find out from that gal they arrested. This is the closest thing to a breakthrough we've had.

Julie sat on the couch next to Ross, afraid to get her hopes up. *Lord, I'm sorry I've been so angry with You. I don't understand why any of this has happened. But please help us find out what happened to Sarah Beth. The thought of wondering for the rest of our lives is more than I can bear.*

Ellen walked down the front steps and out to the mailbox. She reached inside and picked up a stack of mail, and noticed a paper on top that had not been placed in an envelope. The letters had been cut and pasted onto a piece of plain white paper. She held it up and began reading...

Mrs. Jones, you may be fooling your husband, but God knows what you're doing, and so do I! Proverbs 12:4

Ellen could almost feel the indignation oozing from her pores. She went into the house and opened her Bible to Proverbs and read chapter twelve, verse four: *A wife of noble character is her husband's crown, but a disgraceful wife is like decay in his bones.*

Ellen stared at the note and let her ire burn. Who was this person who seemed determined to characterize her as some sort of floozy? And whom else had she told? Ellen took in a breath and exhaled loudly. How was she supposed to fight this kind of enemy—go around the neighborhood, knocking on doors, acting as if she were some sort of gossip gestapo? She wondered when the note had been put in the mailbox and cringed to think the postman might have read it.

Ellen got a pen and paper out of the drawer and opened her Bible to Proverbs and scanned the pages until she found a verse that seemed appropriate. She printed the words of Proverbs

18:8: *The words of a gossip are like choice morsels; they go down to a man's inmost parts.* Then added Proverbs 19:5: *A false witness will not go unpunished, and he who pours out lies will not go free.*

She closed her Bible, then stormed out to the mailbox and put the note inside. She looked up and down the street and wondered if the busybody was watching smugly from behind a curtain.

Ellen went back in the house, feeling childish but hoping the gossip would find her retort and feel ashamed.

She went out onto the veranda, sat in her rocker, and tried to calm down and reflect on her morning with Julie. She had not been surprised at Julie's intense anger at God, but her willingness to turn back to Him was more than Ellen would have hoped for in such a short time. And any doubts she'd had about Ross's past Julie had addressed without any hint of defensiveness or hesitation, and his innocence no longer seemed far-fetched.

Ellen was more and more inclined to believe she had misjudged Ross—and that Sarah Beth's disappearance was the work of someone else. But she no longer trusted her feelings, and Guy's words were ever present.

Just keep in mind that regardless of how he came across, we still don't know whether or not Ross Hamilton's guilty.

Gordy Jameson was delighted to hear the many congratulations Weezie Taylor was receiving about her promotion as he ambled around the dining room at Gordy's Crab Shack, mingling with customers. He looked over at her just as she turned and looked at him. He winked and wondered if he'd ever seen her face more radiant.

"Psst!"

Gordy looked toward the sound and saw a woman motioning him over to a booth filled with ladies.

"Is everything okay?" he said.

"Oh, yes, the food's wonderful," the woman said. "We just wanted to say congratulations."

"Thanks. But be sure you tell Weezie."

The woman seemed almost giddy. "No, congratulations on your *engagement*."

Gordy felt his jaw drop and fought to find words. "I'm not engaged. You must be thinkin' of someone else."

"Oh, dear. I play bridge with Melody Drummond, and a friend of hers knows a friend of Pam Townsend's ex mother-in-law. We heard you and Pam were tying the knot. We were so happy for you."

Gordy felt the heat color his face. "Pam's a lovely person, but we're not engaged. We're not even datin'. You should set the record straight with your friends before this gets back to Pam."

The other ladies at the table avoided eye contact, and Gordy wished he were somewhere else.

"I...I'm so sorry," the woman said. "I guess we heard wrong."

"Guess so."

Gordy left the dining room and walked back to his office and sat at his desk. He recognized the footsteps coming down the hall and looked up in time to lock gazes with Weezie.

"Did somebody die?" she said. "You look shaken."

"Uh, no. I just got congratulated on my engagement."

"Your *what*? And you didn't tell me?"

Gordy sat back in his chair and rolled his eyes. "I didn't tell you because it's not true." He relayed to her the conversation he'd just had with the ladies in booth three. "Isn't that a fine how-do-you-do?"

Weezie dropped into the chair next to his desk. "What're you gonna do? You can't let this go on."

"I'm gonna talk to Melody Drummond, but I need to cool off first." Gordy took a handkerchief from his pocket and wiped his forehead. "If I'm hearin' this stuff, you know Pam is. I should've seen this comin'."

"How could you?"

"Eddie said somethin' about it this morning. I set him straight—guess it was too late."

Weezie squeezed his hand. "I'm so sorry. I know it took a long time for you to build up your courage to even think about seein' someone. The last thing you needed was somethin' this private turned into a three-ring circus."

"The sad part is, I was workin' up to askin' Pam to go boatin' with me this weekend—maybe out to the blue water and do some fishin'."

"So ask her."

Gordy felt as though he had a mouth full of cotton. "I'm too embarrassed now. What if she thinks I'm the one sayin' this stuff?"

"Come on, she won't."

"If I'm seen with her, that'll just add fuel to this stupid rumor."

Weezie leaned over and poked his chest with her index finger, her eyes wide and round. "Listen to me, Gordy Jameson, don't you go lettin' some stupid gossip ruin your chances to move on with your life. Talk to Pam and tell her what's goin' on. Worst that can happen is she won't go out with you. Best that can happen is she'll understand."

Gordy took his pencil eraser and drew imaginary shapes on his desktop. "I don't know if I can handle people talkin' about us. I'm not sure I like Pam that much—or if she likes me at *all*."

Weezie sat staring at him with those big brown eyes that always marched right past his defenses. "Well, one thing I *do* know: you're never gonna know if you don't give it a chance."

Ellen picked up the TV remote and turned on the six o'clock news. She left the mute button on until she saw the anchor's lips moving, then turned on the sound.

"...FBI Special Agent Bryce Moore and Police Chief Will Seevers announced late this afternoon that a woman has been arrested for alleged ties to the vigilante group RISK that authorities believe may have abducted two-year-old Sarah Beth Hamilton.

"Moira McDaniel, a thirty-seven-year-old social worker from Port Smyth, was arrested and is being held without bail tonight in the Beacon County jail. Though Moore and Seevers would not comment on whether McDaniel's arrest is connected to Sarah Beth Hamilton's disappearance, sources inside the police department have confirmed that a taped conversation between McDaniel and an undercover FBI agent led to the woman's arrest. WRGL News is trying to get more information and will bring you the latest minute-by-minute developments.

"Also, this just in: authorities have received a tip from a local man who believes he may have seen Sarah Beth Hamilton here in Seaport. Harold Kaufman, a forty-one-year-old off-duty fireman, told authorities he saw a little girl in a pink dress and hat on the north playground at Bougainvillea Park around twelve-thirty this afternoon. The child was with a man and a woman and there were no other children or adults on the playground. Kaufman told authorities the couple was pushing the little girl on a swing when her hat fell off and he noticed her red hair. The man and woman rushed to put the hat back on the child's head, which caused Kaufman to become suspicious. He walked to a nearby pay phone and called the police; but when he returned the trio had disappeared.

"Kaufman told police he didn't get a good look at the man and woman, but they appeared to be young, and the child seemed happy and playful.

"Police are still combing the area, looking for DNA evidence that might confirm if the girl was indeed the missing Sarah Beth Hamilton.

"Anyone who may have seen this child or has any information as to who the adults with her might be is asked to call the

FBI or the Seaport Police Department at the numbers given on the bottom of the screen.

"In other news tonight…"

Ellen copied the phone number and dialed.

"Seaport Police Department, how may I direct your call?"

"I think I saw the same child Harold Kaufman told police he'd seen at Bougainvillea Park. With whom should I speak?"

"Please hold."

Ellen waited, her mind racing with regrets. If only she had said something to Julie at the time.

"This is Investigator Al Backus. I understand you've seen the little girl in the pink hat?"

"Yes. My name's Ellen Jones. I was at Bougainvillea Park all morning, and around one o'clock, I saw a child who fit the description given on TV. I don't know that I can add to the information Mr. Kaufman gave you, other than I saw her playing at the duck pond."

"I definitely need to get your statement. Are you where I can come talk to you?"

"Yes, I'm at home." Ellen gave him her address, relieved not to be talking to Chief Seevers.

"I know right where that is," Backus said. "I'll be there in a few minutes."

Ellen hung up and the phone rang again. "Hello."

"It's Julie. The FBI left a few minutes ago. Someone saw a little girl who looked like Sarah Beth at Bougainvillea Park—and not that far from where we were!"

Should I tell her? How could I not? "I just heard it on the news… Julie, I think I saw the same little girl. I glanced up at the duck pond right before we left and while you were still pretty emotional. I noticed a little girl in a pink sundress and bonnet. The way she clapped her hands and jumped up and down reminded me of Sarah Beth, but I honestly never made the connection that it might really be her! I can't believe I didn't pay attention to the man and woman who were with her. I'm just sick about it."

Julie's voice was shaky. "The FBI says the chances of it being her are slim, that no one in his right mind would take that kind of chance. But if the two of you saw her, maybe someone else did, too."

31

Ellen Jones sat in her living room and gave her statement to Investigator Al Backus and Police Chief Will Seevers. The chief's presence seemed invasive, and all she could think about was getting the interview over with.

"Anything else?" Chief Seevers said.

Ellen shook her head. "I've told you everything I can remember."

"Okay. We'll comb the area. Maybe we'll find something that will tell us if it was the Hamilton girl." The chief's eyes seemed to be searching hers. "I'm surprised you were with Mrs. Hamilton again today, considering you've had such passionate feelings about her husband's guilt."

"I never implicated Julie," Ellen said. "Actually, she called *me*. She was climbing the walls and wanted someone to keep her company while Ross did his psychological evaluation."

"Sounds like you've become friends."

"I'm just starting to know her, but I feel as though I've learned a lot about this family."

"Has your opinion of Ross changed?"

"Well, it's certainly mellowed."

"Really?" Will lifted his eyebrows. "Why?"

"In addition to the fact no one has found evidence that points to his guilt in this case or any other, I was touched by his plea for Sarah Beth's life. Plus Julie volunteered details about the deaths and disappearances that I and everyone else have been suspicious about. There's a surprisingly reasonable, albeit tragic, explanation for each incident."

"Imagine that," Will said. "The Biloxi police knew what they were doing all along."

Ellen decided she deserved his sarcasm. "Chief, I know I've been an irritation to you, but my true intention was always to make sure Sarah Beth wasn't in danger. I think we agree that what's important now is finding out what happened to her. It might take the cooperation of the entire community, but if that little girl I saw today is Sarah Beth, surely we can find her."

Will's face softened and he looked at her intently. "Well at last, Mrs. Jones, I think we're on the same side."

Julie Hamilton moved from the couch to the Lazy Boy, then got up and went into the kitchen where Ross sat straddling a chair, his fingers nervously tapping the table.

"I feel like we should be out looking for Sarah Beth," Julie said.

"I know. But where would we even start?"

"Well, this sure isn't working." She stared for a moment at the Post-it note on the refrigerator, then picked up the phone and dialed.

"Hello?"

"Ellen, it's Julie. I just had to talk to someone. Ross and I are going out of our minds thinking that Sarah Beth might be here in Seaport."

"Me, too. I gave my statement to Chief Seevers and one of his investigators. I'm so sorry I didn't say something to you at the time. If only I'd—"

"There's no way you could've known. Neither of us was thinking she might be here."

Ellen sighed. "Julie, the little girl's mannerisms were just like Sarah Beth's. I should've been sharper than that."

There was a long period of dead air. Julie wondered if it had been a mistake calling Ellen again.

"I have an idea," Ellen finally said. "It may not work, but it's worth a try. Can you meet me on the same corner in about an hour?"

"Okay. What're you thinking?"

"I'll tell you when I see you. Bring a recent photo of Sarah Beth."

Julie hung up and turned to Ross. "Ellen has an idea. She's going to pick me up at our spot in an hour."

"What's she gonna do?"

"I don't know. But it's got to be better than this."

Will Seevers sat in his office, reviewing the file on the Hamilton case. He yawned and opened his eyes wide and blinked several times. It made no sense that Sarah Beth's abductor would take her out in broad daylight. It had to be a look alike. A knock on the door broke his concentration. "Come in."

"I thought you'd gone home," Bryce said.

"This case is messing with my mind."

"Save your brainpower. It's nothing more than wishful thinking that the Hamilton girl is here *if* she's even alive." Bryce sat in the chair next to Will's desk. "Let's keep working on McDaniel. It makes the most sense to me that RISK was involved in this. And they sure wouldn't have relocated the girl here in Seaport."

"Then you think it's just a case of mistaken identity?"

"Has to be."

"You know I went with Backus to talk to the Jones woman?"

"Yeah, I read the report. She didn't add anything new except the location where she saw the girl."

"In hindsight, she's convinced it could've been Sarah Beth."

"So was Kaufman. But they're going by what, a picture they saw on the news?"

Will picked up his pencil and tapped the eraser on his desk. "Actually, Ellen Jones spent some time with the girl. That's why she came to me in the first place—out of concern for Sarah Beth's safety. When she gave us her statement today, she said she was struck by how much the little girl's mannerisms were like Sarah Beth's."

"And a million other two-year-olds. Come on, Will, the woman was seventy-five yards away. She didn't report it until she saw it on the news. It's just the power of suggestion."

Will shrugged. "Maybe. Or maybe the investigators will find something at the duck pond or on the playground that will prove it was her."

Bryce put a hand on Will's shoulder. "Listen to me...I've been involved in seven of these cases. It's much easier to look at the best possible scenario than deal with reality. But here are the cold, hard facts: there's a better chance of you winning the lottery than us finding Sarah Beth Hamilton in this town. She's either been relocated by RISK—or she's fallen victim to some sexual predator, possibly her father. The sooner you accept that, the easier you're going to handle it when we find her—dead or alive."

Ellen saw Julie standing on the corner of Orange Blossom and Flamboyant and pulled the car over to the curb.

Julie opened the door and peered inside. "I hope you don't mind that Ross came with me."

Before Ellen could reply, a man in a blue cap and dark glasses left the tree he was leaning against and hurried over to the car. He squatted by the passenger door and took off his glasses, his face looking even more drawn than on TV. His mustache was gone, but his eyes had the same beseeching look.

"I know you didn't invite me," Ross said. "Just say the word, and I'll turn around and go home."

"Don't you dare," Ellen heard herself say. "I need all the help I can get."

Julie and Ross crawled into the backseat, and Ellen looked at them in the rearview mirror. If someone would have told her a week ago that she would be helping the Hamiltons search for Sarah Beth, she would have thought them insane.

"This is awkward," Ross said. "I'm sorry to put you on the spot. But I can't go out looking for Sarah Beth in either of our cars or I'll have the media tailing me."

"It's okay," Ellen said. "Did you bring the picture?"

Julie reached over the seat and handed it to Ellen. "It's a professional one we had done when she turned two."

Ellen smiled, thinking it captured Sarah Beth's personality. "It's perfect."

"What do you want with her picture?" Julie said.

"I want to make flyers and distribute them all over the city. I can make them myself at Kinko's. With Sarah Beth's photograph posted in high-traffic areas, surely, if she's here, someone will recognize her and call the police."

"What a great idea," Ross said. "We'll be glad to pay you."

Ellen shook her head. "It's the least I can do. But you can help me get them distributed. This is going to take hours and we need to move quickly."

Gordy Jameson sat next to the phone. He picked up the receiver, then hung it up again, unsure of how to express his disgust without antagonizing Eddie's wife. How did one Sunday dinner get so blown out of proportion? Finally, he picked up the phone and dialed.

"Drummond residence."

"Melody, it's Gordy Jameson."

"Oh, boy. I am soooo sorry, I—"

"How'd you get the idea I'm engaged when I'm not even datin' anyone?"

"You're not?"

"No."

"But I heard the Seevers had you over to their house for a big dinner, and that you gave Pam Townsend a ring."

"Where'd you hear a thing like that?" Gordy said.

"I don't remember exactly who told me."

"Why didn't you just ask Eddie? He knows better."

"I did," Melody said. "He didn't know anything about it. But a lady in my bridge group has a friend who's friends with a friend of Pam Townsend's—"

"Ex mother-in-law. Yeah, I know. You ladies got your wires crossed. Now I'm the one who's red-faced about it. Not to mention Pam."

"Then you've talked to her?"

"No. But if I'm hearin' this stuff, she must be."

"So you're not even dating her?"

Gordy exhaled loudly. "Look, Melody, I don't know how to say this so it comes out the right way, but my business is exactly that—*my* business. You of all people should know how hard it's been with Jenny gone. If and when I decide to date, I'd like the freedom to do it without all these friends of friends of friends talkin' about me and speculatin'. It's not right. And I'm askin' you to put a stop to it."

"Oh, Gordy. I am sooo embarrassed."

"Yeah, well, that's two of us."

Ellen parked her car in the Publix parking lot and picked up a box of flyers. "I'm going to ask the manager if he'll authorize his checkers to give these out with each purchase—possibly as a bag stuffer."

"I don't think they allow things like that," Ross said.

Ellen caught his gaze in the rearview mirror. "Then I'll shame him into it. I can be *very* persuasive. Why don't you two tack some flyers on the light posts around the parking lot and on the bulletin board in Walgreen's? I'll talk to the Walgreen's manager when I'm through in Publix. Let's meet back here as soon as possible. We have a lot of ground to cover."

Ellen went into Publix and walked up to the customer service window. "My name's Ellen Jones. May I speak with the manager, please?"

"He's not here this evening. I can let you talk to our assistant manager."

"All right, thank you."

Ellen walked over to the bulletin board and attached the flyer with pushpins, then stood back a few feet, satisfied it would draw attention.

HAVE YOU SEEN THIS FACE?
NAME: SARAH BETH HAMILTON—AGE: 2
BELIEVED LAST SEEN WITH A YOUNG
CAUCASIAN MAN AND WOMAN
AT BOUGAINVILLEA PARK, TUESDAY, APRIL 14
CHILD WEARING A PINK SUNDRESS AND MATCHING BONNET
IF YOU HAVE SEEN HER, OR KNOW WHERE SHE MIGHT BE,
PLEASE CALL THE SEAPORT POLICE AT 396-9000

"Mrs. Jones?"

Ellen spun around. "Yes."

"I'm Alice Rimes, the assistant manager. What can I do for you?"

"I'm a friend of the Hamiltons, the couple whose little girl was abducted? I came to ask if you would authorize your checkers to give one of these flyers to each customer, perhaps as a bag stuffer."

Alice perused the flyer, then handed it back to Ellen. "I can appreciate the gravity of the situation, but if we start doing this for one, we'll have to do it for all."

"I see." Ellen's eyes searched Alice's. "I'm fairly new to the area. How many abductions would you say happen every year in Seaport?"

"Well, I, uh—I suppose it's pretty uncommon. Actually, I don't remember that it's ever happened before."

"Then surely you can see it in your heart to make an exception, just this once. It is a bit of an emergency." Ellen turned the flyer around so the woman could see Sarah Beth's picture. "She's a precious little girl. Wouldn't it be rewarding if by distributing her picture, you were instrumental in saving her from heaven-knows-what? Putting a flyer in a bag or handing it to a customer with a receipt will take each checker all of three seconds."

Alice looked down at the floor and then at Ellen. "You say you know the girl's parents?"

"Yes. And everything negative you've heard about Ross is either false or has been grossly misconstrued. But this isn't about Julie and Ross Hamilton; it's about an innocent two-year-old who can't help herself. I'm convinced if this community pulls together in the search for Sarah Beth, we're going to find her."

"All right. I'll authorize this for tonight. But I'll have to clear it with the manager after that."

"Thank you." Ellen shook Alice's hand, then gave her an entire box of flyers. "If you're a praying woman, please say a prayer for Sarah Beth—and for her parents. This has been unspeakably difficult."

"I will," Alice said. "Wouldn't it be something if they find her alive?"

32

Ellen Jones walked in the house just after 1:00 AM and heard the phone ringing. She dropped her purse and keys on the countertop and put the receiver to her ear. "Hello, Guy."

"Where have you been? I've left messages all evening. I've been worried sick about you."

"It's a long story. I'm so exhausted I don't think I can articulate it well."

"Let me see if I can stimulate your thinking. I turned on the eleven o'clock news and imagine my surprise when I found out you told police you had spotted Sarah Beth Hamilton in Bougainvillea Park! You might have given me a heads up, Ellen. I've already gotten calls from two of my partners, and I was speechless."

"It was on the Tallahassee news?" Ellen sat on a stool at the breakfast bar. "Things here went into high gear and I've been out all evening distributing flyers with the Hamiltons."

"Hamiltons, *plural*?"

"Yes. Let me explain what happened."

Ellen told Guy what had taken place from the time she heard on the news about Harold Kaufman spotting a girl that looked like Sarah Beth to her distributing flyers with Julie and Ross.

"Guy, it wasn't the kind of thing I could call and explain to you on the run. I didn't know I'd be out so late. And I certainly didn't think this would make the Tallahassee news. I'm sorry you were embarrassed."

"That's all right," Guy said, his voice softening. "You had your hands full."

"You're not mad that I ended up talking to Ross?"

"Not under the circumstances. What were you supposed to do—leave him on the street?"

"My feeling exactly."

"So what's he like?"

"Actually, very nice," Ellen said. "And terribly depressed. It's obvious the man is torn up over losing his daughter."

"How many flyers did you have made up?"

"You're going to think I'm crazy...ten thousand."

"For heaven's sake, Ellen, what are you going to do with them?"

"Well, between the two Publixes, Walgreens, and every light post we could find till we dropped from exhaustion, we've given out two thousand. Tomorrow, I'll talk to the managers at Wal-Mart and other stores and restaurants that have a lot of customers. I'll have Ross and Julie put flyers on car windshields in the parking lots."

"You won't get very far with just the three of you."

"I know. I thought I'd call Pastor Crawford and see if he can help recruit some volunteers."

"Good idea. So you really think you saw Sarah Beth?"

"I *think* so. I'm starting to second-guess myself. But the little girl I saw had her mannerisms, no question."

"I'm proud of you for taking the bull by the horns."

"You are? I thought you'd be angry I got involved."

"Oh, it's who you are: Ellen Jones, righter of all wrongs. Champion of the underdog. I wouldn't expect less of you."

Ellen half smiled. "I do have a way of ending up in the thick of things."

"Yes, you do. I take it you didn't get anything written on your novel?"

"No, but by tomorrow night, I'll have ten thousand flyers in print."

Will Seevers came in the kitchen door and laid the plastic bag from Publix on the countertop. He opened the refrigerator and poured a glass of milk, then sat at the table, opened the package of Hostess cupcakes, and took a big bite. He pulled a rolled-up flyer from the plastic bag, surprised to see Sarah Beth Hamilton's face on it.

"You're back," Margaret said sleepily. "Where'd you go?"

"Sorry I woke you. I was wired and couldn't sleep, so I went out and got something to snack on."

"Your usual artery-clogging comfort food?"

He smiled. "Just two little cupcakes. Here, take a look at this."

Margaret took the flyer and read it. "Where'd it come from?"

"Publix. It was in the sack."

"Boy, the Hamiltons didn't waste any time getting this out. You think it was really Sarah Beth?"

"I don't know. Bryce doesn't think so. Truthfully, honey, what kind of idiot would abduct a kid and then go out in broad daylight. It doesn't make sense."

"No, but it is odd that two different people thought they saw her on the same day. That makes me wonder. By the way, I forgot to tell you Gordy called earlier. Apparently a group of ladies came in for lunch and congratulated him on his *engagement* to Pam Townsend."

Will stopped chewing and looked at her. "Please tell me you're kidding."

"I wish I were. Let's see if I can remember how this goes: The wife of one of Gordy's friends has a friend who's friends with a friend of Pam Townsend's former mother-in-law."

"You couldn't say that again if your life depended on it."

"You're right. Anyway, that's the rumor circulating, and Gordy is just sick about it."

Will popped what was left of the first cupcake into his mouth and washed it down with a gulp of milk. "I can't believe this. After all the time we spent trying to get Gordy out of his shell, promising not to push him, and then this happens? You know how private he is. I hope this doesn't set him back."

"Didn't sound like it to me," Margaret said. "He's embarrassed, but his biggest concern is that Pam is hearing the same rumor and might be upset."

"Have you called her?"

"No, it was too late. I'll try to catch her in the morning."

Julie nestled in Ross's arms, the thought that Sarah Beth might actually be alive bouncing off the walls of her mind. She glanced at the clock. It was three-thirty—exactly one week to the hour that Sarah Beth had been missing.

"Are you asleep?" she whispered.

"You kidding? I can hardly wait for daylight so we can get the rest of those flyers out. I like your friend Ellen. She's the first person in a long time that hasn't made me feel like a loser."

"I've never told you this, but after what Ellen heard Eddie say, she would've been the first person in line to lock you up and throw away the key. She believed all the media hype and had you convicted for everything that reporter in Biloxi put in the article *and* for abusing Sarah Beth."

"Then why's she being so nice?"

"Because she started praying for you instead of condemning you. It's weird, but she swears it changed her attitude."

"Too bad more people haven't done that."

Julie hesitated, then decided to say it. "What about us, Ross? Are we ever going to start praying again?"

"I don't feel like it."

"Are you angry with God? Because I sure am."

"Anger would be a walk in the park compared to how I'm feeling."

"What do you mean?"

"I feel like a reject..." Ross's voice cracked. "It's almost like I can hear God saying, 'You know, there's just something about you I've never liked.' Maybe it sounds stupid, but that's how it feels."

The hopelessness in Ross's voice tore at her heart. Julie turned over and looked into his eyes. "There's no way God feels that way about you. He loves you, Ross. Love is His very essence."

"Then take a look at my life and show me where His love is. Because I don't see it."

In the dim of the nightlight, Julie saw his eyes pool with despair, and was afraid to say anything else.

Ellen pulled the sheets up over her and yielded her entire being to the mattress, her mind racing and her body spent. She closed her eyes and could see Sarah Beth's face and hear her laughter— but also the lifeless expressions on the faces of Julie and Ross.

Guy's words kept playing in her mind. *I'm proud of you for taking the bull by the horns. It's who you are. Ellen Jones, righter of wrongs. Champion of the underdog. I wouldn't expect less of you.*

Ellen felt a twinge of fear. This was bigger than she was. And what if it was all for naught? What if Sarah Beth's body was found and her parents' hopes dashed? Was Ellen willing to stand with them through an agonizing loss? Was she even strong enough? She sensed her role was not merely to be the cheerleader who could throw down her pom-poms when it was all over and walk away. The Lord had called her to be a player. There might be pain. And disappointment. And loss. Was she up to the task? Was she willing to follow His lead even when she might get hurt?

My grace is sufficient for you, for my power is made perfect in weakness. Ellen let the words the Lord had said to the apostle Paul comfort her, and had a feeling they were about to become very personal.

33

Will Seevers arrived at the police station early on Wednesday morning and headed straight for the officer's lounge, pleased to find a fresh pot of coffee already made. He could hardly believe it had been only a week since Sarah Beth Hamilton disappeared. He poured himself a cup of coffee and carried it down to his office, surprised to see the light on and Bryce Moore working at the table.

"Don't you ever sleep?" Will said.

"I never sleep well in motels."

"Might have something to do with the Hamilton case."

Bryce smiled wryly. "Do you think?"

"What're you working on?"

"I'm just going over the transcript of McDaniel's interrogation. She's one tough cookie. We'll never be able to get her to talk unless we can come up with a deal that's attractive to her."

"You don't think staying out of prison is attractive enough?"

Bryce shook his head. "Our profiler says she thrives on the idea of being the heroine for the cause and won't sell out the kids. But we'll think of something."

"Speaking of profiler, have you heard anything from Special Agent Clifford about Ross Hamilton's evaluation?"

"Yeah, he left me a note. Said to check with you and Al and see if ten o'clock was a good time to meet."

"Fine with me. Where?"

"In the meeting room where he tested Ross—unless you have other plans for it."

"No, that'll work. Did he give you any idea of the results?"

Bryce closed the file and got up from the table. "No, but he never does until he's got my undivided attention."

"Well, I'm available at ten. I don't want to tie myself down too much today, just in case something breaks on the Hamilton case."

"You still holding out hope that Sarah Beth will be found here?"

"I wouldn't go that far, but someone is sure making a noble effort." Will reached in his pocket, unfolded the flyer, and handed it to Bryce. "I got this in my grocery bag last night."

"Didn't waste any time, did they?"

"Nope. I'm impressed. It's really a great idea."

"Seems redundant. Most people already know all this and they've been seeing her face on TV for a week."

"Yeah, but they can refer to the picture on the flyer again if they need to. Publix was using these as bag stuffers. My guess is they're not the only ones doing it."

Ellen Jones waited until seven o'clock and then dialed Pastor Crawford's number.

"Hello."

"Dorothy, it's Ellen Jones. I hope I didn't get you out of bed."

"No, we're having our coffee."

"May I speak to Pastor Crawford, please?"

"Yes, of course. Hold on just a minute."

Ellen opened and closed her hand a few times, pleased that her fingers seemed almost well.

"Hello."

"Pastor, you're probably wondering why I'm calling so early. I—"

"Actually, I was expecting you."

"You were?"

"Yes. The woman who came to us before left a note in our

mailbox, suggesting you weren't telling the truth about the affair she's accused you of."

"*What?* Of all the nerve! I've told you the absolute truth!" Ellen paused and softened her voice. "Ms. Busybody also left a judgmental note in my mailbox and made reference to Proverbs 12:4. Of course, she didn't sign it so I have no idea who I should reply to. It's been very disconcerting, but has nothing to do with my reason for calling. I have a huge favor to ask and wondered if you could tell me how I might quickly enlist a core of volunteers."

Ellen told Pastor Crawford about how she had met Julie and Sarah Beth Hamilton, and then quickly recounted all the events that had led to her change of heart toward Ross. She also told him about the flyers she had printed and how she and Ross and Julie had already distributed two thousand.

"Pastor, I feel impressed to help the Hamiltons any way I can. I don't know for sure that the little girl Mr. Kaufman and I saw is Sarah Beth, but how can we afford not to act on it? The police can only do so much. I need the help of a few able-bodied citizens willing to help us finish distributing the flyers. I thought I would start here, with my church family."

"I'm glad you did. I'll get Dorothy to start calling. I'm sure we can round up some volunteers. Why don't you come by the church in an hour?"

Ellen pulled her Thunderbird over to the curb and picked up Julie and Ross, then headed down Flamboyant Street, juggling her attention between the road ahead and the two faces visible in the rearview mirror.

"Okay, here's what I've got going so far," Ellen said. "My pastor is getting some volunteers to help us distribute the flyers, so we'll need to go by the church around eight. In the meantime, let's go to Wal-Mart and I'll talk to the manager while you put flyers on cars in the parking lot."

"Your pastor's gonna help us?" Ross said. "I'm surprised any-one would want to help me after everything I've been accused of."

"I did."

"And we appreciate it," Julie said. "But you're the exception. It's been a long time since people have been kind to us."

Ellen spotted the Wal-Mart Super Store at the next intersec-tion. "I can only imagine the nightmare you've been living. But I think you'd be surprised how sympathetic people might be if you were plugged in at church.

"Oh, please," Ross said. "Like anyone ever gave us the chance. After the article came out, we started getting hate mail and anonymous phone calls and disgusting messages left on our answering machine."

"From the people at church?"

"I don't know who they were," Ross said. "I stopped listen-ing to the messages. What difference does it make? We couldn't go back to that church anyway."

There was a long, uncomfortable silence. Ellen wondered if she'd overstepped.

"Ross, in all fairness," Julie said softly, "we hadn't been to church in a year *before* that article came out. People tried reach-ing us for months. We never returned any of their calls. And after the article came out, even Pastor Helms called several times. But we never called back."

"How could I face him," Ross said, "after his mind had been poisoned by that reporter?"

"That was just a convenient excuse. Isn't the real reason we stayed away from church because we blamed God for letting Nathaniel die?"

The silence that ensued told Ellen that this was probably the first time the Hamiltons had discussed this. And she wasn't about to make ripples in the quiet by throwing in her two cents.

Gordy Jameson walked in the front door of the crab shack and went back to his office, a grocery bag in one hand, his keys in the other. He dumped the contents of the bag on his desk and put both packages of lemon drops in the top drawer. He picked up the paper that had fallen out and noticed Sarah Beth Hamilton's picture on it. He read the flyer, thinking what a shame it was that someone could hurt a cute little kid like that.

He pushed the flyer to one side of his desk and went through a stack of orders Weezie had approved. He double-checked them, feeling confident that soon she would be able to do this without his input. He pictured Jenny, healthy and happy, standing in front of his desk, looking through the in-box that was once hers but now belonged to Weezie. The memory dissipated at the sound of the front door opening.

Gordy looked at his watch: 8:50. He got up and went into the dining room and saw Billy Lewis getting his bucket out of the supply closet.

"You're late again, Billy."

"I will work now."

"Son, look at me," Gordy said.

Billy slowly turned around, his face flushed, his eyes darting from side to side.

"What can I do to help you be on time? I don't want to lose you, but I can't let you do as you please."

"I am sorry, Mister G. I was needed at home."

Gordy shook his head. "You're gonna have to give me more than that. Is there a problem?"

Billy passed his bucket from one hand to the other. "Lisa said we cannot talk about it."

"Is it something you can talk over with your parents?"

Billy turned and started walking toward the door to the deck. "I will work now. I will do an ex-cel-lent job."

Gordy put a firm hand on Billy's shoulder and turned him toward the hallway. "Let's go in my office and talk man-to-man."

Gordy prodded Billy into his office, then closed the door. "You can sit there in that chair, and I'll sit in this one. Okay, we need to get somethin' straight. I know I'm friends with your folks, but you work for me. I'm the boss. Now I can be understanding of just about anything reasonable, but bein' late without a darned good excuse isn't one of them."

Billy stared at his hands. "I am sorry, Mister G. I was needed at home."

"You've said that twice. Wanna tell me what it means?"

Billy shook his head.

"If you and Lisa are having a problem, why don't you talk it over with your dad? I bet he'll have some good advice."

Billy rocked in the chair even though it didn't move. "Lisa said we cannot talk about it."

"The last thing I wanna do is fire you, son. I'm pleased with your work. But you've gotta do a better job of gettin' here on time, you understand?"

Billy's head bobbed, and then he suddenly seemed distracted by the flyer on Gordy's desk.

"That's Ross Hamilton's daughter—the one who's missing," Gordy said. "Two people think they saw her yesterday at the park. The police are searching for her all over town. They may be close to finding her."

"No! The po-lice cannot pro-tect chil-dren from Ross Hamilton! Eddie said Ross Hamilton is dan-ger-ous! He told me to stay away from Ross Hamilton!"

Eddie's the one I wish you'd stay away from. "I promise you, Billy, Ross Hamilton's not gonna hurt you. I don't want you worryin' about this, okay? Why don't you go on out back and get to work."

"I will do an ex-cel-lent job." Billy got up and left the office.

Gordy heard the back door slam and decided he should call Billy's dad and give him a heads up about the sudden change in Billy's work ethic. And give Eddie Drummond another piece of his mind.

Ellen walked out of Wal-Mart, her hands empty and her heart satisfied. She moved her eyes across the parking lot and noticed flyers on every car windshield except her Thunderbird, where Ross and Julie sat in the backseat.

She walked over to the car and looked in the open back window. "Well, that was a huge success. The manager took a thousand and said they'll put them around the store, in the restrooms, and also in customers' bags. Couldn't have asked for a better response than that. Why don't we head over to my church now and see if Pastor Crawford was able to get someone to help us distribute the rest of them."

Ellen exited the parking lot and headed toward the church, aware that Ross and Julie hadn't spoken. She was tempted to break the silence with empty chatter and then thought better of it. *Lord, I'm trusting that whatever is going on with them is Your doing. Help me know when to talk and when to be still.*

Ellen drove about a mile, then turned into the circle drive at Crossroads Bible Church and pulled up to the front entrance where a small gathering of women sat on the steps. The ladies stood and came over to the car, and Ellen recognized a couple of them from her Sunday school class.

"Okay," Dorothy Crawford said to Ellen, her eyes stealing a glance at Julie and Ross. "There are twelve of us, and we—"

"Thirteen," Pastor Crawford said, approaching the window. "Tell us what you want us to do. We've all got cars."

Ellen got out and leaned against the car door. "Okay, everyone, this is Ross and Julie Hamilton." She motioned toward the backseat. "The three of us have already taken flyers to the managers of Wal-Mart, both Publixes, and Walgreen's, and they've agreed to put one in the bag with each customer's receipt. There are seven thousand flyers still in my trunk. Let's each take a box and go a different direction. Put flyers on car windshields, especially in shopping areas where people come and go regularly. Put them anywhere that will draw attention—light posts, telephone posts, front doors in neighborhoods. Surely ten thousand of these in a town this size will produce someone who knows where the Hamiltons' daughter might be."

"Okay, let's do it," Pastor Crawford said. He reached in the open window and shook hands with Ross and then Julie. "We're praying for you."

Ellen opened her trunk and handed Pastor Crawford a box, aware of others talking to Julie and Ross.

"Thank you for doing this," Ellen said softly. "You can't imagine what this will mean to them. They've felt abandoned by God for a long time."

"I'm glad to help. Think I'll head over to Old Seaport."

Ellen handed a box to each of the others. She checked to see which direction each planned to go, then slammed the trunk lid, satisfied that most of the city would be covered with flyers.

"Why don't we meet back here at noon?" Pastor Crawford said. "I'll order lunch in for everyone. But I'd like us to pray before we go."

Pastor Crawford went over to the car and opened the back door. "Won't you please join us as we ask the Lord to help us find Sarah Beth?"

Ross and Julie looked surprised and a little tentative, but they got out of the car. Pastor Crawford stood between them and offered his hand to each. The others joined hands and formed a circle, and the pastor began to pray.

"Father, we're desperate for your help. You who *are* love understand how Julie and Ross feel about Sarah Beth and how much they've suffered, not only by the torment of not knowing what's happened to her, but also by the cruelty and condemnation of others.

"Father, we ask for Your peace that passes understanding to settle on Ross and Julie and comfort them.

"And Father, we ask You to direct us. Help us do whatever we can to bring about Sarah Beth's safe return. We ask these things in the name of Your Son and our Savior, Jesus Christ. Amen."

Ellen opened one eye in time to see Ross's lips form the word, "amen."

34

W ill Seevers left his office at 9:59 and walked down
the hall to the staff meeting room, where Special
Agents Newt Clifford and Bryce Moore and
Investigator Al Backus were already waiting for him. Will went
inside and shut the door, then took a seat in the front row of
folding chairs.

"Thanks for being prompt," Newt said. "This won't take
long. I did the usual testing with Ross Hamilton, nothing more
and nothing less. His profile was a real eye opener."

"Okay, let's hear it," Bryce said.

Newt put on his glasses and looked down at the paper in
his hand. "Ross Hamilton is a man who has lost his way, who
views himself as some hopeless, cosmic misfit who can't do
anything right and who's destined to disappoint those closest to
him. He's ridden with guilt over a traumatic event in his child-
hood and thinks every subsequent tragedy is part of his
deserved punishment. But the punishment actually brings double
jeopardy, since it also inflicts sorrow on those he cares about,
which perpetuates the very guilt he's trying to salve. In short,
Ross Hamilton is stuck in a never-ending cycle of hopelessness—
virtually, a living hell."

"Is he violent?" Bryce said. "Would he act out his sense of
helplessness by victimizing?"

Newt shook his head. "He'd be more likely to hurt himself."

"So you think his suicide attempt was legit," Will said, "not
faked?"

"Yes, I do."

Backus leaned forward on his elbows. "So how do all the deaths and disappearances in his past figure into this?"

"I think they were just freak occurrences that produced and fostered a very wounded little boy who has to be reckoned with. From all indications, Ross seemed to function well in his role as a dad, almost as if it served to protect the child inside himself as well. But with both of his children having fallen prey to tragedy, he can no longer rely on that sense of safety he felt as a father. He's back to being the scared little boy."

Backus shook his head. "Way too deep for me."

Will put his hand on the back of his neck and rubbed the tightness. "So he didn't abuse his daughter?"

"No way."

"Then I suppose he didn't hand her over to RISK either?" Bryce said.

Newt took off his glasses and sat back in his chair. "He's not capable of such a thing. I stake my career on it."

"So the guy's not violent," Backus said. "Is he sane?"

"Quite. With some good counseling and time to deal with the compounded losses, there's no reason why he can't lead a normal life. I know you're anxious to solve this case, but Ross Hamilton isn't your man."

Ellen put the last flyer she had under the windshield wiper of a van in the last row of the Hobby Lobby parking lot. She walked to her car, nursing a blister on her big toe, and waited for Julie and Ross.

Suddenly, she was riddled with doubts. What if she hadn't been following the Lord's leading, but her own? What if her decision to make and distribute flyers had been nothing more than a guilt offering to make up for having judged Ross so harshly?

Ellen could imagine the gut-wrenching disappointment if Julie and Ross were told that Sarah Beth's remains had been found. How could she ever justify her impulsiveness? Was this search for Sarah Beth actually cruel and selfish? Had Ellen been thinking only of herself and her desire to feel better?

She closed her eyes, her hands gripping the steering wheel. *Lord, don't let the enemy turn this into a farce. I stepped out in faith. If I mistook my own thoughts for Yours, please don't punish Julie and Ross.*

She heard the back doors open and in the rearview mirror saw Ross and Julie sliding into the middle of the backseat.

"That's the end of the flyers," Julie said. "I'm anxious to get back to the church and find out where everyone else put them. Imagine: ten thousand flyers! If my baby's out there, somebody's bound to recognize her."

"Ellen, we can't thank you enough," Ross said. "We're finally *doing* something to find Sarah Beth. If it hadn't been for you, we'd still be sitting at home with no hope at all."

Gordy Jameson sat on the back deck with his lunch buddies, trying not to show his irritation at Eddie for continuing to fill Billy Lewis's head with stuff about Ross Hamilton.

Gordy noticed Eddie picking at his lunch. "Somethin' wrong with the food, Drummond?"

Eddie glanced up and then at his plate. "Nah, it's fine."

"You're poutin' about something," Captain Jack said. "Can't blame it on Ross Hamilton anymore."

Eddie looked at each of the faces looking at him. "Can't a guy eat his lunch without havin' to talk?"

"You gonna tell us or not?" Captain said.

"Okay, me and Melody had a little spat. No big deal. I really don't wanna talk about it, all right?"

Gordy shot Eddie a knowing glance.

"Anybody know who's distributing the flyers with the Hamilton girl's picture on it?" Captain said.

Gordy nodded. "The pastor's wife from some local church. Said she's tryin' to help the Hamiltons find their little girl. But I got the same flyer in my grocery sack at Publix."

Eddie stabbed a fried clam with his fork and popped it into his mouth. "If they find that little girl, the cops'll never send her back to her parents."

"Why not?" Captain said. "Nobody's proven anything."

Eddie lifted his eyebrows. "They will."

Weezie Taylor came out on the deck. "Gordy, you've got a call I think you'll want to take."

Gordy wiped his mouth and stood. "Good havin' lunch with you all. If I don't get back before you leave, I'll see you tomorrow."

He walked in the back door and down to his office, picked up the receiver, and pushed the button that was blinking.

"Hello."

"Gordy, it's Chet Lewis returning your call."

"Yeah, thanks for callin' back. I wasn't sure if I should even say anything, but Billy's been actin' kinda strange and comin' in late. I think maybe he and Lisa are havin' marital problems. I told him he should talk to you, but he got all red-faced and flustered. I don't think he's gonna do it."

"I haven't seen him in a couple weeks, but he and Lisa seemed great last time they were here. When did he start acting this way?"

"Last week. I called Hank Ordman and asked if Billy was actin' funny over there. He said Billy's been late almost every day and even stood him up once. Hank's about to fire him. Now, Chet, you know how fond I am of Billy. And he's a great worker when he's here. But I can't have him doin' whatever he wants. That's not fair to either of us. I really think there's somethin' wrong at home that he needs help with."

"Okay, Gordy, I'll talk to him. I really appreciate your taking an interest in Billy. He's a great kid. I'm puzzled, though. He and Lisa seem so happy."

"Maybe it's somethin' else," Gordy said. "But in all the years I've known Billy, I don't remember him bein' late for anything."

Will Seevers sat in the meeting room watching Bryce Moore and Al Backus pacing in opposite directions.

"Okay," Will said, "what do we do now that we know Ross Hamilton isn't responsible for Sarah Beth's disappearance?"

"We don't know that for sure," Backus said. "A psyche test doesn't *prove* his innocence."

Bryce stopped and stared at Backus. "Wake up and smell the coffee, Al. Hamilton didn't do it. We need to find another perp. Or prove RISK did it. I still think they're the best fit."

"I'm not willing to let Hamilton off that easily," Backus said. "I watched him squirm during the interrogation. He knows something."

"Al, you're dreaming." Bryce resumed his pacing. "Unless you've got rock solid proof, you and every one of us involved in this case need to switch gears. I think I'll go over to the jail and put a little pressure on Moira McDaniel."

Will took a sip of coffee. "I thought you said her lawyer won't let her answer questions?"

"Let's just say he's *selective*. I have a feeling he's sympathetic to the cause, but he's no dummy. McDaniel is facing some serious jail time if she doesn't cough up the Hamilton girl or give us something to shake down this group. She might be more willing to admit what she knows about Sarah Beth when we tell her we no longer suspect Hamilton of molesting his daughter."

Ellen sat at a long table in the church hall, enjoying a sub sandwich and watching Julie and Ross Hamilton interact with the thirteen people who had distributed the flyers. Ellen caught a yawn with her hand and decided she would go to bed early tonight.

"May I join you?" Pastor Crawford said.

"Yes, please do."

"Quite a morning," he said. "I'm so glad you called and allowed us to be a part of this."

"I appreciate your help. You can imagine how hard it would've been with just Julie, Ross, and me."

"Guy's still in Tallahassee?"

"He'll be home late this afternoon. I talked to him at one this morning. He's such a good sounding board."

"Ellen…" Pastor Crawford stared at the sandwich on his paper plate. "I'm sorry about this woman who keeps making false allegations. I hope you're able to discover who it is and set her straight."

"Me, too. But that's the least of my worries at the moment. I so want the Hamiltons to find Sarah Beth. I'm afraid I've become obsessed with the idea."

"Of course, you are. We all are."

"But what if she isn't found alive?" Ellen said. "How do we explain that to a couple who already feels as though God has played cruel jokes on Ross most of his life?"

"We'll deal with that if and when we have to. For now, I just want to support them in the search for Sarah Beth. How well do you know them?"

Ellen wrapped her hands around a warm cup of coffee. "Not well. But Julie's been transparent about Ross's disturbing past and how that article in the *Biloxi Telegraph* twisted the truth and turned their lives upside down. I'm finally convinced that a terrible injustice has been done."

"I've wondered about that," Pastor Crawford said. "The police chief made it clear that they've uncovered no evidence against Ross, and anything to the contrary is speculation and gossip."

"For some reason, people just can't seem to resist a juicy bit of gossip." Ellen took a sip of coffee. "You may remember I was a newspaper editor for a decade before we moved here. During that time I came to understand the power of words and the enormous responsibility we have to choose them wisely—and the devastating consequences when we don't."

"Indeed," the pastor said. "I've seen marriages destroyed, careers toppled, relationships severed—all casualties of careless words."

Ellen raised her eyebrows. "I wonder if the lady who's passing false information about me has thought of that?"

"Dorothy and I will be praying that you'll have the opportunity to confront her with the truth."

Ellen mused. "Maybe you need to pray I won't do something I might regret when I do."

35

Julie Hamilton sat in the living room and listened to Special Agent Newt Clifford explain the results of Ross's psychological evaluation, grateful that Ross had insisted she be present. She wondered how a complete stranger could understand and articulate things about Ross she knew intuitively but could have never put together.

"Obviously, the good news in all this," Newt said to Ross, "is we believe you had nothing to do with your daughter's disappearance. But it's going to take some work for you to turn your life around. It's important that you get good counseling."

"How am I supposed to afford it?" Ross said. "Our insurance doesn't cover mental health."

"Most psychologists will work with you on a sliding scale. If you're serious about wanting to get better, they'll do what they can. I'll be glad to put in a good word for you. There's nothing going on inside your head that can't be helped by getting a fresh perspective and taking some time to deal with all the losses."

"Guess I'm not nuts after all."

Newt smiled. "Hardly. Do either of you have questions?"

"What will you tell the media?" Julie said.

"Just that Ross's psychological profile coupled with the lack of evidence has caused us to eliminate him as a suspect in Sarah Beth's disappearance and focus on other leads."

"You think the media will leave us alone now?" Julie said.

"Possibly. There's usually a renegade or two who will want to stay with it. If I were you, I wouldn't comment on this to anyone."

"Has that woman from RISK told the FBI anything?" Ross said.

"No. But she thinks you're guilty of abusing Sarah Beth. Once she's been told you're no longer a suspect, she might mellow and tell us something. But from what I'm hearing, she's pretty callous."

Will Seevers heard footsteps coming down the hall and the jingling of keys. He walked over and sat at the table next to Bryce Moore just as the heavy bars opened and a sheriff's deputy brought Moira McDaniel into the room, handcuffed and dressed in bright orange.

The deputy seated Moira on the opposite side of the table next to her attorney, Godfrey Hawkins.

"I'll be right outside if you need me," the deputy said.

Will sat with his hands folded on the table, studying the woman who appeared no less harsh than the last time he'd seen her.

"How nice you each brought a buddy," Moira said. "I know how you law enforcement guys like to gang up on the helpless."

"Helpless?" Bryce said. "Seems to me you could do a lot to help yourself."

Moira folded her arms on the table. "I've already told you everything I plan to. Why are we here?"

"Ross Hamilton has been dropped from the list of suspects." Bryce lifted his eyebrows. "We no longer think he molested his daughter or had anything to do with her disappearance."

"Bully for him," she said.

Will caught her gaze and held it. "Moira, we want the same thing—justice for the abuser and safety for Sarah Beth."

"Everyone in the system says that. It just doesn't happen."

"We need you to level with us about the Hamilton girl," Bryce said. "If you can help us find her and the RISK safe house or houses involved, we can make the conspiracy charges go away."

"Don't say anything, Moira," Attorney Hawkins said.

Bryce's eyes turned to slits. "We can make you a very attractive deal."

"Pretty hard to deal since I don't know anything."

"Come on, Moira," Bryce said. "You found out about a child you thought was being abused and still living at home, you got caught up in the media hype, and less than forty-eight hours later you removed her in the middle of the night. This abduction had RISK's fingerprints all over it."

"If you had evidence, you would've produced it," Godfrey said. "We're wasting each other's time."

"Okay, here's the bottom line. What we really want is Sarah Beth Hamilton. Give her to us and we'll make the tape go away."

Moira stared at Bryce, her arms folded.

Bryce blinked first. He mumbled a swear word and sat back in his chair.

Will leaned forward on his elbows. "Moira, are you a mother?"

"I've got three teenagers."

"Then you know what it is to love a child. Ross Hamilton is innocent. There's been a big huge mistake and Sarah Beth has been robbed of the only parents she's ever known—the ones who adore her and can't sleep at night, worrying about what might be happening to her. Ross even tried to take his life. I probably shouldn't tell you that, but if you have any compassion in your heart, think about what this is doing to Sarah Beth *and* her parents."

Moira seemed to study Will's face, then leaned over and whispered something to her attorney.

"Okay, gentlemen," Godfrey said, "maybe you could take a walk or something. I need a few minutes alone with my client."

"Ellen?"

Ellen opened her eyes and saw the blades of the ceiling fan going round and round above her. Why she was in bed while it was light outside? She glanced over at the clock: 3:05. She remembered lying down after she took Julie and Ross home from the church.

"Honey?" Guy said, walking into the bedroom. "Oh, I'm sorry. I didn't realize you were taking a nap."

"I just woke up."

"And I just got home. I don't have to go back till Monday." He leaned over, his hands on either side of her pillow, and pressed his lips to hers. "Hi."

Ellen smiled. "Did you end your meetings on a positive note?"

"Yes, but let's talk about what's been going on with you first. I just heard on the radio someone else spotted Sarah Beth."

Ellen sat up on the side of the bed. "When?"

"Yesterday. A lady in Old Seaport read one of the flyers and told police she was sure she had spotted the couple and the little girl along a county road, picking wild flowers. She remembered the child because of the pink bonnet."

"Was she able to offer any more information about the couple?"

"No, she didn't pay much attention to them. It was the pink bonnet that caught her eye. So were you able to get help with the flyers?"

"Yes, it was unbelievable the way people at church joined in."

Ellen told Guy about all the events of the morning and the efforts of the thirteen other volunteers, including Pastor Crawford.

"He was very sweet about the whole thing," Ellen said. "I

was pleased with the way all of them treated Julie and Ross. I never expected that kind of support after all the bad press."

"I'm proud of you and them," Guy said. "It's going to be really something if those flyers help the authorities find Sarah Beth. I doubt there's anyone in Seaport who hasn't seen one."

"Oh, that reminds me," Ellen said. "Our Gossip Queen struck again. This time she left a note in our mailbox, and one in Pastor Crawford and Dorothy's. She told them I was lying about not having an affair. What nerve! I kept the one she left in our mailbox so you could see it."

Ellen reached in the nightstand and handed him the note.

"Hmm…a decay in my bones, eh? If she feels that strongly, I wonder why she doesn't just ring the doorbell and get it out in the open. This note-passing is really childish."

"I'm ashamed to tell you what I did," Ellen said. "I was so mad I left a note in our mailbox with Proverbs 18:8: 'The words of a gossip are like choice morsels; they go down to a man's inmost parts.' And Proverbs 19:5: 'A false witness will not go unpunished, and he who pours out lies will not go free.' I forgot to check the mail when I got home. I don't know whether she got it or the mailman did."

"Either way, she left another one. It's on top of the stack of mail in the kitchen."

"Why didn't you tell me?"

"I just got here. Besides, I didn't realize what it was until you enlightened me on how you've been using your writing talent."

"It's not funny, Guy."

"No, it's not. It's the image of you toting notes back and forth from the mailbox that makes it hard to keep a straight face."

Will Seevers squeezed past the sheriff's deputy and followed Bryce Moore into the room where Moira McDaniel and Godfrey Hawkins were waiting. He resumed his place at the table.

"I've had a long talk with my client, and she's decided against my better judgment to tell you something. All right, Moira. Say what you have to say."

Moira seemed to ignore Bryce and kept her attention directed at Will. "Chief Seevers, I thank you for being genuinely concerned about Sarah Beth Hamilton's well being. Believe me when I tell you I have no knowledge as to her whereabouts. I have never met the child, nor do I know anyone who has—"

"Okay, Moira, that's enough," Godfrey said. "Gentlemen, that's all she has to say."

"Why didn't you just tell us that before instead of running us in circles?" Bryce said.

Moira glared at him. "For one thing, I really don't like your attitude, *Special* Agent Moore. You show disdain for caring people willing to risk everything to protect the wounded children the system has failed time and time again—"

"Moira, don't say anything else," Godfrey said. "You've told them what they need to hear, and—"

"And for another," she said, talking a little louder, "I was furious that Sarah Beth Hamilton had been left in the home with what I surmised from the news to be a sexual predator for a father. I *wanted* the public to think RISK had rescued her so that DCF would come under fire for failing another child."

Godfrey Hawkins threw up his hands and sank back in his chair, his head shaking from side to side.

"However, now that Ross Hamilton is no longer a suspect," Moira said, "I felt a responsibility to Sarah Beth not to withhold the truth. I assure you, it's a waste of your time and resources to pursue RISK in your search for this child."

"Thank you for telling us," Will said.

"This isn't going to get you a reduced sentence, if that's what you think," Bryce said.

"You have no idea how I think, *Special* Agent Moore. That's part of the problem."

Julie watched Special Agent Clifford drive off, then went outside and sat on the porch steps for the first time since someone spray-painted "Child Molester" on the garage door.

All the picket signs had disappeared. Across the street, the sidewalk was crammed with media people, but she tuned out the questions they shouted at her. She just wanted to breathe fresh air—and to thank God she hadn't lost Ross to suicide.

The psychological evaluation made perfect sense and had filled in the missing blanks that had plagued her for years. She had always known that much of Ross's pain stemmed from the accidental shooting death of his little brother. But now that the evaluation had defined the emotional cycle of pain and punishment, perhaps Ross would be able to see it and choose to respond in a more healthy way. She was aware of the front door opening and then Ross sitting beside her.

"I just heard on the radio that a lady in Old Seaport saw the little girl in the pink bonnet yesterday—on some back road picking wildflowers or something! She couldn't give a description of the man and woman she was with, but she was sure the little girl fit the description!"

Julie's heart sank. "Then it's probably not Sarah Beth. That's too much exposure for a child someone's trying to hide. I wish I had seen her in the park so I'd know for sure."

"Come on, this should be encouraging! Old Seaport isn't far from Bougainvillea Park. That's three sightings in the same area. I'll bet the authorities are all over that side of town."

There was a long stretch of silence.

Ross slipped his arm around her. "What did you think of the results of my psyche test?"

"It made perfect sense."

"I would've never put it together," Ross said. "I'm anxious to get into counseling and get my head on straight."

Julie rested her hand on his knee. "Your head's on straight. You just need to let go of the feeling that you deserve to be punished. That's a terrible burden to carry around. Easier said than done, I know."

"I really wanna get better. I can't go through another year like the last one."

"That's two of us." Julie was suddenly aware that the media presence had grown. "Look at them out there, the vultures. I'll bet they heard about the woman in Old Seaport spotting the girl in the pink bonnet."

"Be glad," Ross said. "Maybe they'll work with us instead of against us for a change. It was cool the way all those people at Ellen's church helped us get the flyers out. I never once felt condemned. That was a relief."

Julie looked over at him. "I thought I heard you say, 'amen,' when the pastor prayed."

Ross half smiled and pulled her a little closer. "Eavesdropper."

36

Gordy Jameson sat in his office reading Thursday's newspaper and waiting for Billy Lewis to arrive. He wondered if Chet Lewis had been able to help Billy with whatever was troubling him.

The front door opened, and Gordy glanced up at the clock and breathed a sigh of relief. Ten minutes early. Good for Billy! He hurried out to the dining room and almost ran headlong into Weezie Taylor.

"Where're you goin' in such a hurry?" Weezie said.

"Sorry. I thought you were Billy."

Weezie laughed and held out her arms and hands. "Yeah, I can sure see how you got the two of us mixed up."

Gordy smiled. "He's been comin' in late, and I had to call him on it. I was hopin' he was here early."

"Since when is Billy late? That kid lives by the clock."

"Not right now. Something's on his mind and he's pretty guarded about it. I'm thinkin' it's marital trouble, so I called his dad and gave him a heads-up. Thought he might wanna talk to him. So why're you here this morning? You're not scheduled in till two."

"I just came by to make sure you're not stealin' from the place." Weezie's booming laughter filled the room. "Actually, I wanted to check the schedule. One of the girls is sick and called me at home. I can't remember who I've got scheduled in."

"Okay, do your thing and then scat. You need time away from this place. I'll see you at two."

Gordy went back in his office and sat at his desk, his hands clasped behind his head, and counted each tick of the clock until 8:31. *Darn it, Billy!*

Gordy waited until 8:45, then picked up the phone and called Hank Ordman.

"Hank's Body Shop."

"Yeah, this is Gordy. Let me talk to Hank, please."

Gordy heard the door shut when Weezie left and kept thinking Billy should be walking in at any moment.

"This is Hank."

"It's Gordy. Is Billy still there?"

"Nah, he didn't bother to show. Far as I'm concerned, he's done here."

"Sorry, Hank. I don't know what's gotten into him."

"Me either, but I haven't got time for it."

Gordy hung up and redialed.

"Hello."

"Chet, it's Gordy. Did you have a chance to talk to Billy?"

"No, I called and he was busy. Said he'd get back to me when he had time. Of course, he didn't. Has he come in yet?"

"No, and he didn't show up at Hank's either. Hank's done messin' with him. I don't wanna be hasty. This just isn't like him."

"I really appreciate your sensitivity. Let me get to the bottom of this and call you back."

"Yeah, okay, Chet. Thanks."

Ellen Jones jogged along the surf, enjoying the morning breeze and praying for Ross and Julie and Sarah Beth. She tried to imagine the jubilation if Sarah Beth actually came home alive—and the profound disappointment and grief if she didn't.

Ellen thought she saw Ned Norton sitting next to the water about a hundred yards away. She studied him for a moment, then started running in his direction. When she was a few yards from where he sat, she slowed her pace and waved. "Hi!"

Ned held up one hand, shading his eyes from the sun. "I was hoping to run into you. I heard on the news last night that you were one of the people who spotted the little girl in the pink hat."

Ellen sat cross-legged in the sand and tried to catch her breath. "Oh, but that's just part of it. You're not going to believe everything that's happened since last time we talked."

Ellen put into sequence the events that had happened from the time Julie called her Tuesday morning and they spent a few hours at Bougainvillea Park until the Hamiltons and the people from Ellen's church distributed the last flyer yesterday around noon.

Ned smiled and shook his head. "I'm mighty proud of you, young lady. I haven't seen such a citywide effort since World War II. I think everybody's out looking for that little girl now."

"Well, the print media is what I know," Ellen said. "Seemed like a perfect opportunity."

"So what'd you think of Ross?"

Ellen wondered if she looked as sheepish as she felt. "He's really a sweetheart. Not at all what I envisioned. I'm so ashamed I judged him guilty before I had the facts. But I'm also glad I wised up in time to do something positive."

"Which reminds me, whatever became of the woman who went to your pastor and said you were cheating on your husband?"

Ellen rolled her eyes. "Oh, the gossip queen of Live Oak Circle still lurks about."

Ellen told Ned about the note passing and how silly and unnecessary it seemed. "In the one she left yesterday, she wrote, 'Does your husband know what you were doing till 1:00 AM?' Heavens, I had just gotten home and was on the phone with Guy at 1:00. She must have been watching the house. I wish she'd just come out of the closet and talk to me. I'd tell her how ridiculous this whole notion is."

Ned patted the wet sand around the base of his sandcastle. "What would you tell her?"

"You don't even want to know what I'd *like* to tell her. But if I actually had the chance to confront her, I'd tell her to mind her own…that she should stop…that I would never…" Ellen picked up a handful of sand and sifted it through her fingers. "Nothing I say is going to change her mind, is it? No matter how good it makes me feel to get it off my chest."

"Sometimes gossip isn't even about whether the information is true or false. It's a way for a person who feels inferior to feel powerful—or a person who feels left out to feel important." Ned whistled while he added on to his sandcastle and seemed to avoid looking at her.

"Ned, why do I get the feeling you know who's been gossiping about me?"

Gordy sat out on the deck sipping a limeade and enjoying the salty breeze while Adam Spalding, Captain Jack, and Eddie Drummond finished eating lunch. He glanced at his watch, thinking it was about time for Eddie to get back to the body shop.

Eddie chugged down the last of his iced tea and laid a dollar on the table and set the saltshaker on it. "I've gotta get back to work. See you all tomorrow." Eddie walked to the door and went inside.

"Excuse me, I'll be right back," Gordy said.

Gordy went inside and caught Eddie by the arm. "Can I talk to you in my office for a minute?"

"I'm due back at work. Can't it wait?"

"It'll just take a minute, Eddie. It's important."

Gordy followed Eddie into his office and closed the door. "Have you been fillin' Billy Lewis's head with more stuff about Ross Hamilton?"

"I haven't seen Billy in days."

"He's been actin' strange, and I'm tryin' to figure out what's wrong with him. Yesterday, he was late again and I brought him in here to talk about it. He saw the flyer with the Hamilton girl's picture on it and got upset. Said he didn't like Ross Hamilton, that he was afraid of him, that he hurts children, the police can't protect children from him—and that *Eddie* says he's dangerous."

"Sure, I talked to him about Hamilton, but not since you told me to back off. I swear."

"All right, Eddie. I'm just worried about him."

"I know you like Billy, but he's a handful, being mentally challenged and all. You're wasting your time trying to figure him out. He doesn't see things the way normal people do."

"Yeah, thanks for the psychology lesson, Eddie. I'll let you get back to work."

Ellen sat at the kitchen counter, picking at her salad, staring at the note the mystery woman had left in the mailbox the day before. *Does your husband know what you were doing till 1:00 AM?* She was aware of Guy coming into the kitchen.

"Thanks for the salad." Guy rinsed his bowl and put it in the dishwasher. "How come you're not eating?"

"I am. I'm just distracted, thinking about this troublemaker who seems bound and determined I'm some sort of Jezebel."

"She's a mystery, all right."

"I stopped and talked to Ned while I was out running. He suggested I leave a note in the mailbox and invite her to lunch."

"What an unusual approach. Then again," Guy said, a grin on his face, "you might end up with the mailman."

"I'm serious. Ned thinks she's lonely."

"How would he know?"

"He didn't say, but I think he's figured out who she is."

"And what are you going to do if she accepts your invitation—get her here so you can rake her over the coals for going to your pastor without confronting you?"

"No, I'll prepare a nice lunch. That'll set the stage for what I'm planning to say."

"Which is?"

Ellen smiled. "I'll let you know when I figure it out. But antagonizing a gossip isn't the way to stop her."

Gordy put a stack of invoices in Weezie's in-box and started to leave his office when the phone rang. He went back to his desk and picked up the receiver.

"Gordy's Crab Shack."

"Gordy, it's Chet Lewis. I'm at Billy and Lisa's, and I…"

"You sound shook up. Somethin' wrong?"

"You have no idea. I really need you to get over here—hurry!"

37

ordy Jameson pulled his bicycle into the driveway of the last house on North Third Street and leaned it against the garage door. He pulled a handkerchief out of his back pocket and wiped the perspiration from his face.

Tall pines, towering shade trees, and thick foliage seemed to devour the small yellow frame house that used to be gray when it belonged to Billy's grandmother. Though the dense shade had caused the grass to thin, Gordy thought the place looked even nicer than when Mattie Lewis lived there.

He walked up on the front stoop and started to ring the bell when Chet Lewis opened the door, ushered him inside, then shut the door and locked it.

Gordy quickly scanned the living room, not surprised to see simple furnishings and everything in its place. "Where're Billy and Lisa?"

"Come with me," Chet said. "I need to show you something."

Gordy followed him across the squeaky floor and down the hall and into a stark bedroom where a small blanket lay folded atop an air mattress in the middle of a hardwood floor. The room exuded a faint smell of urine. Chet reached inside the closet, then turned around holding a pink dress and matching bonnet.

Gordy felt his jaw drop and stood staring at the clothes, unable to turn his shock into words.

"They'd never hurt that little girl!" Chet said. "I can't go to the FBI until I talk to Billy. I haven't even told Lena. This is going to kill her."

"Any idea where they are?"

"No, but they must be on foot, their bicycles are in the garage. Those flyers are all over the city, and I'm sure Billy knows the authorities are looking for the girl. There must be a logical explanation for this, but I sure don't have it."

"Maybe I do," Gordy said. "Let's go sit down and see if we can put the pieces together."

Chet went into the living room, seemingly in a daze, and collapsed in the rocking chair.

Gordy sat across from him on the couch, his mind racing in reverse. "This explains why Billy's been actin' so strange. I can't even imagine him and Lisa tryin' to take care of a two-year-old."

Gordy told Chet everything he could remember about Billy's strange behavior and his strong reaction to Ross Hamilton. "Billy overheard Eddie say the police couldn't protect children from Hamilton. Poor kid must've been tryin' to save the girl from bein' abused."

Chet's eyes brimmed with tears. "You really think the FBI's going to care why he kidnapped that girl? People are scared of Billy because he's different. This is going to ruin him. He and Lisa will be separated, probably institutionalized. It'll break their hearts."

Gordy rubbed the back of his neck. "Look, we can't sit on this."

"I'm not going to the FBI until I talk to Billy! Maybe he'll be home soon."

Gordy glanced at the wedding picture of Billy and Lisa on the bookshelf. "Will's a reasonable guy. Let me call him. He'll make sure Billy doesn't get hurt."

Chet rested his head against the back of the rocker. "Billy was doing so well. He and Lisa were happy. I thought he had a future. What was he thinking?"

Gordy got up and laid his hand on Chet's shoulder. "Listen, buddy, we've been friends a long time. We're gonna have to agree on this. We can't wait to call the police. Billy and Lisa aren't emotionally equipped to handle this kind of pressure. They're liable to do somethin' foolish and really get hurt. There are *three* kids out there, and we need all the help we can get to find them."

Will Seevers sat at his desk, thinking about his confrontation with Moira McDaniel and wondering if Bryce had gone off somewhere to nurse his bruised ego.

Every police officer, sheriff's deputy, and FBI agent that could be spared was knocking on doors and combing the area around Old Seaport, trying to get new leads on the couple and the little girl in pink.

The report had come back on DNA found on a candy wrapper at the playground in Bougainvillea Park. It didn't match the Hamilton girl's. And a dozen partial prints found on the swings were inconclusive. Nothing with DNA was found around the duck pond or along the county road where the woman told police she had seen them.

Will's phone rang and he picked it up. "Seevers."

"Will, it's Gordy. I hope you're sittin' down. The Hamilton girl's alive, and I know who's got her! I'll tell you where I am, but you gotta promise me you'll come over here with an open mind."

Will grabbed a piece of paper and a pencil. "Tell me where you are, and don't mess with me. Our friendship can't influence how I do my job."

"I promise I'm not messin' with you. But there're extenuating circumstances you should know about before the FBI gets in the middle of this."

"Gordy," Will lowered his voice, "don't put me in a position to have to charge you with impeding an investigation."

"Hey, I'm not impedin' anything. I think I just *solved* it. I'm at Mattie Lewis's old place. 314 North Third Street. Last house on the block."

"Isn't that where…oh, no…" Will's heart sank. "I'll be right there."

Will grabbed the keys to his squad car and rushed out of the building.

Gordy laid his head against the back of the couch in Billy Lewis's living room and rested his eyes. "That's it. You know everything I know. Call whoever you want."

"Special Agent Moore is already on the way," Will said. "I called him when I drove up. Mr. Lewis, can you think of any place Billy would go—a friend's house? A favorite place?"

"Honestly, I can't," Chet Lewis said. "I've been racking my brain, but nothing comes to mind. Billy loved the park, but I doubt seriously he would've gone back there now."

"We'll check it out anyway."

"Chief Seevers, my son is a gentle young man. His reasoning ability is equivalent to an eight-year-old's. His heart is innocent and good…" Chet's voice cracked. "He wouldn't harm that little girl. I'm sure his reasons for keeping her here made sense to him. Please don't let anyone hurt him. I'm positive he's not armed. I can get him to turn the little girl over to you if we can just find him."

Will looked at Gordy, his eyebrows raised. "You have any idea where he might've gone?"

Gordy shook his head.

"Okay, then. When Moore gets here, we'll map out a search plan and tear this town apart. Those flyers are everywhere. That can only work in our favor. We'll have a team here gathering evidence, so we'll be prepared if Billy and Lisa come back." Will turned to Chet. "Mr. Lewis, you need to call your wife. We'll need to talk to her, too."

Ellen Jones put a ham and cheese quiche in the oven, then turned up the volume on the six o'clock news.

"…Sources confirm that police investigators and the FBI are currently searching a residence at 314 North Third Street, where Sarah Beth Hamilton reportedly has been held."

"Guy, you need to come in here!" Ellen hollered.

"Police Chief Seevers confirmed that investigators have recovered a pink dress and bonnet identical to those described by three local residents who reported seeing the missing child yesterday. Investigators are hopeful that DNA found on the clothing and elsewhere in the home will prove to be that of two-year-old Sarah Beth Hamilton.

"No arrests have been made, but police and FBI are searching the city for a mentally challenged couple who live in the home, twenty-one-year old Billy Lewis and his twenty-year-old wife, Lisa.

"The Lewis's home is situated on a heavily wooded lot at the end of the block and is relatively secluded. Police and FBI have been questioning neighbors, most of whom are elderly, and so far no one on North Third Street remembers seeing the Hamilton girl.

"Investigators won't say whether they believe the Lewises were responsible for abducting the girl or whether the couple conspired with someone else. However, authorities are hopeful that fingerprints taken from the Lewises' home will match those found on Sarah Beth Hamilton's bedroom window after her abduction just eight days ago.

"Chief Seevers told reporters that a huge concentration of law enforcement personnel is using every means available to search the area around Old Seaport. He feels confident that Sarah Beth will be found, and encouraged each resident to be proactive and refer to the picture of the girl on the flyers that are circulating around the city, and to call the police if you think you've seen her or Billy and Lisa Lewis.

"Billy Lewis is described as five-feet-eleven, two hundred pounds, dark hair and eyes, slow speech and childlike demeanor. His wife Lisa is five-feet-two, one hundred and thirty pounds, long dark hair and glasses, and a quarter-size birthmark on her right forearm.

"WRGL news will stay on top of this story and bring you breaking news as it happens."

The TV screen became a blur, and Ellen was aware of Guy standing next to her. She turned and wrapped her arms around him, the side of her face resting on his chest. "I can't believe it," she whispered. "Lord, help them find her!"

Julie Hamilton sat on the couch with Ross, holding tightly to his hand and realizing both of them were trembling.

"How're you doing?" Special Agent Newt Clifford asked.

"I'm terrified someone's going to get trigger happy," Julie said.

"Don't worry, Mrs. Hamilton. No one's going to take chances with your daughter's safety. As far as we can tell, the couple isn't violent."

"Will they let us know when they find them?" Ross said.

Clifford nodded. "Immediately. The search is intensive, and if they're hiding in the area around Old Seaport, the blood-hounds will find them."

Julie felt a wave of nausea and was glad when it subsided. She wondered if she had ever been so excited and so terrified at the same time.

Ross pulled her hand to his lips, then held it to his cheek. "You okay?"

"My heart's racing a hundred miles an hour. And I feel like I could throw up."

"Yeah, me too. Think we ought to pray?"

Julie looked at him and tried not to show her surprise. "Okay." She bowed her head and kept a firm grip on Ross's hand.

"Lord," Ross whispered, "we've been far away from You the way Sarah Beth's been far away from us. Bring Julie and me back into a right relationship with You—and please bring Sarah Beth home—"

Special Agent Clifford's cell phone rang, and Julie jumped, her hand over her heart. She wiped the tears off her cheeks.

"This is Clifford…You're sure…? Want me to tell them…? Okay, thanks." He put his cell phone back in his pocket, a smile on his face. "The fingerprints on the plastic cup in the kitchen are a match. They're definitely Sarah Beth's."

Gordy leaned against Will Seevers's squad car, his arms folded, his skin tacky from the humidity. He looked up when Will came out of Billy's house and walked over to the car.

"I thought you'd left," Will said.

"I wanna go with you to look for Billy."

"Sorry. It's better if you stay out of the way."

"He listens to me, Will. I might be able to help talk him into lettin' the girl go."

"If we run into problems, his parents can do that."

"Maybe. Have you taken a close look at them? They're devastated. They could probably use a little moral support from someone who understands and cares about their son."

Will seemed to search his eyes. "I didn't realize you'd hired him."

"Billy's a good kid trapped in a man's body. He just needs people to give him a break."

"Well, he may not get a break this time," Will said. "He's in big trouble."

"Just keep in mind he thinks like an eight-year-old and should be judged accordingly."

"You think I don't know how to do my job, Gordy?"

"I never said that. Come on, let me go with you. I promise not to get in the way."

Will rolled his eyes. "All right, get in. But you have to do exactly as I say."

"Fair enough."

Gordy got in on the passenger side of the squad car and fastened his seatbelt as Will backed out of Billy's driveway. Gordy wondered if Mattie Lewis could see what was going on, and if she had any pull with the good Lord to bring this thing to a happy conclusion.

"Where are we headed?" Gordy said.

"Old Seaport. There's a heck of a lot of ground to cover. But now that our investigators have the pink dress, those bloodhounds ought to take us where we need to go."

38

Gordy Jameson counted two dozen law enforcement vehicles from the time Will Seevers turned his squad car onto a gravel road behind the warehouse district of Old Seaport, until he pulled into a grassy field and turned off the motor.

"I'm trusting you to stay out of the way," Will said. "This could get real intense, and I can't worry about where you are or what you're doing. Come on, I'll introduce you to Bryce and tell him why you're here."

Will got out of the car and Gordy followed him over to where a man in khaki pants and a sport coat was talking with half a dozen guys wearing FBI shirts. The baying of bloodhounds echoed in the distance.

Will walked up to the man in the sport coat and shook his hand, then patted him on the back. "Bryce, this is a close friend of mine, Gordy Jameson. Gordy, this is Special Agent Bryce Moore."

Gordy shook hands with Bryce, feeling as though his hand were in a vice. "Pleased to meet you."

"Gordy's one of Billy Lewis' employers," Will said.

"How long have you known Lewis?" Bryce said to Gordy.

"Since he was knee-high to a grasshopper. His parents are friends of mine. They used to play cards with me and my late wife."

"And Lewis works for you?"

"Yeah, just over a week now."

Gordy told Bryce exactly what he had told Will and Chet about why he hired Billy, what a good worker he seemed to be, and how his behavior had suddenly changed.

"I figured the kid was havin' marital problems," Gordy said. "I'm as shocked as everyone else that he and Lisa are involved in this."

Bryce turned his head suddenly and put his walkie-talkie to his ear. "This is Moore, over…where…? How far is that…? Yeah, makes sense. We're on our way. Out."

"What's going on?" Will said.

"The hounds are on full throttle and heading across that open field in the direction of the Jackson Caves. Let's drive around and meet them on the other side. Lead the way."

Gordy ran to the car and had barely shut the door when Will backed out of the grass, the rear of his squad car swinging around in the opposite direction. Will pushed the accelerator and raced back to the highway, kicking up a cloud of white dust behind them.

"You ever hear Billy talk about the Jackson Caves?" Will said.

"No, but every one of us goofed off out there when we were kids. Why should Billy be any different?"

Gordy winced when he said it, and was glad Will didn't answer.

Julie sat in the backseat of Special Agent Newt Clifford's car, clutching Ross's knee and feeling as though she could be sick at any moment.

"Where are the Jackson Caves?" Ross said.

Newt looked at him in the rearview mirror. "A couple miles east of the Old Seaport city limits. Apparently, there's a densely wooded area and a number of caves. We'd have a time trying to find anyone hiding in there. But those bloodhounds won't."

Julie's heart pounded and she felt panicky. "How does the FBI know this is where they took Sarah Beth?"

"They don't, ma'am. They're following the dogs. We're going to wait at the edge of the wooded area and maintain radio contact."

Gordy leaned against a tall, skinny pine and looked up at the leafy, green canopy that separated dark and light. How these woods had enticed him as a youngster! The trees seemed smaller now and the hiding places less discreet. But one thing hadn't changed: about fifty yards beyond the caves stood a live oak tree with his and Jenny's initials carved in its bark.

"You're a million miles away," Will said.

Gordy smiled. "Funny, I feel right at home even though I haven't been out here in over thirty years."

"Hear that? The hounds are getting close."

"Poor Billy," Gordy said. "If the dogs don't scare him to death, the guns will."

"Yeah, well, I'm more worried about that little girl."

"Why? Billy won't let her get hurt."

"Don't be naïve, Gordy. We don't know that Billy and Lisa are out here alone. I doubt they were smart enough to pull this off by themselves. We have to be ready for anything. It could get violent."

"I'm sure all Billy was tryin' to do was protect the girl."

"To hear you talk, we should canonize him. Don't forget he kidnapped a little girl and put her parents through hell. You better get over your attachment to him real quick."

Gordy let his anger burn silently and then let it go. How could Will possibly understand what kind of person Billy was or what must've been going through his mind after Eddie poisoned it?

The bloodhounds were really close now, and Gordy knew if Billy and Lisa were hiding in the caves, it would be a matter of minutes before the dogs gave them up. The best he could hope for now was that Billy and whoever was with him wouldn't resist—and no one would hurt him.

Julie Hamilton stood leaning against Special Agent Newt Clifford's car, listening to the baying of the bloodhounds and keeping an eye on the growing media presence about fifty yards behind them.

"You okay?" Ross said.

"My knees feel like rubber and my heart's doing flip flops."

"Yeah, mine too. Agent Clifford thinks the dogs are almost to the caves."

"I'm so scared of getting my hopes up and having them dashed again."

Ross put his arms around her and held her close. "Before we go to bed tonight, we might actually get to hug and kiss our daughter. Concentrate on that."

Special Agent Clifford's phone rang.

"This is Clifford… Now…? What about the others…? Uh-huh… Yeah, that'll work… All right."

Newt turned off his phone and put it in his pocket, then went over and put one hand on Julie's shoulder and the other on Ross's. "Okay, let's go."

Gordy ran behind Will through the woods to the edge of a clearing where officers were restraining the frenzied hounds. About twenty yards beyond the clearing was the entrance to a cave.

Gordy's heart sank when he saw the SWAT team taking their positions.

Bryce waited until everyone signaled they were ready, and then put the bullhorn to his mouth. "This is Special Agent Bryce Moore of the FBI. You are surrounded. You cannot escape. We know Sarah Beth Hamilton is in there with you. Send her out first and then come out with your hands in the air. You will not be harmed."

Gordy kept his eyes fixed on the entrance to the cave. *Come on, Billy. Make this easy on yourself.*

A minute ticked by. Bryce looked at his watch, then raised the bullhorn and repeated the command. Moments later, he picked up his walkie-talkie. "This is Moore, over… When…? Talk about a double whammy. Okay, out."

Gordy heard whispering and turned around and saw the Hamiltons standing with a man who appeared to be an FBI agent.

"I'll give them another minute," Bryce said. "Then I'm sending in the SWAT team."

"Let Billy's dad talk to him!" Gordy said. "Billy will surrender willingly if someone he trusts tells him to."

Bryce's eyebrows scrunched together. "Unfortunately, I was just informed that Chet Lewis is doubled over with chest pains and his wife is staying with him till the paramedics arrive. Billy's going to have to come out on his own or we're going in."

"Then let me talk to him," Gordy said. "He's scared. I doubt he even understands what's going on. Come on, what've you got to lose?"

Bryce hesitated, his eyes searching Gordy's, then handed him the bullhorn.

"Billy, this is Mister G. Don't be afraid. I'm coming in to talk to you."

"What're you doing?" Bryce said, taking back the bullhorn. "You're not going anywhere. It's too risky. We don't know who else might be with him."

Will took Gordy by the arm. "We're not going to hurt Billy unless he poses a threat. Let us handle it."

"The kid's not a criminal, Will. If I can't get him to come out, do what you have to. But at least let me have a crack at it."

Bryce looked at Will and then at Gordy. "You've got three minutes. Go."

Gordy jogged over to the entrance of the cave, his heart pounding and his determination stronger than his fear. He peered inside and thought he saw movement in the back.

"Billy? It's Mister G. Are you in there…? Billy…?"

"I am here."

"Are Lisa and Sarah Beth with you?"

"Yes, they are here."

"Anyone else with you?"

"No. We are hid-ing from Ross Ham-il-ton."

"May I come in? I need to talk to you."

"You can come."

Gordy ducked inside the cave, instantly hit with the cool, musty dampness. He saw two dark forms. His eyes adjusted quickly and he realized Billy and Lisa were sitting together on the floor of the cave and Sarah Beth Hamilton was nestled in Lisa's lap, hugging a baby doll.

Lisa whispered something to Sarah Beth and the girl looked up at Gordy and smiled. "Hi."

"Hi, cutie." Gordy squatted in front of the trio, unexpectedly moved by their guileless demeanor. He swallowed hard and looked at Billy and then Lisa. "I need you to trust me with some-thing very important. Do you think you can do that?"

Billy looked at Lisa and nodded.

"Ross Hamilton is *not* a bad man. The things Billy heard Eddie say are not true."

"Did Ed-die tell lies?" Billy said.

"Eddie was wrong, Billy. He thought Ross Hamilton was a bad man. But the police found out it's not true. And Ross Hamilton is sad. He misses Sarah Beth very much and wants her to come home. That's why the police are outside."

"Ed-die told me the po-lice cannot protect chil-dren from Ross Ham-il-ton."

Gordy gently squeezed Billy's arm. "I know he did, and I'm sorry, Billy. Eddie made a big mistake. Now I need you to do something very brave—even braver than protecting Sarah Beth."

Will Seevers couldn't take his eyes off the entrance to the cave, aware that the three minutes were about up. Finally, Gordy came out, waving his hands in the air. "It's okay! It's okay, they're not armed!"

In the next instant, Sarah Beth emerged from the cave followed by Lisa and then Billy.

Special Agent Moore picked up his walkie-talkie and Chief Seevers grabbed his arm. "No, wait."

Billy and Lisa put Sarah Beth between them, the three holding hands, and started walking across the clearing. Every now and then they lifted Sarah Beth by the arms and swung her, the sound of her giggling filling the eerie stillness. When they were a few yards from the tree line, they stopped.

"What're they doing?" Bryce said.

Will shrugged. "I don't know, but I trust Gordy. Let's wait a minute."

Billy bent down and appeared to be saying something to Sarah Beth. He hugged her, and then stood up straight and started waving. "Bye-bye. Sar-ah Beth will go now."

Lisa let go of the little girl's hand and pointed toward the tree line. "Go see Mommy and Daddy."

"Sarah Beth!"

"Sarah Beth! Over here! Over here!"

Will recognized the voices of Julie and Ross Hamilton and felt them breeze past him as they raced toward their daughter.

Ellen Jones sat watching the TV, batting her eyes to clear away the tears as Julie and Ross smothered Sarah Beth with hugs and kisses. *Thank You, Lord. Thank You!*

"There are no words to describe the elation here," the news reporter was saying. "We are witnessing live what most people thought would never happen: A very much alive Sarah Beth Hamilton being reunited with her parents. And as you can see on the faces of FBI agents, police officers, and sheriff's deputies, this is an emotional moment for them, too.

"But not everyone is convinced this is the ideal outcome. I have here with me Valerie Mink Hodges, the reporter from the *Biloxi Telegraph* whose controversial article about Ross Hamilton may have set in motion events that eventually led to Sarah Beth Hamilton's abduction. Ms. Hodges, do you feel comfortable about this child being returned to her parents?"

"I don't see how anyone can feel comfortable about that with all the mystery surrounding her father."

"Do you feel any responsibility for what happened?"

"Absolutely not," Hodges said, "I'm a newspaperwoman. If what I wrote rattled a few chains, then so be it. If Ross Hamilton wanted me to understand a different version of the story, then he should have returned my calls."

"Then you don't feel you owe him an apology?"

"Look, I didn't do anything *to* Ross Hamilton. All I did was put some facts out on the table that I found disturbing. What other people did with them isn't my problem."

"Will you continue to follow this story?"

"Yes. Until I'm satisfied that every stone has been unturned."

"Thank you. We appreciate your talking with WRGL News. Well, folks, the celebration here continues to be heart-warming, especially in the aftermath of community protest and allegations of abuse against Ross Hamilton. I wonder if anyone could have guessed such a positive outcome to the eight-day ordeal?"

The announcer seemed distracted for a moment as if someone not on the TV screen were saying something to him.

"In just a moment, we're going to hear from Gordy Jameson, the owner of Gordy's Crab Shack and the man who went inside the cave to talk to Billy and Lisa Lewis. I think all of us are wondering how it feels to be a hero. Here's Mr. Jameson now. Sir, do you feel like a hero?"

"Nah, I just know Billy's mental limitations and knew he wouldn't understand why the police and the dogs were there. I went in to explain what was goin' on."

"Can you tell us what the mood was like in that cave when you confronted the couple?"

"It wasn't a confrontation," Gordy said. "Billy and Lisa were very cooperative. And the mood was calm. Sarah Beth even smiled at me."

"Did they admit to kidnapping her?"

"I'm not gonna speak for them," Gordy said. "But I can tell you this: Those kids wouldn't hurt a flea. Whatever happened, that little girl was never in danger."

"As emotionally charged as the situation has been with the Hamiltons, do you think Billy and Lisa can get a fair trial here in Seaport?"

Gordy looked dumbfounded. "Who said there's gonna be a need for a trial? There you go again, gettin' ahead of the facts."

"You sound angry."

"We should all be angry! The accusations made against Ross Hamilton were untrue and hurtful. What a shame most of us fell for it. I'm not just blamin' the media. Maybe if we'd *all* kept our opinions to ourselves until we found out the facts, a nice young man like Billy Lewis wouldn't have felt compelled to protect a little girl that didn't need protectin'."

"Are you saying Billy Lewis was trying to protect Sarah Beth?"

"Why don't we just wait for the *facts* for a change? If you'll excuse me, I need to be with Billy."

"Thank you for talking with us, Mr. Jameson. Well, folks, one thing is certain: whatever the fate of Billy and Lisa Lewis, WRGL News will be on top of the story, bringing you breaking news as it happens."

Ellen watched as Billy and Lisa were led away in handcuffs, looking scared and confused. She was deeply troubled and prayed for them, almost certain that Ned Norton already had.

39

ate the next morning, Police Chief Will Seevers, Special
Agent Bryce Moore, and Investigator Al Backus sat at the
round table in Will's office, listening to Special Agent
Newt Clifford's analysis of Billy and Lisa Lewis.

"By all indications," Newt said, "these are two very honest
kids who are surprisingly well-adjusted, considering their mental limitations. I'm convinced they're telling the truth and that
they acted alone."

"Did they know that taking Sarah Beth out of her home was
wrong?" Bryce said.

"Not in the traditional sense. It never even occurred to Billy
not to leave fingerprints when he opened the window. With
their limited capacity to understand the law, they did what they
thought was right and moral—to protect Sarah Beth from an
abusive father. This was a costly decision, all legalities aside."

"What do you mean?" Will said.

"For one thing, they were ill-equipped to take care of a two-
year-old. Lisa went to the thrift store at the Methodist Church
and bought clothes for Sarah Beth—but not enough, and she
was constantly washing them out by hand and could barely get
them dry before she needed them again. Plus, they don't own a
TV or a DVD or video player. They had no kids' music, no toys,
no books. They literally entertained this child all day long."

"Most *parents* couldn't handle that," Al said.

Newt raised his eyebrows. "No kidding. Billy started being
late for work because he was trying to help Lisa with Sarah Beth.

They couldn't afford diapers, and after a couple days of them cleaning up messes, she pretty much potty trained herself."

Will shook his head. "It's a wonder they didn't turn *themselves* in. Can you imagine this kind of pressure on someone whose reasoning ability is that of an eight-year-old?"

"I think that's the point I'm trying to make," Newt said. "Billy and Lisa's desire to save a child from being abused was more important in their minds than the hardships. That goes to intent. No judge in his right mind would allow these two to be convicted of a crime. They're simply not criminals."

"Are we supposed to just let them go?" Bryce said. "What's to stop them from breaking the law again when they don't understand it?"

"In my professional opinion, we treat them as we would any elementary-age child that makes a mistake. We explain why what they did was wrong and teach them to act more responsibly next time. And we make sure they have adequate supervision. I think both sets of parents learned a valuable lesson."

"Speaking of parents," Will said, "did we hear any more about how Chet Lewis is doing?"

Al nodded. "The heart attack was mild. Not much damage. He'll be fine."

Julie Hamilton sat in the living room and stared at the sight of Sarah Beth asleep in Ross's arms. It seemed almost incomprehensible that their daughter was home again. Julie heard the phone ring and hurried out to the kitchen.

"Hello."

"Hi, it's Ellen. I was out when you called. I've been out of my mind wanting to talk to you! I watched everything live on TV. I'm ecstatic for you—simply overjoyed! I've been thanking and praising the Lord all day."

"Me, too. I still can't believe it. I can hardly take my eyes off her."

"Understandably. So she's all right?"

"Better than all right," Julie said. "The Lewises took good care of her. She's even learned some new songs. And would you believe she's potty trained?"

"You're kidding?"

"I'd sure like to know how they did it. Truthfully, other than crying and being overwhelmed when she first saw us, and being a little clingy, you'd never know she'd been through anything. She doesn't even want her blanky. We put her in bed with us last night, and she slept like a baby. I was almost afraid to close my eyes, as if I needed to stand guard or something. I don't want to let her out of my sight."

"Hopefully, that will pass quickly," Ellen said.

"First thing this morning, we took her to a doctor that DCF recommended. He said she didn't lose any weight and shows no sign of having been abused, physically or emotionally."

"Oh, that's wonderful. So what's going to happen to Billy and Lisa?"

"I don't know," Julie said. "Sarah Beth keeps asking us where they went. I think she misses them. Certainly what they did was wrong. But they told the authorities the reason they snuck Sarah Beth out of the house was because Eddie told Billy that Ross was hurting Sarah Beth and the police couldn't protect her. Maybe the person they ought to throw in jail is Eddie Drummond. I sure hope people learn something from this."

"So do I, my friend. It's been humbling for me. I so misjudged Ross. It's going to take me a long time to get past it."

"Well, at least you weren't out spreading the gossip."

"You're too easy on me, Julie. All of us had a part in this because we let ourselves get caught up in the he-said she-saids. Had we not jumped to conclusions, none of this would've happened. I'm just so grateful that Sarah Beth is home safe and sound."

40

L ate Friday night, Ellen Jones sat in the widow's watch, reliving the events of the past eight days and trying to assimilate what she had learned.

She was struck by the contrast between the comments made on camera by Valerie Mink Hodges and those of Gordy Jameson. She contemplated calling Valerie again and expressing her disapproval of the woman's professional ethics, then decided against it. Valerie was on a mission to make a name for herself, and nothing was going to dissuade her.

Ellen couldn't erase the image of a bewildered Billy and Lisa being led away in handcuffs, or the total trust in Sarah Beth's demeanor when they led her across the clearing to be reunited with her parents.

She turned on her laptop and let her fingers record the thoughts that were racing through her mind.

As a former newspaper editor, I am awed by the inestimable power of words, and how a mere twenty-six letters of the English alphabet give us infinite potential for communicating anything the human mind can conceive.

However, one immutable fact about words is that once they have been shared, we cannot effectively take them back.

Countless careless words have been circulated in this community during the Hamilton ordeal. And they're heavy on my heart, not only because I've come to know and respect Julie and Ross Hamilton, but because I, too, have spoken irresponsibly in judging Ross guilty without having a shred of evidence. How reckless it was for me to read that article by reporter Valerie Mink Hodges and then make assumptions about Ross Hamilton's guilt based on her "implications," and not the collective evidence compiled by the Biloxi police department.

And choosing to believe those implications made it easy for me to believe the abuse allegations about Ross that I had overheard someone telling someone else— gossip that nearly destroyed an innocent man.

Ironically, I have recently fallen victim to gossip myself, and experienced firsthand the helpless condition of a person falsely accused. Though I despise the embarrassment, humiliation, and unfairness, I'm choosing to embrace the experience and pray that I will never again choose to sample the choice morsels of juicy gossip or prejudge a person's guilt or innocence.

I was impressed with Gordy Jameson, who had the courage to stand in front of the TV cameras following Sarah Beth Hamilton's rescue and speak words that few of us would have had the courage to say.

Gordy said that we should all be angry, that the accusations made against Ross Hamilton were untrue and hurtful. And shame on us for falling for it. He went on to say he didn't blame just the media. That if we had all kept our opinions to ourselves until we had the facts, maybe a sweet young man like Billy Lewis wouldn't have felt compelled to protect a child that didn't need protecting.

I'm grateful that Sarah Beth Hamilton has been reunited with her parents—and so very sad that two people as innocent and caring as Billy and Lisa Lewis ultimately will pay for the sins of everyone else.

In spite of my disillusionment, for the first time in the fourteen months I've lived in Seaport, I feel emotional ties to this community. Perhaps it's because I've been part of the problem and would now very much like to be part of the solution.

I can only hope there are others who feel the way I do, and that together we will work to ensure that every citizen is treated with respect and dignity, and afforded the fairness of due process.

Ellen reread what she had typed and then printed it. She turned off the laptop, only her eyelids heavier than her heart, and wondered how long it would be before the sadness left her.

She heard footsteps ascending the winding staircase and then the door open.

"Honey, what are you doing up?" Guy said.

"My mind was on overload. I figured the only way I was going to get any sleep was to write down my thoughts."

Guy picked up the paper she had printed. "Is this what you wrote?"

She nodded, stifling a yawn.

"This is great, Ellen. You ought to submit it to Speaking Out."

"It's just my private thoughts." She yawned again and could hardly keep her eyes focused.

"Let's get you back to bed." Guy pulled her to her feet. "Seriously, unless you object, I'd like to send this in to the newspaper. I think people would benefit from what you had to say."

"Whatever you think…" Ellen nodded off for a second and then jumped, her hands gripping tightly to Guy's pajama top.

He chuckled. "If we wait much longer, I'll have to carry you downstairs."

41

Gordy Jameson opened his eyes to the sound of the gentle surf. He sat on the side of the bed and combed his hands through his hair, a damp breeze moving the curtains on the window.

He pulled on his cutoffs, then stumbled barefoot out to the kitchen, turned on the coffee pot, and went outside and picked up the Sunday paper. He brushed off the sand and removed the rubber band, his eyes instantly drawn to a picture of Billy and Lisa with the caption: Did They Act Alone?

He skimmed the article as he walked back inside and decided he wasn't interested in reading another spin on Billy and Lisa's involvement in Sarah Beth's abduction.

He sat at the kitchen table and read through the advertisements, pleased with the one Weezie had made up for the crab shack.

He read the sports page and the comics, then turned to the Speaking Out section, surprised to see that Ellen Jones had submitted a letter. He wondered if it was the same Ellen he knew.

Gordy read the letter, touched by her transparency and surprised by what she had said about him. He was still amazed he'd had the gumption to say what he did to reporters.

He folded the newspaper and laid it on the table, then finished a second cup of coffee, studying the photographs on the refrigerator of Jenny and him. Why hadn't he noticed until now how faded they were and how the corners had curled up from the humidity?

Gordy got up and removed the magnets, then put the old photos in a drawer, surprised that he didn't feel guilty.

The doorbell rang. Who would stop by on a Sunday morning? Gordy went to the front door and opened it, surprised to see Eddie Drummond.

"Can we talk?" Eddie said.

"Yeah, I suppose." Gordy held open the door, and Eddie went into the living room and sat on the couch, his foot jiggling and his fingers tapping his knee.

"What's on your mind?"

"Come on, Gordo. Did you think I wouldn't see you on TV—or read that Jones woman's letter in the paper?"

"I didn't intend what I said to be personal, Eddie. But I'm not apologizin' for it either."

"I never meant to hurt Billy Lewis. How was I supposed to know he'd do something that stupid?"

"It may seem *stupid* to you, but in Billy's mind, it was a very brave thing. I told you to stop fillin' his head with stuff about Ross Hamilton, that you were scarin' him."

"Gimme a break. He talks to other people. He watches TV. I wasn't the only one talking about it."

"You're the only one he ever quoted. Billy heard everything you spouted off down at Hank's. And just so you'll know, Billy doesn't watch TV. Anything negative he heard about Ross Hamilton, he most likely heard from you."

"Look, this wasn't my fault."

"You can't tell me you don't bear some responsibility. We all do—every one of us who decided Ross was guilty before we had the facts. But you're the one who started the rumor, Eddie—and kept it goin'. At some point you're gonna have to own that."

Eddie looked out the window and cracked his knuckles. "So what's going to happen to Billy and his wife? Has Chief Seevers filled you in?"

"Will's not gonna talk to me about the specifics. But my gut feelin' is everyone close to this case wishes the Hamiltons would drop the charges."

"Would Billy and Lisa go free?"

"I don't think it's that simple. There has to be an arraignment and some sort of court hearing. I don't understand how it all works. But I think if the Hamiltons would agree to drop all charges, the DA would work something out for Billy and Lisa. I don't know that the Hamiltons are willin' to do that, though. Especially after all they've been through."

"What a mess," Eddie said. "I'm really sorry."

"Yeah, I believe you. But *sorry* won't do Billy any good."

Julie Hamilton sat with Ross on the patio, watching Sarah Beth play in the sandbox. The child sat on her heels, filling plastic cups with sand and singing a song Julie didn't recognize. What had happened in her daughter's life the eight days she had been away from them? Julie wondered if she would ever know. Surely Sarah Beth was too young to remember it for long.

Julie closed her eyes and let the sound of her child's singing seep into her soul. She was aware of the back gate creaking and Ross tapping her arm. She opened her eyes and saw Eddie Drummond standing just inside the gate.

"I tried ringing the bell," Eddie said. "Nobody answered."

Ross stood, his arms folded. "That's because nobody wanted to. What're you doing here?"

"We need to talk."

"No *we* don't. Go away. I've got nothing to say to you."

"Just hear me out," Eddie said. "It wasn't easy for me to come here."

"I don't really care, Drummond."

"Ross, look...I made a big mistake, okay?"

"Is that what you call it? You almost ruined my life! Nothing you can say will make any difference to me!"

"Not to you. But what about to Billy and Lisa Lewis?"

"What about 'em?"

"Could I come closer and talk to you and your wife?"

Ross turned to Julie, his eyebrows raised. "Your call, hon."

Julie nodded. "Let's hear what he has to say."

Eddie trudged over to the patio, his hands buried deep in his pockets. "I'm not going to make excuses about what I did. No matter what I thought I overheard Hank say, I should've come to you and given you a chance to explain—or to set me straight. I'm sorry. I know that sounds lame considering what all you've been through. But I really am."

"I couldn't care less how you feel. What about the Lewises?"

Eddie rocked on his feet, heel to toe. "It's my fault Billy was afraid of you. He overheard me running my mouth and took everything I said as gospel."

"Chief Seevers already told us that."

"But do you realize Billy's harmless? He didn't know he was committing a crime."

Ross's eyes narrowed. "Why do you suddenly care so much about Billy? You treated him like a dog—fetch this, fetch that. I heard the wisecracks you used to make about him: He's in the gene pool, but there's no lifeguard on duty. Sound familiar?"

"Yeah, I know. I can be a real moron. But it bugs me to think that Billy's going to be punished for trying to protect your daughter. He thought he was doing the right thing."

"That's for a jury to figure out," Ross said.

"Unless you do first." Eddie glanced up, then looked at the ground. "The two of you could get the DA to drop all the charges against the Lewises."

"Why, so your conscience can feel better?"

"No. Because you of all people know what it's like to suffer unfairly."

Julie slipped her hand into Ross's.

"Look," Eddie said, "I'm going to give notice in the morning.

We can't both work at Hank's, and I'm the one who messed up. But please at least *consider* dropping the charges. One injustice has already been done. Punishing the Lewises would make it two. And that's a heck of a way to even the score."

42

E llen and Guy Jones waited at the end of a fast-moving line that had formed in the foyer after the Sunday morning service at Crossroads Bible Church. Ceiling fans kept the air circulating and sent a stack of bulletins sailing across the floor where several young children scurried to pick them up. The line moved quickly, and soon they were face to face with the pastor and his wife.

"Well, look who's here," Pastor Crawford said to Guy. "It's good to have you back. Ellen told us you've been working on a big case."

"I have. But it's time I put my priorities back in order. I plan to be there for the Thursday Bible study."

"Glad to hear it." The pastor shook his hand, then turned to Ellen. "Your letter in the newspaper this morning was very well put. I'm sure it has caused many of us to do some soul searching."

"Thank you."

Guy put his arm around Ellen. "I insisted on hand delivering it to *The Messenger* yesterday morning. I'm surprised they got it in so quickly."

Dorothy Crawford took Ellen's hand. "Have you seen Ross and Julie since Sarah Beth came home?"

"No, I haven't wanted to intrude on their family time. But I have talked to Julie on the phone several times. They're all doing great. Sarah Beth seems unscathed by what happened. That's the best news of all."

"I want to invite the Hamiltons to come to church," Dorothy said. "You think they'd be open?"

Ellen smiled. "I have a feeling they just might. Julie told me they were deeply touched that people from our church were so willing to help them."

"What an amazing ending to the saga," Pastor Crawford said. "God's hand was certainly evident. And that Gordy...I was so proud of him. I'm glad in your letter you reiterated what he said on the news. I'm sure going to be praying for Billy and Lisa Lewis."

"Thank you. So am I."

"Well, Mrs. Jones," Guy said, "what do you say we go out for lunch and then spend the afternoon being a couple of beach bums?"

"In broad daylight?" Ellen said. "Now that should throw our gossip queen into overtime."

Ellen walked into the kitchen from the garage, Guy on her heels, and set her Bible on the countertop. "I'm so full I may not want to eat again today."

"Me either," Guy said. "Next time I'll order from the menu instead of indulging in the buffet."

"I'm so disappointed Gordy wasn't there. I was anxious to tell him in person how proud I am of him."

"I'm sure you'll catch up with him when things settle down. Would you mind if we wait a while before we go to the beach? I'd like to let my lunch settle and finish reading the newspaper first."

"That's fine. I'm in no hurry."

Guy left the kitchen, and Ellen took her sermon notes out of her Bible. She reread them, then jotted down a couple of key points she wanted to remember.

The doorbell rang. She finished writing her thought, and

then hurried to the front door and opened it. A petite woman with curly blue-gray hair and thick glasses stood on the porch. She wore a pink silk dress—and a troubled expression.

"Mrs. Jones, my name is Blanche Davis. I read your article in the newspaper this morning, and I—well—oh, why beat around the bush? I'm the person you think has been gossiping about you."

Ellen stood dumbfounded and studied her for a moment. Why hadn't Ned told her the Blanche Davis he mentioned was also the woman who had been walking her poodle on the beach?

"I wouldn't blame you if you threw me out, but—"

"On the contrary, won't you please come in?" Ellen heard herself say.

The woman stared at her blankly. "You're kidding, right?"

Ellen held open the door and Ms. Davis stepped inside. "Would you like something cold to drink: lemonade, Diet Coke, bottled water?"

"No, nothing for me. I'd just like to get this over with."

Ellen led Ms. Davis out to the veranda and offered her a seat on the wicker couch. "Don't you have a white poodle?"

"Ah, you do recognize me from the beach. Did you figure out I'm the one who went to your pastor?"

"I wondered. But of course, I had no idea who you were."

Ms. Davis wrung her hands, and Ellen noticed she wasn't wearing a wedding ring. "I felt so bad after I read your letter in the newspaper. I wanted you to know I never really *gossiped* about you to anyone."

"Other than my pastor and his wife?"

"I suppose he told you what I said?"

"Yes, he did. Both times. After you confronted him in person, and then when you left a note. I assume you got my reply in the mailbox?"

Ms. Davis's face flushed with color. "Yes, but as defensive as you were, it just made you seem all the more guilty."

Ellen bit her lip. *Lord, don't let me lose it.* "Ms. Davis, just so you'll know, the man you saw me with on the beach the first time was my husband. We'd been out jogging, sat down to rest, and fell asleep. Chief Seevers discovered us there and asked us to leave. It was excruciatingly embarrassing for me. Guy, on the other hand, thought it would make a cute story to tell our grandchildren someday.

"And the other gentlemen you've seen me with is Ned Norton, a very wise eighty-seven-year-old man I met while I was out walking and who's taught me a great deal about how to love and pray for difficult people."

Ms. Davis's eyes matched her hair and looked huge through the lenses of her glasses. "What a coincidence. Ned goes to my church. In fact, he made me the most unusual shell necklace. I didn't recognize him as the man you were with. Then again, I don't see as well as I used to."

"Perhaps now you can understand my indignation and embarrassment when you accused me of being unfaithful to my husband, whom I dearly love, and then went to my pastor without even confronting me—*and* followed up with a note implying I was lying. I had no way to defend myself. It was terribly disconcerting, especially not knowing how many people might have been privy to the gossip. I'm assuming you've told others about this?"

Ms. Davis shifted her weight. "I may have mentioned your name in my prayer circle at church, but it certainly wasn't gossip. They don't even know you—well, except for Lucille Morley at the bank and Helen Ratliff who lives next door to me, but I can go back and clear it all up."

"Let's hope so, but it usually doesn't work that way once the seed of doubt is planted. I'm curious, how did you know where I go to church?"

"I found the church newsletter in your mailbox."

Ellen took a slow, deep breath and counted to ten... eleven...twelve. "You went through my mail?"

"You have to understand that until I read your letter in the newspaper this morning, I honestly thought you were fooling around on your husband. It never occurred to me that I might be wrong. I don't blame you for being angry, but I'd like to explain my actions."

"Yes, by all means. Go right ahead." *This ought to be good.*

"When I was a young woman, I married a real Mr. Nice Guy whose sales position kept him on the road. I stayed busy at first, but after years of living that kind of life and having no kids to take care of, I got lonely." Ms. Davis folded her hands. "I started seeing someone. My friends all knew it, but pretended they didn't. I really wanted someone to confront me with it because I wasn't strong enough to stop on my own. But no one ever did. Maybe if they had, I would've felt pressured to do the right thing. Eventually, my husband found out and divorced me. And back in those days, a divorce was really humiliating. Everyone treated me like a Jezebel. About the only thing they didn't do was stone me."

Ellen held Ms. Davis's gaze. "If you felt that strongly, why didn't you just confront me to my face instead of passing notes and talking to my pastor?"

"Since you didn't know me, I didn't think it would matter who it was that knew your secret—just that someone did— someone who would make you accountable to your pastor."

Ellen was taken aback by the audacity of this woman. Had she no respect for personal boundaries?

"I can tell by your silence how upset you are," Ms. Davis said. "I don't expect you to forgive me for this, but I really am sorry. I should probably leave."

Ellen noticed how her glasses magnified the lifeless look in her eyes. "I'm not going to lie to you and say everything's fine. I feel violated. And you're kidding yourself if you think mentioning my name in your prayer circle wasn't gossip. You could have prayed for me without ever revealing my name and casting aspersions on my character. But I do appreciate what it cost you to come here. It couldn't have been easy." Ellen paused for a few moments, and then decided to say the words and trust God that the feeling would come later. "And I *do* forgive you."

Ms. Davis stared at her in disbelief. "You do?"

"Well, yes. I imagine we'll be running into each other again. I assume you live around here?"

"At the end of the block. I inherited the big gray house with white Bahamas shutters. My parents left it to me to salve their guilt since they as much as disowned me after my divorce."

"How long have you lived there?"

"Thirty-two years. But I've never fit in. I've been accused more than once of meddling. I know what I am, Mrs. Jones. But I promise to go back to your pastor and the ladies in my prayer circle and set them straight. Thanks for not giving me the third degree. Frankly, I didn't expect you to be this nice." Ms. Davis rose to her feet. "I'll get out of your way so you and your husband can enjoy the rest of your weekend."

Ellen got up and walked Ms. Davis to the front door, and Ned's words came rushing back to her. *I suspect Blanche Davis needs a touch from God. And we're His body. Isn't that what these hands are for? It's a whole lot easier not getting them dirty.*

"You know, as long as we're neighbors, why don't you call me Ellen? Sounds a bit friendlier, don't you think?" Ellen offered Ms. Davis her hand.

The elderly woman's eyes turned watery and she looked down at the marble floor, her hands clasped in front of her. "I wish I'd been friendlier, Ellen—and kinder."

"Then let's start over. If there's ever going to be harmony in this community, it's got to begin with each of us."

Ms. Davis put her hand in Ellen's, tears dripping from behind her glasses. "Thank you…and by all means, call me Blanche."

43

Ellen Jones opened the front door and threw her arms around Julie Hamilton, not even trying to hold back the tears. "It's so good to finally *see* you! Can you believe that at this very moment three weeks ago we were out distributing flyers? It's amazing what the Lord has done!"

She let go of Julie and looked at Sarah Beth who stared up at her with those bright blue eyes. "Hi cutie. I'm so happy you came to see me."

Sarah Beth held something in her hands, and Ellen realized it was the *National Geographic* she had taken home.

"All done," Sarah Beth said, handing it to Ellen.

"Why, thank you. Come see what I have for you out on the porch."

Ellen led them out onto the veranda where she had put up a card table, covered the top with waxed paper, and set a place for Sarah Beth.

"What's all this?" Julie said.

"I've got something healthier than cookies that she can play with *and* snack on."

"Looks interesting," Julie said. "What's that in the bowl?"

"I made it with peanut butter, honey, and powdered milk. Those are just raisins in the other bowl. Sit here, Sarah Beth. Let Miss Ellen show you how I used to make honey bears with my boys." Ellen took a small lump of the mixture, formed it into a ball, and flattened it on the waxed paper to make the face, then took two smaller lumps and did the same to form the ears. She used raisins for the nose and eyes. "Here, taste."

Ellen pinched off an ear and popped it into the little girl's mouth.

Sarah Beth's eyes were wide and round and she seemed to savor it for a moment, then reached for the bowl. "My turn!"

Ellen smiled. "You can have all the turns you want. Your mama and I will be right here."

Ellen sat in one of the wicker rockers, and Julie sat in the other. "So how are you doing? How's Ross?"

"Happier than I've seen him since Nathaniel was alive. Somehow this crisis has gotten us out of grief and into gratitude. We're actually enjoying Sarah Beth instead of fighting depression. Ross started counseling last week. The two of us are talking again and thinking about the future. Would you believe we've even made amends with my parents? Ross invited them to come stay this weekend; and truthfully, we can hardly wait to see them."

"That's wonderful," Ellen said. "I can't get over how terrific you look."

"Thanks. It's been a long time since I let myself be a wife and mom. It feels great."

Ellen smiled at Sarah Beth singing a random medley of "The Farmer in the Dell," "The Wheels on the Bus," and "The A-B-C Song."

"Have you decided whether you'll be staying in Seaport?"

Julie lifted her eyebrows. "Where else would we go? Biloxi's out. My folks want us to move to Meridian where they are, but Ross has job security at his Uncle Hank's body shop. And now that Eddie's gone, Ross has made friends with the guys and is really enjoying working there. Uncle Hank's even talked about the possibility of Ross taking over the business in a few years."

"I'm so glad you've decided to say!" Ellen said. "Now that things have settled down, have you thought any more about going to church with us?"

"We definitely want to start going again. I'm ashamed to say Sarah Beth has never been to Sunday school." Julie glanced over at her daughter. "And the Lord's certainly chosen an interesting way to humble us about that."

"What do you mean?"

"Sarah Beth, sing your special song for Miss Ellen."

Without hesitation, the little girl began to sing with gusto. "Jesus wuvs me, this I know, for the Bible tells me so. Wittle ones to Him belong. They are weak but He is stwong. Yes, Jesus wuvs me. Yes, Jesus wuvs me. Yes, Jesus wuvs me. The Bible tells me so." She stopped singing and glanced over at Ellen, looking as pleased as if she had just performed an aria.

"Very nice!" Ellen clapped for several seconds. "Good job, Sarah Beth."

"Sweetie, tell Miss Ellen who taught you the Jesus song."

"Wisa and Billy."

Julie dabbed her eyes with her thumb and forefinger. "It's humbling that our daughter's first introduction to Jesus didn't come from Ross and me, but from the kidnappers we were so worried would harm her. We've prayed about it and decided to drop the charges. You were right. Why should two people as innocent and caring as Billy and Lisa suffer for the sins of everyone else? Not even Eddie Drummond disagrees with that."

Ellen got up and put her arms around Julie. "What a generous and compassionate decision. I'm so proud of you."

Gordy Jameson went in his office, closed the door, and looked at Pam Townsend sitting at his desk. "Okay, everybody's here."

"Tell me again their names," Pam said.

"Adam Spalding's the rich young hunk, Captain Jack's the one with the anchor tattoo on his arm, and Eddie Drummond's the wise guy wearin' a Goodyear Tire shirt."

Gordy pulled her to her feet, then kissed her hand, his eyes recognizing the uneasiness in hers. "Don't be nervous. I'm anxious to show you off."

"I want them to like me."

"They will. Come on."

Gordy took Pam by the hand and walked through the dining

room. He winked at Weezie and then went outside on the back deck and walked up to the table where his friends were seated. The conversation trailed off and then stopped, all eyes on Gordy and the woman in a blue sundress standing next to him.

"Okay, everybody. This is Pam Townsend. Pam, this is—"

"You must be Adam," Pam said. "And you're Captain. And you must be Eddie."

Each of the guys shook hands with Pam, and then Gordy seated her at the table. "You guys be nice to my lady. I'll be right back."

He went inside and caught Weezie's eye and nodded toward his office. They got there at almost the same time.

"So what'd you think?" Gordy said.

"I couldn't be happier for you. I haven't seen that sparkle in your eyes in a long, long time."

"Sometimes I feel guilty, like I'm bein' unfaithful or somethin'."

Weezie took her index finger and poked his chest. "Then you better be remindin' yourself of what Jenny said: that you shouldn't keep your love bottled up for long or you'll self-destruct. She knew how important it was, that's why she said it."

"It's still feels a little weird goin' out with another woman."

"Apparently not *too*. Pam's crazy about you. And I can tell you like her—a lot."

"Now don't go puttin' the cart before the horse. We've only been seein' each other for a couple of weeks."

Weezie lifted her eyebrows, her hand on her hip. "Uh-huh. And what do you expect me to think when you come in here wearin' that fancy yellow shirt you brought back from Brazil?"

Gordy threw his head back and laughed, then put his arm around her. "I expect you to think positive, Weezie. Somethin' tells me life is just gonna get sweeter."

Ellen stood in the alcove of the widow's watch, her eyes drinking in the glistening blue waters of the gulf. Off in the distance on her favorite stretch of beach, she could barely make out a couple walking hand-in-hand along the surf, a child riding on the man's shoulders. She put the binoculars to her eyes and smiled, her heart overflowing with gratitude for the restoration God had allowed her to be a part of.

She dabbed her eyes and went back to her desk and turned on the laptop. In the past couple of weeks, it was as though her novel had taken on a life of its own and she was merely along for the ride. Everything she had experienced about gossip, about prejudging, about the smallness of people and the greatness of God seemed to flow through her onto the pages, coming to life through her characters.

It occurred to Ellen that perhaps her novel was meant to do more than entertain, that God had given her an opportunity to let her characters articulate the truths she had struggled so to grasp. Perhaps her job was to listen well and tell their story.

She sat quietly for a long while, trying to think of a title; and then it came to her as unexpectedly as the new direction of her novel. She brought up the title page on the screen, a smile of satisfaction on her face, and typed in the words: *A Shred of Evidence.*

Julie Hamilton nestled on a beach towel facing Ross, Sarah Beth sound asleep between them. She gazed into her husband's eyes and felt no need to spoil this sacred moment with words.

Julie rested her hand on Sarah Beth's chest and felt the rhythmic beating of her heart. She imagined the Creator having placed within her daughter at conception a precision timepiece, which could not be stopped until the days ordained for her were completed. There was no doubt in Julie's mind that Sarah Beth had been in the hollow of God's hand the eight days she was missing. But she still hadn't reconciled Nathaniel's untimely death.

"What are you thinking about?" Ross said softly.

"Our children. Why one was spared—and the other

wasn't. I have a lot of questions to ask the Lord someday."

Ross covered her hand with his. "One thing I *do* know: He would've been there to comfort us if we'd let Him. I'm glad you talked to Ellen. I'm so ready to get back in church."

"Me, too. We had the nicest morning. I think we're going to be good friends. Of course, Sarah Beth sang 'Jesus Loves Me' and got tickled with herself. Ellen thinks she's the cat's meow."

Ross smiled. "Ellen's right."

"I also told her we've dropped the charges, and she seemed pleased. Once the legalities are behind us, I'd like us to think about meeting Billy and Lisa."

"Funny you should say that. I've been thinking the same thing."

Sarah Beth yawned, her tiny hands turning to fists while she stretched one side of her body, and then the other. She batted her eyes sleepily and then looked over at Ross, an impish grin spreading across her face. "Water get me!"

He chuckled. "Okay, baby doll, let's go do it again."

Julie sat upright and hugged her knees, overjoyed at the sight of Sarah Beth riding atop her daddy's shoulders, her hands clinging tightly to his, her beautiful curls aglow in the afternoon sun.

"It's gonna *get* you!" Ross shrieked as he ran away from the approaching surf, the sound of Sarah Beth's belly laughing ever so reminiscent of her brother's.

Julie's thoughts drifted back to an afternoon much like this one, when she had sat on the beach in Biloxi, watching Ross play this same game with Nathaniel, and wondering if the child in her womb would bring them as much happiness as Nathaniel had.

She leaned back on her palms, her face tilted up toward the endless blue, joy trickling down her cheeks, and thanked God she didn't have to wonder anymore.

AFTERWORD

Dear friends,

How powerful words are—not only those we speak, but also those we listen to! Gossip comes cloaked in many disguises, but its function is always the same: to pass on information that the recipient doesn't need to hear, and which most often results in diminishing the person being talked about.

In today's world, the media can often be intrusive, eager to meet the people's demand that they have "the right to know."

But the Scriptures don't support that type of conduct in our relationships with one another. Ephesians 4:29 couldn't state it any more clearly, "Do not let any unwholesome talk come out of your mouths, but only what is helpful for building others up according to their needs, that it may benefit those who listen."

Webster's defines gossip as, "Idle talk or rumor, especially about the private affairs of others." Based on that definition and the words of Ephesians 4:29, I wonder if we aren't guilty of gossip far more than we realize.

I'd like to think most Christians avoid *malicious* gossip. But do we engage in idle talk about the private affairs of others? Do we talk about the negatives instead of the positives we see in others? And when we share prayer requests with other people, do we simply dress up our gossip in a different costume the way Blanche Davis did?

But what should we do when we hear gossip that suggests someone might be in danger? Ellen's conscience and good sense wouldn't let her simply ignore the allegations she'd heard about

Ross. And though she might have done better to confront Eddie first instead of going directly to his boss and then the police chief, her motives were pure. Her downfall came when she allowed the gossip to win her over without facts to prove Ross's guilt.

Gossip produces bad fruit. So why do we let it entice us? Perhaps the best way to avoid being seduced by gossip is to run from it—to refuse to listen. The time to decide how we will respond is *before* it happens.

In our twenty-first century world of computer hackers, spyware, security cameras, and in-your-face media coverage, personal privacy is more precious than ever before. Maybe one of the greatest acts of love we can offer each other is respecting each other's boundaries by doing what Ned Norton did: praying for people and giving them space to be imperfect and the Lord space to work. We don't have to know what's going on behind the scenes of someone else's life.

The words we choose can be immeasurably powerful. Let us use them to build up the Kingdom of God, not tear down those He created.

I invite you to join me for book two in the Seaport Suspense series, *Eye of the Beholder,* where we will meet some interesting new characters and revisit some we've already gotten to know. It promises to be a page-turner, so catch up on your sleep!

I love hearing from my readers. You can write to me through my publisher at www.letstalkfiction.com or directly through my website at www.kathyherman.com. I read and respond to every e-mail and greatly value your input.

In Him,

Kathy Herman

DISCUSSION GUIDE

1. To qualify as gossip, does information have to be untrue? Can revealing truth about someone be just as detrimental? If so, can you give an example?

2. Can you explain Proverbs 18:8 in your own words? "The words of a gossip are like choice morsels; they go down to a man's inmost parts." Why do you think gossip seems so palatable?

3. Have you ever been gossiped about? Was the information passed on true or false? How did it make you feel? How did you handle it? Did you confront the offending party? If so, did that put a stop to it?

4. Have you ever been guilty of gossiping about someone? If so, did the person find out? How did it make you feel? If the person didn't find out, were you bothered by your actions? Should you have been?

5. Do you think Ephesians 4:29 also applies to gossip? "Do not let any unwholesome talk come out of your mouths, but only what is helpful for building others up according to their needs, that it may benefit those who listen." Is it possible to gossip without realizing it? Or is gossip a conscious choice? Do good motives lessen the damage? Should they?

6. What was Eddie Drummond's motive was for passing on information about Ross Hamilton? Do you think his concern was laced with jealousy? Could he have handled the situation better? If so, how?

7. Was Ellen Jones justified in going to Eddie's boss with the information she'd overheard? The police? Was she guilty of gossip? Where do you draw the line between gossip and repeating information out of genuine concern?

8. What do you think Blanche Davis's motive was in asking for prayer for Ellen's supposed adultery? Can prayers be gossip? Have you ever left a prayer circle feeling as if you learned something you shouldn't have about someone? Have you ever revealed more about someone than you should have when asking for prayer? Have you repeated something you heard in a prayer circle even though you knew it should be kept confidential? If so, why?

9. What reaction did you have to Valerie Mink Hodges's article about Ross Hamilton (Chapter 7)? Not knowing anything more than what you saw in print, would you have been swayed by it? Do you think media reporting can be gossip?

10. Did Ellen have the right motive when she called Valerie Mink Hodges to discuss her suspicion about Ross Hamilton? Would you have handled it differently?

11. Could you relate to Gordy Jameson's disgust at being gossiped about? Did he feel any less violated because the gossip wasn't malicious? Do you think he handled it the right way by confronting Melody Drummond? What would you have done?

12. What are some of the reasons people engage in gossip? Which character's gossiping annoyed you the most? Why? If you could confront that character, what would say to him or her?

13. Did this story cause you to broaden your understanding of gossip? If yes, explain.

14. Was there a thought, a principle, a scene, or a character from the story that will stay with you?

Available
NOW!

Don't miss
another one of
KATHY
HERMAN'S
page-turning
novels!

Poor Mrs. Rigsby

Nursing Assistant Sally Cox is about as happy to be at Walnut Hills
Nursing Center as the patients are. But it's work or starve, now that
her husband has found a younger companion. Sally's new crowd
skews toward the elderly—ninety-year-old Elsie Rigsby, for
instance, whose dementia comes and goes with her gold-digging
son and grandson's visits. Elsie's not going to tell those vultures
where she stashed her money. Still, she's not getting any younger,
and someone besides her needs to know. Three deaths later, is
anyone watching Sally?

ISBN 1-59052-314-8